The Chronicles of Salduwe

Book One

Dave Scorza

authorHOUSE™

1663 Liberty Drive, Suite 200
Bloomington, Indiana 47403
(800) 839-8640
www.AuthorHouse.com

© 2005 Dave Scorza. All Rights Reserved.

No part of this book may be reproduced, stored in a retrieval system, or transmitted by any means without the written permission of the author.

First published by AuthorHouse 12/19/05

ISBN: 1-4208-7588-4 (sc)

Printed in the United States of America
Bloomington, Indiana

This book is printed on acid-free paper.

Contents

Chapter 1	Fearful Intrusion	1
Chapter 2	Cryptic Messages	14
Chapter 3	The Sacred Mountains	28
Chapter 4	The Caves	46
Chapter 5	Amazing Adventure	62
Chapter 6	Escape From the Goblins	81
Chapter 7	Elven Patrols	95
Chapter 8	The Elven Council	112
Chapter 9	The Dwarves Join the Alliance	128
Chapter 10	Mountain of Death	147
Chapter 11	Shades Attack the Camp	157
Chapter 12	The Raiding Party	171
Chapter 13	Tales in the Dark	187
Chapter 14	The Hermit of Lake Salduwe	201
Chapter 15	Mountain Pathways	212
Chapter 16	Surprise Attack	223
Chapter 17	The Passing of Two Great Warriors	239
Chapter 18	Wesip is Captured	256

Chapter 19	Salvation from the Skies	269
Chapter 20	A Pleasant Relationship Develops	286
Chapter 21	A Day Too Late	299
Chapter 22	Night Attack	313
Chapter 23	Broken Paths	324

Chapter 1

Fearful Intrusion

The heat of the day was past. The high mountain air began to cool as the sun eased its way toward the distant crags. A few scattered clouds drifted from the west towards the knoll where a young woman stopped momentarily. Her long dark hair was neatly braided, hanging down her back, over the leather jerkin she wore. Her left hand held a bow, an arrow nocked carefully onto the string. Slung from a belt on her right side were two small quail she had snared earlier. With her knife she had bled them, but had not yet gutted them. In her haste she had simply tied them to her belt, planning to attend to them later. She was a long way from her rendezvous.

Her quiver held five arrows, still unused, bearing the design of her clan, Tinosik. The crest of the Bird of Paradise on display was the emblem their house-line had chosen centuries earlier. The clan to which she belonged was the dominant line among the seven other groups making up her village.

Meri's mind was no longer on her lineage now. Something unusual was happening again. The birds had ceased their happy chatter. The cicadas had stopped their noisy afternoon ritual. She knew from experience this signaled a presence. She had lived in the forests too long not to notice. Carefully glancing about her she stared intently, but was unable to locate the source. Meri felt the hackles on her neck rise in response. Her heart began to pound as fear pumped adrenaline into her chest. Acting more like a startled deer than a girl, she glanced furtively toward the wooded slope. This was the trail she had intended to follow. Now she was unsure. Sensing something amiss, Meri blended as best she could with the shrubs and trees. She desperately wished for better cover. Hardly daring to breathe, she waited, staring intently. Her eyes were on a patch of wood down the slope, off to her right. She had seen something moving as she crested the knoll. Now there was nothing. Angrily, Meri thought it only her over-wrought imagination again. *Yes, that must be it, she mused. I'm just upset.* But dealing with that issue would have to wait until she was safely away from here.

Hesitantly, she stepped toward the path leading to the wooded patch. Keeping an eye on the trail, and an eye out for further movement, she continued cautiously. She breathed out evenly, trying to slow her heart beat and dispel the effects of her agitation. She had promised to meet her brother, Bili, down at their private swimming hole. That is, if she had managed to bag any quail. They were his favorite birds. Whatever was out here was threatening her time with him, yet she dare not make a mistake. It could cost her her life.

Her mind drifted uneasily back to her brother. These days Bili had no time to hunt on his own. He was being warrior trained. That took up most of his day. When he was done, he was too exhausted to hunt. Handling the sword and shield in the morning was hard enough. Now he was kept afternoons, training in the secret martial arts. These were taught to those assigned to protect the shaman priests.

Meri knew the sessions were arduous, draining the young men as they landed roughly in the sawdust pits. She'd also heard they were training with iron tipped sticks, both long and short. Bili himself had confided this to her. She longed to watch them practice, but women were forbidden near the men's camp. Putting these thoughts aside, Meri looked forward to sharing these quail with him. It would also give her time to share the pain and uncertainty that were nagging heavily on her heart.

Meri savored their time alone. Though younger, Bili had always been special to her. They had hunted and fished together, even when there was pressure for her to follow more feminine pursuits. Their father, Weno, had allowed Meri to learn to shoot the bow while yet a child. To his great delight, he watched his daughter develop into the finest marksman in the village. He was careful to praise her in private, for the entire community frowned on women making themselves equal to their men folk. Weno knew Meri bore the prophetic mark on her arm. Those few in the village who knew of the mark were sworn to secrecy. One who bore such a mark was believed to be "Kimat", a chosen of the gods. They must be left alone to develop according to their interests or abilities - one of the unwritten laws handed down through generations. The shaman priests observed these rules with unusual strictness.

Approaching the wooded area where she had seen the shadow of movement, Meri bent down, placing her hand on the ground, checking the ferns and lichen next to the old cedar. She was disappointed. She found nothing. No tracks, no bent blades of grass, no torn lichen. *Nothing! Just as I figured*, she thought angrily. *It's my imagination again*! Yet as she straightened up and stepped out into the open again, a faint odor tickled at the edges of her senses. Not of decay or humus; a rather strange scent. It was something new, like a sword being pounded in the forge, yet somehow burnt in the process.

Shaking her head in confusion, Meri looked up, scanning the area once again. Fear once again gripped her anxious heart, bringing with it a deep feeling of exposure. She had been spotted; that much was obvious. But by whom and to what purpose? She also knew she had seen someone. This was definitely the place! Yet, there was no other sign of passage. *What could this mean?* Fear continued to tug at the corners of her mind. With a bold sigh of resignation, she straightened once again, and continued working her way to the appointed rendezvous.

Nearing the path, Meri stumbled momentarily over roots belonging to the bushes that concealed the entrance. Hurriedly she slid down the overgrown track, hanging on to vines and branches to slow her descent. She looked back over her shoulder to see if she had been followed. *So far so good. Now to locate my brother!* Meri muttered audibly. She forced her way through heavily entwined vine and broomstick brush, shoving branches aside in her haste. Catching her toes in a hidden cluster of small roots, Meri sprawled clumsily across the trail.

Wiping the dirt from her eyes and mouth, she sat for a moment, trying to catch her breath. Fear was taking its toll, making her careless in her haste. Meri was embarrassed at falling like this, but glad no one had been around to observe. She was annoyed with her lapse, especially when she was attempting to leave no trail. Putting that aside, she brushed off her jerkin, got up and continued.

"Screech!" A raucous call ripped violently across the silent forest! A battle hawk fell heavily into the brush right in front of her, its shredded body blocking her way. Startled, Meri stifled a cry, staring at what lay in front of her. Sidestepping the lifeless body, she looked about anxiously. A battle raged above. Not far ahead, hawks were viciously attacking a large roc. They circled, dived and dodged its huge talons. For all its size the roc was surprisingly quick. The hawks did well to keep their distance.

Aware that something was very wrong, Meri abandoned all caution and stumbled recklessly along the trail, trying to stay with the battle. She just managed to keep her balance as she ran, her eyes scanning the trees above. Goose flesh appeared on her arms as she became aware of something happening ahead in the clearing. She spied hawks flying over the forest canopy in full battle armor *They never fly this far east and never around one of those giant rocs.* Meri's "gift" began yelling a warning within her. This should have been enough to startle her into hiding, but Meri was stubborn. She ignored all the signs overhead and the pounding in her head, signals alerting her of extreme danger. She defiently dared expose herself to them. Her insatiable curiosity drove her. Trees temporarily blocked her vision, so she pressed to the clearing ahead. Her eyes were riveted to the hawks. Suddenly a hand reached out, grabbing her, pulling her into the brush. Another hand covered her mouth. "Sh-h! There's someone up ahead. Be quiet and stop fighting!"

Meri's startled heart relaxed as she turned to stare into the eyes of her brother. *So he was here already! I should have known it,* she thought. *Never mind! I've got some important news that can't wait.*

Bili released her, and motioned for her to stay where she was. Then he moved carefully ahead, his eyes on the tree the stranger had used to watch the fight. He advanced soundlessly, years of training helping him move unseen through the brush. He approached the tree where the stranger was hidden, but there was no one. No telltale prints marked his passing. Only a strange scent seemed to cling to the space where he had been. Bewildered, Bili let out an oath of surprise, searching the ground again. Nothing! Meri joined him and smelled that same odor she had encountered back by the meadow. She tucked that information into her heart, then turned her eyes back to the trees. The noise of the birds had become deafening.

Over the clearing the battle continued. More hawks appeared from nowhere, darting in and out, attacking the roc. "Why are those hawks so intent on attacking the roc?" whispered Meri. "I've never seen anything like this in my life!"

Bili was already upset and nervous. Meri's comment served to further his irritability. *Why did women always have to ask the obvious,* he thought sourly. *Couldn't they just be quiet and wait for the outcome? Certainly at a time like this?*

Meri was two years older than he. In many ways she was more mature than he. This rankled, for Bili felt he had been raised in her shadow. She was their father's favorite, Bili knew, and for good reason. But lucky for him she was a girl. *Yes, she is a girl*, thought Bili, and *that is all. The men are the important ones. They always make sure that things get done. Important things - Battles, gardens, new houses, bows and arrows, spears, swords. These are men's work, and she will never share that.* Still, Bili had to grudgingly admit she did have qualities he liked. She wasn't like the other girls. She knew a lot more than she let on, but acted quiet and unassuming. That was one of those special qualities that helped them remain close as they grew up.

Breaking free from these thoughts, Bili whispered, "Look! The roc is hurt", pointing a finger upwards. "It's not fighting the hawks as it did earlier. Those metal rakes attached to their battle harnesses must have some sort of drug or poison in them. See! It's starting to lose altitude."

Though it was hurt, the roc was still dangerous. Two more hawks tried to move in and rake again, but the roc's beak cut one in half. A talon tore the wing from another. Both fell into the clearing.

"Why do the hawks keep coming"? Meri whispered. "Does the roc carry something so valuable they've been sent to recover it?"

As Bili watched, it certainly did appear as though they were trying to dislodge something the Roc held in one of its talons. Screeching out a harsh warning, a call born of desperation, the roc flew over the clearing, dropping a small bundle from its claw. It fell in a slow arc to land in the deep pool of water immediately behind the great Cyprus tree growing its the edge. Several hawks dived for it, but the bundle splashed safely into the pond beyond reach.

Bili's eyes followed the bundle, watching it sink into the pool. Then he turned his gaze back to the roc. Three hawks had attacked its open side, raking him mercilessly. Unable to remain aloft, it settled heavily into the clearing, still roaring its defiance to the hawks. They continued to swoop, trying to finish it.

Bili watched momentarily as the hawks descended upon the roc. Before he was aware of doing so, Bili had joined battle against them, drawing his sword and cutting two of the hawks in half. They never knew he was there. Others screeched a warning, veering from the roc. They flew over the pool a couple of times, then disappeared as suddenly as they had appeared.

Hesitantly, Meri made her way to the roc, fearing she herself might be misunderstood and attacked. The roc watched her coming through blurring eyes. She had heard of these great birds, but had never been close to one. She sensed the roc was trying to communicate. She lost her initial fear when she felt the mind contact it offered. She came right up to its head. She placed her hand around its neck, lifted it up and turned the eyes fully toward her. Bili stiffened protectively, fearing she would be torn to pieces.

Images crowded her mind. Her thinking was askew. The roc was trying to mind link with her. She had some knowledge of mind melding, but this practice was expressly forbidden in her village. The roc was insistent! What was it saying? Meri tried to concentrate.

The bundle! The bundle! she thought. *It must not fall into the hands of the hawks. It must be delivered into safe hands. Safe hands....*

Meri was jolted. The mind link had been severed. She turned to see the huge eyes staring emptily into the sky. The great roc was dead. The poison had done its work. Angry and disturbed, Meri gently lowered the majestic head to the ground.

Bili lowered his sword and began wiping it on a hand full of bamboo leaves. Then, approaching his sister he spoke, breaking the eerie silence. "The roc fought well. Is it dead?"

Meri nodded. " It mind linked a message. It said to take the bundle in the pool and deliver it into safe hands...whatever that means. It didn't want the hawks to get it."

Glancing toward the pool, Bili made a quick decision. "I think I'll dive and recover it. Must be something pretty important for a roc to make a special trip like this."

Leaving his sword in the care of his sister, he trotted over, diving into the cold water. After coming up for air more than once, he surfaced with the bundle successfully clasped in his right hand. Meri watched anxiously as he unwrapped it.

Inside was the strangest stone they had ever seen. It looked to be made of black obsidian, but the shape was what drew their attention. "This stone has been cut into an octagon," His eyes filled with wonder, Bili managed "It has buffed edges on all sides. And it's unusually heavy. What could it be?"

Meri looked at it curiously for a moment, and then turning to Bili she whispered, "I'm frightened. I feel we should bury the roc and the hawks", an edge of worry in her voice. "Those hawks might return and bring others with them. I don't like the looks of all that armor. They belong to someone I don't think I'd care to meet right now. Let's make this place hard to find."

Wrapping the stone in its cover, Bili reluctantly agreed. "You're right. I'll dig a trench with my dibble stick and sword, and then we'll bury them. Watch out though. Don't scrape yourself with their rakes. There must still be poison lodged along their edges."

Together they buried the hawks and dug a shallow trench for the great roc. It took much longer than they thought to hide the huge bird. Bili would like to have raised a stone cairn above the grave, but Meri reminded him that they were trying to hide everything, not advertise that a battle had taken place.

Taking brush and rubbing out the final signs, Bili looked around at the clearing. Everything appeared natural again, with the exception of a few more humps than normal. No casual observer would notice a fight had occurred here recently. All pools of blood and torn feathers had been carefully removed.

"Well, that's done. Let's get out of here."

As they started, Bili turned to Meri, "By the way, did anyone see you arrive? You know you're not supposed to come here unless you're sure you're not being followed!"

"No one that I know of," she replied thoughtfully, keeping her feelings about the incident in the meadow to herself. That had been unsettling enough. Now they had faced another crisis of greater proportions here closer to home. It was unsettling.

Then Meri paused, remembering the occasion that had brought her to the clearing. She wasn't looking forward to going home. That's why she had come running to their private hideaway. "Father came to me and said that he had made arrangements for my betrothal to Hanasih over in Warin village," she blurted out hastily. "Bili! I don't want to get married and have to live there! They are so backward compared to our people. All my freedoms would be taken from me and I would be unhappy all my days! They expect a woman to simply be silent and bare children. There's no room in their minds for change, or creativity. They've the worst reputation for the way they treat their women, especially at the Yam harvest festivals. All they can think about is male Pride. They always taunt the other villages with the size and power of their yams. And I don't even know this Hanasih!"

Bili stopped in shocked surprise. He turned around, putting a hand on her shoulder. He stared into her dark eyes and saw the anguish there.

"Has father promised you to their clan? He said nothing to me about it! I know some of their young men. They are a rough lot! You really would be unhappy there. That's a fact! I've seen some of their men and the way they treat the women. I wonder what Father has in mind to do that to you?

"Still, father has spoken and I don't know what we can do about it. Once a vow is taken, it's great shame for us not to make good on our promise. Even though you've been born a girl, you're different. Father recognizes that. I've always lived in the shadow of your light. You're better with a bow than any of our men. At first the men used to scold father for letting you try, but he always stood up for you saying, `Someday it may be that she will save our village from destruction. Don't be so hasty to condemn my decision. Remember the prophecies." Then he would confide, "After all, she does have the mark!'

"Father has always looked on you as special. You also have a keen inquisitive mind. I've seen his look of admiration when you've found the answer to something that has stumped everyone else. Or when you've created something unusual. He's quite pleased."

"Then what is he doing trying to make an alliance with the people of Warin and using me as bait!" Meri complained. "We've always grown giant yams and been leaders in the ceremonies. No one has ever brought shame to our village. Father has always managed to keep peace through the yam confrontations. Twice now he has made the Warin people accept our yams, and they haven't been able to turn them down!"

Bili was baffled. *What is father planning that he would upset Meri like this; especially by not consulting her first? She turned down other opportunities twice, and he honored her feelings. Now he had done something highly unusual.* "Well", mused Bili, "I guess he has his reasons. I'll talk with him when we get home. Then maybe I can find out what this is all about. Anyway, I'm sure something can be worked out. I'd rather have you marry someone in our village, than see you sent off to some disdainful family."

Meri remained silent. It was little consolation, but she felt it better to drop the subject. Better to keep her brother on her side than antagonize him with further talk. Maybe more information would shed light upon this very scary situation.

As they hurried along the familiar path, Meri thought back on all the things she had been allowed to do as a girl. She was always happy to help her mother with the chores, but her times alone in the meadows were her favorite memories. She had made friends with the woodland creatures, and actually managed to understand their feelings- fear, pleasure, anger, pain- things forbidden to explore, at least that's what the village elders said. Meri knew she was gifted in this area, and discreetly worked at it when she had occasion to be alone. Who knew when a gift of this nature might prove useful?

Her other pleasure came from shooting the black palm bow her father had given her as a young child. She was proud of that bow and worked hard learning to shoot well. She knew how to make and fletch her own arrows, chip and hone stones into sharp points, and braid split vine over it all to hold the sharp heads in place. She'd made many for her father, who proudly carried them in his quiver. She spent many hours at practice, often with her brother as company. They would walk to the meadows, set up targets and set arrows around the meadow. Then they would run from target to target, nocking each arrow quickly, and shooting the various targets. When they were able to put all arrows in the targets on the run, they would collect everything and return home. Sometimes Meri would shoot wide, allowing her frustrated brother to win. This helped their relationship.

At length, Bili and Meri reached the village. Making their way to the house, they noticed a crowd of men gathered outside the ceremonial house, deeply engrossed in a heated discussion. Rather than stop to listen, Bili passed by, intent only on getting to the house before someone could stop the two of them.

"Hello Mother. Is Father home yet?" asked Bili.

"He came home, but went out to the garden to gather some greens to go with the wild bush hen he shot today, " Mayit commented quietly. "He shouldn't be long."

Meri looked at the bush hen, which reminded her she had two birds of her own. Untying them, she gave them to her mother to add to the meal. The bush hen had been plucked and gutted, and Meri knew she would have to prepare the two quail.

Bili interrupted her thoughts. "Mother, I want to take Meri with me to find father. We have something to ask him. Do you mind? It's a matter of some importance. I'll help her prepare the quail for dinner when we get back."

Not awaiting the reply, Bili looked at Meri and together they raced from the house, heading toward the garden. This was what they had hoped for- to get Father alone and ask him about the strange things that had happened today. Meri also looked to Bili to approach their father about the strange betrothal that was purported to have been made between her clan Tinosik and those of the Muruk. She hoped desperately this was only rumor, but was fearful that this might have in fact occurred. This would mean she might be bound by an oath of promise. Her heart pounded with anxiety as they neared the garden.

Chapter 2

Cryptic Messages

Weno pulled off the last cane shoot growing on the stalk. He placed it in his string bag with the others he had collected. He felt good about the day's catch and was anxious to finish gathering the greens and vegetables to garnish the table. It had been a bad season for wild game. Something was frightening the animals away. Even the birds, loud and raucous in their flights, weren't coming around. Maybe they knew something he didn't. This had been eating at him for some time now, and he was unable to put his finger on the problem. His father before him had mentioned something similar when he was but a lad, yet he had paid scant attention in those days. There were on-going tribal wars, and his thoughts had been wrapped up in the challenge of fighting. *Funny,* he thought, *that such a thing should be occurring again. I wonder if there is any significance between what came to pass in those days and trouble that might erupt among us now?*

His reverie was short lived.

"Father! Father!" Bili's familiar voice interrupted his disturbing thoughts. *The boy is growing more like a man all the time,* Weno mused. He had just begun to take notice of his son. His voice had deepened and he was putting on some weight. His frame was beginning to fill out toward his manhood. *If I can just can spend more time training my only son,* he thought sagely, *he will definitely be leadership material one day.*

"I'm over here by the garden house," Weno answered. "Why don't you come and help me stuff all this food into another string bag. I've dug up too much for one meal-yes, even too much for one bag."

Both Bili and Meri trotted over to where he stood. Weno knew from the looks on their faces they were bursting with news. He watched as Bili withdrew a small bundle from his carrying bag. Whatever it was he had wrapped in leaves and tied together with bits of twine.

"Father, the strangest thing happened to us today," Bili began, looking over at Meri. "I was done with my training, so I went to cool off at the secret pond. I was about to pull off my shirt for a swim when a roc flew overhead! It was closely pursued by battle hawks. They fought, and the roc dropped this into the pond. The hawks had poisoned rakes and managed to bring that great bird down."

Weno stood there patiently listening, his head tilted in his typical cynical pose. A lesser personality would have been frightened into silence. Undeterred, Bili continued.

"I killed a couple of those hawks with my sword and the others flew up and disappeared just like a morning fog. I dived into the pond and retrieved this," he smiled nervously, holding up a small package. "No one else knows about it. We thought it best to keep it hidden until we could show you. Do you know anything about this?"

Meri chipped in, lending support to her brother's story. "I was on my way to see Bili when one of the hawks fell dead at my feet. I was startled and Bili grabbed me before I could be seen. With hawks so far east like this, surely something important must be happening."

His hands beginning to shake with excitement, Bili quickly unwrapped the stone, then gave it to his father. Weno took it, looking tentatively at its shape and color. Then he turned it over carefully. He took his time with the stone, noting especially the strange runes. Thinking carefully, he could recall nothing of a stone as this in their oral traditions. Could it possibly belong to a neighboring enemy to the North? They were known for their sorcery and hid many things from outsiders. A chill began to creep up his spine as he thought of the implications.

Squinting, he looked up at Bili. "You say the roc had this in its talon and dropped it purposely into the pond?"

"Well, that's what we think, Father. It tried to communicate with Meri, and placed words into her mind. It said, uh, what was it Meri?"

"It told us not to let the hawks get the stone," she explained. "It seemingly went to great lengths to flee from the hawks, but they cornered it as it flew over our forests. After it fell to the forest floor, it remained alive only for a short time. After it died, Bili and I buried it along with the hawks that we killed. We covered all traces of battle as best we could in the short time we had. We hope no one from the outside is after this stone and comes looking for it."

This last news was particularly unsettling. Weno felt deep fear welling up in the pit of his stomach. He knew nothing of this sort had happened in these isolated forests. They were a people unto themselves, quietly trying to avoid contact with outsiders. This certainly did not set well with him, nor would it with the other elders in the village. Outsiders always brought trouble! Their fathers had found this to be only too true. The Great War had shown them the importance of remaining unobtrusive, blending in with the great forests that had protected them.

"This stone is obviously an important artifact to someone," Weno grumbled at last. "It resembles the talisman we won from the Goblins in our last wars against them," Weno shared with them. "I suggest we take it and place it in the men's ceremonial house with that stone. We'll call a meeting of the village elders tomorrow and explain these strange events. If any of them has an idea, I'd like to hear it. They're certainly not going to accept this strange news we bring to them.

"It's getting late. Let's get back to the house."

After the family had eaten, Meri cleared the plates and utensils from the rough-hewn table. Carrying the wick lamps from the dining area, she placed one atop the fireplace mantle. The other she took with her to the outdoor kitchen where water was already heating. Here she joined her mother, Mayit, who had stacked and carried the dishes, and was beginning to pour water for washing up.

Inside, Weno lit his pipe, set his feet up on the stool and puffed. He savored his tobacco and sweet-bark pipe. He would not be hurried. This was more than an evening ritual. This was a basic principle governing Weno's lifestyle. The world could wait while he extracted his simple pleasure from it. The sun would rise again in the morning, bringing with it fresh opportunities and life's challenges. There would be time to worry about life then.

Bili sat anxiously to one side, wondering how to approach his father about the subject of Meri's betrothal. He seemed distracted enough without adding this new dimension to an already confusing picture.

Several minutes went by. The room began filling with the sweet aroma of blended tobacco. The men of the Eastern Mountains prided themselves on their tobacco. They went to great lengths to produce what they considered the finest leaves grown anywhere. Care was taken to protect their crops from undue cold, rain or insects as the leaves ripened for harvest. Bili's father, as the leading village elder, always had a ready supply to hand. This was especially important when infrequent visitors from other clans showed up unexpectedly.

Meri returned and coughed as she encountered the smoke. "Thank you for the meat, father," she expressed gratefully. "It's always nice to have. It breaks the monotony of just vegetables."

Weno uttered a distracted reply. She noted he was obviously preoccupied with the stone and the hawks. He sat tranquilly, mulling over the events of the day, well at least until the tobacco ran out. Then he turned slowly, unhappily, tapping his pipe against the chair, knocking ashes onto the wooden floor.

"Guess it's time to take this over to the men's house," he groaned in resignation. "You all stay here. I don't want to attract any more attention than I have to." With that he got up off the chair, took the stone from Bili's hand and went through the doorway.

Once Weno left the house and had worked his way across the clearing, Meri moved over to where Bili was sitting watching him go.

"Did you get a chance to ask him anything?" she queried? "I suppose not, huh?" she asked, already sensing the answer. "Father seems too engrossed with what we told him. Never mind! You can try again later. I think I'll turn in early tonight. It's been a long day for me."

"I'm going over to the men's house after father's done," Bili informed her. "I'm going to study that talisman again. Maybe I can figure something out. I've never seen father react so strongly or appear so.., uh, unsettled. It's as though he's hiding something from us that has caused him deep pain. I have a gut feeling that what we've seen today is going to bring some uninvited changes, and possibly soon."

Bili left the house, ambling across the yard along the narrow path. He looked up and saw the quarter moon slowly sinking in the early evening sky. The weather had been clear for the past week, and only an occasional cloud dotted the horizon. It wouldn't be long before summer arrived. Even the mountain air was starting to warm.

Weno walked through the doorway of the men's house. There were no men sitting on the porch yet, neither had the fires been started. He took a lantern off the hook and opened the latch. Taking out his flint, he scraped it across the short piece of steel taken from the goblins. Sparks showered outward onto the wick, catching the fuel oil alight. Weno closed the latch, trimmed the wick, put the flint and steel away, and then moved toward the center of the room.

Hanging in the center of the trophy case, the goblin talisman made a bold impression. In contrast to the blackness of this strange stone, it reflected a brilliant blue. The two stones were also shaped differently. The black stone had been cut along its cleavage lines into a perfect octagon. The stone of the talisman was shaped more like a prism, long and narrow. Weno put his hand behind the talisman and drew the stone upwards and to himself. He stared at it for a while, looking intently at the strange black object in his other hand. He placed the two stones side by side, as if attempting to assess their relative merits. Shaking his head and knowing he was not up to such a task, he put the talisman back in its resting-place. Then as an after thought, he grasped some rawhide strings from a nearby basket, then deftly wove a net and placed the black stone inside. Holding the ends and tying them together, he suspended the stone from a wooden hook near the talisman.

"We'll see what comes of all this," Weno muttered to himself. Then turning, he walked over to the bench and sat down heavily. Putting his hand to his bearded chin, he stared at the ground. He shuffled his right foot back and forth, absently attempting to whittle down a dirt bump he found on the floor of the men's house.

Here again was proof that something sinister was happening on the outside. *How long,* Weno pondered, *can we continue their isolation?* It had been the proper thing to cut off ties with those of the cities. There was too much corruption, too much intrigue at the courts of the outsiders. If they wanted to maintain their integrity, their ethnic purity, and their customs uninterrupted, this was certainly the only logical alternative.

Nearby, a door slammed. Footsteps approached the house, and shortly someone mounted the stairs to the porch. Weno recognized the footfalls.

"Who dares to desecrate the sacred portals of Meli the Undivided?" Weno's voice rang out in challenge.

"One of the sons of the sacred forest mound upon which Maibor bested Yilwo in the ancient battle," came the reply.

"Enter, worthy son of the sacred forest. Be at peace and rest within the portals of this haven."

The ritual over, Yenwe stepped across the threshold. From of old, this custom had been observed. The first man into the house was duty-bound to challenge the next person to approach after his arrival. No one could say where the custom had evolved, but the men observed the ritual religiously.

Soon others began arriving, and before long those men who had seen the hawks fly over their part of the forest were deep in speculation.

"They came from the North I tell you!" protested old One-Eye. "I may not see as good as t'others, but I know what I saw!"

"I heard nothing until they were directly overhead," asserted Tolepai. "I say they just materialized and were somehow teleported by whoever owns those cursed things."

Weno had not been there nor had he seen them. Bili's report was all he had to go on. He allowed the men to continue uninterrupted.

"An those things had some sort'a pree-tekshun on their sides an all," interjected Tabinis, as he spat betel juice through an open hole in the floor. "I seen-em wunts or twice during the times we fought them ole Goblin things. They ken get down right testy!"

Bili arrived unnoticed. Standing to one side, he listened as each man contributed what he knew about hawks. He made mental notes about each word he felt to be genuine. This was his first encounter with something from the outside. A thrill of excitement raced through his body. *It would be great to be able to see other parts of the world than these mountains,* Bili mused. *There must be a lot of interesting people and things I've never been exposed to. But I'm a clan leader's son. I'll never be given the opportunity to do something like that*, he thought deep in his heart.

Shifting to his other foot, Bili felt ready for more challenges than he had been given. The more he listened, the more he wished he could fly like the great roc or those hawks. Then he could escape the prison of his ordered life here and seek adventure on the outside.

The conversation rose and fell as each man had his say, and discussion about the meaning of this intrusion slowly died out. Finally after a few men had made their beds at the far corner of the house and were already snoring, the talking finally came to a stop altogether. Weno stood up and promised, "We'll meet in the morning and then go to the site and look around. Maybe then we can make sense of what has just happened to us today. Let's rest on it, then maybe we'll be able to think more clearly in the morning light."

With that, most of the men left the ceremonial house to find what sleep they could in their own houses. Bili decided to stay and sleep near his father. Maybe he would have a better opportunity to talk to him in the morning about Meri and her concerns. He grabbed a blanket from a shelf and curled up near one of the still smoldering fires. He tossed a couple of logs on the glowing embers, rolled over and was soon asleep.

It seemed to Bili that he had been asleep but a moment when someone stumbled over his prone body. He rolled over again trying to sleep, but an eerie glow forced its way under his sleepy eyelids, probing, burning. Irritated, he turned from the glow. It didn't help. It wouldn't go away. It was insistent! He groaned and sluggishly sat up. Peering around, he let out a gasp of surprise!

"Meri! What are you doing in the Men's house?"

Meri's eyes were glazed as she stared dumbly upon the stone. She made no reply.

"Meri!" Bili's shouted whisper persisted. "Meri!"

Getting no response at all, Bili flipped off his covering. Placing a hand on the floor, he pushed himself heavily upright and walked over to his sister. Peering at her, he took her shoulder, and shook her gently.

"Meri, are you all right? Meri?"

Still no response. Bili looked at the talisman that had started pulsing. Then he noticed the black stone too was glowing, the runes pulsing brightly.

Bili, open you mind and let the knowledge flow into you, a voice broke into his mind. *Your sister is receiving instructions. Allow her time. Don't interrupt.*

Bili, dumbfounded, stepped back in alarm, but had enough sense to listen.

Staring intently at the talisman, he did what he was told. He tried to blank out his mind. Impressions began to form, vaguely at first, then taking definite shape. *A gravesite? Yes, up on the Sacred Mountain. Huge boulders, a rockslide, caves, yes-definitely caves, several of them. Strange sounds- almost like wailing, strange apparitions moving freely through the walls. A probing eye. It's staring at me-full of malicious intent. Must get away. Now*!

Bili cupped his face in his hands. The visions stopped. Heart pounding, thoughts reeling, he slumped to the ground, momentarily disoriented. Fearfully he opened his eyes, praying desperately not to see the specter of that horrible eye drawing him into itself.

Someone was pulling him to his feet. He turned as he felt his father's hand tugging at him.

"What's going on Bili? How did Meri get in here, and why are those stones pulsing?" he asked in a tone that betrayed the alarm he attempted to mask.

"I don't know, father. One moment I was sleeping, and the next I was awakened by someone stumbling over me," Bili burst out awkwardly. "I awoke to see Meri staring at the black stone. She seems to be in some sort of trance. I started to shake her, but a voice told me to leave her alone until she had received the message the stone has for her."

Bili stood confused, knowing his father wouldn't be able to understand any of this.

Meri collapsed unexpectedly to the floor startling them both. Weno knelt and put his hand under her head. He lifted her gently, tenderness replacing the anger he felt for her violation of entering the sacred men's house. *Women have never been allowed inside. The spirits will be angry. Such a thing is unheard of. It has never been allowed! What is happening here?*

He started to leave the house, but turned to talk to Bili. He started to speak but stopped. He was shocked by his son's strange behavior.

Bili had noticed that the black stone had stopped pulsing. The talisman, however, continued its eerie glow. It seemed to beckon to him, drawing him in, demanding he take possession of it. Reaching out a tentative hand, Bili lifted the talisman from its hook and slipped it over his head. The pulsing stopped. He turned and stared into the eyes of his father watching him.

"Let's get her over to the house," Weno whispered hoarsely. "Something unusual has happened to both of you. We need to talk."

Once in the house, Weno laid Meri on a cot. She babbled incoherently a couple of times. Slowly she turned her head then opened her eyes. Awakened by the noise of Weno and Bili's entry, Mayit got out of bed and joined them. She put a cup to Meri's lips and let water dribble into her mouth. Meri sputtered, then sat up abruptly. She appeared disoriented, fearful. She stared around her, trying to understand what was going on.

"Would you two youngsters like to tell me what this is all about?" Weno demanded, fear and worry lacing the tone of his voice. "First you come home reporting a story that has the whole village upset. Then you bring home this cursed stone. Now somehow you've got them both glowing. If they're owned by someone outside, it won't take them long to mobilize and locate them."

A frown creased Meri's forehead. She laid a hand on her temple as though trying to clear her thoughts. She looked blankly at her father, then to Bili. When she saw the talisman hanging around his neck, she whispered, "Then it's true. Everything the stone said is true."

"What's true?" Bili interrupted, fearful of what she might say next.

"These stones do not belong here.'" Meri stated flatly. "They must be taken far away to the west. Someone there has great need of them. They must be returned," she exclaimed with great conviction. She stared from Bili to Weno. Then she turned to Mayit.

"What is all this nonsense?" Mayit queried suspiciously? "What stones are you talking about?"

"She's talking about the black stone and this talisman, mother," Bili said, defending his sister. "I received a message from it while it was pulsing. Meri must have been drawn to the men's house by the power of the black stone, and she woke me when she stumbled on my blanket as she came in. The stone was glowing all over. There was Meri standing before it. A voice told me to leave her alone when I tried to wake her."

"Enough!" shouted Weno. "That kind of talk is forbidden in this house! Those dark arts were banned hundreds of years ago, and I won't allow them to start now. I knew it was a mistake to keep that cursed Goblin relic around. And now you're wearing it around your neck. Give it to me at once! I'm going to destroy it!"

As he reached out, Meri cut in sharply. "No, father, don't touch it. You will only hurt yourself and bring down the wrath of the Dark Lord. What I'm saying is true! And, yes, the talisman has spoken to Bili. It has filled his mind with the landmarks we will need. We've been given a quest: return these stones to their rightful owner."

"That's nonsense!" Weno huffed. "First you tell me that these stones have spoken to you. Then you plan to cross hundreds of miles through uncharted wilderness and enemy territory to return them to Krell knows where! Do you have any idea what a trek like that would involve?"

"Weno, maybe what Meri says is true," Mayit said to her husband. "When we were both young, that old woman, the seer from Wityap said that one day two young people would re-direct the course of our lives. Remember? Maybe this is what she was predicting would occur."

"Woman, this is no time for futile speculation," Weno chided, frustration evident in his grating voice. "If I even allow myself the freedom to think that these cursed stones can communicate, I don't want to have to consider allowing my only children to make the journey. That's the same as giving my blessing for them to go out and get themselves killed."

"Father, if these prophecies are true, there will be other powers at work helping us fulfill them," Meri suggested. "Maybe that is to be our destiny. Why else would I receive the mark?"

"Besides," Bili chimed in, "who's better with a bow and arrow than Meri. And I'm getting better with the sword and dagger. Old Aldrex says I'm the fastest and smoothest youth in all the villages. He said himself he is planning to promote me to the last training level."

"I don't want either of you going," Weno grumped. "I'm very fond of you both, and don't want to lose you." He turned as he spoke again, "It's out of the question."

Drawing his pipe from its bag, Weno went out on the porch intending to smoke. The stress of what possibly lay before him was frightening. What if his two children were the ones? How could he best protect them on their journey? No! This was crazy. No telling what dangers lay across their path; and this business about the Dark Lord. Where had Meri gotten that? What Dark Lord? No one had heard even a rumor for five hundred years. That Dark Lord was destroyed in the great battle on the Plains of Desolation. "Yes, that's what it is," he concluded. "Nonsense!" He lit up his pipe and stared off into the darkness.

Chapter 3
The Sacred Mountains

Early the next morning, Meri got up, washed her face, and donned her hunting clothes. Selecting her best arrows, she wrapped these in her jacket. Then she went to see if Bili was still asleep. He stirred as she entered the room. Seeing her in those clothes brought back all last night's memories.

"Bili, something's happening to me!" she whispered. "I had more dreams during the night. I couldn't sleep because of them. It's urgent we go back to where the giant roc fought those war hawks. My dreams have all centered on the pond and the stone. I've got an uneasy feeling about yesterday. Something dreadful is going to happen. I can feel it!"

Bili rolled out of bed, pulled on his trousers and began buttoning his shirt.

"Why do you say that, Meri?"

"Strange things are going on, Bili. Can't you sense it? Look at what's happened to you now. Doesn't that mean anything?"

Bili, rubbing the sleep from his eyes, thought a moment. "Well," he began, clearly uneasy, but still not fully convinced, "ever since I put on this talisman, I haven't been able to remove it. I've tried, but I can't! Maybe that says something. I feel the power in the stone compelling me to wear it, you know, as though it has become a part of me. And..., I just thought about it. The stone woke me up just before you entered the room," he said, looking puzzled. "Maybe there is something to what you say. I'm not used to this kind of communication. It's never happened to me before. I think it is part of what the shaman has been attempting to teach me. But he said this kind of power is evil, Meri."

"I don't think whatever is trying to communicate with us is evil, Bili. Nor was the message the giant roc gave to me before it died there by the pond. It's just a different way of hearing messages. Bili, don't be afraid of the stone. Try being silent and letting it impress your mind with what it needs to tell you."

Feeling very threatened and uncomfortable, Bili resisted his sister's advice. "I don't know, Meri. The Shaman says that in the old days when people tried that kind of contact with magic, it was uncontrollable and sometimes destroyed those who attempted to use it. I don't know whether I want to trust these stones or not; especially when this one places a compulsion on me to keep it on. I don't want to be possessed by something I can't understand. I don't want to end up like those people of long ago. Magic is dangerous!"

"Bili, think about it," Meri suggested in her most soothing manner. "I've been able to communicate with the animals of the forest. The Shaman says that's absolutely forbidden. Has that destroyed me? Do I seem different to you because of that?"

"No, I guess not," Bili admitted reluctantly. "But these stones are different. One came to us from the goblin wars, and now this other comes to us from the outside as well. Why did they pulse when we brought them close to one another? I'm not sure I want to trust my life to these strange stones!"

Meri thought a moment before answering. What her brother said made sense, yet somehow these stones felt safe in spite of the power contained within. She could detect no threat. *Possibly I am too trusting*, she thought philosophically. *Yet, these dreams are filled with urgency.*

"Bili, maybe they contain the same type of magic, or maybe the source of the magic is the same. I don't know. I just have a feeling that the stones are not out to either hurt or possess us."

Dropping his defenses at last Bili replied, "I'm sorry to be such a doubter, Meri. I've just been brought up to fear magic in any form. You may be right. I'm allowing my prejudices to cloud my thinking. I'll try to keep an open mind."

Bili finished dressing, then moved over to the basin filled with water. Splashing his face, he could feel the shock of the cold liquid stir his system fully awake. Taking a cloth, he dried his face, and pulled a wooden comb roughly through his thick dark hair.

"I suppose you'll want me to get the stone from the men's house? Well, I can be in and out of there without anyone seeing or hearing me."

"If we hope to do anything against whoever sent those war hawks, I'd like to be ready. Yes, I need the stone, Bili. While you're busy getting it, I'll get some food packed, get our forest cloaks and put everything in our traveling packs. Then I'll meet you down by the old cedar at the edge of the village. Try not to run into father though. I don't want him to get more upset than he already is. I don't know what he'll do when he finds out that we're going back to the pond to investigate. He asked us to stay away from there until the shaman can check everything over and ward the area against intrusion from the outside. He'll be angry with us if he discovers we've disobeyed his orders."

While Meri packed, Bili, true to his word, slipped in and out of the men's house unnoticed. He placed the stone in a small leather pouch and put it in his jacket. Covering his tracks, he hurried to the appointed rendezvous, proud that he hadn't awakened anyone. It was still dark when Meri joined him.

"I think I got everything," she said, short of breath from running the last two hundred meters.

"Your sword is hooked to the pack and the dagger is inside with the flint and tinder. I also put in some dried jerky and fruit. If we have to flee the village, these provisions should last us until we get out of the mountains. I don't think we can get too far without something to eat along the way."

Bili reached into his pocket and took out the leather pouch. Handing it to Meri he smiled, "There's a rawhide strip sewn into the pouch if you want to wear it around your neck."

Meri took the pouch and slipped the thong over her head. It felt warm, and despite its bulk proved to be rather light. Bili had felt its heaviness when he had first retrieved it from the pond. Now its properties seemed to have changed and it didn't seem to be a burden. This gave her an odd sense of comfort.

"Thanks," she said as she gave her brother an affectionate hug. "What would I do without your help and oneness of spirit?"

They became silent as they started down the hill. Meri looked ahead carefully, using the tracking skills she employed when hunting game. She couldn't help wondering what lay ahead. Would she ever see home again if they were forced to run for their lives, taking these strange stones with them? They stepped carefully on the trail, placing their feet on stones, avoiding the grasses that would leave traces of their passing to any skilled tracker.

Dawn found them working their way around the pond. There was an unusual silence. The forest was normally alive with the sounds of birds, greeting one another in the treetops. Today it appeared something was upsetting the inhabitants.

Keenly aware of this change, Bili signaled Meri as they pushed their way warily to the stands of bamboo that served as an enclosure to the pond. These poles were also a source of siding used by Bili's clan in building homes. Sometimes Meri made spearheads from the sharpened bamboo and fitted them into her shafts. These she used while hunting the wild boars that lived in the lower swamp areas southeast of the village. She used her father's dogs to track and rouse the pigs. These hunts were seasonal, and she went only in the company of her father or brother.

Ahead, Bili could just make out the clearing where he and Meri had buried the roc and the hawks that died in yesterday's battle. As he approached, he noticed movement just beyond them. Stopping in his tracks, he crouched, fear beginning to make his heart race.

Meri noiselessly joined him. They hid, watching as men in strange robes prodded the ground with their staffs. Meri crowded closer beside him, intent on seeing what the strangers were doing. Soldiers dressed in forest green moved in behind them, examining the brush nearby. Bili knew if they looked hard enough, they would soon find evidence that a battle had indeed occurred.

"Meri, do you recognize any of those people up ahead?" Bili whispered. "Whoever they are, it won't take them long to find the bodies that we buried yesterday. Do you think we can work our way closer and hear what they're saying?"

Meri nodding her head in mute agreement moved forward, under the shelter of two old cedars. They were gnarled and low to the ground, bowed with greatness of age. As Meri approached, she heard the sound of voices. They obviously belonged to these strangers, but she had a difficult time understanding what they were saying. The words were familiar, but the way those strangers pronounced them was new. Meri followed their speech closely, but most of it eluded her.

Bili, who had made trips to the other villages to the north, fared little better. He glanced at Meri, who shrugged her shoulders in hopelessness.

Bili nudged her to move toward the east, where they could cross the trail without being seen. As they shifted positions, one of the robed priests turned in their direction. Meri froze. Cocking his head to one side, he seemed to be listening for something. Then suddenly he turned back to the others. One of the solders had dug up the body of a hawk. Meri's heart began to pound as she saw him hand the body to the priest. Horrified, she moved quickly across the trail, followed closely by her brother. When they were a safe distance away, Bili gripped Meri's arm.

"They found the hawk, didn't they? Now they'll know that the people in this area saw what happened. When they uncover the body of the roc, they'll find the stone missing. They'll probably probe the pond, and when they don't come up with anything, they'll start searching the villages closest. Someone is bound to tell what he saw yesterday, and then they'll attempt to recover the stones. Meri, our people are in danger. What should we do?"

Meri was silent. The messages she received through those dreams were right. They would have to make a dash for it if they had any hope of getting away.

"Bili, our only hope lies in getting away from here as quickly as we can. The dreams I had last night showed us fleeing through the sacred mountains. I'm afraid to go there, but that's the direction we appeared to be traveling."

Bili started to protest, but a loud outburst from one of the strange robed priests cut him short. Peering more intently through the brush, they saw the priest lift a metal object suspended from a chain hung around his neck. He began chanting in some strange tongue, turning slowly as his incantation filled the air. Crackling sounds filled the air- the kind one sensed when lightening struck a nearby tree. The hackles on Bili's neck rose involuntarily.

Meri shivered, feeling her stone pulse within the pouch. Panic filled her mind. The priest was tracking the stones!

"Bili, we've got to get out of here. The priest is using that object around his neck to track the stone. We're too close. We've got to get further away, or he'll locate us. My stone is pulsing."

Bili, frozen in fear, stared at the priest. Terror attempted to grip his mind. He felt himself begin to slip. He reached for his own stone. To his dismay, it too was radiating a signal. He could feel it now through his hand. Jerking away suddenly, he began stuffing it fearfully into its pouch. Freeing his hand, he nodded tersely. "Let's go! You're right about the sacred mountains. That's the only place that might throw them off the track. Enough incantations and spells have been called upon over the years to provide some kind of interference. We might have a chance if we take that route."

Silently, they melted back into the forest, picking the quickest route to the burial mounds. Still careful to leave as little trace as necessary, they hurried east. Bili followed Meri so he could check their back trail. He brushed out marks several times as they passed over soft ground. Twice he stopped and purposely made false trails leading north. At least it would slow them down, he thought anxiously.

Within the hour they gained the heights. Here the burial mounds started. The beds, placed above ground, were mute testimony to spirits who guarded the groves. Small tables dotted the fringes, some fallen with age. The sending feasts were held here, ensuring that the spirits of the departed would be assisted safely on their journey deep into the mountains. Sometimes a spirit would refuse to go, and would haunt the groves for weeks. They would even venture into the forests near villages and attack the women and children as they were foraging for nuts and berries. Bili hoped that there were no such spirits here now. He was glad it was daylight, when the power of those spirits was weakest. They would need to hurry to be out of the reach of anything accidentally left lurking around. The day would pass quickly, because the trails were unknown and they would probably have to backtrack several times before they gained the fastness of the mountain forests.

Glancing back along the lowlands above which they had ascended, Meri saw no trace of pursuit. Yet, the stone continued to pulse. Concerned, she stopped and spoke to her brother.

"Bili, this stone continues to radiate power. Is your stone active as well?"

Bili fished out the stone, still amazed at the brilliance of the blue colors. "Only slightly. It's a lot less than when we were back there near the pond. Do you think that means they are following us?"

"I'm not sure, but that would be my guess. Maybe we've thrown them off the track temporarily. At least, I hope we have. Have you ever been beyond this point?"

"No, this is as far as I've gone. I've been told about the trails into the Sacred Mountains, just as you have, but I have no idea where they begin."

Meri could barely contain her disappointment. "Well, if that's the situation, we'd best get moving. We'll have to hunt for a major track, or follow animal tracks until we run across one. What do you think?"

"You're right again, Meri. Let's skirt these clumps of juniper, and move off to the lower side. Maybe we'll find an easier way to get across to that ridge with the huge boulder on the top."

Soon they were working their way through the scattered trees at the far end of the groves, which ended abruptly at the face of a cliff. Bili looked down and found a rough track leading into the dense brush below. Holding onto rocky handholds, he started down. Meri followed, her soft shoes conforming to the shape of the rocks which formed the footholds she used.

Within the hour they were climbing up the other side toward the promontory they had seen back in the groves. A narrow track led toward the back of the ridge. Following this, they wound their way to the top. It was late morning when they finally broke out into the clearing they had been trying to reach. Here they stopped to drink from their water flasks. Meri pulled out two pieces of dried jerky, handing one to Bili.

"From here we command quite a view of those groves," Bili said admiringly. "I wonder if we should wait a bit and see if we can expect company anytime soon?"

"That's a good plan, Bili," Meri said. "I think, though, I would move off to one side. We might be too easily spotted standing here as we are."

Bili grinned at her in spite of the seriousness of their situation. "Yes, you're right of course, but the sun sure feels good. Wonder how cold it will get in these mountains tonight? And whether it's going to rain? We're on the other side of the water shed now. I don't know much about this place."

"Well, we've got our cloaks in any case," Meri sighed. "At least we'll keep somewhat dry. Maybe we can find an overhanging ledge to shelter under if rains do start."

They sat side by side for almost an hour, scanning the hills and groves behind them. Eventually, seeing nothing, they decided to move on. Hiking another two hours brought them to the base of the forbidden heights. Few people ventured here, and then only in the company of the village shaman. In spite of this fact, this path was the one that they had been forced to follow to protect themselves from discovery. The magic supposedly contained here would easily shield them from anyone searching out their tracks.

Further up, the trail split. Bili paused a moment as he decided which path to follow. He was tempted to place his hand over the talisman to seek direction. As quickly as he thought to do so, he pulled his hand away. He had no desire to become dependant on magic. He'd heard enough about magic to make him cautious. Finally deciding, he took the left fork. It wound closely around the mountain and led, as Bili had been warned, ultimately to the dreaded caves. Only shaman ventured there, and some never returned. It was a dangerous place. Dread gripped Bili's heart. Were they going to have to go that direction to keep the stones safely from those strange priests? Bili desperately hoped that would not happen. He knew their lives hung in the balance once they committed themselves to this path. He wisely kept his thoughts to himself.

In the distance, they heard the sound of a village horn. Three long blasts. Danger! Meri now knew the strangers had been discovered. Soon they would be missed as well, and a great hunt would begin. Meri shivered at the prospect. Would those priests track them here? Would her father and the villagers decide to fight with the priests? Did those priests have powers that would destroy the people among whom she had been raised? Would they force the truth out of the people and then track them?

Her heart beating wildly, Meri moved up the trail after Bili. She tried to stop shaking, concentrating instead on leaving as little trail as possible. They climbed for another hour. Then, taking a rest, they sat down on two stones opposite each other on the trail. Meri took a handkerchief from her pack, and wiped her forehead and neck. The sun had just now gone behind the clouds and the day began to cool a little. The hike was difficult because they were climbing steadily, gaining height quickly. Looking back over the trail, they could spot the groves far in the distance. Bili smiled approvingly.

"Meri, we've sure come a long way in the past couple of hours. I wish we were close enough to see if anyone has come to the groves."

"Maybe it's just as well we can't," his sister replied. "If we knew they were definitely on our trail, we'd panic or do something foolish and get caught anyway."

While she spoke, her stone began pulsing. She put her finger to her lips. He stopped and she showed him the stone. He nodded, then moved to her side.

"What does it mean?" he asked.

"It senses danger ahead, and is trying to help me understand the nature of the danger. Wait a moment," she warned. She stood silently for a while, then took the stone out of the pouch holding it openly in her hand. "You must create a diversion for me, Bili. I have to do the rest. Go up the trail to that boulder, and pry it loose. Send it down the side of the mountain, then bang the trees nearby with your sword. Something will come after you. Don't run from it; just hold your sword in front of you."

Wondering what was going on, Bill moved quietly toward the boulder. He found a short, dead limb suited to his purpose. Wedging the limb under the boulder he pushed with all his might. At first the stone refused to budge. As he continued to pry upward, it grudgingly slipped forward a couple of inches. Bili wedged the limb again, and pushed hard. The boulder slipped a bit further, then began to roll forward. With a loud crash, it gathered speed, crushing everything in its path. Bili quickly drew his sword, and banged it against several saplings growing nearby. He yelled and stamped the leaves and brush.

He felt the presence before he saw it. It was malevolent and angry. Disturbed, it left its lair and came to claim the intruder. "A guardian," thought Bili petrified.

No one with any sense came this way. Stories of the Guardians had made their way into local folklore. No one had ever seen one, but the wise didn't attempt to disprove those stories either. Leave a sleeping dog lie. It was always the safest path. Now Bili was face to face with a living legend.

Terrified, he turned, placing his sword in front of him. The creature was huge and ugly. Dark scaly flesh covered its limbs, grotesque and deformed. The stench was overpowering. Panic and confusion filled Bili's mind. He tried to run, but was rooted to the spot. The creature was projecting into his mind. He could feel the probe penetrate his senses, and fill him with darkness. He tried to scream, but nothing came. He tried again, and yet again. The creature just moved inexorably closer, reaching out with those ugly limbs.

Meri waited for the right moment. The creature passed without sensing her presence, his mind on Bili. She took the stone, and pressed it against the side of its body. She muttered two brief words, *talo yapri* which the stone supplied her, then she stepped back. The Guardian, stopped, turned, let out a roar of anger, and suddenly slumped to the ground. Meri waited but a brief moment, making sure the creature was indeed asleep. Stepping carefully around him, she hurried to Bili. Placing the stone on his forehead, it pulsed, causing all the darkness to recede. He looked at Meri, then at the creature. He sagged to the ground in relief, dropping his sword.

"I thought I was finished," he whispered hoarsely. "It filled my whole mind, and I couldn't do anything against it."

"I know," Meri admitted. "I could feel it probing. The stone protected me and guided me in disarming it and putting it to sleep. Had I known, I could have instructed you to hold your stone. But maybe it was best you didn't. It might have been alerted of the danger and might not have gone far enough toward you for me to stop it. Let's check its lair."

She moved off in the direction it had come. She had only to follow her nose to find the entrance. She held her breath, and together with Bili ventured inside. The rough cave was dark, and leaves and brush partially covered the opening. Bili grabbed several branches, and hauled them outside, allowing more light to penetrate.

Inside were old bones, rusted weapons, dried vines and leaves. Obviously, it wasn't a very clever creature; just one that could blind men's minds and destroy them. They ventured a bit further into the cave. Suspended from several vines was something huge shaped like a cocoon, wrapped up in leaves and brush. With a sweep of his sword, Bili severed the vines and the bulky cocoon landed heavily to one side. Meri began unwrapping it. Bili stood by and watched. A foot appeared, then another. Bili, holding his nose in disgust, looked on in horror, wondering if he would find a half-eaten corpse. Against his better judgment, he bent down and began helping. It took time to unravel all the coils the guardian had spun around the body. They were tough and thick. Neither of them was sure what they would find when they unwrapped this package.

After struggling to free the body for some minutes, they broke his shoulders free of the final harness. To their amazement, they found a very heavily drugged man. Reaching down into her pack, Meri pulled out the container of water she had filled at the stream. Pouring some into his mouth she said, "Try and drink this." He sputtered and then tried drinking. He managed to swallow a little at first, then more. Bili propped up his head, and tried to help. The man lay there, groggy and babbling incoherently. Meri forced more water through his lips. He stopped for a moment, then relaxed.

In a short time, the man was able to sit up feebly. He stared at them in the darkness, then suddenly tried to stand. He fell heavily at first, but after a few more tries, and with an assist from both Meri and Bili, he managed to remain upright. They helped him walk toward the entrance, the stench forgotten for the moment. The fresh air was delightful. All three of them drew it hungrily into their lungs.

Now that they were in the light, they had a good look at the man they had rescued. His pants and shirt were covered in mud and grime, with stains where he had bled from several wounds inflicted by the guardian. He was a couple inches taller than Bili, and heavier. His complexion appeared to be lighter than theirs, but with all the dust and filth on him, it was hard to tell. He had penetrating brown eyes, clear and strong. His nose was well formed, but a bit sharper than their own; yet he looked manly for all that. His thick brown hair fell neatly into place as he brushed his hands through it trying to shake out the debris that had lodged there. He was well proportioned, and thickly muscled, with those knotted cords on his shoulders and arms standing out prominently. Meri thought he must be a warrior, or at least a well-traveled woodsman. His hands were big, yet his fingers were slender. There were large calluses on both hands, the mark of someone used to heavy work.

Moving away from the Guardian, they made their way slowly along the trail. Coming to a clearing, the man stumbled again and fell to the ground, panting. Meri offered him more water, but he refused. "I'll be all right again in a moment," He whispered. He lay there panting. Bili went over and cut a sturdy limb from one of the nearby trees. He brought it back and offered it to the man on the ground.

"Here, use this cane until you're feeling stronger."

The stranger accepted it and struggled to his feet. "Guess I'm not as strong as I'd hoped I'd be," he mumbled. Meri offered him part of a biscuit, and he nibbled on it. "Sure tastes good! I haven't eaten anything for days. I've no idea how long I've been hanging in that nasty cavern."

"We'll talk about it later," Meri insisted wisely. "Right now we need to get as far away as possible. That creature could wake up any time and come after us."

"You don't have to ask me twice," the stranger replied as he struggled with his footing. With

that they continued on, at a pace the stranger was able to keep. By nightfall, they had covered only a couple more miles. Finding a secluded shelter underneath an overhanging boulder behind some scrub brush, they made camp.

Bili got a small fire going, to keep the stranger warm. He had no pack, no provisions, and no weapons. Bili wondered what could have happened to them. He noticed nothing in the cave of the Guardian. Surely the creature wouldn't have thrown them away. Meri made some soup, part of which she handed boiling hot to the stranger. He accepted it gratefully, cupping it in both hands. He sipped it slowly. Bili threw a few more twigs on the coals. As the branches flared, the stranger finished the soup.

Looking at Meri, the stranger said, "I owe you my life. Twice that beast injected me. I thought I was going to die from the pain alone."

"Yes, you were in pretty rough shape back there. You looked like tomorrow's dinner," Bili interrupted. "And I didn't like the look or smell of the one who was planning to dine."

"Bili!" Meri scolded. "Don't be so insensitive! You weren't in such great shape either."

"It's okay," said the stranger. "I'm just glad to be alive."

Looking again at Meri he volunteered, "You're probably wondering how I ended up in that cavern. Well, from my features you can tell I'm not from around here. I was sent on a mission to the Western Lands. I was trying to take a short cut, when I spotted a giant roc from the West flying overhead. I wondered what it was doing this far east, so I hurried to follow it. I got careless and wasn't watching where I was going. The guardian surprised me.

"I don't like traveling through goblin country. That's why I'm so far south. My name is Wulpai. It means 'Favorite Son.'" He waited expectantly for a response.

Bili's eyes began to betray him. Meri saw he was about to blurt out information she didn't want known. "We assume, then, that you come from up north," she asserted. "Have you been often to the Western Lands?"

"I've been there several times as a courier for my king," Wulpai replied, noticing Meri's quick thinking. "It's quite a journey. This time, however, I'll be further south. I'll still use the same landmarks, but have to find new trails."

Bili looked puzzled. "If you've been traveling these paths, where's your gear. I didn't find any pack, food or weapons back there in the cavern."

Wulpai laughed. "I put them in a safe place just a bit further ahead. I was searching for a trail that would lead me south around these caves. That's when the Guardian surprised me." His answer seemed to satisfy Bili for the moment.

The fire began to burn lower, and Bili broke out the blankets they brought. "Here, you can use this blanket. I'm planning on keeping watch for that Guardian, or any other surprise this place might have ready for us."

Wulpai took the blanket gratefully, curled up near the fire and was soon fast asleep. Meri took the other, wrapped up in it, and propped herself against one of the boulders. She wondered about Wulpai and these strange circumstances. Was he all he seemed? Well, they had rescued him, he was grateful, and for the time being that was all that mattered. So far, they had eluded anyone who might be trailing them. That at least was a positive sign. She just hoped that the three of them would be up to tomorrow's challenges. She felt the warmth of the stone through the pouch as she drifted off into a light sleep.

Chapter 4

The Caves

Toward morning, Bili gently shook Meri. "Could you watch for a while?" he asked quietly. "I need a little sleep." Meri unwrapped herself, stretched her stiff body, and got to her feet. She gave Bili the blanket, took her bow and quiver, and moved off soundlessly to the edge of the camp. Bili lay down where Meri had been and felt the warmth of the ground under him. He was soon sound asleep. Wulpai still lay near the fire.

Shortly before dawn, Meri entered the camp, and stirred up the coals buried under the ashes. She coaxed some branches into flame, then spitted the game animal she had snared, skinned and gutted.

Wulpai was awakened by the smell of roasting meat. He turned over, sat up, and stretched, glad to be alive.

"How are you feeling this morning?" Meri asked quietly.

As he stood up, Wulpai replied, "I'm doing better, thanks. I still feel a bit weak in the legs. Sleeping with my head up instead of down seems to have done wonders for me otherwise," he smiled.

Bili stirred and flipped Meri's blanket off, folding it neatly. He placed it into the pack, then joined them near the fire, an appraising eye checking Wulpai before he glanced up into the early dawn sky.

"Looks like the weather is still holding. We should be able to lose anyone trying to follow us," he suggested tentatively, trying to sound more confident than he felt.

Meri took the meat from the fire, and cut off a couple of pieces, handing them to the two men.

"I had another dream last night, Bili," Meri started. "The stone is directing us through the caves. I've heard nothing but terrifying stories about that place, and I'm scared to go in," she admitted.

"Are you sure that's necessary?" Bili asked, apprehension lacing each word. "Surely we could find a way around them and still get where we need to go?"

"What stone are you talking about," Wulpai asked innocently.

"It's an involved story," Meri replied evasively. "I'm not sure you would understand, or agree."

"Time to break camp and move on," encouraged Bili. "The sun is beginning to bring the valley below into bold relief." Placing his hand on the talisman under his shirt, Bili swore! He yanked his hand away, licking it with his tongue to cool the pain. The stone had suddenly become hot. Quieting his spirit, he tried to listen. Impressions began to build. He sensed rather than saw those strange priests. There were others with them as well. Three were the soldiers he had seen earlier, but there was someone with them who radiated power. He had a sense of evil and cruelty about him. Bili shivered in-spite of the warmth of the sun peeking over the hills below them. It was obvious they were being followed. They must be very near for the stone to pulse so strongly. Bili turned to Meri.

"Meri, we've got to get out of here. Those strange priests are following us. They have someone with them who radiates power. He seems to be the leader. I can sense cruelty and evil radiating from him."

Meri nodded, kicking though the cold ashes on the ground. "The fire's out, so we can take a few branches and cover it. I wonder if there's a way out of this canyon other than the caves?" she muttered, more to herself than the others.

The thought of those caves sent shivers of fear through Bili's whole body, but he shouldered his pack, and helped Meri into hers.

Wulpai looked from Bili to Meri, confusion showing clearly by his expression. He knew they were being protective about these 'stones', whatever they were, but wasn't about to interfere at this point. They appeared afraid and under a lot of stress. He was prepared to let it go until a more appropriate time, but at this point he began to wonder if there would be another time.

"Wulpai, let's retrieve your gear before we head into those caves."

"Yes, it's only a short walk from here." Wulpai replied, pulling himself from his short-lived reverie. "I'll go get my stuff if you don't mind waiting."

Bili looked at Meri. "Why don't you stay here and wait. I'll go with him in case there's trouble."

Meri nodded, and Bili dropped his pack again. The two of them started off toward the trail. Meri tried to familiarize herself with the landmarks. To the east were more hills, but nothing worthy of note. To the Southeast, from where they had come yesterday, the land sloped away. This would be where the priests and those with them would be coming from. North, there were high mountains, some of them rugged and forbidding. West lay their only safe destination, the enigmatic caves. Meri was nervous. She had heard stories about them, none of them encouraging. She attempted to put these thoughts from her mind as she waited impatiently for her brother's return.

Not long afterward, the two men returned to the campsite. Wulpai had a full pack, a sword and a stout pole. Bili helped Meri into her pack again, and the trio started off at a fast pace. A short distance down the trail, a path led westward. Bili took this without hesitation, and worked his way steadily upwards toward the caves. As they topped a rise, the sheer wall of the caves rose threateningly above them. The jagged stones, like broken teeth, leered at them, mocking their puny strength. The wall rose in a breath-taking sweep that seemed to fill the sky before them. A narrow track traversed the Southern edge, twisting its way toward the top at the northern end.

"We've had it now," said Bili softly, staring uneasily about. "We must be insane to think we can survive this ordeal."

"We're going to have to trust ourselves to the maker of this stone. I don't see any way we'll survive otherwise," Meri stated for them all. "I'm scared to death."

Wulpai decided this might be a good time to encourage these young people.

"From what I've been told, there's nothing to fear inside but what you take in with you," he said simply, surprising them both. "Our people have many stories from of old about these caves. They are meant to reveal your true inner self, not destroy you. I don't know what you've been told, but trust the directions you've been given."

Bili started forward again, thinking as he walked. When the opportunity presented itself, he determined to question Wulpai. He seemed to know a lot more than he let on. *Who is he? Where does he really come from? And,* Bili thought finally, *can he really be trusted?*

Kicking aside the newly cut branches, the priest turned to the others. "The fire can't be dead more than two hours. They were here all right. I sense the residue of power as the stone activated. I'm sure they have the stone we're looking for. The sooner we locate them the better. From what I can tell, these trails lead up to the cursed caves. We must stop them before they can lose themselves inside. There's no way we can enter and survive."

Baalkorth cursed and spat angrily into the fire. "They've led us a merry chase, but that ends now! Gather close together. I'm going to teleport as close to those caves as I dare."

Once the group was clustered together, Baalkorth closed his eyes and the entire party disappeared, teleporting to the location Baalkorth had placed in his mind.

The vibration of power used to send such a large party disturbed the guardian. He awoke with a start. Realizing that he had been bested, he sullenly moved off to his lair. Smelling the air as he went, he was aware that others had come and gone as well. The smell of one of the strangers upset him. He sensed power had been wielded and he shrank back from it. This was one of the makers. He felt threatened. Gaining the entrance to home, he hurried to hide himself from danger.

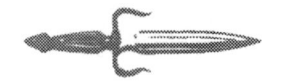

By mid-morning the trio had reached the base of the cliffs. The caves loomed above them. They sat down planning to have a short meal before going inside.

"Have you ever been inside these caves yourself?" asked Bili bluntly.

"No, I never have," replied Wulpai.

"Then how can you be so sure they're safe?" he asked smugly. "There might be all kinds of unexpected surprises waiting for us, ... like the one yesterday," Bili accused.

"Surely you don't believe that!" Wulpai chided. "If those kind of beasts entered, they would destroy themselves by their very nature. They wouldn't survive the pure kind of power that fills those caves because of the things from which they have been created. That's not to say though that some creatures created time out of mind might not be lurking inside."

"He's right Bili," Meri interrupted. "It's only the guilty who are always looking over their shoulders ready to run when no one's after them. Remember what father always told us. 'Those who aren't guilty have nothing to hide.'"

They finished their meal in silence, struggling mentally to prepare themselves to enter the caves. Bili felt totally inadequate. He had been scared and apprehensive when he had gone through the humiliation of initiation to become a warrior. Now he was facing another ordeal where he would probably be forced to look within himself. He hid a lot of his insecurity behind a mask of pride. He was fearful of what he might find once the mask was taken from him.

Meri looked up at the trail, squinting into the sunlight. A sense of expectancy and excitement passed through her as she realized there were more to these caves than just a test of oneself. There must be more than the goal of having us pass though here, Meri thought to herself. She was as interested and anxious to begin as Bili was loath to enter.

"C'mon Bili," she encouraged. "Let's get this over with. We'll be here all day if we don't hurry." With that, she started up the hill toward the entrance. Bili reluctantly followed her, plucking up what courage he had left. Wulpai followed at a distance, checking their back trail. As far as he could tell, no one would even think that they had taken this route. No one in his or her right mind would voluntarily go through these caves.

The entrance to the caves was wide, with a high arching dome. The sides were formed of jagged limestone protrusions, resembling the teeth of a dragon. The floor, by contrast, appeared smooth, as though someone had taken time to lay pieces of tile together. Meri went in a short distance, and the light got dimmer.

"Boom!" As she reached into the side of her pack, a tremendous blast of power hit the wall above her. Instinctively, she fell and rolled to one side, the debris spattering her back and legs. The smell of ozone and cordite filled the air. Bili and Wulpai, who had been behind her, were hurled backwards toward the entrance, chunks of limestone rock clattering noisily about them. Wulpai bled from a cut to his forehead, his eyes blinded by the dust of the blast.

Bili, skinned and bruised by his fall, picked himself up and turned around, staring fearfully down the wall. Those fearsome priests were there, looking up toward them. The cruel looking man Bili had seen in his vision was moving up the wall rapidly, triumph written across his cruel face.

Shocked from his stunned disbelief, Bili grabbed Wulpai by the arm, lifting him to his feet. He half dragged Wulpai to where

Meri was pulling out two small sticks wrapped in oiled cloth. She thrust out her arm, and waited for Bili to take one of the sticks.

"We've got to get into the caves now! I only made up two," Meri apologized. "But if we can stick together we can conserve our light. We've got to get away from that dangerous man at all costs!"

Nervously, and with one eye on the entrance, Bili got out the flint and tinder, and started a small fire. Meri then ignited the torch from the shavings. Bili shoved everything back in his pack, and the three of them hurried onward. Wulpai seemed at ease in spite of the tension. He followed close behind, careful not to lag lest he fall in the gloom and slice himself against the stone shards strew across their pathway.

Looking back, Wulpai saw the cruel looking man rushing closer to them. As he breached the entrance, he was thrown violently backwards. Not deterred, Baalkorth the Bold picked himself up, and sent a red beam in their direction. It smashed harmlessly to the left, splintering more rock from the stony bed. Wulpai turned from that scene to catch up once again.

Further in, Meri, who was holding the torch, rounded a corner and stepped into a small running stream. She looked upstream then down, wondering which way to go. The wind was blowing softly in the direction of the flow, so she decided that this would be safest.

Bili let out a grunt when his feet hit the water. "I could really have done without this," he moaned. "Maybe I should look on the bright side, and say, 'Oh, now we'll have water to drink' if we survive the night! Hope it's not too mineralized to drink."

The channel continued to lead gently downward. It turned first one direction, then another, as it snaked its way into the mountain. A series of terraces formed a natural stairway leading off to the left. Sediment had built up here and made the bed slippery. Bili almost fell twice as he twisted around trying to get a good look at the walls and the formations of stalactites hanging from the ceiling. He began to feel a bit claustrophobic, as the walls became narrower; the ceiling seemed to press down on him.

After what seemed like hours, they broke out into a large chamber. The wind had picked up noticeably, and the little torch was almost blown out. "Meri, watch out! The wind is about to leave us in total darkness," Bili said, a worried look on his face. "No telling what might happen if we try to move without a light. I'm sure there are some deep sinkholes around here. If we fell into one of them, we'd be killed or starve to death before anyone found us."

Meri continued to look around. "Wulpai, what do you think?" she consulted him. "You've no doubt been in caves before. What appears to be the most likely route to you?"

"At this point, I'd say we should continue going down. If these caves actually go right through the mountains, we'll have to get as low as possible to catch an exit."

With that, Meri turned again and took the right fork. It seemed to be going down. Shortly, she stepped into water again. "This must be the same stream we left just before we entered the main room back there." She was comforted and felt they were on the right path. They continued on for some minutes, then found the water growing deeper. Soon it was running above their knees, and the cavern began twisting in both directions. The ceiling got lower, and the water higher. It now reached their waists. They waded on. If it got any deeper, they would have to swim. Meri wasn't looking forward to swimming with a pack on her back.

Rounding another corner, they bumped against a stairway leading away from the water. Meri turned aside to check it. Who would carve stairs here in the middle of a cavern? She looked at Bili and Wulpai, an expression of disbelief crossing her face briefly.

"What do you think of this?" She said in wonder. "It looks similar to stairs leading up from a great wharf." She looked down the stream and noticed that water was filling a greater portion of the cavern. It didn't look safe at all.

"Meri, I've got my hand where I want it," Bili said cryptically. "I get the impression we're supposed to climb these stairs. It looks like a dead end for us further down anyway. What do you think?"

"You're probably right, Bili," Meri agreed. "My torch is about out, and I don't relish swimming with a pack on my back and trying to keep a torch above water. I'm game to try the stairway if you two are."

Two heads nodded, so Meri started climbing. The stairs were wide from side to side, easily measuring 20 meters across. The slope of the stairs was gentle, rising vertically at a measured pace. It seemed to be made for people bearing heavy burdens. The trio continued climbing. The stairs appeared endless. They stopped to catch their breath twice before going on.

"I've counted over 375 stairs already," remarked Bili. "I wonder how much further they go?"

As if in answer to his query, more stairs appeared as they turned another corner. Bili kept count. They mounted another 125 stairs, and stopped on a landing. The stairs narrowed here and turned again, this time to the left. They continued to climb. After another interminable space, they came to a second landing. Here, there were no more stairs; only three doors. There were strange runes on all three. Bili stepped up to the door, attempting to read it. There was a buzzing in his head as he touched the talisman again. He pressed the left door tentatively. It wouldn't move. Then he shoved harder on it. It still wouldn't move. He relaxed and spoke what came into his head.

"Hi hatput heriuwe menmen iuwe me nan im, ti ekeisiu."

Slowly the door ground forward, opening about halfway. Bili poked his head around the entrance, and exclaimed, "It's lit up by small torches. C'mon!" As he went through the door, it slammed shut, sealing him inside. Bili turned to pull the door back open, but there was no handle. The door was smooth and the crack where the entrance had been vanished.

Meri watched with astonishment as the door slammed shut and became a solid wall. She looked at Wulpai in alarm, "What happened? My brother's trapped on the other side. We've no way to join him or help him!"

Wulpai laid a hand on her shoulder and tried to calm her near hysteria. "Easy Meri. I've heard that in these caves, each person must finally take his or her own path. Bili obviously found his. Now you must find yours."

Meri, still upset, turned then to look at the remaining two doors, then took a couple of deep breaths, letting the last out with a slow hiss. "Of course! That makes sense. There were only three doors here anyway. Now there are two. When I go, you'll take the last. Good luck to you, Wulpai. May the creator of the stone guide you to journey's end."

With that she gathered her thoughts and touched the stone. She felt compelled to push the door to the right. At her touch it swung open freely. She entered serenely, looking back at Wulpai. He smiled briefly, encouraging her. Then the door closed, leaving her alone.

Dave Scorza

Wulpai stepped up to the only door left. He touched it lightly and it swung open. He too moved apprehensively, as the door closed behind him. He walked down the dim corridor until he came to a main hall. Here he stopped, set down his pack, and sat with his back to the wall. He knew he would be tested, as would the others. He closed his eyes and seemed to drift off into deep sleep. Calling on his former shaman training, he slowed his beating heart. Concentrating, he began to shut out thoughts of panic as he had been taught. Peace began to replace panic. Anxiety gave way to clear thinking. Wulpai knew he would be able to face whatever confronted him as he moved through the corridor.

Bili got over his initial panic at being confined against his will when the door had slammed shut. He began to explore the shaft he was in. A draft gutted the torches once or twice. He thought about Meri. Her torch was almost used up. He hoped she was able to enter one of the other doors, just as he had this one. Wulpai would be happy for the challenge. He simply took everything in stride working with what came. Bili wondered how he himself would have survived hanging upside down for days in that foul smelling cave. Not very well, he concluded.

Bili wandered on. He came to a turn and followed it. Passing through the lowered archway he came to a dead end. He couldn't go back; the door had disappeared. He couldn't go forward because there was no opening. He was stuck. He quietly sat down and tried to clear his mind. Was there a door, or was this some kind of illusion? His first thought was to consult the talisman. He held it, but received no impressions. Apparently he would be on his own for this ordeal. Sweat dotted Bili's brow. What was expected of him? Staring at the wall, he noticed it beginning to change. It glowed and then shimmered, turning into a mirror. Bili saw himself reflected in that mirror. He stood up and approached the mirror. His reflection, however, did not. The reflection shimmered and changed. Before Bili stood a semblance of himself, yet someone altogether different. Bili watched intently as his alter ego began to portray to him his personality. Scenes from childhood flashed on the mirror, revealing ugly pictures of pride and competition, lying, stealing, cheating, and bullying others. The long buried act of vengeance came to life before him, showing him how cruel he had been to his former friend, Wiyon, when Wiyon had made public that he and Bili were the ones responsible for destroying the totems of a rival clan. Bili had only meant to scare Wiyon. Instead, he ended up crippled in one leg, never able to walk straight again. Wiyon's leg had almost been torn off by the trap Bili had set for him.

Filled with shame at seeing what he was really like, Bili buried his head in his arms. He couldn't face things he was now ashamed of. Bili wondered how he could have done some of these things. But there they were in front of him. He couldn't deny he had done them. Shame and remorse filled his heart. He cried at what he saw. A lot of what he had done stemmed from his jealousy of others, and his insecurity at home. Bili was glad the others were not here to see. He wept openly.

As suddenly as the pictures appeared, they vanished. The mirror faded away, and in its place was an archway leading deeper into the mountain's heart. Bili finally stood and stumbled through. He became disoriented and began falling down a long narrow shaft. He screamed out in fear as he fell. Then he got hold of himself, reached out and steadied himself against a wall. He hadn't really fallen at all. It was another illusion. He chuckled nervously, righted himself and started on. He rounded a corner in the cavern and came face to face with an ugly goblin. Freeing his sword as quickly as he could, Bili backed up ready to fight. With a roar, the goblin attacked. Bili parried the blows, trying to get over his shock. The goblin kept coming. Bili stopped backing and started pressing the advantage of his greater reach. He broke through the goblin's defense and ran his sword through his chest. The goblin howled loudly, as blood poured from the wound, and hissed upon striking the floor. Bili watched in horror, as the blood turned into snakes which rushed toward him. He jumped over them and tried to run past the goblin. He only managed to bump into him and trip. The goblin started howling, this time with laughter, as Bili fled up the other side of the cavern. He stopped and looked back. The goblin had evaporated and disappeared. Another illusion! Bili was relieved, but ashamed. It had all seemed so real. He had failed again. There was nothing to do but go on. Painfully aware of his inadequacies, Bili clutched the talisman and silently prayed this nightmare would end.

His next choice was a stairway leading down or a small trap door going up. He chose the stairway. He hurried down it, careful not to trip on the slippery surface. Placing his foot on the last stair, he felt something grab his ankle and plunge him headlong onto the slimy surface. He guessed at another illusion, so he did nothing. The Guardian that confronted him smelled and looked just like the one back on the mountain. Bili waited, holding tightly to the stone.

The Guardian moved its tremendous bulk right over Bili, then reached out a grotesque arm, hooked him around the waist and lifted him up. Bili tried to calm his mind saying, "This is only an illusion. It will pass." He desperately clutched the talisman under his shirt and waited. The Guardian injected him with its stunning juices. Unbelievable pain wracked Bili's body. He screamed, then struggled to get free. The Guardian held him fast, then began encasing him in a web like substance. Bili became groggy, and went limp. He awoke hanging upside down, suspended from several strands hooked to the cavern roof. He took stock of his options.

If this was a real situation, what could he do? Amazingly enough, his arm was still against the talisman. He could feel it under his hand. He knew it had a rough edge, so he slowly worked it up through the opening in his shirt, then twisted it against the webbing. The webbing began to tear, and soon Bili had his arm free. He continued to cut until most of his body was free. Looking around, he saw no Guardian, so he cut his legs loose, gradually lowering himself to the floor. He was groggy and his head hurt! Bili wondered if this was not an illusion after all. Leaning against a wall he rubbed his temples. He continued this way until the pain and pressure lessened. As his eyes began to clear and he could think normally, he went forward, this time, dagger and sword in hand. He would not be tricked again. The stench was still strong, and grew stronger as he reached a fork. The last thing Bili wanted was to have another run-in with the creature. He stopped for a moment trying to think. He knew that one of the two forks led to freedom, the other contained the Guardian. How could he make the right choice? Examining the floor, he looked for marks to show the Guardian had passed one way or the other. The floor was too hard and showed no signs of passage. The air smelled the same in both openings. "I don't want to go through either opening," Bili spoke aloud to him, frustrated at having to make a choice. He stood there momentarily, then instead of choosing, he put his hand on the wall in front of him, and pushed. Nothing happened. He took the talisman from around his neck and touched the wall a second time. It shimmered, then a door appeared. "Ah, another illusion," he yelped triumphantly. He took hold of the latch, and pulled hard. It slowly swung open, creaking on ponderous hinges, rusty from years of disuse. Relieved, he found himself in a main hall. Closing the door, he looked around to find Wulpai slumped against a wall to one side, but there was no sign of Meri. Concerned, Bili set his pack down, collapsing next to Wulpai. He seemed in deep sleep, so Bili left him alone and put his own head down waiting for his sister to appear. He too soon fell asleep, exhaustion and the injection of the guardian's venom overcoming his will to remain alert for the arrival of his sister.

Chapter 5
Amazing Adventure

Bili opened one eye. The sleep had felt good. He'd been exhausted. Gazing down the hallway, it took a moment to remember where he was, but was he unable to figure whether it was day or night. Time had no meaning here in the caves. There was no sunlight, no stars, no movement, or so it seemed. *Maybe there is only time,* Bili reflected. He had no idea how much time had passed since he had entered these caves. There hadn't proven to be a short cut anywhere, if that's what people's legends said they were supposed to be. A testing ground, yes definitely. Bili thought back over what had occurred up to this point. If he were being judged, he'd be a miserable failure. Thoughts of his early life and those things that had occurred brought regret and this saddened him. *I wonder how Wulpai fared as he worked his way here?* Bili mused.

Looking over, he saw Wulpai stir. He sat up, stretched himself, scratched the side of his neck, then looked around.

Sometime as they slept, Meri too had arrived and had placed herself near them. Now she too was beginning to wake. Lifting herself off the floor onto her elbows, she peered out from between strands of beautiful dark hair. She gave the two men a lopsided grin. "Looks like we made it this far without getting killed. Maybe we've a chance of survival yet." Smiling at some inner thought, she got up, folded her blanket and placed it in her pack.

"I don't know what happened to you two when we parted, but I don't want to relive any of my adventures. I've had enough of this place. I just want to get out!"

Bili swore softly to himself then said, "I'm feeling like you, Meri. I didn't know when to take my experiences seriously, or to ignore them. I failed on all counts. The mirror was the most awful thing for me. I have no false ideas about myself now. Did you experience anything like that?" Bili asked hesitantly, looking over at her.

"As a matter of fact, I did," Meri replied shortly. "I feel better not talking about it either. I'm sure that I too have failed whatever tests were meant to help me back there. I'd rather not dwell on them."

Pulling out the last of his jerky, Bili offered a piece to Meri. "Thanks, but I'm just not hungry."

Wulpai, however, took a couple of strips and began to let one melt in his mouth. Then he ripped off a chunk of another and began chewing slowly, releasing the flavors locked within. Bili too took one of the last pieces. He needed something after all he had been through.

Getting their gear together, they walked to the end of the hall and went through the only exit available. They entered a narrow cavern with a low ceiling, and immediately spun into disorientation. They were falling and spinning at the same time. They all screamed and yelled as they fell. Just as suddenly as it began, it was over. They lay sprawled on the floor.

"What was that all about?" muttered Bili, picking himself up again.

Looking around, Meri peered at the walls. "Something is really different about this place. Wonder what we're up against this time?"

Wulpai was last to get up. He stood studying the cavern for a short time, then turned and looked at the archway they had crossed. He stretched his hand out trying to shove it through the opening. A tremendous burst of energy hit Wulpai, knocking him across the cavern's narrow space into Bili. They both fell heavily into the wall. Meri, concerned, rushed over and tried to help by rolling Wulpai off of Bili.

"I'm okay, Meri. See what you can do for Wulpai. That looked really nasty." Meri checked his eyes, which were rolled up in his head. She put her ear to his chest. He was barely breathing, but his heart was beating. She waited anxiously for him to regain consciousness.

Meri lifted his head off the floor, tears running down her cheeks. "We know so little about him, yet he seems so brave," Meri whispered worriedly. "He always fills our hearts with hope when we should cringe with fear. I hope he's going to be okay."

"Maybe we could use these two stones somehow to help him," offered Bili. "Don't you think we could try joining our minds or wills through these stones, and see if we can bring him around?"

"I don't know if we should try something like that," cautioned Meri. "The stones are so new to us, we might do more harm to him."

"Just try," begged Bili. He took out the talisman, held it in his hand and began to concentrate, forming a picture of his injured friend.

Meri watched Bili for a moment, empathy evident in her soft looks toward him. Then she too took the stone from the pouch clutching it tightly. She closed her eyes, trying to see a whole, alert Wulpai. The stone began to glow faintly as her mind entered its power field. An echoing reply came from the talisman. Soon both stones were quietly humming. Meri passed her stone over Wulpai's head and chest in a circular motion. Bili moved over and pressed his stone against Wulpai's heart. Laying the stone on Wulpai's forehead, Meri chanted words welling up in her.

"Harmony and concord sustain life;
love dwells underneath to give life to both.
Pain and discord flee, disruptive and destructive.
Be banned to the nether realms where darkness begets evil spawn.
Power of light, enter. Repair, restore, retrieve, replenish,
and relieve: Re-light the spark which yet remains."

The stone pulsed in a steady rhythm, like a beating drum. The talisman took up the beat, pulsing in accompaniment. Wulpai seemed to relax, released by the power that gripped him. His eyes shut, his body went limp and an audible sigh escaped his lips. Meri removed the stone and placed it carefully in the leather pouch. Bili stuffed the talisman back inside his shirt. They waited and watched.

After anxious minutes, Wulpai moved his left hand. Jerky at first, then smoothly he lifted it to his head. He opened his eyes hesitantly, looking around at his companions.

"Got any medicine for a headache? I feel like I fell off a cliff and hit my head on the only stone in the pond." Wulpai commented.

Even though he sounded light-hearted, Meri knew he was still experiencing a great deal of pain. She rubbed her hand lightly over his forehead as he lay there. Bili pulled out his water bottle and poured a little for Wulpai. He drank a few drops, then lay back again.

"Looks as though our return passage has been canceled," Wulpai grinned. "I don't think I care to try that again!"

"We're so relieved that you're all right," Meri smiled. "It certainly does appear as though you're correct. We'll stay until you feel well enough to move on. Bili, we might as well stay here for a while. Get the blankets and..."Ro-o-o-ar!"

A deafening roar shook the cavern, cutting off further conversation. Bili slipped out his sword and spun around. Wulpai sat up in spite of the pain.

"I think we'd better plan on camping elsewhere," he winced. "Seems like this space has been spoken for."

He struggled to his feet, grabbed his pack, and put a hand out to steady himself. Bili moved down the cavern to where it made its first bend and peered around. He saw no monster, but rather the beginning of a twisting road. Meri joined him, holding on to Wulpai. They stared at one another.

"What are all these funny turns?" asked Bili? "It looks like someone took a bunch of stones and stood them up in crazy patterns."

"It's called a maze, Bili," Wulpai explained, his voice gruff from his brush with death. "There are many twists and turns, some which bar our way. If we follow the wrong one, either we come to a dead end, or have to face that noisy beast out there. We may find other unpleasant surprises awaiting us as well."

That was little comfort to Meri or Bili.

"I can't wait to get out of here!" Bili hissed, anger and fear replacing his shattered composure. "I don't know who has the warped sense of humor, but I don't think it's funny anymore!"

Meri put a hand on Bili's shoulder. "Just trust the stones, Bili. They'll see us through safely."

"Sure, just like they helped me defeat the goblin and get away from the Guardian back there," scoffed Bili. "Big help!"

Wulpai started forward. "When we enter the maze, we should make a right turn whenever possible. If we come to a dead end, we'll go left, then start on all right turns again. That way, we should eventually find our way out, even if it takes a little longer than lucky guesses. Watch out for trip levers along the wall. They may open trap doors to pits, or release arrows from within the walls. Anything can happen. Be alert."

Baalkorth cursed loudly, shaking his massive fists at the mountain. He stopped to wipe the blood from his temple where he had been so violently thrown into the wall. Turning to the Sanguma he bellowed, "Don't just stand there! Bring me a cloth, you dolts!"

One of the priests hurried to him proffering a towel. Grabbing it roughly, Baalkorth wiped the blood from his head then tossed the cloth back at the priest. Glaring around, he desperately sought to formulate an alternate plan. The Master wasn't going to be pleased with him. The trio had safely eluded them and was beyond reach. At this point there was nothing to do but report back to the palace and try to locate possible exit points from those cursed caves. Picking up a jagged stone, he angrily hurled it at the entrance, venting his rage. Turning his gaze from the mountain, he gathered his group together and teleported out of the area. The strange odor of burnt metal filled the air, lingering in the mid-day sun.

Wulpai moved on, followed by Meri. Bili scowled softly then reluctantly trailed them.

The first several hundred feet brought them slowly downward as they negotiated the turns, all right ones. Wulpai stopped and reached out a hand. It went through part of the wall. Meri let out a terrified gasp, afraid he would be hurled again against another wall.

Wulpai turned around and said, "This is the hardest part about a maze. Sometimes you don't know if what you're seeing is real. You have to test everything you're not sure about." He stepped through the illusion, and led them on. Bili looked around apprehensively before he stepped through the wall. Fear etched itself across his features before he shoved through the entrance.

As the trio continued to advance, Bili was first to notice a change in the walls. He yelled ahead to Wulpai. They stopped to inspect the way ahead of them. Embedded low in the wall was a trip lever. If any of them had brushed against it, it would have released something lethal. Taking her bow, Meri reached forward, tripping the level. A shower of darts sprayed across the path, embedding themselves in the opposite wall. The companions went on, finding and disarming two more. Further down, they came to a dead end. No illusions here; just no path! They retraced their steps, turned into a left-hand corridor, then continued to turn right as the maze deepened.

Another great roar froze them in their tracks. This time the harsh bellow was much louder. The monster was quite near. It sensed their presence. It was agitated. It wanted them, but couldn't find them. It lumbered its way toward them. Meri nocked an arrow on her bow. Bili drew his sword and dagger. Wulpai decided to set a trap rather than run.

"You two move ahead, but don't trip this lever. Hide in the right corridor until I attract its attention. When you hear it bellow from the pain this trap inflicts, come back quickly and see if you can get a clear shot or sword stroke in a weak spot."

Bili gave Wulpai his sword. "I'll be behind him. I can't get a good stroke in, but you may. My dagger will be enough for anything I might be able to do."

Wulpai took the sword, and felt its balance. There was a trace of blue as the runes shimmered slightly at his touch. He seemed satisfied. He handed Bili the dagger he had taken from his belt.

"Use this if you miss the first time," he said. "It's been a life saver on a couple of occasions."

Limping in obvious pain yet, Wulpai moved to the center of the path, motioning them on. Bili and Meri stepped carefully through the trap, then hid in the right hand corridor.

They didn't have long to wait. The monster emerged from the left, its powerful body glistening of slime and sweat in the glare of the low-burning torches.

Wulpai yelled loudly, causing it to turn in his direction. With huge jaws clacking, it moved on all fours toward the hidden trap. It brushed the lever, and sprang the trap. A huge sharpened log impaled itself in the side of the beast. It bellowed its rage, but was unable to withdraw the stake in the narrow corridor.

Wulpai worked his way to a shallow ledge, swinging the sword as he gained his footing. He caught the monster under the chin and split the skin right across its throat. A thick ichorous blood spilled out.

Meri appeared from the side and shot an arrow into its ear, quickly nocking another onto the bow. The beast turned to see it's new foe and Meri drove the second arrow deeply into its eye. Again it bellowed in rage, this time at being blinded.

Wulpai stabbed hard into the throat as the beast turned away, and drove the sword into a vital artery. More blood gushed out, making the floor slippery and dangerous. Wulpai withdrew the sword and backed away.

Bili slipped along its side and slashed quickly along its underbelly, the only soft place on it otherwise formidable body. He tried to get to the opening toward the left, but part of the beast's body blocked the entrance. The beast kicked out, sending Bili sprawling senseless for a few moments.

Wulpai looked for another opening, but finding none, decided to make one of his own. He feinted to the left, drawing the beast's attention in that direction. Then he charged forward, feinting again, this time jumping to the right up on the ledge- the beast's blind side. He stabbed hard up under the chin, driving the sword deeply into its neck. Then wincing, he leaped toward the back, narrowly escaping snapping jaws.

He joined Meri and Bili. Together, they waited to see whether the creature would die. It continued to thrash and bellow, finally breaking loose from the stake that had held it. It moved forward a little, then with astonishing agility climbed the side of the ledge and turned about to face them.

Meri drove another arrow deeply into the remaining eye, blinding the beast completely. He roared a challenge, then advanced, despite his blindness. Wulpai shoved them quickly through the left opening and they hurried down the narrow corridor.

"Sorry about the sword, Bili. I hope we can find some more weapons somewhere," Wulpai said hopefully.

In her haste, Meri missed a trip lever. It tripped the hidden trap and opened a huge pit door. She fell heavily through to a lower level. She twisted her ankle against the rocks below. Bili fell too, bruising his shoulder and back, but was otherwise okay. Wulpai, walking last, fell, but managed to hang on to the edge of the pit and pull himself up again. "Hey, are you two all right down there?" he inquired anxiously.

"Yes, just a little bruised, I think." Bili laughed nervously. "How about you Meri?"

Meri winced and said, "I think I've hurt my ankle. If I can't walk, I won't be much good if we have to run from another monstrous surprise."

"Bili, do you still have a rope in your pack?" he yelled. "If you do, toss it up to me."

Bili rummaged in the dark and came up with the short rope. He tossed one end up to Wulpai, then turned to Meri. "Tie it around your chest, and I'll support you as Wulpai tries to lift you out," Bili said, handing her the rope.

Meri looped it quickly under her arms and Bili lifted her in his arms as high as he could.

"Go ahead and pull her up, Wulpai. She's ready," called Bili. Wulpai took up the slack, then pulled. Meri dangled helplessly as she was drawn upward. Wulpai soon had her out. Then he threw the rope down to Bili. Bili looped it around himself and waited to be pulled up. Despite her bad ankle, Meri helped pull. Bili was quite a bit heavier than she, and it took both of them to get him to the opening. Bili grabbed hold of the side of the pit and pulled himself out.

"Thanks." I was afraid we would all end up down there. I couldn't see any way out."

They moved more carefully. Twice more they ran into traps, but avoided tripping them. Three more times they had to backtrack as they ran into dead ends. Finally, tired and worn out, they decided they'd be safe from the beast, if it was still alive. Collapsing, they all fell into a deep sleep.

The pulsing of the stone awakened Meri. She woke with a start from another bad dream. She felt the heat through the leather pouch. She looked around, but saw nothing. She shook Bili hard.

"Wake up! The stone is pulsing again. Something dangerous must be coming this way. Hurry!"

Bili jumped up, grabbed his blanket and stuffed it hurriedly into his pack. He drew out his dagger, but felt half-naked with no sword. Wulpai too got up, quickly straightened his pack and got ready to move on. Meri took out a short length of cloth and wrapped her damaged ankle, then lifted and shouldered her pack, wincing at the extra weight it created on her ankle. She stepped on it gingerly, testing it to gauge whether it would support her. Then satisfied that she could safely hobble, she stopped, reached out with her mind attempting to sense the direction from which the threatening thing was coming. Alarmed, she gasped!

"There is more than one of whatever is out there!"

There were no more torches in the corridors. Now an eerie glow from the walls illuminated their path.

"Time to make another right turn," Bili grimaced. "I hope that direction is clear of more 'friends.'"

They moved down the corridor and turned to follow the right corridor. Nothing appeared in their path so they went on. Always alert for levers, Bili concentrated on the walls. It was Meri who first saw their danger.

"Bili, stop!" she yelled. "Whatever they are, they're coming."

Bili stopped and looked up. Three hideous creatures were making their way toward them. Green slime oozed from their heavily plated sides. Twisted horns stuck out from the tops of their heads. Huge tusks like those of a pig extruded from the sides of their mouths. They slobbered in anticipation of a meal.

"Follow me!" ordered Wulpai. "There's more room to maneuver down toward them." He bolted ahead running at these vicious creatures. Just before he got there, he stopped. Meri and Bili were trailing behind, slowed by her bad ankle. To their left they found a small opening. Meri crawled through and found a full sized cavern.

"Quickly, in here!" she called back. Bili ducked through, then Wulpai. They moved down the cavern quickly, as the frustrated creatures began bellowing and smashing the small exit, trying to force an entry.

They ran until they were out of breath, Meri leaning heavily on her brother. The corridor forked again, and they took the right one. It went on for some length, coming to a dead end. Bili touched all sides to see if they were merely illusions. They weren't. Another dead-end! They quickly retraced their steps and took the left fork. Meri began limping lightly again. She was feeling frustrated that she was slowing them down.

The left fork led down again. They ran on. The bellowing stopped. Did that mean the creatures were on their trail again, or had they given up? The stone continued to pulse, so Meri refused to stop. Bili kept a sharp eye out for traps. Wulpai guarded the rear, so they wouldn't be taken by surprise. Another dead-end! Feeling around, Meri put her hand through another illusion-covered exit.

"Through here," she yelled, and took off, stumbling whenever she had to put too much weight on her swollen ankle. Rounding another corner, she broke out in a huge hall. She stopped. Bili and Wulpai joined her, looking around in awe.

"This must be the main hall." Bili suggested. "Wonder who lived here before it filled with enchantments and monsters?"

They crossed the center and made their way toward the far end. The largest passage sat off to one side.

"Look at the confluence of passages! There must be at least 25 caverns leading to this hall," Meri whispered. "This place must have held thousands of people."

Here they stopped for a moment, exploring the ledges and stairways carved into the walls on all sides. Bili noticed a carved statue in a nook near one of the stairs. Walking over to it, he felt it. He'd never seen anything like this before

"Meri, come and look at this thing." He whispered excitedly. "It looks just like a short fat man with a beard. Is this what the dwarves are supposed to look like?"

Meri joined him, followed by Wulpai.

"Yes, Bili, that is a statue of a dwarf king. This must certainly have been carved by them, and then abandoned," said Wulpai. "It shows all the marks of their workmanship. See the way they have pieced the stairs together. Just like a master mason."

Bili fingered the stone statue all around. Something at the back moved when Bili pressed on it.

A loud rumble sent them stumbling backward. The stairway parted, and formed yet another cavern. Bili hurried down and was stopped by a door. He pushed and tugged, but it wouldn't move.

"Dwarves make doors move by writing runes on them," Wulpai explained. "You have to find the right words to speak for them to operate the door." He looked around the stone that framed the door. "Here's something. It's written in the old tongue. I think I can make it out.

`If in need, any friend can open this door,
and to him will be given that which he lacks.'

"Well, I guess we would be considered friends, but I'm not sure what the word to be spoken is."

Meri looked intently at the runes. "Open door, for we are friends," she commanded quietly. Nothing. Just moments of silence. Suddenly there was a loud *'snap!'* Then a crack appeared at the top of the ledge. The crack spread down both sides and with a harsh grating of stone, the door slid back, allowing them passage into the dark room.

Surprised, Bili stood there as Wulpai stepped through first, finding flint and tinder to one side. He struck the flint until the tinder caught. Then he lit a small torch he took from the nearby holder. All three of them were unprepared for what they found. Upon the wall hung old shields, armor of all kinds; swords, daggers, helmets with plumes, both of silver and steel. Several bows stood unstrung against the far wall, with arrow filled quivers.

"Looks like enough weapons for a small army," Bili said, eyeing it all approvingly. "Wonder if they're real and we can take what we need?"

He stepped over and touched his finger to a finely wrought blade. Its light color reflected the torch. Bili grabbed it and lifted it from the wall. Swinging it a couple of times brought an exclamation of amazement to his lips.

"I've never felt anything so well balanced; and it's so light!" he exclaimed as he swung it in several directions. He thrust, then recovered, spun and sliced forward at knee level.

The swords Bili's people forged were dark, and tended to be heavy. This was light and easy to use. Wulpai too picked up a gleaming sword, runes running the entire length of the blade. He took it as well as a leather scabbard he found hanging nearby. He strapped it to his waist.

Meri had made her way to the bows. She strung one of them and tested its strength. It was slightly longer than hers, but felt good. It was very resilient, yet light, and made of some type of wood that seemed as hard as steel. She took one of the quivers and slid out an arrow. The fletchings were different from what she knew, but they were well made and had good balance. Sighting along its length, she replaced the arrow, obviously satisfied with the craftsmanship. Then lifting the quiver, she said, "I intend to make good use of these. I'm almost out of arrows anyway, and haven't had time to gather feathers or reeds to make new ones. These are well made and quite straight"

Bili stood besides her, eyeing the other bow. "I think I'll take this one too, just in case."

Stepping over to one side Meri noticed two small vials. Both had writings that she could not read. Being raised a healer, she was curious. She picked them both from the shelf, then brought them to Wulpai. "Have you any idea what these might be?" She asked him.

"From the writing, it looks to be some kind of medicine. I can't be sure, but one says, 'Life's blood', and the other says 'Foe Changer.'"

Meri opened them and smelled. The odor was faintly medicinal, but smelled more of earth and herbs. She closed them deciding they might be useful in the days ahead.

"I think we'd better be moving again," Wulpai suggested. "Those `friends' might have smashed through the wall by now, and be on our trail." He stepped from the room, and out beyond the stairway. Bili followed him.

Meri stopped for a moment and said, "Thank you for the gifts. Door you may close now." She turned her back and left. A small grating sound issued from the corridor, then the stairway rumbled together again.

Bili stared at her, a look of curiosity wrinkling his features. He hesitated only a moment, then shaking his head, followed her. His sister was beginning to amaze him. *Where did she get such knowledge*? He wondered. *How could she know the proper etiquette for dwarven lore as though she had been raised among them? Had the stone prompted her to do so*?

Looking across at the corridors, Meri voiced what they were all feeling.

"Which exit do we take now?" They had been steadily working their way downward, and most of the passages now seemed to be moving upward, or at least remaining level.

"It appears there are only three tunnels now that lead downward, and they are all on the same wall. I suggest we take the middle one and see where it goes," suggested Wulpai.

"Good idea," replied Bili. "I hope we eventually get out of here. I've had enough of caves to last me for some time to come!"

He walked off, taking the lead, his newly acquired armor making faint squeaking noises as the leather stretched whenever he moved. His sword bumped against the leather creating a faint metallic noise. It was assuring to Bili. He also carried the new bow in his left hand, an arrow nocked, ready for use.

Leaving the main hall, the light began to dim again. Bili stopped and took out one of the torches he had taken from the dwarf storage room, along with the extra flint and tinder. It took a few moments to get the torch going, but it was necessary. No glowing walls and no torches burned in this section. It was quite dark. The talisman and the stone were dark, no pulsing to warn of dangers. After an hour of anxiously wending their way through the corridors, they came to a dead end. There were no turns right or left.

Frustrated, they felt for illusions. Poking the walls they found none. They decided they might have to retrace their steps and try another passage. It was strange that this shaft in the mountain would go so far and end nowhere. *Why would anyone make a tunnel like this*? Bili wondered.

They started back up the tunnel. Not far, they ran into a wall blocking their path. "Guess we've stumbled into some sort of a dwarven trap," Meri speculated. "I wonder what we're supposed to do?

"Look for a trip lever or something that we can manipulate?" suggested Bili. He looked all around with the torch, but spotted nothing. Wulpai put his hands out, but found no illusory openings anywhere nearby.

"I think we're going to have to rely on the stones again," Meri fretted. "Besides, mine is beginning to pulse ever so lightly. I think we're headed for trouble again."

Bili placed his hands on the talisman, and felt warmth in the stone. He tried to blot out all thoughts from his mind.

"Be one with the stone and its power," he heard a voice say inside his head. He tried to relax and allow his thoughts to follow the same pattern he felt in the talisman stone. Soon, he was relaxing! Sounds akin to light music filled his head. His mind began to fill with impressions of elves, dwarves, cave dwellers, men from far away and men living along the grassy plains south of the great mountains. Peace and beauty were interrupted with shouts of war, pain, killing, and death. Someone shouted in his head and he felt bound to repeat the words.

"Shadow of doom, feeling of gloom,
Ebony clad, filling the room,
Partition a wall, archways and all,
Open a way to exit this room."

Even as the words come from Bili's lips, a shimmering mirage appeared before them, an archway into a hidden corridor. Bili gaped at the apparition, but Wulpai leaped through.

"C'mon," he yelled. "It's real," he shouted.

Meri grabbed Bili's arm and pulled him through as the archway shimmered, becoming a solid wall once again. Regaining their balance, and taking a couple of deep breaths to quell their pounding hearts, they reluctantly turned their backs on the wall and started walking. A faint but familiar smell greeted their nostrils. Shortly, they found themselves in a main hallway. To the left they saw daylight. Bili quickly extinguished his torch, and headed that way. He had gone only a short distance, when Wulpai grabbed him from the back, pulling him aside.

"Look out!" he whispered. "Don't you see what's up ahead?"

Bili looked again. "I can see something there, but what is it? And what's that strange smell?" he asked.

"Those are trolls!" Wulpai informed him. "Don't try to fight with them. Their skin is like armored leather, and they are very strong. You'd have no chance against them."

"It looks like they're guarding the entrance to this cave." Meri said. Do you suppose we came out where we shouldn't?"

"No, I don't think so," Wulpai guessed, looking around at the surrounding walls. "It appears that they or someone else has taken over the use of these long abandoned caves. I'm surprised we didn't run into them sooner.

"C'mon, we're going to have to figure a way around them." Moving to one side they crowded near a boulder that hid them from the trolls. They crept closer and listened.

Chapter 6
Escape From the Goblins

Four trolls stood near the entrance to the cave. The first two wore leather hauberks covering their chests with matching helms. Armed with long shafted spears, and holding shields, they appeared a match for any intruder. They were obviously in charge. The other two were slightly smaller and had no hints of armor covering. Wearing course burlap thick material of woven brown cloth, they were covered only from the waist downward. Carrying thick clubs, roughly hacked from limbs of black oak, they loitered near their larger cousins.

The wind had begun to gust, the up-drafts pushing cool air from the cliffs below. The sun was partially covered, but shining too brightly still for the nervous trolls. They were talking among themselves, their voices and smells carrying on the wind to the back entrances.

"Be glad wen dat ugly orb goes down. Dis cursed light hurts me eyes," grumbled one. "An der beta be plenty o' grub an ale fer us when we git dun wit dis shif."

"Yah, how'd we end up pulin dis gad duty? Diz slimey lit'l gobis is always tryin' to boss ya aroun', an I don' like dat."

Bili edged back, disgusted by the stench of the trolls. He wiped his hand across his nose stifling the urge of his stomach to bring up everything he had eaten.

"Easy Bili," Wulpai urged with a grimace. "It takes some getting used to being around trolls. It can be as bad as cleaning out horse stalls. I've never gotten used to troll smells. It can be overpowering." He handed Bili a small cloth to put over his nose and mouth to make breathing easier, until he could adjust to the rancid odors.

Bili was able to settle down again and studied their situation. He was aware they would be unable to sneak past those sentries and get clear of the entrance, at least not until there was a change of guards. Maybe they could manage some ploy to pull the guards away from entrance. Bili moved over near Wulpai and Meri to solicit their support.

Meri had been listening intently as the trolls conversed. "I've an idea that might work," she whispered softly, interrupting what Bili had in mind. She began outlining her plan. As she quietly talked, she lifted the stone from its leather pouch, cupping it carefully in her hands. Closing her eyes, she concentrated, intent on bending her will to the stone's pulsing. Once she tuned inward, she brushed her hands forward, projecting that force outward. Bili and Wulpai could feel something passing through them. The three of them waited breathlessly, knowing that whatever it was would shortly reach the trolls.

"Hey! Did'ja hear dat nois ova der?" said the big troll with the wart on his cheek. "Sombody's comin. Hey, der it is again! I tink somebody's makin' a fus. Les get ova der an see wat it's all about."

All four of them ducked quickly back into the entrance running down the corridor, anticipating a good fight. Chuckling over the rouse, Meri looked up. "Guess it's time to make a run for it." Putting the stone back into the leather pouch, she picked up her bow and quiver, and darted out from behind the stones. Bili and Wulpai followed closely behind. With a final glance around, Wulpai made sure no one saw them leave.

It felt good to be in the sun again, now on its journey toward the distant crags. The air was cool in spite of the sun, but it was refreshing. Meri breathed in lung-fulls of it. Off to the right a trail opened, moving away from the cliff. Meri nocked an arrow, and moved silently down the path. Bili loosened the beautiful sword he now possessed, ready to draw at the first hint of trouble. Wulpai stepped lightly behind them, constantly watching their back trail.

Reaching a narrow corner, Meri edged around the cliff face keeping her balance on the narrow ledge. Bili hugged the stones, mildly afraid of heights. Wulpai stopped to check for passage of others before them, puzzled by what he saw. There were light footprints on the outer edge, almost blown away by the wind. He hurried to catch up with the others.

Meri entered a narrow defile barely wide enough to squeeze through. Bili was about to enter when he heard a rustling above and behind him. He spun, his hand on the pommel of his sword. A goblin, braced on a rock, was drawing a bead on Meri's back with his bow.

"Whoosh!" An arrow flew through the air, embedding itself in the goblin's neck. With a garbled cry, he fell headlong into the defile, landing on top of Bili. They both went down in a tangle of arms and legs. Bili shoved and kicked him off, then looked him over. The goblin was dead.

Bili looked at the arrow, got up and looked for the other archer. Meri startled by the commotion ran back.

"Oh gosh!" She croaked, stifling a gasp as she saw the goblin! Then looking up she saw an elven warrior dressed in forest green, his head bare, a crooked grin on his face. Leaning on his bow he addressed them.

"He almost had you," he chided, looking directly at Meri. "You should look up once in a while! Didn't you notice his tracks back there?" The elf didn't trust the trolls, and had taken up a position here, just in case they were up to some ploy.

"What are you talking about?" Meri yelled back up to him. "You talk as though they were expecting someone to pass through here."

"They are!" the elf replied. "The Dark Lord sent some Sanguma priests here to warn the goblin nation. He believes that someone may try coming through the passes to this side of the mountains. They must be in possession of something pretty valuable. He wants them, plus whatever it might be they have with them."

The elf hopped lightly off the rock, landing nimbly in front of them. "My name is Yilmai. I live some miles south of here. Three months ago, I set out with an elven patrol to scout out the movements of the goblin. Somehow they got wind of our mission and ambushed us along the rim of the passes. Four others and I escaped by moving north, rather than toward home. I got separated from the others, and have played a cat and mouse game with these goblin guards since. They know I'm around, but are unable to corner me."

Bili interrupted. "My name is Bili. This is my sister Meri, and our companion, Wulpai. We are deeply in your debt. If you hadn't shot when you did, my sister would be dead. I saw him too late."

Yilmai stared at the three companions, ignoring the comment. As he gazed from one to the other, Meri asked, "Is something wrong?"

"Oh, ah, no!" Yilmai replied abruptly. "I had a dream two nights ago. No, it can't be, can it?"

"What can't be," pressed Meri.

"Sheer coincidence. Surely! Well, uh, in this dream I was shown that three humans would come out of the caves. They would be able to aid us elves in our fight against a coming darkness. You three are a very unlikely group anyway. Still, I haven't been able to get the dream out of my head. So I thought to come here and watch, just in case. Now you three show up and make the dream come true. We elves just don't have anything to do with humans-haven't for many years now."

Wulpai spoke up. "We have been through the caves of testing, and are newly come to this entrance. How else would we appear in the middle of the lair of the Goblin?"

Yilmai rudely cut him off replying, "If it weren't for that cursed dream, I would laugh and leave you to your resources. No humans have ever been into our sacred forests; at least not to my knowledge. You say you have come through the Caves of testing? Indeed!"

Wulpai countered, "How do you explain, then, our sudden appearance at this heavily guarded entrance? You yourself have said it's heavily guarded, and no one's been past here except goblins."

"Well it is true, I can't explain your sudden appearance," Yilmai grudgingly admitted, "But it's out of the question to take you to elven lands. Your lives would be forfeit if you dared to cross our borders."

"We are on a quest of some importance," Wulpai replied, a hint of irritation edging his voice. "So we are in need of help on our way. Our pathway lies south toward your homeland. Then we must go west over the Witsiunuk Mountains into the Western Lands. Believe me, we are those people you saw in your dream. Please, set aside your prejudice and your preconceived notions about outsiders. We need your skills and assistance. Will you help us find our way?"

Something inside the young elf seemed to give way. The hardness seemed to fight with the impulse to believe these strangers. For a long moment he seemed uncertain, struggling to find truth. Suddenly he abruptly pushed this all aside and a pliable spirit appeared in its place. "Well, you are in a rather precarious position, I'll admit, he voiced skeptically. I'm not fully convinced about what you've said. But it's dangerous standing here any longer than necessary. I'm willing to help you escape, but about the elven lands, I'll make no guarantees."

Noise along the trail interrupted them. The trolls were coming back and one of them started making his way down to where they were standing.

"Quick, help me throw this goblin over the cliff," hissed Yilmai. Quickly reclaiming the arrow from the dead body, Yilmai wiped it on a leaf nearby and placed it back in his quiver. Then with Bili's help, they lifted the goblin's body and heaved it over the edge. They brushed their trail clean, then climbed behind the stones the goblin had used.

They all felt rather than heard the heavy footfalls of the troll as he rounded the corner. He stopped suddenly, sniffed the air, and then moved a bit further down the trail. Sniffing again, he returned and stumped rapidly back toward the cave entrance.

"We must flee quickly. He has your scent and will bring the others." Opening his pack, Yilmai pulled out four silken capes. He looped the lower catches through his legs, tying them tightly around his ankles. Passing the upper part through both arms, he secured them around his wrists.

"Do as you have seen me do, quickly! These are special elven capes. They will enable you to float down the cliffs to the edge of the river, and hopefully escape the trolls."

Passing the capes around, he helped Meri into hers. Bili watched and followed his lead. Wulpai seemed to already know something of their use, and was finished before either of the other two. Yilmai noticed this but kept silence.

Leading them quickly to the cliff's edge he explained, "Don't be afraid. These capes will hold your weight. Simply cast your arms out as though you were an eagle in flight, and spread your legs. Just follow my example, but hurry!"

Leaving them, Yilmai threw himself into the up draft and was borne slowly downward. He looked up and motioned them to jump. Meri spread her arms and leaped from the rock. She suppressed a cry of fear as she fell a few feet before the wind caught her and she began a controlled descent. Wulpai jumped to one side and went down. Bili, last but not willing to be left behind, cast himself over the rock, joining the others.

Four hundred feet below, Yilmai landed soundlessly on the rock scree near the base of the cliffs. Removing his cape, he folded it quickly into his pack. Meri landed near him, stumbling awkwardly as she found her footing. Wulpai and Bili landed near her, both bumping into the base of the cliff as they glided to rough landings. Apparently, humans were heavier than elves so the capes maneuvered differently for them. On the ground and stable at last, they removed the capes, which Yilmai took from them, placing them with the two others in his pack.

"This way." He whispered hoarsely. "I don't think we've been seen. It may give us a couple hours start before an alarm is raised. They may spot the goblin body during the night, but we'll be miles from here. Let's go."

He headed off at a brisk trot. Meri and Bili quickly tightened their packs and started after him. They had to run to keep up with him. Wulpai, jogging quickly and lightly, followed at a distance, covering their back trail from time to time. Yilmai glanced back several times but if this surprised him, he didn't let it be known.

The path wound through the brush that grew next to the river. Water flowed out of the mountains at the base of this cliff, making its way toward the lower lands to the south. Yilmai was familiar with this area, and led them past forking trails and obstacles.

Noise of an approaching patrol brought them up short. Yilmai led them off the trail toward the river, into a sheltered bank. Here they huddled while the patrol moved noisily past. When Yilmai could no longer hear them, he broke cover, checking their trail. It seemed safe. He signaled to the others and they resumed their march. They traveled another hour before they heard voices and the heavy stomping of boots. This time Yilmai led them away from the river into a sheltered patch of fallen trees. They waited anxious moments, for the goblins decided to rest nearby. The patrol milled all around, some striking at tree branches with their swords, others relieving themselves near Yilmai's temporary hideout. When the call came, all the goblins fell in line and resumed their march back to the cliff stronghold.

"Am I ever glad they decided not to explore further," said Meri, happy to be rid of their smelly enemies. "I was sure they were going to find us."

"They didn't though," said Yilmai. "I've been living like this now for three months. It gets pretty scary at times. Let's keep moving." With that, he shouldered his pack and moved toward the trail again.

Toward dusk, they spotted some overhanging ledges a good ways off the trail. Another goblin patrol sounded a horn in the distance. "I think we should camp over there under those ledges," Yilmai suggested. "There are more patrols coming this way. We may be caught by one of them if we continue. Hiding at the ledges until morning may be the safest thing to do."

Without asking the others, Yilmai left the trail, heading for the ledges. Bili glanced uneasily back at Wulpai, raising his eyebrows in question. Wulpai shrugged his shoulders then tilted his head toward the ledges in reply. They moved quickly into the brush.

Yilmai took them around to the back where there were some good overhangs. This would shelter them from any rain that might come during the night. Clouds were moving in and the moon, fortunately, would be partially covered giving them a better chance of not being discovered.

Since no one had any fresh meat to cook they decided against a fire. Yilmai volunteered to take the first watch. Wulpai would relieve him. After the elf climbed to the top of the ledges to keep watch, Bili turned to Meri. "What do you think? Will he be able to get us past all these patrols and on to the edges of the elven forests?"

"I'm hopeful that he will," replied Meri. "He's managed to evade them this long. I don't see why he won't be able to do it."

She brushed her hair in the fading light, trying to get the snags and knots out. It had been a long time since she had been able to think about her appearance. She felt dirty and would have loved to bathe in the river. *Well, maybe I can wash it when we get out of goblin country,* she mused to herself.

"Meri," Wulpai said quietly, interrupting her thoughts. "You may find that you have need of the stone again before we get out of here. You should spend more time trying to tune your mind and will to it, so it becomes automatic. It may save your life."

Meri turned, looking at Wulpai. She was tempted to be resentful, but chose not to react, wondering how he came into such knowledge. *This man is an enigma. He seems just like any ordinary man from the outside, but his knowledge and wisdom speak otherwise.*

Curious, she asked him, "How is it that you know so much about this stone? Have you seen one like it before?"

"It's a long story, Meri. I have seen such a stone as yours up north. I saw several people in their time try to master it, but either had no gift or no patience. You appear to have both. I have also read some of the ancient prophecies concerning the Dark Lord. He hopes to gain total power over all nations, using these kinds of stones, bending everyone to his will. If that happens, this will be a bleak world indeed. Any who survive will be twisted just as he. You and your brother are part of a growing force set to oppose him in his bid for power."

"How do you know all this? What growing force are you talking about?" Meri asked, quite shocked. Hearing Meri raise her voice, Bili moved over to hear more of their conversation. He too was curious to hear answers to the mysteries surrounding the objects they carried.

"Look at the mark on your shoulder, Meri. Its pattern matches the descriptions of the first prophesy written in the *Codrin*. You do know about the *Codrin* and the *Tiwei Mamkepai* don't you?"

"We've heard about these books," interjected Bili. "But we know little of them. Only the shaman in our village has ever seen the Codrin. He spent two years away learning from that book. He has kept most of this knowledge to himself, except for the few parts he's shared with our father. He was intrigued by the strange mark on Meri's shoulder. He told our father that this might be something significant someday."

"It will be very significant, and soon," replied Wulpai. "The Codrin tells of a woman to be born in the later years who will bear a mark on her shoulder that will set her apart from other women. She will be the rallying point to draw the other orbs into position against the Dark Lord. He will do his utmost to obtain the orbs and join them into one so that he may conquer all peoples and races on this planet and make his move against the Great One."

Unconvinced, Bili queried, "How do you know those prophesies refer to my sister? We are from the mountains in the East, not a part of the mainstream civilization in the West. Maybe other women have a similar marking as my sister. Possibly it's common."

"Further in the Codrin there are references alluding to the origins of this woman and they refer to someone living beyond the mountains in the Eastern Forests. It sounds only logical that your sister fits these descriptions. Think about it Bili.

"What can you tell us about the Dark Lord, Wulpai? " Meri interrupted, coming back into the conversation. "We've not been outside our area, and few strangers venture in. What's the origin of this Dark Lord, and how did he come to be so evil? Since I'm prophesied be part of this adventure, it might help if I knew what part I'm supposed to play."

"Rightly so meri," Wulpai conceded putting up a hand. He smiled to himself, the humor of the situation lightening his mood.

"Let's start from the beginning. According to legend, the Dark Lord was not evil in the beginning. He was pure and good. He had a high position in the court of the Great One. Actually, he was the most important personal attendant. The Great One created him to serve and be a companion. This went on for many years. The Great One created others, and they too served in various capacities. Each of these carried out their assigned responsibilities, trying to satisfy the Great One's creativity with the gifts and the abilities they had been given. It was sheer delight just to be in his company. They dwelled together in unity."

Bili looked over at Meri, amazement and disbelief written on his face. Wulpai continued.

"One day, the Dark Lord began to change. No one can say how this came about. In some way he allowed envy to enter his heart. He became jealous of others, feeling his own secure position with the Great One threatened. He became dissatisfied with who he was, and felt a strong need to possess the gifts of others. This finally led to a desire to have his master's power. He attempted to draw as many others to himself as he could, and made a bid to become the Supreme Being. He planned to dislodge the Great One himself!

"After careful planning, lies, deceit and coercion, he won a great following. Then he started a war. The Great One tried to change their minds, but they ignored his bidding. Since his arbitration and attempt to regain their cooperation was totally rejected ,the

Great One took it upon himself to create another world on which to live if he was overthrown.

The Great One called on his own special forces during this period, and was able to defeat the rebels. It broke his heart, but he had to banish them to this alternate world. It is here that they were sent, and in the long years following, they have grown in hatred and power. The Dark Lord who leads them hopes to become strong enough through conquering this world to go back and challenge the Great One and unseat him from his throne."

Meri shifted uneasily at these unexpected turn of events. Leaning on her other arm, she moved to a more comfortable position. Maybe this was part of what the Shaman had been trying to share with her after he found out about her special mark. *If only I had been more open to him instead of being afraid of him*, she thought suddenly, *maybe things might have turned out differently*. A sudden chill overtook her and she shivered in the damp evening air.

"Three stones of power were taken from the Great One's kingdom," continued Wulpai. "The Dark Lord intended to use them to conquer his enemies, but he was struck down, and the stones were taken and hidden by one of his underlings. It seems these stones were brought here, and the Dark Lord wants to recover them and master them. He was badly hurt by one of them several hundred years ago, when he attempted to master it. He's now looking for the others, so that he can re-unite them. Only in this way can he hope to master them and thus do battle with the Great One. I believe that you and Bili are in possession of two of those stones."

Meri sat stunned! Bili took out the talisman, looking at it and fingering it again. "You mean this stone our people recovered from the goblins in the war is actually one of these power stones? No wonder it was activated when Meri's stone was placed next to it."

"We were told in dreams and visions that they must be returned to the Western Lands," Meri admitted at last. "We didn't tell you because we weren't sure we could trust you. I guess that was foolish, but we had to protect the stones at all costs."

"After what you've been through, I don't blame you," Wulpai said equitably. "I might have done the same thing if I had been in your place. But now, may I suggest that you begin working on tuning yourself to that stone. Bili, you need to do the same. Both stones are part of a bigger unit. Each of them functions in a different manner. You must learn to listen to what your stone attempts to share with you. It will take work, maybe more than you might think; but if you practice carefully each day, you'll tune yourself to it and hear the message. I've said enough. I'll leave you two alone so you can decide for yourselves."

With that, Wulpai promptly stood up and walked silently into the darkness.

Chapter 7

Elven Patrols

The night deepened. Bili decided to take the second watch, spending tense moments when three different goblin patrols passed by unseeing. Yilmai had picked a good camp, and Bili knew the elf was gifted in wood lore. He decided he would put aside his feelings about Yilmai's briskness and scorn for outsiders, and learn as much as he could from his new companion.

Wulpai relieved Bili in the early hours, but Bili found it hard to sleep. He lay awake, too excited and nervous to relax. Toward morning he managed to doze fitfully, jumping at every sound.

Morning arrived at last, bringing with it a bleak day. The weather turned foul, hurling scudding clouds and strong winds in their direction. Occasional drizzles made the trails slippery. Covering their tracks became an ever-increasing impossibility. At least fewer patrols ventured out now, so traveling was somewhat safer. They trekked without incident on into the early afternoon. Stopping only briefly for a bite to eat, they hurried on, anxious to find sanctuary in the elven woods.

Meri felt rather than saw the stone pulsing. Reaching into the bag, she recognized its warning glow. "Yilmai," she called softly, "The stone is glowing again."

Yilmai stepped off the trail, halting the others. Quickly hiding themselves, they waited. Goblins came running along the trail, shouting loudly and cursing. Obviously something important to them was in progress. Here at the juncture where they had hidden, the trail narrowed, forcing those behind to spill out to the sides. The rush of bodies from behind pushed them, stumbling right into the hiding place of the four companions. Before anyone could draw a sword or nock an arrow, startled goblins stumbled, falling on them, everyone becoming entangled together. Others from behind barreled into them, barely managing to remain upright.

Howls of surprise and excitement erupted from the crowd that quickly gathered. Pinned down as they were, the companions had little chance of escape. Goblin hands overpowered them by sheer numbers. In no time at all, Yilmai and his friends were disarmed and securely bound. The babble between the goblins increased as they recognized Yilmai. Slapping him around and kicking him, they leered at him, gleeful they had captured another elf. It was obvious they were quite pleased. The others they roughly hauled to their feet and took to Borgmoth, leader of the patrol. He shoved the elf aside, staring intently at the three humans standing before him.

"Word was out about you humans. We knew you was headin' westward." Then he grinned, "Sanguma will reward me handsomely fo you two," he boasted, as he nodded at Bili and Meri. Grabbing rope from a nearby pack, Borgmoth knotted it securely around their necks, handing the excess to his second in command. With harsh guttural commands, they were roughly pulled forward. The goblins continued their wild pace, stopping only when Bili or Meri stumbled, sprawling headlong onto the wet trail. They traveled swiftly upriver the better part of an hour.

"Clang!" The sound of steel rang through the air. Suddenly all was confusion around them. Bili and Meri were pushed to the ground. There were shouts and curses, as Borgmoth attempted to rally his troops against the ambush. Yanking his blade from its sheath, he charged into the brush, followed by others. The din of more steel on steel filled the air. Bili and Meri lay still as whistling arrows embedded themselves in the throats and sides of the goblins standing guard over them. Those that didn't fall broke toward the river, madly attempting to escape the deadly hail from around them. Loud cries followed as their pursuers chased them. The captives were abandoned in the headlong rush to get away.

Yilmai rolled over, a grin cutting his elven features. "Those are my people," he shouted happily. "A patrol must have been coming this way chasing the Goblins when they ran into us. We are lucky indeed! I shudder to think what might have happened had the Sanguma priests laid their knives to us!"

More elves dashed into the clearing, releasing arrows at the backs of fleeing figures. Elves near the end of the group stopped when they saw the captives lying on the ground. Looking in surprise and then in jubilation, they lifted Yilmai their brother and untied him. Yelps of joy and astonishment filled the clearing.

"We gave you up for dead, Yilmai!" One of them exclaimed. "You've been missing for months, and the patrols we sent out came back with no word of survivors. How did you do it?"

Yilmai gave a brief account of what had happened during the months he had been gone, and how he had managed to stay alive. Then he turned and said, "These are the people who came through the mountain and the caves of testing. I met them as they were about to encounter the trolls up on the mountain by the 5 waters. Help me release them."

As others helped release his three companions, a young elf burst into the clearing. He stopped abruptly and stared.

"Yilmai, is it really you?" shouted the young elf. "We thought you had been killed with the others in the massacre! We worked our way up here with a much larger patrol trying to find any survivors. We've run into nothing but goblins everywhere. And"… abruptly he stopped and stared. "Who are these humans and what are they doing with you?"

Yilmai, delighted at seeing his cousin replied, "Kusai, am I glad to see you! I've been hiding and harassing these Goblins for three months now. I got cut off from the rest of the patrol when the fighting started. I looked for any of them who might have survived. Sadly I found no one, but I stayed in the area trying to find news of any they might have captured. I hoped to rescue them and head for home again."

Kusai turned to the strangers, using his free hand in a gesture toward Yilmai "Again I ask you, who are your companions, cousin?"

"These humans actually came out of the caves!" confided Yilmai. "Can you believe that? They are on a quest to the Western Lands, but want to stop and talk with our high Lord about battle plans. They seem to know what's happening up North with the Dark Lord."

"Then we must take them to Uncle at once! He'll know what to do," Kusai shot back.

The four companions walked back along the trail, hurriedly picking through all the things that had been dropped. Fortunately for them, their weapons had also been discarded in the fighting. Bili found and strapped on his new sword and also retrieved his daggers and bow. Wulpai picked up his sword and walking stick. Meri found her bow and quiver. They recovered all but one pack- the food pack. Yilmai rummaged through his things and found nothing missing. There hadn't been time for the goblins to forage through their packs.

Returning from the river, the elves gathered around the small group to hear Yilmai's story. As he was repeating it, uncle Tulemai arrived and interrupted them all.

"Yilmai, are there any other survivors of your patrol?"

"No sir," the young elf answered. "As far as I know, I'm the only one left."

"Right! I think this patrol has accomplished its mission. Let's return south immediately. Those goblins will bring reinforcements with them to overpower us and wipe us out… Uh… what? Who are these humans?"

Yilmai yet again explained as briefly as possible how he met his friends. When Tulemai heard they wanted an audience with their elven king, his face grew shadowed.

"No humans have come to our lands for hundreds of years. Our enchantments alone might cause your deaths, even as you risk crossing the magic boundaries. We'll have to think on this. But for now, we must travel quickly. Gather whatever is yours and let us march."

Elves retrieved spent arrows, and picked up abandoned weapons. They then began a hasty retreat along the paths they had followed. All too soon the afternoon shadows grew long. The trails were well packed from many feet pounding them, so their footing was secure. They made good time. The clouds were clearing.

Meri's stone began pulsing yet another time. She informed Yilmai, who relayed the news to Tulemai. He stopped the patrol, urgently ordering them off the trail. Shortly, a large goblin patrol rounded the bend, marching swiftly in pursuit of some unseen enemy. They passed by, and the elven patrol continued its march south. Tulemai called his aids to his side.

"This is too dangerous. We can't afford to get pinned down by another patrol. It would give the others time to catch us from behind. I feel it might be safer to travel along the river. It's only another four miles to where hidden several canoes await such an emergency. Let's move."

By the time they reached the river, darkness blanketed the skies. The moon occasionally peeked from behind thick clouds; otherwise it remained allusive. Six elves went to prepare the canoes.

Bili looked at Meri as the canoes were taken to the water. "These people have carved out trees to use to float upon the water! I've heard of such things, but never thought I'd see one."

"Nor float in one," added Meri nervously. "Wonder how they keep from tipping them over? I wouldn't step in one if I didn't have too! Surely we'll end up in the water before long?"

"They are a lot more stable than you think," Wulpai assured them. "I've been in them before, and they ride well. Just stay toward the center until you get used to the rocking motion. Then they won't feel so unstable to you. Hurry, they're ready for us."

Once in the water, the patrol paddled silently into the current, just out of bow shot away from the bank. They worked their way swiftly downstream, everyone lending a hand with the paddles. They hoped to throw any pursuers off their trail and outdistance them at the same time.

Toward morning, they reached the shallows, and abandoned the canoes to continue their flight on foot. Further down the rapids were too rough, so portage was out of the question.

Carefully concealing the canoes among the reeds and bushes, the patrol warily took to the paths once again. They'd had no rest and were beginning to feel the exhaustion of forced travel. But they'd agreed among themselves they would rather do that than risk another encounter with goblins. At mid-day they stopped to rest and eat. Those who could, caught a few minutes sleep, then resumed the forced march.

An hour down the trail, Meri's stone pulsed yet again. Marching near Tulemai, she advised him of impending danger, this time coming from the west. Tulemai sent two scouts to spy out activity in the long reeds that dotted that area. He also sent another pair south to see what danger lay along that path.

Soon they came back, running. "Sir, the further shores of the river are teeming with goblins. It looks as though someone saw us moving and sent word ahead. They managed to set a trap for us there, believing we would risk the rapids to gain the time we need to get back to our forest homes."

The two scouts sent south into the canyon returned reporting that goblins held the pass and were also awaiting their arrival. Tulemai thought quickly, decided that the pass held their best chance of breaking through.

Wulpai heard the discussion, and then approached Tulemai with a plan. After hearing this plan and discussing it with his closest advisors, Tulemai was pleased to agree to it. He divided his forces, using the smaller unit as the decoy. Yilmai and Wulpai went with the decoy unit. Bili and Meri were commanded to remain with the larger unit. The main group began climbing the edges of the cliff at the back of the canyon. Once they were well on their way up the side, Tulemai ordered the decoys to move down the path. They knew they'd be caught in a pincer thrust, but were counting on the main body to cut down most of the battle group positioned at the far end, opening a way for them to escape.

While they climbed, Meri concentrated again on the stone trying to be one with it. The sun had dropped below the horizon, and the few clouds in the sky reflected the dying light. As she reached a small shelf near the top, she was amazed to find she could see things clearer. Gazing up toward the top, she spotted two goblins with their backs to the climbers. She nocked an arrow and aimed at the closer one. She drew a bead on him and released smoothly. The arrow flew true to its target, embedding itself in the scruffy goblin's neck. He clutched at the arrow for only a second, then plunged sideways down the side of the cliff. She waited with another arrow nocked. The second sentry came over and leaned out, looking down the cliffs. Meri released the second arrow and this one caught him full in the chest. He gave a startled cry, then plunged to his death. His body fell near the elves, who had been watching Meri. Murmurs of "Well done! That's good shooting," rose from her companions.

"Meri, how could you see those goblins?" Bili asked incredulously. "I couldn't even see their silhouettes against the sky."

"The more I work with the stone, the more things it shows me," replied Meri. "I could see both those sentries sitting there facing toward the path. They weren't expecting anyone from this direction. The stone has given me a sort of night vision."

Moving on, they continued scaling the wall until they gained the heights. Meri thrust her head up over the edge to look around.

They were directly behind a group of goblins waiting to attack the unsuspecting elves along the trail. Further to their right another group had spread out waiting in ambush.

Meri signaled the others to silence, and they carefully crested the lip, crawling soundlessly into position. Bili stayed near Meri, not trusting her safety to mere elven archers. He too nocked an arrow to his bowstring and waited.

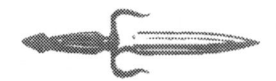

The decoy party made their way into the narrow canyon. They knew they would be set on from above and possibly along the trail as well. Those who had chain mail had put it on over their shirts, placing a jacket over to dampen the sound. They wanted as few casualties as possible. The growing darkness wasn't helpful either, because the goblins had better night vision than they.

As the elves became fully boxed in the canyon, the goblins above let out war cries and began to fire. A rain of arrows descended on the decoys, who sought the cover of nearby bushes and rocks. At the far end of the canyon, another group of goblins emerged, swords and spears at the ready. They had laid their trap well. The decoys spread out in groups of four to engage the enemy. They shot arrows up at their attackers, and then turned to fire in back of them and in front of them. Some of the arrows struck goblins, taking them down. A hail of arrows from goblins above rained down on the vulnerable elves, striking two of them.

When the main party of elves above heard the shouts of battle, they hurried forward standing as closely as they dared, and began firing arrows into the backs of the goblins lined in front of them. As the unwary goblins fell, the elves quickly advanced, shooting more arrows into their ranks. They also fanned out, shooting at the goblins to the right, who were just now realizing they had been out-flanked. There was confusion all over the top of the ledges. Goblins began running in all directions, trying either to escape or hurl themselves on their attackers. Bili had to drop his bow, draw his sword and parry several blows, killing two aggressive goblins who rushed him. The sword he had picked up in the caves of testing began a slight humming as others tried to engage him. Every time he swung, he felt the sword had a will of its own. It pulsed from the pommel into his arms. This freed him to use the sword as though it bore no weight at all! Amazed, he found he could out-swing, out-thrust and jab faster than any goblin. He waded into their ranks, killing as many as came within reach of his blade.

Soon the hail of arrows from above ceased, only to be replaced by the roar of battle. Wulpai led his group of elves, advancing on the goblins from the far end of the canyon. The impact of their meeting was painfully audible, leather jerkins smashing heavily into chain mail. Curses and grunts met the elves as they waded into the goblin ranks. Wulpai, an experienced swordsman, took on the largest of the goblins lining the front ranks. These were obviously seasoned warriors, used to leading forays in battle. He stepped in, pirouetting to the left, parrying blows from the first of these huge warriors, then turning aside his blade and thrusting him through. Backing off and moving to his right, he had only a moment to raise his blade as the next one engaged him. One by one he worked through them, disarming and destroying them.

Before long the trail grew slippery with goblin blood. Wulpai continued relentlessly onward, followed by his elven friends. They began to clear a pathway through the goblins, who fearful for their lives, began to turn and run. Only a few managed to reach the sanctuary of the open woods again. Elven arrows brought down most.

Tulemai held off the band of goblins at the north end of the canyon, and began driving them back. Then seeing that Wulpai and the others had opened a pathway, he shouted to his warriors, "Enough! Run for the far end. The way is open!" He stood with a sword in his hand while the others began running down the canyon. He followed them, keeping an eye on the goblins gathering together in pursuit. A stray arrow found its way into a chink in Tulemai's armor, wounding him in the side. He broke off the arrow as best he could, then continued hurrying toward the far end.

Wulpai saw them coming, and called "cover the retreat." They shot several arrows into the approaching goblins. This slowed them enough to allow Tulemai and two assisting elves to reach the south entry. The others remained behind shooting arrows at those goblins bold enough to defy chance in hopes of taking down more elves.

"Tulemai, you're wounded," yelled Wulpai. "Go on quickly through the canyon exit. We'll join you shortly."

"Thanks, friend," Tulemai replied. "This arrow hurts, and is slowing me down."

He hurried on while Wulpai waited for the group of goblins along the canyon floor. The elves continued to shoot more arrows at them. Some found their mark, others bounced harmlessly off wood and leather hauberks. As their number grew, they kept coming.

From above came an avalanche of stones, brush and other debris, falling squarely on top of the goblins beneath. Many of them went down in a cloud of dust. The ones in the rear turned around and fled. Wulpai and his group quickly turned and ran through the exit on the heels of the others, as more stones came cascading down the narrow defile.

The battle was a rout, with goblins running for their lives. This gave the elves above the opportunity to bolt for the far end of the ledge, running down to join their companions. They took stock of their wounded. Three were hurt from up top, and three from the decoy group. They stopped just long enough to tend their wounded, then hurried on. They would be pursued again once the goblins regrouped.

Tulemai was hardest hit. He was unable to hurry. The more he exerted himself, the deeper the arrow seemed to embed itself. Wulpai stopped him to have a look. The shaft had indeed embedded itself in a lung. He would bleed to death if they continued on.

"Do you have any more canoes hidden along the river?" Wulpai asked. "If you do, we need to get you there and travel to your homeland that way. Any more exertion will drive this shaft through your lung and kill you."

"Yes, we have more canoes," Tulemai replied raggedly. "They're hidden about two hours walk away. But we'll never make it with all these goblins around."

Let us try," suggested Wulpai. He picked the elven commander up in his arms and started off at a brisk walk. He caught up with the others and announced that they should head for the river once again. After a few complaints, and a reprimand from Tulemai, they started in that direction.

Twice they hid from goblin patrols roaming the trails. It took almost three hours walking in darkness to find the river and the extra canoes. Everyone was beginning to feel exhaustion coming on again. Once in the water, only part of the group paddled. The others rested. Meri rested while Bili paddled. They made good time, and weren't spotted by any goblins.

Toward morning they approached the gorge, where the river narrowed and rocks jutted dangerously up out of the riverbed. Water cascaded over these rocks, but further travel by canoe was no longer possible. The elves once again hid these canoes, only to make their way on foot. They crafted a stretcher for Tulemai, now very pale and weak. They carried him along as best they could.

Toward mid-morning, they spotted another Goblin patrol heading their way. There was no place to hide. They would have to fight. They placed themselves in battle position and waited. The goblins rounded the bend, spotting the elves. A great shout went up and they charged. The elves shot their remaining arrows at the goblins as they closed on them. Several went down, but others kept coming. Wulpai and Bili stood near each other and began hewing with their swords. They killed several of the leading goblins trying to penetrate their ranks. An unusually large goblin took Bili from the side, knocking him from his feet. He swung a heavy club intending to crush Bili beneath it. Wulpai stepped in and thrust his sword through the goblin's eye, killing him instantly. The club fell harmlessly to one side. Bili got back up and kept fighting.

A great shout from the rear caught their attention. Looking back they realized a large patrol was attacking from the rear. The elves were now hemmed in. Their situation looked hopeless.

Tulemai shouted, "Leave me here and run for your lives. There's yet hope toward the east. Quickly before they surround you."

Yilmai and his cousin moved in, refusing to leave Tulemai, their uncle. They picked up his palette and began running with it. Others began shooting arrows as a rear guard action. They jogged about half mile as a group, while the goblins continued to press them. Then they set the palette down to catch their breaths.

Bili and Wulpai were at the rear, fighting with their swords, continuing to slow the goblin advance. Being off the trail, the brush was now a handicap. There was no more room to swing. Wulpai put his sword away, and yelled to Bili to do the same. Then they turned tail and ran to catch up with the few elves that had arrows left. Continuing their retreat, they moved further into the forests.

Finally, as the goblins moved to surround them, the elves reached a small bluff, and raced frantically, scrambling desperately to reach the high ground in their attempt to defend themselves. Goblins rushed headlong, bent on stopping them. Shouts and cursing rang out again as the two sides engaged, leather crunching, and weapons clanging. Bitter hand-to-hand fighting broke out, each side using short daggers, cudgels, even broken branches as weapons. Yilmai and Kusai managed to drag Tulemai to the top of the bluff before they were overrun. There were arms and legs flying in all directions.

The loud blare of a trumpet cut the early morning air. Arrows began flying, this time into the goblins. The confused goblins halted their advance. Facing them was a fresh elven patrol, well supplied with arrows. They poured down from the back of the bluff, yelling battle cries of encouragement to their exhausted companions. For a time determined goblins held to their battle lines, but it soon became evident they were no match for this patrol. They broke into ragged groups and fled deeper into the forests, intent on escaping the wrath of these fresh young warriors.

Finding themselves free of the fighting, Wulpai and Bili wearily worked their way to the top of the bluff. Here they picked up the palette and doggedly tramped off with Tulemai between them. Both were bleeding from cuts they had received during the fighting, but there was no one else nearby to assist them. The others were hotly pursuing the retreating goblins. Wulpai had an especially nasty cut near his shoulder, and it was obvious it was bothering him as they worked their way down the trail. At last they reached a small river, and stumbled across. Climbing the bank on the far side, they moved into the safety of the forests. Meri joined them, and after a short rest, they began walking along a common trail again.

"That was really close," Bili mumbled breathlessly. "I thought we were finished."

Wulpai was too winded to reply, but wearily nodded his head in reply.

Meri stared at the two of them, then looked down at Tulemai, sudden shock registering across her sweat-streaked face. He seemed to be fading!

"Wulpai!" she cried, "Look at Tulemai. He's fading! He's dying! What can we do for him? I know only the natural medicines that I learned in our mountains. I picked up some things in the caves of testing, but I can't read their labels, nor do I know anything about them."

"Open your pack and let me see what you've got," replied Wulpai, spreading his hands out in a calming gesture, attempting to bring Meri down to rational thinking again. She took a deep breath and let it out slowly. Then she did as requested, pulling out the vials and packages she had taken. Wulpai checked a couple of them, then handed one back to her.

"This is an old remedy used by dwarf healers. I'm not sure how much good it will do for an elf. I'm going to pull the arrow out.

Bili, you hold him as still as you can. When I do, Meri I want you to pour some of this ointment right into the open wound," Wulpai instructed. "After that, lay the stone on the wound, and blend your mind with it."

Meri did as instructed. Wulpai turned Tulemai gently on his side with Bili's help. He was unconscious. Wulpai felt for the shaft, held it for a moment, then gave a slight twist and pulled. An audible groan escaped the lips of the unconscious elf. Meri quickly poured some of the strange ointment into the wound. It seemed to her as if it bubbled ever so slightly as it worked its way into the hole. Meri placed the stone over it firmly, closing her eyes. The stone began glowing steadily. She reached within her mind, placing the stone at the center of her thoughts. Finding its core, she joined her mind with its pulsing force, trying to feel its cadence. She worked to picture Tulemai as whole, free of this dreadful wound.

She remained frozen in this position for some minutes while the returning elves crossed the river. They gathered silently, watching. They showed great respect for these two healers, and watched curiously to see what was being done. Slowly color began to return to Tulemai's near translucent skin, covering the veins and capillaries that had become so prominent. His ragged breathing slowed, becoming regular and even. He sighed deeply, suddenly relaxing into a normal sleep. The stone stopped its pulsing so Meri lifted it from Tulemai's body and stood up.

"The stone has done all it can for him. The rest is up to him now. How much further is it until we reach the safety of the elven forests?"

Yilmai looked astonished. "You're already in them," he insisted. "And nothing has happened to you!" Puzzlement gave way to genuine delight.

The leader of the other patrol, Paiyu, returned and quickly took charge of the war party.

"Lift that bed lightly and go carefully now. In under a day's journey we could be at the capital, but since it is evident he is healing, we must slow down and allow Tulemai time to rest. We'll make camp at dusk and wait until daylight to resume our travel."

Two young elves picked up the bed and began moving down the trail. Meri trailed close behind, concerned that the wounded elf leader be handled gently.

Bili looked at Wulpai, noticing for the first time the nasty gash he had in his left arm.

"You'd better bandage that wound soon. It looks bad."

"I hear a stream up ahead. I think I'll bathe it there," Wulpai replied, nodding in the direction of the noise of cascading water. They walked on until they reached the stream. Both men stripped off their shirts and chain mail. The water stung the many cuts as it cleansed away dirt, sweat and caking blood. Bili had been lucky. He had but one minor cut. It would heal. Wulpai, on the other hand, had several small cuts and a severe wound on his arm where the armor ended. It would take stitching and an elven healer's care.

Chapter 8
The Elven Council

Morning dawned clear and cool. The rains had moved eastward during the night and left the forests smelling refreshed, renewed, pure. Meri was first to notice the change. The birds sang differently here. The sounds were somehow nobler, sweeter - a near recklessness to their enjoyment of life. Softly clutching the stone in her hand, she spotted a beautiful rainbow colored lorikeet above her on a nearby branch. Willing it to land on her, she extended her free hand. It cocked its head, hopped a couple of steps toward the end of the limb, suddenly fluttering down, warbling and chirping excitedly. Jamming its claws around Meri's hand, it stared at her in wonder. Meri, not daring to move, reached out tentatively to touch its mind, finding there a simple one, filled with happiness, thoughts of flights, juicy worms, bugs, insects and a full belly. Meri laughed out loud, unable to contain her amusement at images it sent her, frightening its fragile spirit. Flying up, it scolded her, then settled once again upon her hand.

Bili looked around him as he walked, his mouth agape in school boy wonder. Hidden in the trees were elven watchtowers, manned by young elves dressed in the green and grays of the forest. Holding up bows in salutes to their friends, they returned to the business of guarding their threatened forests.

The trail began to climb slowly, winding along the sides of the forested hills. As the sun reached its zenith they broke from the cover of the forest, looking directly into a lovely meadow. There were daffodils and daisies along a streambed that rambled across the upper edges of the meadow, surrounded by clover and soft grasses. Does and fawns grazed quietly, looking up at the approaching elves. Conies and their little ones were chewing grass off to one side, keeping a wary eye on an old badger clawing angrily at some roots along the far bank.

The sun felt good to their tired bodies. They set Tulemai down near the stream. He stirred, turning his face to one side, then opened his eyes, squinting as the sun touched his cheek. He stretched his arm, placing a hand over his wound. Sliding it across his ribs, he began exploring for the hole. He struggled to sit up as he began probing. He frowned. There was neither arrow, nor wound. One of the young elves rushed to help him stand as he struggled for his footing. Quickly pulling off his shirt, he looked at his side. He stared incredulously. There was no wound. His side was tender, but there was no wound! He looked around confused.

"How long have I been asleep?" he asked, panic showing in his eyes. "How could my wound be healed? I was shot with a goblin arrow. Only elven herbs and medicines can draw out that poison!"

Wulpai stepped over and began quietly, "It was medicine from Meri's pack, along with the power of the black stone that seems to have drawn the poison from you, Tulemai. You've been asleep less than a day. Look! The sun hasn't started sinking yet. Here, have something to eat."

"Speaking about healing, let me put a little of this on your arm, Wulpai," interrupted Meri. She had noticed bleeding from his left arm, and saw how Wulpai favored it. She got him to sit down and peeled off his shirt. The nasty cut still had not closed. She poured a small portion of the healing medicine into it, then placed the stone over it. Wulpai winced visibly as the stone touched his skin. Its pulsing seemed to tear at the very fiber of his being. He held still as long as he was able, then turned away, unable to bear further pain.

Meri stared, not comprehending. "It worked for Tulemai," she burst out in frustrated surprise.

"Why isn't it helping you?" She looked at the stone, disappointment and confusion written on her features. Then reluctantly she placed it back in its leather pouch around her neck.

Wulpai smiled, relief showing plainly on his face. He placed the hand of his good arm on her shoulder.

"Maybe the stone is only meant to work for certain people," he suggested. "We'll be at the capital soon, and the elven healers can do the rest. Don't worry about me. I'll be all right." He left her there. Walking over to the stream, he kneeled down and took a long drink.

Tulemai, still unbelieving and amazed, tested his strength. He decided maybe he wasn't ready to walk very far after all, and allowed himself to be carried again. Two fresh elves lifted the palette and began following the trail. Not long after, the whole party joined them and everyone was on the move again. The trail continued to wind slowly upwards, following a ridge leading to a heavily forested plateau. The air grew cooler as the afternoon wore on, but it was refreshing. Everyone felt well rested, so they hurried along.

By late afternoon, they crested the ridge they had been following, and were well along the plateau. Huge boulders were strewn at random on both sides of the trail, as though spilled like marbles from a bag by some giant hand. Here the trees were sparse, and small pebbles and odd looking stone monuments overran the soil. Years of wind and rain had swept most of the cover away, exposing the harsh bed beneath.

Yilmai stepped off the trail and waited for Meri to catch up. As she approached, he walked with her. "Have you noticed all these boulders?" he began. "They are believed to be the ancestors of our people. There was a time long ago, when they had to fight evil in the land. With their magic, they beat back those who challenged their right to exist, but many of them were killed. Instead of burying their bodies, or sending them along the silver road, the lords turned them into stone and placed them here as a memorial. Some of our greatest leaders still come here just to listen, gathering wisdom and power. I hope to achieve that someday when I come into responsibility in our nation."

"I was wondering how such huge stones appeared in a place like this," Meri replied. "There's nothing like this along the whole trail. Uh…, you mentioned a `Silver Road'. I don't understand. What is that?"

"That's simply where our people go when their time on this earth is done. We are immortal unless outsiders kill us. It's always been our way to send our old ones on the road to join the others who've gone before. There is a special ceremony held twice a year. Those are the only times the road is open."

Meri was silent, reflecting on what she had heard. Nothing in her culture mentioned anything about a 'Silver Road.' That disturbed her; yet in some small way also gave her hope about the future. She thought to herself how much she had learned already just being away from her village. She pondered this, wondering how much more she would learn before this adventure was complete?

At sunset, the elves arrived at a small encampment. Tulemai got up from the palette and greeted the caretaker. He explained to him that this company would be spending the night, but needed to make an early start for the capital. The caretaker nodded, and hurried off obediently to prepare a meal for the travelers. He glanced furtively at the three humans standing there as he turned his back to leave.

Tulemai joined Meri and Yilmai, who were discussing elven healers. Meri was still concerned about Wulpai.

"I'm sorry," Tulemai said. "I had no idea Wulpai had been hurt. I'll speak to the caretaker. There is a healer stationed here for such an emergency."

He hurried to join the caretaker, and soon returned with an elderly elf, slight of build, but his step still strong. He carried a small bag in which he kept herbs, ointments and elven medicine. The two of them went to Wulpai who was sitting on a carved tree trunk shaped into a chair. Wulpai got up, greeted them, then took off his shirt as requested. He sat down again as the healer probed the extent of his injury. With much clucking, and with the help of two young elven girls, he set about sewing up the torn muscles, stopping the new flow of blood that had started from all his probing.

After thoroughly bandaging the wound, he set Wulpai's arm in a sling. "Try not to move the arm for a few days," he commanded matter-of-factly. Gathering his implements, he walked away as quietly as he had come, flanked by his two assistants.

"Thank you for attending to my wound, Tulemai," Wulpai said graciously, still staring at his shoulder.

"The least I could do for a friend who saved my own life," replied Tulemai appreciatively, as he laid a hand on Wulpai's good shoulder. "We should arrive in the capital by noon tomorrow, and I believe I can gather the council together the following day. They will be very interested in hearing what you three have to relate to them. "

As darkness laid a gentle shroud across the last rays of light touching the crags, the caretaker returned to invite everyone to diner in the modest but spacious hall. They came in groups of two or three, talking quietly among themselves. The hall was lit with candles set in sconces on both walls, throwing spectral shadows across the tables that were set with meats, nuts, fruits and elven mead.

Tulemai settled himself at the far end, inviting Paiyu, Wulpai, Bili, Meri and Yilmai to sit near him. Others found places around the room, waiting for Tulemai to give the signal to begin the meal. Small gusts of wind blew in through the open windows, gutting the candles, causing the shadows to leap and dance before them. Glancing at their host, Tulemai lifted the traditional mead cup in thanks and salute, then took a short drink. He placed the cup down on the table, raised his hands, palms spread outward, and called out the awaited elven blessing.

Once finished, Yilmai leaned over to Bili and said, "Now we can eat."

Bili watched in silence, interested in learning all he could about his new friends. He liked the idea of special communal living and the camaraderie that it brought-*sort of like being in the elven army-* he thought to himself. He glanced over at Meri who was busy dishing up some fruit for herself. She seemed at ease among the elves too. Bili wondered if this was due in part to the influence of the stones. Did they possess some quality that drew the good will out of others toward those who carried these special stones? Bili tucked those thoughts away until a more convenient time. He would find time to talk with Wulpai and Meri about this.

There were quiet conversations all through the meal. The patrols were glad to be back safely in their own borders, but saddened to have found only one survivor in enemy territory. There was hushed speculation about the strangers, and what business they had inside their enchanted lands. They heard rumors about an elven council to be convened to talk about the war-like activities of the goblins. There was even rumor that a delegation of dwarves might be arriving to join the discussions of the council. No dwarves had entered elven lands in living memory. Something unusual must be happening if dwarves were coming!

Before dinner was over, Tulemai stood up, addressing all present.

"I want to praise you all for your courage these past few days and for all the help you gave to our friends here in the daring rescue. I'm proud of each one of you. In the face of overwhelming odds, you showed your skills and proved your loyalty. I speak especially for Yilmai and I'm sure for the others with him."

Tulemai went on to remind them they were scheduled to move on to the capital in the morning. Finally he encouraged them to get a good night's rest and be ready to march at first light.

He left the room first, in the company of the caretaker and Wulpai. Bili followed Yilmai and some of the other young elves.

Meri excused herself, and hurried to the quarters assigned to her. As it turned out, the caretaker had a daughter, who took Meri in. They talked a while outside, then climbed the stairs to the room nestled among the branches of a sturdy ash tree.

Sleep was interrupted with black dreams. Goblins leered, trolls swung clubs at their feet, the ground fell away, and the river was swollen. Bili tossed and turned, trying to avoid capture. He was surrounded with no chance of escape. He struggled furiously as the enemy pressed him, driving him to the ground. He struggled helplessly as they continued to pile on him.

Bili awoke and sat up with a start, sweating and irritated. Realizing he had been dreaming, he lay back down and rolled over, willing himself back to sleep. It was no help. Sleep eluded him. Resignedly he sat up, found his boots and slipped quietly outside. The cool night air helped clear his mind. He padded across the veranda and worked his way down the stairs. Something was bothering him. He stopped and sat on the last step, trying to make it surface. Trying to concentrate only seemed to drive it deeper. He worked to relax his agitated mind and feelings, and allowed his mind to go blank. The stone around his neck, dormant since the fight earlier that day, began gently pulsing. Bili stilled his mind further, listening hard. Impressions of a room full of books, an elderly elf, an ancient scroll spread out on a table; heads pouring over the scroll; strange runes and writings from past ages. Images tumbled through Bili's head. He lifted his eyes up toward the stars as he mulled these over in his mind. He had no idea what they portrayed, nor who the people were or where he was, but they must be important he reasoned. Tomorrow, he thought, he might have the answers that he sought. At last he yawned, then climbed back up the stairs, re-entered the room, and soon fell into a dreamless sleep.

Movement in the room awakened Meri. She opened an eye and stared vaguely around. It was still dark, but morning was not far off. She groaned inwardly, rolled over and got up out of her sleeping cot. Gathering her few things, she put them back into her pack. Then she went outside with the caretaker's daughter to wash the sleep from her eyes.

Everyone was gathering in the hall for breakfast. It was a simple meal, with elven cakes, honey and a steaming kettle of Nauke, the elven coffee. No one spoke as they hurriedly downed the food. Bili looked up to catch Meri's eye as she entered. She gave him a brief smile, then sat down to eat.

Tulemai's strength returned with the new day. He got everyone on the trail before the sun made its grand entry over the cliffs east of them. Birds tittered in alarm and flew from the branches that had been home to them the night before. Deer looked up and scattered as the party walked through yet another meadow. They spread out as they crested the far plateau, then started down again. Here the trail was steep, with scree covering the footpath so thickly in places, even the elves were forced to find bushes to slow their sliding descent.

Toward noon, the trail leveled off becoming more heavily enclosed by Cottonwood and Aspen, which grew in groups, providing plenty of shade. Looking up, Bili noticed more hidden towers. They must be approaching the capital, he thought. He nudged Yilmai and asked,

"How much further is it now?"

Yilmai smiled and pointed. "About an hour's journey and we'll reach the outer fences. Then it's only a short way into the central part of the city. Are you getting tired?" he asked.

"No, I just want to be fully awake to appreciate everything I'm going to be seeing," Bili replied.

Tulemai stopped beside a clear flowing brook, taking time to drink water again. He had lost quite a lot of blood, which lowered his stamina. Rising slowly, he continued along the trail. Wulpai filled a water bottle he'd made from a gourd, and put a stopper in it, while he waited for Meri. She too stopped and drank deeply. It tasted as though this water had life of itself. It not only refreshed. It filled her with a feeling of strength and vitality again. She commented about it to Wulpai. He nodded and said something about the elven magic making it that way. Meri didn't catch all he said, but she heard enough to piece together an image of power among these people.

They started climbing again, and in a short time came to the outer fences surrounding the city. The fences were woven of heavy bramble thorn bushes clustered together, sealing the city off from intruders. The magic interwoven with the thorns made it impossible to breach. High gates led to a short bridge spanning a sparkling stream. Young elves stood sentry duty, two on either side of the gates. They stood at attention as Tulemai approached. He took his party right on through. They watched wide-eyed as the strangers entered their beloved city.

Beautiful parks and ponds dotted the landscape along the roadway. Benches and shelters were placed every so often, where others could best enjoy the views before them. Bili and Meri stumbled over each other several times, their eyes darting from item to item. They had never imagined such a place of beauty could exist. Soon there were houses arranged in neat rows, built slightly off the ground. Children played along the lanes, throwing balls and chasing one another.

Tulemai turned up a wide lane, leading them to the city's center. Here tall buildings made of wood, faced with stone, and held together with magic circled another parkway. Real gates of wrought iron marked the estate of the elven king. Guards blocked their entry until Tulemai spoke to them. They parted, allowing the party to pass through. Walking up the flower-lined pathway, the senior member of the elven council met them. Tulemai introduced the three guests, as they continued making their way toward the palace.

Yilmai nudged Bili, and whispered, "What do you think of our city now?"

Bili gawked at the palace before answering. "If I weren't here to actually see it, I'd say I'm having a dream which I hope never ends."

This answer seemed to satisfy Yilmai who kept moving with them toward the palace. Meri, walking a short distance in front of them stopped suddenly. She put her hand to the pouch, withdrawing the black stone. It was pulsing. Bili almost bumped into her.

"What's wrong, Meri?" Then he, too, noticed the stone.

"I'm not sure why the pulsing, but it's definitely hot." Meri said alarmed. "Surely there's nothing here to threaten the elves or us?"

Wulpai noticing her distress turned and walked back to her. "I think the stone senses something here tuned to its frequencies, and in some way is communicating. If this is true, it should stop in a short while. The elven council is assembled and awaits our entry."

Relief flooded Meri's face. She decided to put the stone back in the pouch. Moving forward, they climbed the stairway, walked across the marbled porch, and entered the large portals of the palace. They were guided on ahead into a large hall, where tables lined the walls. At the front of the hall the elven king awaited them, sitting on an ornately carved throne of kinosen wood, a rare dark wood grown only in the elven forests. Beautiful sapphires, rubies, topaz and amethysts were tastefully inset. A huge mural carved in ivory covered the back panel above the king's head. It portrayed an ancient ceremony, with a young maiden in attendance to two venerable looking elves seated on ornately carved toadstools.

The humans were brought before Duranmin. They all bowed low as they were introduced. The king was the first to speak.

"We've been informed of all that happened from the time you left the goblin caves until you reached sanctuary among us. All three of you are obviously gifted, and we consider you 'elven friends.' No humans in recent history have passed through our enchantments untouched as you three have." He continued. "We would learn of your quest and give you what aid we might." He peered intently at Meri. She felt his gaze probe beyond her eyes, searching for sincerity, honesty, and answers to questions he had as yet not asked.

She moved forward nervously, curtsied slightly and began a hesitant narration. "Your Majesty, members of the council. We express our gratitude to you for the patrols. Against great odds and personal peril to themselves, they brought us safely here. It has now been 16 days since we left our homeland beyond the eastern mountains. Many strange things have occurred to assure us that our quest is both urgent and necessary.

"Battle hawks flew over our forests, fighting one of the large golden rocs from the Western Lands. It was badly outnumbered, and realized it had little chance of escape. It threw a small package into a pond near my feet, hoping I would be able to keep it from falling into the hands of the hawks and those who own them. My brother drove the hawks off, and we retrieved the package, carrying it to the village. We showed it to our father, but he was unable to discern its origin or use. During the night the stone and also the talisman stone which my brother carries, gave us dreams, warning us that we must return these stones of power to the Western Lands where they would be given into the hands of those who know best of their use against the Dark Lord."

At the mention of the Dark Lord, the elven king's eyebrows raised ever so slightly. He had been alive when the wars along the plains had caused so much destruction. No one had seen or heard anything more about the Dark Lord for several hundred years. They figured him dead. Now these young humans were telling him that the Dark Lord yet lived. He allowed Meri to continue.

"We talked it over with our parents, but they were against our making the journey. The stones communicated with us in no uncertain terms, and we were given instructions to follow. We decided it was best to leave immediately and not be encumbered with others traveling with us." Meri paused briefly, then went on.

"We left for the sacred mountains and rescued Wulpai when we encountered a guardian. Then we were directed to the caves of testing. We've no idea how much time we spent there, but we underwent some rigorous testing, and had to fight our way out to safety. When we met Yilmai outside the goblin caves, he realized that we were under special protection. We shared with him our need to see you and also the nation of Dwarves, to alert you to the fact that the Dark Lord is preparing for war."

There was an audible gasp from the council members.

"Your majesty," started the head councilor. "This might explain, at least in part, the growing activities of our enemies to the north. There is a lot of traffic, and we've not been able to get to the bottom of it. This young girl's explanation could possibly account for a lot we've seen in recent months."

"How can we know these things are true?" countered the king. "Do we have proof these aren't merely idle rumors?"

Meri flinched as though she had been struck. She reached into her tunic, pulling out the stone. It was pulsing evenly. She turned to Bili.

"Is your stone active?" Bili pulled out the talisman stone, and saw its light growing. Together they began a tentative mind-link. As the pulsing began to grow in size its force field began shoving the two of them apart.

As they were pushed apart, a holographic video developed between them. Soon the hall was enveloped with dark figures roaming about an old castle, shouting orders and preparing for battle. As the scenes shifted, they witnessed awful destruction, tremendous carnage- the dead lying everywhere: humans, elves, dwarves, rock dwellers, goblins, trolls, and strange beasts having no names.

The hall broke into an uproar. There were shouts on both sides. Some interpreted the holograph as prophesy; others roared angrily, yelling about sorcery being brought into the hall and using it to dupe the unwary.

After the head councilor had restored order, the king encouraged Bili and Meri with these words. "We've been told strange tales. We have also seen strange visions this day. We must take time to consider the meaning of all this. Until then, you are to be our guests. Enjoy your stay here in our capital, Yasainik."

From a side door, a beautiful young elf appeared. She was dressed in a simple frock, with a flower in her hair. She approached the throne, bowed low, then walked to Meri. "I have been sent to show you the city," she smiled. "Please, come this way."

Meri looked over her shoulder at Bili, and began following the girl. Bili, not sure if he was to follow, trailed behind, continuing to stare at the hall with its designs and craftsmanship. Wulpai stayed with the king, speaking privately with him over some matter. Then he too left the hall.

"My name is Rimwai," the young maiden said quietly. "My father has asked me to help you in any way possible, making sure you're comfortable while the council debates the information you've presented them. Come over to the park. Food and drinks have been prepared for you."

Moving down the path, Bili waited for Wulpai to catch up with him. He began sharing his impressions of elven architecture. Wulpai smiled, listening patiently. Soon Yilmai, bursting with news caught up with them, then excitedly started jabbering.

"You people are the talk of the town! News of what happened in the council has spread all over the city. The council hasn't been in such confusion in recorded history."

"It's hard for the elves to come to grips with the need to cooperate with humans," Wulpai replied, not unkindly. "Years of isolation and memories of the great wars have made them wary.

It's going to take time for them to digest the reality that the Dark Lord still lives. They were sure he'd been destroyed."

"How is it that you know so much about the elves, and the wars from the past," asked Yilmai. "Are you a historian in your country?"

"No, not exactly," countered Wulpai. "You see, my father was a member of our council. He often took me to the library where he researched documents. I was allowed to browse through whatever interested me. I had heard about the elves, but never saw one. So I thought that I would learn what I could. As I grew older, I learned to read well enough to struggle through the records we had of the ancient wars. There I learned much about the nations- dwarves, elves, cave dwellers, trolls, goblins- I was inquisitive."

"You also told us that you've been to the Western Lands on missions," interrupted Bili. "You must have seen a lot of things there too?"

"I was warrior trained as I came to manhood," Wulpai smiled. "It was natural that we accompany our leaders as they moved about the country. I was assigned to the elite palace guard as captain, so I went every time a delegation was sent out. I've seen a lot of unusual things in the past 12 years, Bili."

Rimwai brought over cups made of leaves, filled with cool drinks for them. She invited them to come pick whatever pleased them to eat. The conversation came to an end, as the hungry visitors tasted the wonders of elven pastry.

Chapter 9

The Dwarves Join the Alliance

During the next two weeks, Meri and Rimwai became close friends. They went everywhere together, spending many hours down by the river talking, getting to know one another. Rimwai shared her heart and dreams with Meri, things that every girl hoped for as she grew toward womanhood. These special times opened Meri's mind to wonders she delighted in being shown. She had dreams of her own, but the scope of them reached little further than her own culture and local area. Since her people had chosen to isolate themselves from outsiders, they had become ingrown and stagnant. There was no chance for interchange between people of other cultures. Preservation of what they once knew became the dominating factor in survival; and survive they had.

Here she was now in the heart of a city whose beauty and diversity had never entered her imagination. And yet, as Meri reflected on all these sudden changes, she was surprised how much two young women could have in common who had come from such diverse cultural backgrounds.

A deep bond began developing between these two young women, a bond that Meri sensed would carry them through some hard experiences, maybe even dangerous situations. Thinking about the things that meant the most to her since she had arrived, and what had touched her heart with sheer pleasure was finding the same predilections toward herbs, healing and medicines. Meri was able to share without reservation or fear of rebuke what she had learned. This also included the unusual ointments she had acquired in the Caves of Testing.

Rimwai, in her turn, was fascinated by Meri's ability to communicate with the animals, especially the way she could use the stone to assist her in virtually getting into the body of the birds, sensing their feelings and communicating with them. Meri worked with Rimwai, helping her to augment her innate elven talent to mind meld with the animals, showing her various ways to get at what she wanted. Rimwai wished the council meetings would go on forever. She was learning so much and everything she experienced brought shouts of joy within her soul!

"Meri, these past days have been filled with such wonder and delight, the young elf confided. "At times I can hardly contain myself. I feel as though my body may burst if this continues any longer! My spirit feels at times as though it is soaring high into the clouds, or racing over the tops of the hills or wending its way through the boughs and branches of the forests! Your coming here has been a fortuitous occasion for me especially!" She leaned gently, putting her head on Meri's shoulder.

"Oh Rimwai!" Meri whispered back, "You have no idea what coming here has done for me. I don't think I'll ever be satisfied with living in a simple yam culture again. The world is so much bigger than what I grew up in. Yes, it has its beauty in its simplicity, and

I appreciate that. Relationships too are a vital part of being a part of a larger whole. But sometimes that whole moves in directions that are not healthy.

"Here I have been given vision. I now see what can be, and maybe for some cultures, what should be. For me, I feel I have been brought here for a larger purpose, possibly something that has been planned from of old, maybe something as old as the mountains themselves! It is such a sweet thing to dream and touch no boundaries! I too feel so full of wonder I could burst!"

They sat near the old bridge, reveling in the beauty of their surroundings and the wonder of discovery.

Yilmai took it upon himself to entertain Bili. His impetuous behavior embarrassed Bili, as the elven girls giggled and teased his friend constantly. Bili realized now how somber and conservative he himself was compared to his gregarious friend. And he blushed furiously every time one of the elven girls took it upon herself to draw him out with lighthearted teasing. This pleased the girls deeply, and endeared him to them. Yilmai refused to rescue him. Rather he was found encouraging them at every turn. Bili felt like a cornered wood deer, desperately searching for a way out. This only amused them further as they learned of his weaknesses.

In spite of the social blunders he made, the enchanted wonders of the city captured Bili's heart. He was deeply drawn to the elven architecture, which at times displayed broad sweeping movements, and at others, careful attention to detail. Bili stared in awe at the finely chiseled busts of unusual animals he had never encountered that adorned the eaves of the more important buildings at the city's center. The intricate balance of brick and sculptured wood around the doorways and windows was as intriguing as it was confusing. The harder Bili attempted to trace out the designs, the more optical illusions appeared to baffle his senses.

He was thoroughly fascinated by the way they fashioned their bows, and the way they rubbed their arrows with certain oils as they slid them back and forth in the heat of their fires to permanently straighten the shafts. Fletching too was a very polished art among the elven elders. They took pride in mounting the feathers and tying them down into their knife carved slots. Some of men adorned the shafts with elven runes depicting former battles, or placing magic upon them that they might fly true toward their intended targets.

What touched Bili's heart most were the times he was able to pull Yilmai to the library. It was here at the library that Bili made his most important discovery. An older elf was caretaker here, with the must and dust of books etched upon his gentle personality. As he and Bili became acquainted, Bili engaged Wulmakai in conversations, plying the elder with stories of the past, especially related to former wars. He was anxious to glean anything that might help him understand the circumstances that had brought him, along with Wulpai and Meri here into the heartland of the elves. He wanted desperately to discover what was happening, and know what his or Meri's part might be in all this.

Wulmakai, being of a kindly disposition, took time to sit with Bili and share what he knew. He educated Bili in history from his elven perspective. He taught him the principles of elven architecture and how magic was cleverly interwoven into the very fabric of daily life. Bili was an avid pupil, drinking in the river of information that seemed to burst forth in an endless stream from the mouth of the elder.

Eventually, he guided Bili to the *Codrin*, a sacred book of ancient prophecy. Revered by the elves, the *Codrin* had been carefully copied in the West, and purposely brought to be stored here in these well-protected walls.

Bili's reading skills were rather weak, just like the rest of his formal education. He hadn't even been given time to complete his training under the village Shaman. He was able to read the script only with difficulty. Wulmakai would help him from time to time with words or ideas that were foreign to his experience. Bili, determined to improve, decided he would make reading a part of his morning routines. He set aside time to come here and learn all he could, while the council continued its debate.

Wulmakai was pleased to find Bili a quick learner, and a determined pupil. Yilmai, spurred by Bili's enthusiasm for learning, decided he needed to brush up on certain areas he had neglected. These were areas that held little interest to a young boy who would rather have been hunting deer in the mountain's fastness. Books were so formal, so lifeless, and all too boring. Now that he was older and had nearly lost his life among the goblin, his values had shifted noticeably, so he willingly joined Bili as they poured over the manuscripts.

One morning, as the young men were engrossed in a particular battle fought in the Northron Mountains, Wulmakai took out an ancient volume with special runes inscribed on its cover. As he approached the table where Bili and Yilmai were studying, Bili's talisman began pulsing. Surprise gave way to Intrigue; Bili decided to remove the stone from its cover and he stood up, placing it atop the book. To his astonishment, the meaning of the runes became clear to him. Excited, he looked at Wulmakai and shouted,

"I can actually read the runes on the cover. I can understand their meaning!"

"Open the cover then, Bili," encouraged the elf.

Hesitantly, Bili opened the book, his heart pounding. A prophecy prefaced the main text. It had been written in special ink manufactured with elven magic. As the pulsing stone lay nearby, the runes seemed to take on a life of their own. They stood out in bold relief, magic adding to the special elven calligraphy.

Bili read through it out loud, slowly, and deliberately. He could read the words, but much of the meaning eluded him. He looked up rather disappointed, only to find Wulmakai smiling.

"Bili, outside of myself and two others, you are the only other person to have read the prophecy. Its meaning has been hidden for eons. Many a scholar has tried to figure out the symbols. They always come to a futile end."

Bili looked over at his friend Yilmai for support, but Yilmai, having tired from his own reading, had fallen asleep.

"I would talk further of this with you," replied Bili, suddenly subdued. "But first I'd like Wulpai with me when we do it. He seems to have unusual discernment for someone his age. He might be of invaluable assistance to us."

Later that day, Bili, Meri and Wulpai were alone for a time. Bili shared his morning adventure. "It was hard to believe, but I actually saw those runes take shape in my mind. It was an old book, the one Wulmakai gave to me. I found I was able to read the letters, although I couldn't understand much of the meaning. Wulmakai encouraged me to stretch my mind as much as I could. I feel that book may contain some of the answers to what the stones have been trying to communicate to us."

"I would appreciate the opportunity to accompany you to the library Bili," Wulpai said. "I wouldn't miss this chance for anything. I'm sure I can get permission to miss some of the debate when they understand this is surely related to the events that must soon to come to pass."

Both Wulpai and Meri agreed to accompany him the following morning. Bili found it difficult to sleep that night. He tossed and turned, impatient for morning to arrive.

As soon as breakfast was over, Bili met the others at the library. Wulmakai was waiting with the book. Bili took the talisman out of its cover and it began to glow as he laid it on the book.

"Wulmakai, does this book have a name?" Bili asked. The old elf smiled. "When I was young, I heard the elders call it '*The Ruler.*' In elven talk, that's *Graemwai*. It doesn't appear to follow any time orientation. Parts came to us over many years and have been placed in the book of prophesy in the order received."

Wulpai took a seat next to the elder. Staring at the runes for a few seconds, he read, "That which is yet to be". He gently lifted the talisman, and turned the cover. Seeing the prophecy, Wulpai asked, "Can you understand this?"

Wulmakai replied, "I can read the words, but some are from other languages. I'm afraid I must admit I feel unsure of much of their meaning."

"Would you mind translating some of it for us," Wulpai asked, "transliterating the words you can't translate?"

Slowly, haltingly, Wulmakai began:

..."Dark upon the mountains broods the evil,

Waiting for its time. Ripe it grows in

Shadow, peeling skin and rind. Pouring
Out its ugly spawn, the seedlings spread
Afar, covering field and hollow, filling
Oak and yar. When the lesser light floods
The hidden way, casting full its brightness
On the holy bay, let the chosen's blood flow
From hearts plucked yet alive, to be devoured
By the power soon to be derived.
Then let all upon the earth who yet remain,
Embrace the darkness, the agony, the pain.
This may yet be stayed, by hearts open to the
Light, listening to the voice of those who walk the
Night. The battle will be fought *glaepinkau kentar
Nan, keruwa yipo na nasi*. Thus will the power be
Broken, *ta glaupokni pika kakno wit karak napai
Kirak kan*. Forces must be joined, and the power
Be made whole. Then will the cleansing be complete.
Yi aiyisas menmen im o manman ap ta mamnen taau."

Wulmakai finished reading, then stared at the others. "Well, have you any ideas?"

"Actually yes," Wulpai smiled. "The part about the battle says that it will take place under the earth in a place of stones. The battle will be fought on two different levels."

"How can you know that?" questioned Meri. "What language is that anyway? And how is it possible that you understand it?"

"It's actually the language of the people north of where I come from. My father married a woman from that language. She spoke it to me often when I was young, and I've remembered much of it. Years ago she took me there a few times visiting relatives."

The Chronicles of Salduwe Book One

"What about the rest of it?" interrupted Bili. "Is it the same language?"

"No, but the languages are related. This must come from the west. It's hard to understand, but I think roughly translated it says, 'These conditions must be met or the things will not come to pass.' I don't know whether that's a message for the dark side or for those of the light. It could go either way."

They spent the rest of the morning pouring over other pages of the book, trying to piece together what they could. Finally, exhausted, they closed the bound volume of the *Cordin*. A feeling of accomplishment settled over them. "Well at least it's a start," grinned Bili. Wulmakai nodded.

Wulpai broke the mood with a practical suggestion. "I'm hungry; anyone for some elven pastry?" The library was soon abandoned. Wulmakai smiled as he turned the key in the lock to leave on errands of his own. *Ah, the exuberance of the young*, he smiled to himself as he walked up the pathway.

Late that afternoon, the four of them were invited to a private interview with Duranmin the elven king. saw them in a private chamber. He listened with interest to their findings. He too was aware of the prophecies, having studied at the library when he was younger. After considering their ideas, he mulled them over in his mind.

"It would seem you've made fair progress toward unraveling several of the mysterious prophecies. It's too bad we have been so short sighted these many years, isolating ourselves from the rest of the world. We all could have benefited greatly by allowing our mutual scholars to work together periodically. We would have been much further ahead in both our understanding and preparations for what is about to befall us."

Smiling sadly he continued, "Never mind what might have been. We must make sure there is plenty of wax on our bowstrings as we step carefully into the coming months."

Duranmin stopped suddenly, a far away look in his eyes as a slight smile touched the corners of his mouth. He gestured toward the hills beyond the city. "A delegation of dwarves has just entered our forests," He informed them. "They should be arriving here early tomorrow. I would like you all to attend the council sessions later in the day to explain the urgent need to form an alliance."

Bili glanced nervously at the others as he heard Duranmin's explanation. Suppressing a loud "Whoop", he smiled, pleased that their quest was being taken seriously. Wulpai winked at Bili but said nothing. Meri nodded her head, acknowledging the news, yet sensing at the same time the power of these stones, setting in motion events that would soon turn their world upside down.

Her Reverie was interrupted by Rimwai's timely arrival. She brought them tea and elven biscuits before they left the chamber.

The dwarves made a lot of noise as they arrived amidst the bustle of the city, huffing and wheezing as they set their packs and weapons on the ground. They were short, but heavily muscled. Their features were thick, with wide foreheads and bulbous noses. Their hands were gnarled and wide, used to handling picks, shovels and heavy axes. Their beards were neatly trimmed, some of them tightly braided. Other younger men were clean-shaven, but some braided their hair into pigtails, while others formed theirs into a queue.

Some wore the plain baggy trousers of the eastern clans, heavy belts, studded with stones, cinched at the waist. Others, obviously from the hills to the north, wore well-tanned leather, created from cattle hides. These thick trousers were more suited to moving through the thorny brush dotting the drier lands toward the plains.

A large dwarf, a mace dangling over his shoulder, was conferring with a smaller but older companion, obviously the leader of the group. Bili watched with interest as they gestured, pointing first to the equipment, then to the council chambers. They looked to be a hard lot, he thought. Turning to Yilmai, he nudged his companion "Have dwarves ever come into the capital before?"

"Yes," Yilmai replied, still keeping his eyes on the big dwarf Bili had been watching, "but this is the first time I've seen this many of them at once. Years ago my grandfather brought me to a meeting with two dwarves. I was too small to remember detail, but these men look larger than those I saw before."

"Do you think they'll listen, Yilmai? They look to be a rough lot, used to following their own counsel."

"If anyone can persuade them, Duranmin will. His reputation for wisdom and right judgment is known among all who dwell in these parts. I've been told the dwarves question everything and take the other side of the argument just to see how strongly you believe something. Yet, they may believe as strongly about something as you do."

"That is an interesting concept. I never thought about doing something of that nature. I wonder if that is what happens at home when the clans get together. They usually argue loudly about anything they discuss. Wish I'd been older when the last council was convened."

To Bili's trained eye it was obvious these dwarves had traveled hard when they had received the summons from the elven council.

Later he was informed that they had fought their way past the goblins, with only minor losses. The goblins usually gave them wide birth unless they had far superior numbers. Dwarves weren't tackled lightly. Many a goblin fell to the dreaded short axes the dwarves were so good at wielding.

After being allowed time to bathe and change clothing, the dwarves were ushered into the council chambers. Then the doors were tightly sealed. Elven guards were posted on all sides, keeping close watch around the perimeter. They wanted no accidents, took no chances.

Later that same day, Wulpai, Bili and Meri were asked to join the council and were escorted to the council hall. They presented their stories about the stones, the caves, and the journey to Yasainik. The dwarves were skeptical. They too demanded proof.

"Meri," Duranmin requested quietly, "Would you and Bili be willing to awaken your stones as proof of your stories? This delegation of dwarves requests more than words."

Meri nodded assent and turned tentatively to Bili. "Are you up to this, Bili? We've only tried something such as this once before. I have no idea what kind of response will be kindled this time."

Bili nodded and began removing his stone. Meri watched as the stone cleared its cover and began its gentle pulsing. Quickly she did the same, and they tuned their minds and wills inward, touching the very heart of that pulsing. What followed shocked them all. The stones burst forth in brilliant light, this time filling the hall and reproducing the dramatic holograph that the elven council had witnessed. Howls and angry protests filled the air as the drama unfolded. The startled guards hastily opened the doors, fearing for the lives of the councilors within. The compelling scenes filling the chamber overcame them as well.

When the holograph finished, the dwarves found it hard to control their emotions. As one they were determined to combat this menace, and readily agreed to an alliance, with conditions.

Duranmin brought Wulpai into these private sessions, for he was known to some of the dwarf chieftains. Wulmakai served as advisor to the elven king on matters of historical importance. They closeted themselves in the hall for the next two days, debating hotly over tactical planning, then placed their differences aside as they worked doggedly to draft an agreement and draw up plans related to the impending war.

The council, well aware that Bili and Meri were determined to return the stones to the Western Lands, decided it was of the utmost importance that the stones arrive safely. After some discussion, they hand picked a group to accompany them. Five dwarves and five elven warriors were chosen. The group was purposely kept small, hoping to remain unobtrusive while achieving maximum mobility.

Each was included in the expedition because of special knowledge or ability. These 10 would be responsible to ensure the humans reached the Western Lands with their precious cargo. The Dwarves included their leader, Daniray and his son Brell, Wabran the huge warrior and his cousin Breagle, and Brell, a close friend and a council member from the Northern Stronghold. The Elven warriors included Yilowen, son of Paiyu, Kusai, second son of Tolepai, and Durathor, chosen to lead to delegation of elves. Once they reached the Western Lands, they would represent their nations to the leaders of those countries. Rimwai and Yilmai were included as personal companions for Bili and Meri. Wulpai suggested that Wulmakai make the journey if he was able, that he might bring along copies of the *Codrin* and *Graemwai*. He himself would act as personal guard to the librarian.

Two days later, after careful preparation and the presentation of introductory documents, the party left Yasainik to begin their journey to the western forests of Yasinpien. They carried well-laden packs, filled mostly with food for the arduous journey. Arrows had been replenished, knives sharpened, swords and maces oiled and honed. Specially wrought elven chain mail was offered to each member. Wulpai and Bili needed none, for each wore the special armor he had acquired in the Caves of Testing. Others accepted these precious gifts willingly. They knew only too well the value of such a gift. The dwarves were long in expressing their gratitude. Finally they made their departure.

Walking along, Bili commented to Meri, "We spent 18 days among the elves. I've grown to love their way of life. It's different from what we know, but they have so much to offer. I wish our people had not cut themselves off from outsiders. We could have learned so much had our ancestors chosen otherwise."

"Maybe we can help bring change to our village when we return from the Western Lands," Meri suggested. "That is, if there is any home to return to when this is all over. In some ways I'm glad this was forced upon us because of what father was planning for me. Yet, in other ways I feel badly for him because it will look as though we have run off. After he had made those marriage arrangements, father will have suffered deep shame. I hope he can find it in his heart to forgive me."

"Relax, Meri. We had no choice! I have no regrets!" said Bili protectively. "It was run away and take the stones with us, or stay there and have an army of outsiders come in and destroy our land and people. I know these stones are very important to them. Nothing would have stood in their way. Our people would have been as chaff cut down at the end of harvest. No! Our people have some growing to do as well. They had no right to cut themselves off from others. Knowledge should be shared and used to help one another, not hoarded." Running out of intensity, he finished gently, "Besides, we both would have been killed had we stayed any longer."

Meri nodded sadly in agreement and said no more. It was comforting, though, to hear these words from her brother, and with such intense feelings. She felt deeply supported.

They hurried along the trails through the afternoon, then made camp in a clearing near a fast running stream. Watches were set as darkness engulfed the land. Everyone turned in early, anxious to be up at first light. Bili lay awake thinking of home, wondering again if his parents were safe. He wished he could contact them to let them know he and Meri were all right. *On second thought*, he mused, *maybe we wouldn't be in a day or two, but at least we are among worthy companions.*

Dawn came, bringing clear skies, and the group broke camp. Chewing elven cakes and raisins, they covered their tracks and cleared the campsite. Noon found them cresting a shallow depression filled with late spring flowers. Daffodils and buttercups grew tenaciously above the steep sides of a ravine, cheering the narrow opening with their bright colors. Yilmai, noticing the two girls had grown silent, worked his way to the edge and picked several flowers for them. Then hurrying back, he gave them to the girls. This brightened their spirits. They began talking quietly again, thinking ahead to what they might do when the quest was completed. The dwarves kept mostly to themselves, always alert for the unusual sound or signs of others. Two of them accompanied an elf as they ranged ahead, scouting to keep the main party from possible ambush.

Later toward evening, clouds began to gather, creating a brilliant sunset. The elves seemed pleased. The dwarves, however, disagreed saying it would bring rain before they reached the mountains.

Dinner was a quiet affair, each one looking inward. They were well aware they would be approaching the dreaded Plains of Desolation late tomorrow. Just the name struck terror into the hearts of those who dwelled nearby. In the past, many had tried to enter the fallen city in search of treasure. Few had returned. It was rumored to be inhabited by the ghosts of those who had not been buried in the great wars. People who managed to escape from the plains again often went mad, or became bereft of the will to live, and soon took their own lives.

In the morning the trail forced them to descend through thick forests, along narrow paths, rutted deeply by the run-offs of spring storms. Meri stumbled once or twice, but managed to keep her balance. Only the elves seemed quite at home, stepping lightly from root to root, avoiding the worst of the erosion. They stared continually upward, occasionally spotting hidden towers housing their fellow warriors who watched silently for intruders.

The forests ended abruptly at a small river. The scouting party sat anxiously nearby awaiting their arrival. There were several elven warriors there with them. Wondering what was going on, Meri turned to Rimwai.

"What's happening? Is there something wrong?" she asked, confusion wrinkling her forehead.

"I'm not sure," Rimwai countered, "but we may have reached the outer boundaries. That would explain the extra escort."

As they approached, the elves stepped first into the water. The dwarves, scowls of fear etched across their heavy featured faces, followed them. Meri wondered at their apprehension. She stepped lightly off the shallow bank into the water and began crossing. Suddenly the whole world seemed to sway before her. The trees began a ridiculous dance from one side to the other, as though blown to frenzy by some unseen wind. Meri staggered and fell. Her head went under the water where she felt the heavy oppression of the waters closing in to crush her. As darkness closed in around her, she felt strong hands lifting her from her prison.

As quickly as the sensation had begun, it ceased. Meri's head cleared and she found herself staring into the face of Wulmakai, the old librarian.

"Are you alright now?" he asked, concern showing on his smooth face. "I failed to remember that this particular boundary has been warded to keep the night prowlers from the plains from entering our sanctuary. It has strange effects on various races. You're the first humans to cross here, so we weren't sure what might happen."

Meri, relieved that it was only elven magic, let out a sputter of water, coughed, then grinned. "I'm glad I'm among friends," she said gamely. "Had you left me in the water a few moments longer, I think I might have drowned."

Yilmai warned Bili after they saw what had happened to Meri, so Bili clutched the Talisman around his neck tightly until he had crossed to the other side. The dwarves, pre-warned, knew what to expect and had made quick short jumps to get to the other side before the magic could take full hold of them. Nevertheless, they were clearly shaken as they reached the further shores.

The elves became much more alert. Now they were out of their home territory. They began murmuring among themselves about the flatlands. It was their turn to be uneasy. The dwarves, although unhappy about getting this close to the dreaded plains, accepted it. They stopped momentarily to confer with one another. Wulpai helped them decide on the route. He had been north of this area, and knew where it led.

"The safest route," he suggested, "Is to turn north, and follow the river until it turns east. Then we'll have to strike out across the plains until we reach the foothills."

The dwarves grumbled among themselves, still unhappy being in open country. Realizing they had little choice, they reluctantly agreed, knowing there was little cover outside the elven forests.

They hiked until dusk, when they came upon a natural wooded area. They crossed the river and voted to make camp a short ways in. They built a fire, cooked soup with dried meat soaked in river water. After the meal was finished and the utensils were put away, the dwarves decided to bed down together and clustered together along the river side of the clearing. The elves for their part decided to sleep toward the side bordering the forest. The women were positioned in the center for safety with Yilmai and Bili sleeping nearby.

As darkness came on, they put the fire out. Best not let others know we are camped here, the group decided. Besides, no one seemed in a mood to talk. Each was in his own private world filled with thoughts and fears of what lay ahead. Among these battle-hardened veterans keeping a fire going was likely to be viewed as an open invitation to strangers. Dwarves especially did not take to strangers. So the less people knew of them and their mission, the better.

The decision proved to be costly.

Chapter 10

Mountain of Death

Dark mists covered the crags of the mountains. In this glacial waste nothing grew. Nothing, that is, except the ever-increasing slag which oozed its way down the side of the once majestic hill. This was home to the Northern Cave Dwellers. Hiding from the light and preferring the dank darkness of the caves, they lived their lives in sight of the ancient castle built on top of the old mound. When they had first come to these mountains, people had called the mound *Wonanara*, "Mountain view". Now everyone called it *Wonarali*, "Death view."

From time to time screams accompanied by high-pitched laughter would burst from the depths of the castle. There seemed to be a lot of that lately. Kolbak, seventh son of kolrak, leaned on his pickaxe, staring out across the frozen plain. His clan had come three generations past to live in this barren waste. There had been the promise of gold and wealth under the rule of the lord of the old castle. Shortly after their ancestors had arrived, the whole warren, as their cave dwelling was called, had been overrun by troops from the castle. Now they were little better than slaves, held in check by the Sanguma. These priests were everywhere, instilling fear in the hearts of great and small. There was no hope of escape, except through death - a slow ugly death at the hands of the cruel priests who also demanded a life in sacrifice every year from their clan.

Kolbak wondered what it must be like in the warrens to the south. He heard occasional stories of warmth, food in great measure, and freedom to roam the hills at night, hunting for the small animals that dwelled in those forests. That was hard to believe. There was no such land near here. No animals other than an occasional hungry wolf ventured into this country. It was barren, cold, and smelly. Sometimes the sun poked its head from behind the mists and clouds, but it was horrid. It hurt Kolbak's eyes. He would flee indoors whenever it appeared.

Turning from the entrance, Kolbak hefted his pickaxe over his right shoulder, and walked back into the warren. His family, along with two others would be bringing the black rock needed by the Dark Lord to keep the old castle running. Twelve bags would need to be dug from the old quarry before the sun went down. Then it would have to be carried the two miles across the plain to the kitchens of the castle. If they were late, they would be whipped or beaten with canes. It didn't pay to disobey the overlords.

Materializing above the castle, three mounted Sanguma circled on their riding beasts, great ugly birds, with long wicked beaks. Their wings looked like flimsy leather, stretched thinly over gaunt bony frames. One got used to the smell after being around them, but their breath reeked of carrion. They resembled the great pre-historic birds, the pterodactyl, said to have once inhabited the northlands thousands of years earlier. Each was capable of carrying three riders, and could fly for a whole day if the thermal currents were right.

Gliding to an abrupt stop near the decaying buildings where the birds were stabled, the Sanguma dismounted and hurried across to a dirty side entrance attached to the castle. Two trolls, trained to handle the great birds, took the reins and dragged the unruly beasts toward shelter and food. It was rumored that the trolls and the birds fought for the food - more often than not, dismembered limbs of those unfortunate enough to have been captured and held prisoner within the palace dungeons.

The Sanguma entered the heavy doors, guarded by two powerful goblins from the Northron Mountains. They were not small, like their southern cousins, but beefy, thick through the legs and stout through the neck. Their group also guarded the filthy dungeons, and supervised the cooking in the great kitchens.

The castle doors were of burnished brass, now grown black through years of neglect. Two ancient animals were carved on the panels: one a unicorn with wings, the other an omnivox with two heads. They were pitted against one another in mortal combat, separated only by a woman in chain mail. She held a scepter high above her head with both hands. The symbolization was lost in antiquity.

Passing through the doors, the Sanguma entered the great hallway, intent on finding the Dark Lord. Rumor had it that the people who built the palace were a race that creatively worked with ice crystals, and shaped granite into mosaics which they inlaid along the floors. Their craftsmanship was the best throughout the land, and in years gone by, delegates from the four lands had visited, partly on business, but more so to view the beautiful creations these people had made famous. The race of crystal makers was made up of five different groupings all clustered in the quiet valleys surrounding the Mound. They prospered until the War of the Plains, at which time their territory was invaded and many of them were killed or simply vanished. Those remaining migrated to the West and were assimilated into the cities along the coast. Lesser races moved into the area to claim what they could of this once beautiful land.

Hurrying along, they barely took note of the gray stone walls, ornately carved into squares filled with flowers. These represented the flowers that once covered the surrounding hills and mountains in days of long ago. Some of these panels had become chipped and discolored with age. The Sanguma ignored them, having only one thought on their minds: 'report to their Lord and master'. Turning right down another hallway, they stopped before a large door made of heavy oak, reinforced with heavy timbers studded with large nails. Looking at one another for reassurance, the leader stepped past the guards and knocked, hard. The tattered tapestry that hung in broken sheets near small alcoves that once must have held ornate carvings muffled the sound. Now they were bare.

The door swung open from the inside, and powerful Malrok scowled at the priests.

"What is so important that you bother the Dark Lord?" he bellowed. Groveling before the mighty being, the Sanguma faltered, then gained courage to speak

"We are recently come from the mountains where we sought the stone his Lordship requested."

Grabbing the unfortunate Sanguma by his collar, Malrok lifted him bodily from the floor, staring him in the face. "And what do you have to report, scum?" he growled, enjoying his position and the discomfiture of the underling.

"Ah, great sir, the hawks brought down the lone roc which had been sent to deliver the stone to the South. Alas, the stone landed in a body of water and was recovered by a race of men in the mountains. By the time we traced its whereabouts, the stone was taken west, into the Caves of Testing. We were unable to follow, but we have word from the Goblins west of these caves that the stone has been taken to the elves. We do not know whether it is still there or has been taken elsewhere."

Frowning, the Dark Lord rose from his chair behind the great desk. Putting out a restraining hand, he said, "Malrok, let them go. We have the information we need. You can play another time."

At this word from his Lord, Malrok released the Sanguma with a hiss, watching him crumble to the ground. Smiling cruelly he growled, "You have failed to gain the stone. If we had no further use for you, I would hang you from the turret as a warning to others. Go now, and await further orders."

Shoving the Sanguma roughly through the door, Malrok turned to the Dark Lord. The Sanguma, glad to have gotten off with their lives in spite of their failure, hurried down the hallway, toward the kitchens where they intended to bully the cooks into feeding them.

The Dark Lord looked thoughtfully out the window. When he spoke it was with quiet penetration. "There is a large library in the elven capital. It holds the key to information about the stones separated so long ago. They are obviously trying to keep the stones apart a while longer until they understand enough about their power to begin bringing them together again. We must prevent that. Some of those mountain people have been attempting to use the stone. It almost feels as though there is more than one stone, but maybe I'm getting too sensitive now. The urge in me to possess those stones grows greater with each passing day.

"**I must have the stones soon**!" he shouted suddenly, slamming his huge fist on the desk! Staring angrily at the map he gripped his head, and started rubbing at his temples. "The pressure is mounting. It may drive me to move prematurely. I want everything ready before I move."

Turning as he finished speaking, he stared malevolently out of black unreadable eyes. His face was shrouded in a dark cape and only his eyes and nose could be seen. He was tall and powerfully built, his shoulders filling out the folds of the cape. His very presence inspired fear in those around him, and his deep voice penetrated through a body like a huge drum being beaten. He confided in no one but those who had been with him in past attempts to rule former empires.

He used the Sanguma to spread his gospel of fear and conquest. His minions included the goblins, the trolls, certain groups of men from whom he had gathered mercenaries, and the hidden peoples-the cave dwellers. The northern groups paid allegiance from long years of tradition and veiled promises. The southern groups were neutral but could be won over by displays of power and threats when necessary.

The Sanguma were his chief means of keeping the people in thrall. They spread throughout the northern regions, living as priests, teaching the people the religion of the Dark Lord. He would one day be supreme ruler over all the earth. The Sanguma demanded yearly human sacrifices, ensuring that his power would continue, under the guise that it kept the solar system and weather patterns stable. To promote obedience, the Sanguma would arrest people from time to time on charges of disloyalty. They would be brought to the castle for interrogation. These people were never seen again, but the cries of those tortured could be heard in the darkness. They were often hung from the walls and lashed mercilessly, lead pieces and bone woven into the gruesome whips. After severely beating them, their torturers took salt and rubbed it roughly into their torn bodies. This would go on several days until their victims died. Then their bodies were thrown outside the stables to be devoured by the huge birds.

With a measured stare at Malrok, the Dark Lord said quietly, "I will have those stones again at all costs. We must move carefully. We have powerful enemies in the West. If they understood what I intend, they would do all in their power to stop me. If they manage to gain the stones, they may yet keep us from our quest. They could hide them in the corridors of time where I might never locate them. Send more Sanguma out into the lands, to contact our spies. We must know where the black stone is and if there are others. We must also be informed of any plans to move the other stones. Notify me if any groups are sent as emissaries to other nations. Keep a tight rein on all our allies and inform me of developments constantly."

Malrok, fiercely loyal and as cruel as his master, bowed and left the room, anxious to help the Dark Lord find the stones. He sensed that things were building to a climax and that soon his master would move his armies into position to challenge the powers in the West. If they could be conquered, there would be no other nations to stop him. The elves and dwarves had long kept to themselves. The races of men were constantly fighting among themselves and would pose little threat. No alliance could be made fast enough to challenge his thrust for world domination.

Striding down the hallway, Malrok turned and entered an anteroom where a delegation of goblins had been waiting. They had been seeking an audience with the Dark Lord. These were the ones from near the Caves of Testing. They could be useful in what he had to do. Putting on his best behavior, he greeted them

"Welcome to the castle of the Dark Lord. We have been awaiting your arrival. We are honored by your visit and wish you a pleasant stay."

The ambassador from the goblin nation bowed low. "We have come in response to the Sanguma who were sent to make known our wishes to the Dark Lord. He is aware, we are sure that we are ready now to move against the elves to the South. We have been running patrols in that area for some time. Some of our people have encountered humans traveling through our forests, and feel this may be of interest to our Lord."

"I, Malrok, speak on behalf of our great leader. He has promised to help you eliminate the elves, those bothersome folks who keep you from your rightful lands. In return, he wants you to form an army that will also be able to help him in his conquest of the races of men in the West. You must come with me at once to see his Lordship. He will be very interested in what you have to tell him."

Leaving the main body of the delegation in the anteroom, he escorted the goblin lords to the room of the Dark Lord. Nothing would be hidden from him. He could probe their minds almost without their knowledge, and would be able to see through their eyes what had transpired. The anticipation of the encounter excited him, for the Dark Lord would pull out information that could only strengthen their position in the coming struggle.

Until recently, the goblin clans warred with each other for supremacy. They came from three clans, located in adjoining mountains. From time out of mind they had fought one another for the resources these mountains offered. Diamonds and rubies were the chief sources of the bitter rivalry. The goblins loved gaudy baubles. With the discovery of two new veins of the precious stones, peace had become all but impossible. The alliance with the Dark Lord had changed that now. Knowing that the elven nation had mines as well set their greedy hearts to cooperating. Malrok knew that once the war was over, the goblins would fall upon one another in an attempt to possess or at least control the elven lands with their precious mines. That was of no concern to him. They would be discarded once the battles were over and the land was plunged into the beautiful darkness that his Lord offered.

These goblins had also brought in some very interesting prisoners lately. They had been made to talk, revealing recent events taking place in the West and to the South. Allowing the Sanguma to have the power to teleport from once place to another wasn't such a bad move by the Dark Lord after all. Giving up a small bit of power to gain so much more was a wise plan. Malrok envied his Lord's wisdom and cunning. He would some day be like him, but for now he must concentrate his abilities on helping his Master achieve his goals.

Approaching the door, he spoke to his master of the goblin leaders, and the door swung open of its own accord. The Goblins were led in, and the door shut firmly behind them.

Kolbak and his family, along with the other cave dwellers arrived at the kitchens with their bundles. Knocking loudly on the closed door, Kolbak's father, Kolrak, stepped back, waiting. It seemed an eternity before the door was opened. Seeing the bundles there, the goblin overseer motioned them to bring the sacks inside. As they filed through the door, the odor of food cooking on the great stoves struck their noses. They were hungry after the trek across the plains, and hoped maybe they would be allowed food before they returned. Kolbak noticed the dark hallway off to the right. He often wondered what lay in that direction. Was it the way to the main building, or did it lead to some special rooms for the guards, he wondered. Possibly it led to the dungeons.

"Stop gawking and put yo sack ova de wit de rest o' dem. Dat is, unless yu wana spend yo time down dat dak hol like de rest o' dem prisonas."

A swat across the head brought his wandering mind back into reality. Kolbak hurried to comply, now knowing that the dungeons lay along that route. He had no intention of joining them at all. He hurried toward the door and ducked the heavy arm that was aimed at him as he departed. Kolrak had asked for food, and several moldy loaves, along with some foul tasting broth were given to them. They ate outside in silence, returning the bowls and utensils when they had finished. Then they set off in the cold night air, anxious to get home to the relative warmth and safety of their warren.

Chapter 11
Shades Attack the Camp

Toward midnight, the wraiths came. Quietly, insidiously they flowed over the uneven ground, sirens in the night. Their mournful cries began as low, deep guttural moans. Rising in intensity, they approached the camp, hesitant, searching. Those on guard were struck first. Bombarded with illusions of war, death, fear, hatred, revenge, they screamed in terror. Dropping their weapons, they put their hands to their ears, attempting to block out the sounds of death. Closing their eyes, they groped to shield their minds from madness.

The whole camp was awakened. Unreasoning fear gripped them, filling each with panic. No one escaped their touch. Bili grasped the talisman. Looking down, he saw a hideous face grinning up at him, not a pure blue stone. He screamed and covered his face.

Meri pulled the black stone from its pouch, desperate to escape the visions confronting her. She looked into the stone and screamed as writhing serpents coiled about her wrists, striking again and again.

The camp was in confusion. Elves, dwarves, humans… the spirits of the unburied dead attacked them all. Wulpai began building a fire the moment he heard the screams. Once before he had been forced to move through this area. He knew the dangers. That's why he'd quickly started the small fire. He bore the agony of the assaults by these nightshades, forcing himself to think beyond the horrible faces that shoved themselves in his face, the stench of their undying breath causing him to gag involuntarily. He focused all his will into building the fire. No matter that ogres and trolls were laying about the camp with their clubs; that a dragon had raised its ugly head, spewing fire that washed over the body of gentle Rimwai. She should have been incinerated. She was not. He continued to coax the small flame into something useful.

Someone rolled right into his fire! Brell the dwarf kicked out viciously, almost knocking Wulpai over in the process. Gaining his feet, he yanked out his battleaxe, laying about him dangerously with one hand, all the while shoving and punching at the enemy with the other. Wulpai watched out of the corner of his eye for others heading his way as he quickly gathered the pieces, desperately trying to keep the fire going. Blowing hard and holding his hands steady he managed to keep it alive, barely. As the little flame grew, he started adding small limbs. It seemed an eternity before his fire grew to manhood. When it did, he acted quickly. Turning to the scene of madness, and grabbing several firebrands, he shouted, "Take one of these limbs. Hold it high and light our campsite. These shades can't live in light. They become powerless. Hurry, before they capture your imagination and you become as one of them."

Rumors of people driven mad and now living in the underground city abounded. Few who entered this cursed region ever escaped. Wulpai was not about to let that happen to his friends!

The elves were first to respond, long used to dealing with illusion. Old Wulmakai took a brand and ran among the confusion, yelling encouragement to the dwarves. The other elves grabbed more burning limbs, and held them aloft. Meri ran, breathless to snatch a brand, still trying to shut out vivid images of snakes. Wulpai placed a burning stick in her hand as she groped. Raising the flame she found control beginning to return. She chanced a quick glance at the stone. To her relief the serpents were gone. She looked up to see Bili holding two sticks above his head, waving them wildly as he recklessly pursued the shades into the shadows. Yilmai, brand almost out from the wind blowing on it, intercepted him before he went beyond the boundaries of their camp. Grabbing him by the arm, Yilmai yanked him around.

"Bili, it's me, Yilmai. Stop! Don't go beyond the bank here! You aren't strong enough to take them on. Come back! Come Back!"

The hot fire of anger began to cool in Bili's eyes as he turned to his friend. "Yilmai! It's you! I thought I'd been set upon by one of them! Phew! They are ugly stinking vile creatures! They even turned my stone against me!"

"Its all over now. You're safe Bili. Come back to the camp!"

The dwarves were last to respond. The shades had found them easy prey. Though the dwarves were not afraid of darkness, they had no exposure to magic or any other type of wizardry. They were overwhelmed... and drawn away. As the shades were repelled, the dwarves slumped to the ground motionless. Wulpai left them while he made sure that the camp was once again secure. He could feel the resentful presence of the shades seething beyond the lights. What unnerved him most were those other un-namable creatures beyond the wraiths, which were watching, patiently waiting their chance to invade. The elves, less affected than the rest, recovered quickly and broke off all the dry branches they found, piling them in heaps around the camp.

Meri, fully recovered, decided to try a mind meld to help the hapless dwarves. She gripped the stone in her hand, and sat among them. She tuned her mind to its pulsing, then quieted herself. As she felt the stone taking over, she reached out. She wasn't prepared for what she found. Shrouded by layers of darkness, the souls of the dwarves were tightly encased. She stretched out with the aura of her will and began unwrapping these layers, starting with Daniray, their gruff leader. As she touched each of the dwarves in turn they struggled violently at the intrusion, making it all the harder to free them. She fought on, layer upon layer, until each soul recognized her touch and was able to help. She moved from soul to soul, until she had helped them all. Then she quietly withdrew.

She found Wulpai kneeling beside her. "Have you been able to touch them all?" He asked.

"Yes, but it was so horrible to see them all bound up by those evil things! I'll have nightmares for weeks!" Meri shuddered. She huddled against him, more for protection than warmth.

"Meri, this was my first real contact with the Shades. I had no idea how strong they really are. This quest is going to be a growing experience for me as well as everyone else."

Slowly at first, then with gathering speed, the dwarves began to break free. One by one, they uncurled from their fetal positions on the ground. Then blinking away the pungent smoke, they began to sit up, holding their heads. Daniray, the stocky leader, stood and stared at length into the darkness. Turning away, he muttered an angry curse in his dwarven tongue. Walking over to the others, he helped them to their feet. They were a badly shaken lot. They kept to themselves the rest of the night, grouped in a circle, keeping a wary eye on the fires and the darkness beyond. One of the larger dwarves, Wabran, left the circle and approached the edge of the camp. Holding his battleaxe high above his head, he shook it angrily toward the darkness. His armor shook with the fierceness of the tremor from his bulky arm. Abruptly he stopped, stared momentarily into the black void, then turned his back and returned to the group.

After a night of little rest, the companions broke camp early, and moved silently into the morning mists, glad to be rid of such a place. They planned to put as many miles between this place and themselves as possible. They kept close to the river, which wound lazily through the plains. They crossed the river several times attempting to shorten their road, but by mid-day, they had only covered a quarter of the distance to the foothills. Dismayed, they realized this meant spending another night on the plains, exposed to those merciless Shades. No one spoke of it. They had little choice.

Two of the Elves ranged ahead, hoping to find a place suitable for camp. They happened on a young buck drinking at one of the fords. They surprised and shot it, skinned and dressed it out by the time the others arrived. The dwarves were encouraged. At least they would eat well if nothing else. They were used to going long stretches with little sleep, but depended on hearty meals to give them strength. They took over the preparation of the venison, and added special herbs and spices they carried with them always. The party ate well that night.

Watches were posted, and in spite of the obvious dangers, they kept the fires burning brightly. Wulpai and Bili took first watch, followed by the dwarves. The elves slept quietly until after midnight then relieved the others. Meri and Rimwai slept close together ringed by the elves, each assured by the presence of these resourceful warriors. Toward morning there was movement in the darkness beyond the camp. Pairs of yellow eyes could be seen staring into the light. Yilmai nocked an arrow to his bow in readiness, but nothing advanced. As silently as they appeared, the eyes were gone. At first light, Yilmai and another of the elves searched the ground for tracks or footprints. They found none. A chill of fear ran through them.

Spirits rose as the group moved further from the ruined city of the plains. As they traveled closer to the foothills, more shrubs and grass dotted the countryside away from the river. The air became less oppressive, actually smelling clean. A few clouds blew in from the west, bringing a sprinkle of rain with it, giving them relief from the heat. Stopping for just a few minutes every hour or so, they made good time. They stopped briefly for lunch, eating a cold meal.

Bili and Yilmai sat down next to Wulpai, asking him about the mountains ahead. "We'll be spending the night at the fork of the river," he began. "We won't be able to actually get into the foothills until tomorrow, but we'll be beyond the range of those Shades. Hopefully anyone who saw our fire will think that we were headed south toward the ruins. They'll shake their heads in disbelief, and go about their business. If the goblin patrols are this far west, they may investigate. We'll have to keep our eyes open."

"How far is it over the mountains? How long do you think it will take us?" asked Bili.

"If we make good time, we'll reach the lake in two days. Another day will take us to the top, maybe down the other side a ways. Then three days hard travel will bring us to the eastern most outpost of the Western Lands."

"Then we'll be on the road for another week! Are the trails hard or easy?" Bili asked again. He was anxious to get to the Western Lands and be shed of his burden.

"The early parts are hard. There are a lot of ravines, gullies and switchbacks. If there have been a lot of landslides since I was last here, it may take us an extra day to gain the lake. From there the trails are straight to the pass, but we'll have to be careful. The trails and pathways are narrow and we could easily run into an ambush."

"Have you been among the western elves?" Yilmai pressed.

"Actually, yes. I was sent there three years ago on an urgent mission. Why do you ask?"

"I've heard stories about our kin there. Do they actually live in grand cities like I've been told, with the special gardens?"

Wulpai chuckled softly. "You haven't heard the half of it, Yilmai. It's beyond description. You'll do better to wait and see it for yourself on our return trip- provided that we survive this one," he added rather somberly.

Conversation ended as they started hiking again. All eyes were on the hills ahead, searching for signs of others in the area. It wouldn't be long before they reached the fork. The trees began to thicken as the ground rose before them. Small game animals scampered to the safety of cover as the strangers passed. The elven scouts sent ahead waited for their companions.

"The fork is just ahead," they reported. "You can hear the roar of the confluence of the rivers up around the next bend. We've spotted no one so far."

"There is a good camping area about another two hours walk ahead," remarked Wulpai. "If it's all right with the rest of you, we'll hike until we reach that point."

Everyone seemed agreed, even old Wulmakai, who had done remarkably well keeping the pace set by the younger people. Wulpai carried his books for him, leaving him with a light load, mostly food. Two hours later, they arrived at the site of which Wulpai spoke. They cleared away the debris, fallen limbs, and rocks that had slid down from the hill above them. Yilmai and Bili went to try their luck in the west fork of the Waikar River. By dark, they had landed eight small bluegill and two good-sized trout. They cleaned them, and brought them into camp, laying them on hot stones to cook. The aroma of fresh fish filled the clearing.

After dinner, Wulpai gathered everyone together, explaining the road ahead. Amid mild protests from the dwarves, he assigned pairs of dwarves and elves to do scouting, figuring both styles of tracking would be best for the mountain country. There would also be a set assigned to cover their back trail. They wanted no more night surprises. He set the watches and everyone rolled up in their blankets. The fire was allowed to burn to coals, ready for use as needed.

Toward morning, a ground fog rolled in from the river. By first light, it cloaked everything in a veil of white. Wulpai had everyone on the trail before the sun began burning the mists from the forests. Visibility was poor, so they took no chances, moving slowly, cautiously. The scouts ranged only a short distance ahead, carefully checking potential danger spots. Those in the rear covered tracks, and made false trails when possible. By mid-morning, the fog had lifted, making the way ahead visible for some distance. Hiking on, they watched as the river gradually fell away further to the right. Now they were gaining altitude, and as they did, forward progress slowed somewhat. Some parts of the trail were very steep, while others tended to level out a bit so the hikers were able to get their wind again. What pathway they found had became overgrown and rough, but fortunately there were no traces of other travelers.

At midday, everyone stopped for something to eat- dried meat and elven bread with some cheese. They drank from the water they had put in the water-skins.

"Have you ever been out to this area before?" Meri asked Rimwai.

Shaking her head, she replied, "Once when I was small, my father and several of the elders brought us near here to meet with our elven cousins from the west. We stayed only a couple of days, then returned. That was long ago, when times were more secure. We were far north of the ruined city and had no trouble with the Shades. Those spirits still make me shiver. I hope we never run into anything so horrible again."

Looking around, Meri confided, "The stone was nearly my undoing. If Wulpai hadn't been there shouting encouragement, I wouldn't have survived. I'll never forget the serpents writhing all over the stone. It was disgusting. I wonder why I wasn't able to use the stone? It's helped me other times when I needed it."

Wulpai walked by and Meri stopped him. "The trail is getting rougher now. Is it worse up ahead?"

"I'm afraid it is," Wulpai apologized. "This trail has gone unused so long, there's almost nothing left. We may have a couple days of this before we meet the trail leading east and west. But the good news is our scouts say there are no signs of anyone's passing. So no one has been spying on our movements. We should also find a good-sized stream up ahead. We can camp near it later this evening." Smiling he moved off again.

"Well, I'm ready to hike again, if you are," said Meri. She got to her feet, shouldered her pack and stepped in behind others who were starting along the trail. Rimwai followed her, smiling, shaking her head at some hidden humor she found in Meri's remark.

Bili talked quietly with Wulmakai through the afternoon, prying old stories from him about the goblins, the trolls, and the ancient wars as recorded in the *Codrin*. Patiently, Wulmakai shared what he knew, explaining battle plans, exploring motives and carefully placing events in perspective. Yilmai listened too. Today neither he nor Bili were covering back trail. Wulpai had paired them together so that each would learn from the other. Tomorrow morning would bring their chance to scout ahead.

Afternoon wore into evening, and as the sound of the stream could be heard ahead, the party cast about for a place to camp. They hiked a while longer, until the sound of the stream became louder and they saw the area where it dropped away to the right to begin working its way toward the river they had left behind earlier in the day. Just below the trail Daniray found a rock ledge, which would provide them shelter if the weather changed during the night. He called to the others, and they followed. He built a modest fire to roast the two small game animals the scouts had shot. They found they had to make more soup on dried jerky to have enough. Wulmakai found some mushrooms down toward the stream, and added those to the soup.

Low clouds scudded across the night sky, bringing wind and colder weather. By morning drizzle had started which turned into a persistent rain as the group broke camp. The going was hard. With no sure trail to follow, Yilmai and Bili had to use all their wood lore to find safe passage. Thoughts of security gave way to the immediate concern of not getting lost. More than once Wulpai helped them make decisions about the path. Crossing the top of one of the hills, they were able to see far enough ahead to note that their path led through a series of gorges. They would have to follow some razorback trails to get through.

Progress was slow. The mud didn't help either. It was hard not to slip on the steeper descents. They grabbed at every bush or tree to slow their sliding. Thankfully they knew the rain would wash away most of the sign of their passing. They wrapped their capes closer about themselves and moved on.

The rain cleared about four in the afternoon. The sun peeked out from the clouds a few times, then went down in a blaze of glorious color. It didn't touch the shadows of the gorge.

Finding no ledges in this area, the group dropped down almost to the stream and made camp, cold, and tired. They found a few dry pieces of wood, most still attached to trees. These they broke and used to warm themselves. The elves tried a little fishing, but caught nothing. Wulpai promised them that tomorrow would bring them to the main crossing; things should improve.

The black stone pulsed lightly, awakening Meri during the night. She turned restlessly, dreams filling her sleep. Something was wrong, but she couldn't find it. Bili too, unsettled by his blue stone, vaguely sensed something amiss, but rolled over and slept on. Meri felt indecisive. Should she wake Wulpai and tell him something wasn't quite right? Or was she just imagining it? She decided on the side of safety and went to awaken Wulpai. He was already up, his keen ears listening for any sound.

"My stone was pulsing and awakened me. What do you think is happening?"

"We are near others, but I can't tell what's happened. We'll have to wait until first light to investigate."

"Do you think we're in any immediate danger then?"

"No, no one knows we've come from the south, and we're down below the trail anyway. It would be very difficult to find us."

Reassured, Meri returned to her blankets and her thoughts. She feared what tomorrow might bring. Rimwai stirred, and saw Meri crawl back into her blankets. "Is anything wrong?" she asked.

Not wanting to upset her unduly, Meri whispered, "The stone was pulsing for a while, but now it's stopped. We're safe for the moment from whatever's out there."

The morning dawned clear, with fog moving only along the gorges down along the stream. They climbed to the trail again, and with the scouts ranging ahead, continued their march. At midday, they reached the main trail. Wulpai directed them to the left, and they moved on. Here the terrain changed.

"We're well into the foothills of Witwaunak." Wulpai informed them. "For the next few miles, cover is going to be scarce. Everything around here is made of rock, so watch your step. We don't want to start any landslides, or make so much noise that we alert others to our presence."

The scouts came back. "We've found tracks ahead, leading down a small trail to the north. Something must have happened on up ahead. Should we take others with us, or move as a group?"

"If tracks are leading away from the site, it should be safe for you to go on ahead." said Wulpai boldly. "Take two others with you. We'll keep our eyes on our back trail. We'll meet you at Rimon Rock. That's about two hours walk from here."

They moved on ahead, loosening knives in their sheaths, and nocking arrows on their long bows. After they were gone, Wulpai turned to Wulmakai.

"I want you and the girls to stay in the middle. I can't risk anything happening to you."

"Bili, you and Yilmai follow immediately behind them. If anything happens, get off the trail, and move up toward the top, not down. That's important."

Yilmai checked his bow, and loosened his arrows in the quiver. Bili released the strap off his sword and took the bow from it cover. He strung it and placed an arrow loosely on the string. He knew he had fast reactions, but didn't trust himself to do the right thing. Both girls carried bows, but didn't string them, feeling that they would have enough time to do so with the men covering them.

They met no one on their way to the rock. There were plenty of tracks, but whoever had been here were gone. As they crested a small rise, they saw the four scouts ahead milling around. Walking closer, they came upon an ugly scene. *A battle has been fought here all right,* thought Wulpai, uneasily. *Sometime yesterday from the looks of things.* A couple of headless trolls, several men, pack animals, goblins, armor, some discarded food and other supplies lay scattered across the hill.

Breagle, younger brother to Wabran, approached Wulpai.

"This looks like a common battle between the races, but I found this." He handed a ceremonial knife to Wulpai. Looking at it, Wulpai frowned.

"Looks as though we have a few Sanguma priests along on this raid. Wonder who they were looking for? It doesn't look good."

The others joined them, looking around. There seemed nothing of value, so they left everything lying there. Yilmai nudged Bili and went off to one side.

"Let's see if there are any tracks ahead. Maybe some of them managed to get away." Bili nodded agreement, and they walked quickly over the hill, looking carefully as they followed the trail.

After 15 minutes of quick walking, they did notice some tracks and a bit of blood. Yilmai pointed it out.

"What do you think? Should we go on?" Bili questioned. "The others may get worried if we're gone too long."

"Let's go on just a short way and see if we can find anything. Then we can run back if we need too."

The two of them hurried down the trail stopping every so often to check sign. There was plenty. They went another ten minutes when the tracks suddenly veered off the trail toward a sheltered ledge above. Quietly they started working their way up.

"That's far enough unless you want to get shot!" a voice challenged them. "Who are you and what do you want?" It was the voice of a girl.

Chapter 12
The Raiding Party

Surprised at hearing the voice of a young woman, Bili responded, "We are traveling west. We saw the results of the fight. There's no one back there. Is there anything we can do to help? We have food and medicine."

The young girl's head peered over the rock. She eyed them carefully, then said, "My companion has been hurt. Maybe you can help him. Come up, but no tricks. I'll shoot."

Bili took his arrow off his bow and set it down as he approached the girl. She was clad in warrior's garb, with a finely tooled helmet covering her head. This didn't hide the golden hair that streamed out the back though. Her skin was light, and her small hands held the bow steady. Bili's blood began to race. He'd never seen anyone so fair or pretty as she. Realizing that he was staring at her, he looked away, embarrassed. She suppressed a smile.

Yilmai followed Bili, and the young girl gasped when she realized she was face to face with an elf. He smiled briefly attempting to put her at ease. He pushed past her and moved with quick light steps over to the man who lay on the ground. It was plain to see that he had lost blood; the ground beneath him was soaked with it. An ugly wound festered near his groin. A bandage had been roughly tied across it, but still it seeped. Bili offered him water, which he greedily swallowed.

Bili and Yilmai discussed the situation keeping their voices low. "If we leave him here, he may die. We need to take him to our group. They may be able to help him."

So Yilmai went down the hill below the trail, and returned with a couple of young saplings. With these and some rope and shirts, he made a rough stretcher for the wounded warrior. Then he and Bili gently placed him on the palate, and lifted him carefully, making their way down to the trail. The young girl collected what things they had and followed. She began to warm to them along the way and finally introduced herself as Wesip, daughter of the Commander of the Eastern Fortress. They had gone but a short distance when pounding footsteps sounded ahead along the pathway. Before Bili or Yilmai were able to put down the wounded man, Wabran and Breagle came running along the trail. They stopped abruptly when they saw Yilmai and Bili.

"Here, let us give you some help," Wabran said, moving around the back to take the stretcher from Yilmai. Breagle relieved Bili and they continued on.

Trailing behind the wounded man, Wesip smiled in spite of the circumstances. Since yesterday she had received shock after shock. First, goblins and trolls had attacked her group, but these she had seen before. The Sanguma priests who accompanied them were new to her and she feared them greatly. Now she had come face to face with an elf and a darkly handsome warrior from the Eastern Mountains. To top if all off, here were two dwarves, the stuff of legends, walking before her, offering their help. This truly was an unusual trip. Wesip shook her head in wonder in spite of all that had happened. She wondered what else she would encounter.

She knew she shouldn't be here, but she had forced her way into the delegation, wanting to prove her courage and her ability to her father. *Maybe this who journey has been a mistake*, she thought ruefully. *It has proven to be much more dangerous than I could have imagined.*

It didn't take long to get back to the camp. When they arrived, a worried Wulpai chided them both for running off ahead of the others. But he softened when he saw the young woman and the stretcher, and realized the situation.

Introducing himself as leader of the group, he made Wesip welcome. Then he left her to tend to the wounded warrior, calling Meri over to help. Meri came over and introduced herself and Rimwai. Wesip was again shocked to meet two women among these men, especially an elven maiden. Rimwai quickly unhooked her pack and pulled out a small container and gave Wesip something to drink and some elven way bread.

Meanwhile, Mary unpacked her bag of herbs and medicines. Taking out certain potions, and making use of the stone, she applied her skills to the wound. In a short time the stone was humming its familiar healing frequencies. The warrior winced at the invasion of his body by the pulsing stone, and began to squirm. Please try to lie still, Meri cautioned him. "You'll heal much faster if you don't fight the power of the stone. She continued to sooth the man and he finally relaxed, realizing it was helping to slow the bleeding. Wulpai was kneeling down nearby talking in low tones to Meri, encouraging her in how she was proceeding. Meri listened attentively, but deep frowns furrowed her brow.

The young woman Wesip listened to the two of them talking and realized from her accent that she must be from the eastern forests. As she tuned in to Wulpai's accent and use of words, she realized he was from the north, but had a broad accent, which she recognized as one spoken by someone who traveled a lot. Wesip continued to watch as Meri worked, fascinated at how quickly the wound was healing. She also noticed from the dark features that this woman must be from the same people group as the olive skinned young man. She wondered if they were related, but held her questions for another time.

"Where did you learn such knowledge? Are you a healer?" she inquired, a touch of awe in her tone. "These wounds are closing so quickly! I've never seen anything like this!"

"I was taught herbal medicines by our local shaman in the eastern mountains." Meri smiled. "But it wasn't until recently I acquired these other dwarf medicines. They seem to work well with this special stone. It doesn't work on everyone, but your friend here seems to be responding splendidly. By morning, he may be able to travel, if he goes slowly."

After Meri had completed her medical work, Wulpai suggested they make camp away from the scene of carnage. They moved forward toward the shelter west of their present location, and finding flat ground, gathered sticks for a fire.

After dinner, the warrior related the story of the massacre. Lying on the stretcher near the fire, he identified himself as Hagred, first sergeant of the wall defense, assigned to the Eastern Outpost of the Western Lands.

"I had been collecting water below the trail," he related, "when I heard shouts and the din of battle. So I dropped my water buckets and ran back to the camp. I had no weapon and by the time I arrived, most of the fighting was over. Two trolls lay dead, several goblins, our pack animals, and several of our company. The remaining trolls and goblins took the girl here, and the three men who survived. They left the extra weapons and hurried off. I looked around and picked up a couple of weapons. I intended to trail them.

"During last night's storm, I was able to slip among them and free Wesip here, and one of our men. We were both wounded in the escape, but got away. In the following darkness and rain, we got separated and weren't able to locate each other. For fear of being caught again, I grabbed Wesip and started back west. We didn't stop, even though I was bleeding badly. We both knew it would be only a matter of time before the Trolls tracked us down. They can smell blood a long way off, you know."

After hearing their story, Wulpai decided to try and find the wounded man. A quarter moon was starting to lower in the western sky, so there was some light. He took Wabran, Breagle, Bili, and Yilmai with him. The dwarves could well see in the dark and Wabran was a formidable warrior. Bili had the talisman stone, which would help locate the goblins and trolls, if not the wounded man. He left Daniray in charge and set watches of the remaining dwarves and elves, then headed quickly down the trail.

In an hour of forced walking and trotting, they reached the fork. They turned north and continued at the same brisk pace for another hour. The dwarves checked the path carefully for sign. They found nothing so they pressed on.

When the moon went down over the mountain crags, it became difficult to see. They decided to wait the few hours to daylight. They got off the trail and posted hourly watches. They slept fitfully.

At first light, they were up tracking again, checking streams and small sheltered places. The talisman began to glow slightly. Bili warned the others. They got off the trail and watched. In a short time a man with a badly torn shoulder and side limped into sight. He was trying to hurry, but in great pain. Stumbling over a tree root, he fell heavily, unable to get up again. Wabran rushed out, grasped the now unconscious man and carried him back into the brush. Wulpai checked him, finding he was still alive. They moved back out onto the trail and started back to Rimon Rock. Breagle and Yilmai covered their tracks while Bili gave the powerful dwarf a hand in carrying the wounded man.

In a short time, they reached the main trail. Breagle and Yilmai came running from behind.

"We've heard the sounds of trolls." Breagle stated breathlessly. "They're a ways behind us, but we've got to warn the others to be ready to move out quickly. Someone should run on ahead to warn them to move on."

Wulpai made some quick decisions. "Yilmai, you're the fastest runner. Dash ahead and have the women and Hagred work their way toward the Witsunuk Mountains. Have Daniray send two dwarves and two elves with them. Have the rest set an ambush at Rimon Rock to help us if we can't lose those trolls. We may be only minutes ahead of the raiding party.

"All right. Let's get moving! Breagle, you and Wabran take the stretcher the first mile. Bili and I will relieve you. We'll switch then and move as quickly as possible."

Yilmai paced himself, and began a running pattern he figured would carry him all the way to the Rock. He was soon out of sight down the trail. Wabran set a killing pace for everyone, but to him this was normal. Breagle struggled to keep up, barely holding his footing on the wet trail.

After the first mile, Wulpai and Bili took the stretcher. They weren't able to keep the pace of the dwarves, but hurried along nonetheless. As they crested a rise where the trail forked, Wabran looked back. He saw the trolls trotting in their peculiar lumbering gait. The two had begun running ahead of the raiding party, hoping to catch the wounded man. They were sure of their quarry.

Wabran hurried to warn Wulpai they were coming. Rather than move on, Wulpai decided on deception. He knew the trolls would overtake them before they could reach the Rock.

"Wabran, you and Breagle take our wounded friend down this path a short way, then you take his shirt and run with it holding it high above your head for half a mile or so. Then leave it, double back and go with Bili and Breagle along the new path. When you come to the end, come back up on the main trail and go as fast as you can. I'll join you when I get free. Now move!"

While they took the right trail, Wulpai climbed a large stone near the fork. He pulled off his shirt, and pulled a long hood from his small backpack. Smearing a bit of grease on his face, he reached down and collected some dust from under the rock. He spread this liberally on both hands, then on his face. He found an old bent stick, set it on the rock beside him and waited.

The jarring pounding of feet preceded the trolls. As they came around the bend, they stopped short. The look of anticipation and conquest fell from their faces. Slowly they approached the rock. Looking cautiously at Wulpai, they stopped and bowed low.

"Ol won," began the first troll. "We be honoed by yo presens. Ow may yo amble sevants be of hep?"

Wulpai feigned madness in the style of the ancient priests, the Sanguma. Smiling stupidly, bereft of wit and understanding, he leered at them. "Hungry you look, and fast you move. Looking for someone you are." Wulpai cackled to himself, and scratched under one armpit. "Want to know secrets they do. Won't help them though. Think me mad they do!" He leered again at them and let the spittle drool down his unshaven face.

The first troll looked at his companion, nodded, then said, "Ole won. I hav 'in my han a bag o preshous stons I duz. Yu tek 'em. Thez fo yu." He tossed the bag at the old man's feet.

"Thinks to buy my knowledge with riches, he does," spat Wulpai. "But I won't tell. He was full of blood, walking slowly. Didn't see me on the rock. But saw him I did. Won't tell. No, won't tell." Wulpai scratched the other armpit, grinning. The trolls waited.

"Along the main trail, don't go. Waste your time you will. No one goes there now. Many dead lie on the rock. Nasty trolls want the human they do. Not find him on the trail. Hiding he is. But won't tell! No won't tell nasty trolls!" He leered again at them and scratched.

Both trolls took off at a trot down the right fork, sure now they would find their prey. Wulpai waited until they were out of sight then ran west along the trail hoping shortly to rejoin his companions.

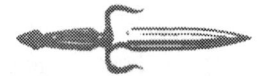

They were running. Wabran was carrying the man as though he was a child. He was running with reckless abandon. Breagle had the stretcher, and Bili had the backpacks. Wulpai saw them in the distance and kept a steady pace until he had caught up. They continued running. Bili looked back at the filthy garb of his friend, stopped and shook his head at what he saw. He then turned around and continued running. It took them several minutes to reach the Rock, breathless and worn out. The two elves and dwarves, took the wounded man, placed him once more on the stretcher and trotted down the trail. Catching their breath for a moment, Bili turned to Wulpai.

"What did you do back there? You look like the crazy man from our village back home," he grinned.

Taking a wooden comb, Wulpai ran it through his beard, taking out the mud and the tangles.

"It's an old trick. Trolls aren't noted for their ability to think. I imitated one of the mad Sanguma hermits from up north. The trolls believe they have been touched by the gods and would never harm them. They do try to pry information from them from time to time though. They should be thoroughly confused by now, but it won't take them long to scent out the trail again. Lets get moving."

Wabran and Breagle decided to stay behind to size up the raiding party's strength and numbers. From their vantage point they would see the raiders long before they themselves could be seen. Meanwhile, Bili and Wulpai trotted off to catch the others.

"Do you have a plan in mind?" Bili asked as they trotted.

"Only part of one. About five miles up the trail is an old bridge. It spans a deep gorge. If we cut the ropes and chop out the stakes, it will give us half a day's start on them. We can plan a much nastier ambush with that much time," Wulpai grinned. "We'll also have a greater advantage there than taking them on at Rimon Rock."

In just over an hour they reached the bridge, helping to get the wounded man across. Bili helped carry the litter for a while, moving carefully between the huge boulders dotting the landscape. Wulpai stayed behind with a broken axe he had salvaged from Rimon Rock. He waited for the dwarves. They weren't long in coming. Moving out of the trees, they approached the bridge, slowing to a walk. Crossing over, they met Wulpai, axe in hand.

"There are two trolls, 15 goblins, and two Sanguma priests." Wabran reported. "They have two male prisoners from the Western Lands by the look of their clothes. They're bound up pretty tightly, but look unharmed. The priests appear to have lost something and are trying to locate it. Guess they can't teleport their prisoners until they find it. They're pretty angry, and the trolls are afraid of them."

Breagle looked at the axe. "Want some help?" He grinned. "It will take them some time to cross after us when you get finished." He moved out of the way.

Wulpai lifted the axe and cut both sides. The useless ropes and planking fell away, banging the other side of the chasm. He proceeded to smash the stakes below ground level so thrown ropes would have nothing to grasp. When he was satisfied, the trio hurried off in pursuit of their companions.

They rejoined Bili and the others two miles down the trail. They hurried on until Bili caught sight of Yilmai waving from a rise ahead. He waved back and broke into a trot. By noon they were together once again. Wulpai and Wabran explained the situation to the rest of the group, then made plans for a surprise. The site they picked was wooded high ground. They would certainly have the advantage, if indeed, they managed to surprise their pursuers.

Meri broke out her medicine kit and began working on the unconscious warrior. Hagred assisted her, explaining the wounded man was Hargreth, his cousin- and he felt responsible for him. Meri worked on him for two hours; there was limited response.

Bili came over and asked if there was something he might do to help. They tried a mind meld between the two stones, which hummed happily together, but it didn't change much. Bili gave it up and went to help Yilmai roll boulders against the log barricade above the trail.

It took most of the afternoon, but by dark, the elves, dwarves and men had made some pretty deadly traps.

At dinner, Wulpai explained what he had in mind. "I want you dwarves to man the stones to be dropped on the trolls. You elves, Bili and Meri must wait for the goblins to go past, then start shooting from the rear. With the landslide of stone, the only way out will be through the box canyon off the left. Here we will try to finish off the raiding party."

Everyone seemed satisfied with the plan, so two elves were sent to watch the crossing and alert everyone when the raiders gained the western side. The rest of the group turned in to get what sleep they could. The moon cast few shadows before it went down because high clouds scudding across the otherwise empty sky obscured it. Knowing tomorrow would bring a fight caused Bili a restless night. He tossed and turned, at times moaning softly, anxious for it to be over. He thought of his folks in his home village, and wondered again if they had been harmed. He still felt twinges of guilt at their quick exodus. He hoped, not for the first time, that there might be a way of letting them know they were all right and nearing the end of their quest.

The sound of stones being piled on top of one another awakened Bili with a start. He rolled over, still groggy but sword in hand, ready to parry a blow he imagined was being aimed at him. Yilmai noticed him and laughed. "Hey, sleepy head! Aren't you interested in the fun and games we've got planned today? I thought you were going to sleep all day and miss the fun!" His smile widened as he teased Bili.

"Why didn't someone wake me?" Bili asked, rubbing the sleep from his eyes.

"I heard you tossing and turning last night, and knew you wouldn't get much sleep. You had a big day!"

"Well, I think today's going to be worse, "Bili grumbled as he pulled on a shoe. "Hope we catch them by surprise." He folded his blankets and stuffed them hurriedly into his pack. Then he wandered over to the last of the hot nauke coffee in the pot. The fire was already out in preparation for their expected visitors.

The unconscious warrior they carried in earlier was awake now and sitting up. He drank bits of liquid, then relaxed against a tree trunk. He looked a lot better than he had yesterday, but still weak. He stared curiously around the camp site watching the frantic activity of those nearest him.

In a short time, one of the scouts loped breathlessly into camp. "They're on their way." He shouted. "One of the trolls launched a goblin across the gap and used him to tie lines to the bridge and onto some nearby stones. They've mended the bridge and have all gotten across. Their two prisoners have been left on the other side with 4 goblins guarding them. I think there's a dozen or more of them all together."

Wulpai organized everyone, some hiding among the trees, others behind the deadfalls. The Trolls came first, sure of themselves, and anxious for battle. Their clubs were held in front, ready, as they rounded the corner. They stopped for a moment, sniffing, then let out low growls as they hurried down the path.

Arriving at a point directly under the deadfall, one of the trolls glanced up. The dwarves were already pulling out the stakes. He managed only a hoarse shout when the landslide of stone crashed into him and his friend. They were buried under several tons of debris.

Bili and Meri moved out from their hiding place among the elves and released arrows at the back members of the raiding party. Two went down with arrows through their necks. The others turned in time to catch a hail of arrows from the elven archers. There was panic then. The raiders left the main trail in an attempt to flee, turning down toward the box canyon. The Sanguma saw the mistake too late. With no option, they hurried down the trail and got ready to destroy whoever had set the trap.

Reaching the dead end, the Sanguma turned, and began chanting, honing their deadly powers. A low red colored beam burst forth from between them. It bounced off the unreleased deadfall above the remaining goblins. They aimed again, striking a limb just above Wabran's head. He ducked, swearing loudly at the priests. Again the beam charged out, this time catching Breagle on the side of the leg. He screamed, rolling over out of harm's way. He looked at his burnt pants, then at the leg inside of them. He had an open bleeding wound. He bound a bit of cloth around it and stayed low.

With the aid of the Sanguma, the remaining goblins began to advance. They knew they were well covered and lost most of their initial fear. Meri saw what was happening, so she whispered for her brother Bili. He heard and scrambled over. Together they discussed the use of their stones. If we are to have any chance of escaping," Meri suggested urgently, we'd better try a mind meld." Bili agreed, so they moved where they could get a good look at the Sanguma- then began their meld.

Soon the stones were humming. Bili concentrated on the scene before him, then pushed his will toward the Sanguma who were firing at anyone they saw up on the rim. Meri felt a sudden surge of power ripple through her as a blue light shot out from the two stones, engulfing the Sanguma and their rings. It shimmered for only a moment. The shimmer exploded into a blinding flash! **Whoomp!** The Sanguma lay humped on the ground, a charred mass. With whoops and war cries, the dwarves descended upon the goblins, using battle-axes to finish them. Once the battle was over, Wabran clasped Bili by the shoulder. "Those priests deserved everything they got. Don't feel badly boy. You and your sister have done us all a powerful favor. We'll clean up the remains!" He moved off to give Bili a bit of time to come to grips with what he and Meri had just done. Bili felt a bit dizzy and stumbled as he turned around toward his sister. She was staring at the burnt bodies of those priests. She sat down involuntarily as she felt the drain of power hit her. Pain began to lance through her neck and shoulders as her muscles cramped violently. She hugged herself in response to that pain, burying her head into her knees. She began moaning softly to herself as she rocked forward and backwards.

Wulpai hurried over to her and knelt beside her. "It's all right Meri. We're here with you. We won't leave you. You are safe. Nothing can harm you now! Relax and let go of the pain. Relax!

As Meri tried to relax, she convulsed violently falling to one side. Then she lay still. Bili hurried over, fear clouding his mind. He grabbed his sister and pulled her to a sitting position. "Meri! Meri! Can you hear me?

"Leave her alone a little longer Bili. She'll come out of it. It has been quite a shock on her system. She took the brunt of the thrust because she is the channel. Give her a little time."

Bili backed off and let Meri slip to the ground again. She lay there some minutes and then stirred, moaning again. First one eye opened and then the other, She turned her head toward the sky, then she seemed to regain her senses. She lay there for a short time yet, then struggled to sit up. Bili helped her to a complete sitting position, and she laid here head on his shoulder. "Thanks Bili! This has been a bit overwhelming. I never expected this kind of power to flow through me as we melded our minds through the stone. It was all I could do to direct the power as it burst forth I felt as though I was on fire. Yet the sensation left me as soon as I felt the power blow out from me."

Meri sat there for a couple more minutes, then was helped to her feet by Wulpai who had stooped down beside her. "Let me get you toward your feet. You should be all right again momentarily." He pulled her gently up and she stood straight, stretching up to the sky and rising on her toes. Then she dropped her arms and turned toward the others gathering around her. "I'm glad this is over. This is the first time Bili and I have used our power to destroy something. Its rhythm is altogether different from healing and infinitely more draining. It doesn't have a good feel about it. Maybe because it's the opposite of what we two have been used to experiencing?"

Meri, stay here and recover. I'll take the elves and Bili with me and attempt to rescue the other captives."

Returning to the rim with Bili and the elves, Wulpai directed them toward the bridge. They hurried across as quietly as possible, then with the elves, surprised the goblins who were half asleep in the morning sun. The fight didn't last a minute. The elves threw the bodies of the goblins into the nearby canyon, along with the few remaining weapons and camping equipment. After Bili and

Wulpai freed the two remaining prisoners and checking them for wounds, the four of them hurried back to the elves. After crossing the bridge again, they, destroyed it so the war party following would also have to rebuild it before crossing. This would ensure their safe camping further down the trail.

Wabran, who had stayed behind had directed the hastily dug graves, placing the goblins and charred Sanguma inside. They left the trolls covered by the stone cairn. Gathering their packs, weapons and food, they hurried along the trail, hoping to cross the mountains without further delay.

Chapter 13

Tales in the Dark

Elves, dwarves and men reached the edges of the pass just before dark. It had been a long arduous climb, and the wet slippery trails hadn't improved the dark mood of the dwarves. They had spoken little and seemed to prefer appearing taciturn as a group, so Wulpai decided to make camp right there along the trail. He posted guards above, some several hundred yards out. They all had a clear view of the trail on both sides. Making a small fire in the shelter of two large stones, they cooked some nauke coffee, and soup.

When the meal was over, and pots and plates had been put away, Bili approached Wulpai. He was tired, but the expression on his face belied the miles of hard trekking he had recently completed. Unasked questions brought wrinkles to his forehead. He sat down heavily, tired from the past two days of fighting and running. Picking up a couple of small stones he found laying nearby, he began to absently spin them around in his hand, clicking them together as they passed each other on an endless quest.

"It appears you are trying to relieve tension with a traditional stone pair," Wulpai observed. "People of the North Country use rounded metal balls in much the same way as you. Those who teach martial arts usually need something to relieve all the stress generated by constantly focusing on ways to hurt an enemy. It's not healthy to always be forced to view life from such a perspective. Some say it generates depression, which lowers the spirit and tends to make it difficult to learn new things. It slows the flow of the body in actual fighting and opens the warrior to the blade of his opponent.

"Sorry for that digression, Bili. I couldn't help but notice the similarities. Anyway, what's on your mind?" Wulpai asked.

"Nothing really, I guess." Bili managed to mumble, trying to sound a lot more casual and disinterested than he really was.

"The pace too slow for you? Are you wondering why we're resting here along the trail tonight instead of going on?"

"No, it's not that. Ells knows we could all use some rest after these past couple of days. It's not been easy! No, Wulpai, something's gnawing at the back of my mind but I can't make it surface. It's been bothering me since we met those spirits on the plains of desolation. I have an uneasy feeling that won't go away. You explained who they are and how they came to haunt those ruins. That's unsettling enough. I hope they don't play a part in any future we're likely to have in the coming days.

"Well, I guess I need to ask some other questions that might spark what I'm really feeling. What kind of things are we likely to run into over the next few days? More trolls, or Sanguma, monsters, or something worse? I'm getting nervous, I guess. This Dark Lord seems to have a lot of power and we're apparently fighting something that has been around for several hundred years. Do you think we really have a chance against him if he decides to declare all-out war?"

Wulpai sat there in the fading light. He didn't seem to be in any hurry to answer. Bili stared at him for a moment, then looked back at the stones in his hand. He was very aware there had been no choice in the timing to start this quest. He also understood that many in his village would have died had he and Mary not spotted the Sanguma and the warriors with them at the pond. They had no choice but to flee and draw off those intruders. His father had been right to be concerned, but wasn't aware of the dire situation in which the stones had placed them; at least not at that time anyway. No matter, there was no turning back. These outsiders had invaded their homeland. They were in the thick of it now, and far away from home. How they responded to each encounter would determine whether they lived or died.

"But why are these two stones so important, Bili pondered outloud? "What is the significance of their power anyway? Once they are brought into the hands of the right people, what is likely to happen? Will the fighting be over? Will our quest really end? Will there really be peace again?"

Wulpai stirred, shuffling his feet a bit, like a man trying to find a more comfortable position. He coughed slightly then turned to Bili.

"You pose some pretty tough questions, my friend. I'm not sure I have the answers you're looking for."

Meri finished giving medicines to the men and the dwarves, who needed them, then spotted Bili and Wulpai sitting alone by a fire. She slipped quietly to Bili's side as Wulpai started his story.

"Good of you to join us, Meri," Wulpai spoke softly. "Bili has brought up some tough questions. I hope I may bring some of them to rest.

"To help you both understand the significance of this mission, you need more background information on the Dark Lord. He wasn't always evil. I mentioned this earlier, but I would like to expand on it for you both. Let me pick up that thread again.

"There was a time when, according to legend, he was the most beautiful creature that ever existed. He was the Great One's favorite. In time he became his constant companion. They shared many secrets, and spent days talking; debating about things that could or could not be, possible futures, purposes, goals, plans, even dreams. Uh, there is a specific section in the *Codrin* that talks about him. Let me see if I can recall it. It's been a few years now since I had occasion to memorize it.

'Great was your beauty. your wisdom was beyond all others. you were created by the great one himself to be a guardian of all that was his. You were mighty in power and wise in your dealings. All who knew you praised your wit and humor. Your garments seemed to be an extension of your very being, reflecting your moods, shining out brightly when your spirit rose in joy and adoration of the Great One. You were hard to look upon without awe and inspiration erupting from those who saw you as you passed by. Your position with the great one gave you access to the very mountain where he dwelled. You were even allowed to walk along the sacred groves where the stones of fire sparkled and burst forth its breath-taking colors as they lit the heights of the heavens, dazzling those in the far reaches of the kingdom.

'Alas, you focused on your beauty and power, forgetting you were but a created being, meant to serve the Great One. You became like a bush of brambles and briars, tearing and ripping at the very fabric of the universe. Stars began to fall from their places, and the mountains were shaken. Whole forests were engulfed in raging

flames as the heavens touched them. Great was the chaos created by your need to conquer, your quest for power.

'The Great One invited you to return, to be healed and restored. But you refused. Instead you raised a rebellion against him. This was your undoing. Your clothing, once brilliant with colors, now became drab, even dull. The excited glint in your eyes grew to become an all consuming fire. Everywhere you went destruction followed.

'In sorrow and distress, and with great reluctance, the Great One created an alternate world, one that might serve as a retreat if the rebellion could not be quelled! It was here, in the end, that the usurper and his remaining rabble were thrown. How the mighty have fallen and the foe vanquished! Is there no one to look upon such horror and mourn? The fabric of the worlds is torn. Is there no one to repair all that has been damaged? Woe to those who are subjected to the outcasts! Woe to those who must pay homage to the deceiver and destroyer of all that is good. Woe to those who hope for peace only to find a sword.'

Meri, quick to pick up the gist of this tale became agitated, interrupting Wulpai. "Are you saying then that this world on which we live is the one created by this Great One of whom you speak?"

"Yes Meri. The story finishes up with *Apollyon*, at least that's what he's called in the volumes, losing the struggle and being cast out of the realm in which he had lived since his creation. He vowed to get even and find a way to gain power to challenge the Great One again. I believe that is what he is attempting to do now."

"Wulpai, can you tell us how the Great One managed to overcome the forces of *Apollyon* and keep his throne?" Bili asked. "I've never heard any of this before. Our own people have their legends, but we've heard nothing of this struggle. Maybe it's been lost through the generations of storytellers."

Wulpai sat a moment pondering. "You may have something there, Bili. It's entirely possible that the Sanguma have been commissioned to cut off all knowledge of those events, and they've worked for years trying to erase any evidence which points in that direction. Maybe that's why so few people outside the Western Lands know about these facts."

Meri, impatient to hear the rest of the story interrupted their reverie. "Wulpai, can you get on with the rest of the story? Don't leave us hanging like this"

Wulpai, after a short apologetic grin and a nod of his head continued. "From what I remember, the rest of the story goes like this:

'The battle raged. Fierce and long was the struggle. Apollyon, the champion of the dark path, was quite crafty and highly skilled in administering his followers. They appeared to win every battle. As a result, there were many defectors among the ranks of the Great One. He appeared to be losing. Fully one third of the greater and lesser beings were rallying to Apollyon's dark banner.

'Unexpectedly, and unknown to those around him, the Great One quietly called upon one who guarded the frontiers of his realm. He was little known, for he had spent eons in the far reaches of the kingdom. His recall came silently as the Great One privately brought him to the mountain. He came on paths known only to those who guarded the vast borders. His assignment was a simple one: Drive Apollyon and his followers from the realm.

'His very appearance radiated untapped sources of power. When he spoke, the mountains seemed to tremble, sliding and scrambling to obey. He took immediate command of the several factions of *greater and lesser beings of the Great One, and culled from their midst a core-group of warriors. They had special powers that lent themselves uniquely to his battle plan. Uniting their wills as one, they began to first isolate, and then drive the forces of Apollyon from the mountain. Slowly, one by one, they were pushed from the halls of the assembly, the vast parks, and finally from the center of the city itself.*

'In a last desperate attempt, Apollyon gathered his troops and held council. He knew the secret ways to the mountain. He would go and steal several stones of fire from the very throne of the Great One. With these, he could call upon powers that no one before had tried. These might prove to be the key that would assure his victory.

'His troops prepared once again to do battle with the warriors of the Great One. As they fought, Apollyon slipped from them, wending his way through the dense growth of the secret ways. He worked his way to the stones of fire, lifting several of them from their places, and setting them carefully in his bag. He drew the strings and hurried back to his troops. As he had envisioned, they were being relentlessly pushed back. He drew out the stones and focused all his strength upon them, binding them as one, attempting to bend them to his will. As he concentrated, the stones started to glow, slowly at first, then gradually building to a great blinding light that burst forth from them. Everyone stopped fighting and covered their faces. Some fell to the ground stunned. Others began to run. The mountain of the Great One began to rumble and heave.

'In great anger, the Great One himself stood up, pointing his finger at Apollyon. A single beam of light pierced the air as it streaked its way to the stones in Apollyon's hands. He gave a startled scream and fell to the ground senseless. The stones scattered and the light

went from them. The Great One commanded that Apollyon and his followers be banished from his realm. They were herded to the borders and hurled far out into the darkness. The powerful forces generated by the vortex the Great One had placed there violently sucked them into the alternate world that he had created. Thus was the kingdom cleansed from the terrible rebellion that occurred.'

Bili shifted uneasily, glancing at Meri as he did to gauge her response to this bizarre tale. She seemed totally engrossed, so he changed to a more comfortable position and decided to hear things out.

Wulpai explained further,

'Unknown to the troops of the Great One, one of the lesser beings had rushed to pick up the stones of fire, placing them back in the special bag which Apollyon hung at his side. He hid them well. No one suspected they had been taken; but the Great One felt the loss and wondered what had become of them.

'Apollyon lay unconscious as he was hurled out into the darkness. He was many days upon this strange world before his senses returned. When he awoke, he was angered to learn he had been defeated and cast from the very presence of the Great One. He swore he would have his revenge.'

"That's all I can remember. I know there should be more, and possibly there are some manuscripts which will give us more light on what the Dark Lord has done down through the years. We don't have those manuscripts in our libraries, but possibly something might exist in the Western Lands. That country has never been overrun in all the years of war. I don't know how they've managed to avoid it, but it simply has not happened."

"That must be why we were given those dreams. That makes sense," reasoned Bili. "The Western Lands must hold the key to our defense and the defeat of the Dark Lord. That would mean the sooner we get these stones to the right hands, the sooner we can get back to our own people!"

"Bili, something tells me it's not going to be quite that simple," Meri said pensively, staring at her brother. "From what I've seen so far, I'd say that things are just now warming up. There's no guarantee that any of us will get out of this quest alive, let alone be allowed to return to our own lands."

Breagle, the dwarf who had taken the first watch, returned interrupting them. "Wulpai, there's something wrong up ahead. I can't put my finger on it, but I've seen some owls flying around toward the south. Would you come with me and look?"

Bili was upset by the intrusion, but at the same time feared to dwell more on the dangers that lie ahead. With his questions half answered, he got up and along with Wulpai, hurried after the disappearing dwarf. They reached the spot Breagle had used as a lookout.

"Over there, by those trees. See the owls? What do you make of it all?" asked Breagle.

Wulpai moved slowly around the rocks and trees, working his way toward the owls. He was gone for what seemed to Bili a long time. Suddenly the owls screeched, spreading their wings, and flying right to where Bili and Breagle were hiding. On impulse, Bili drew out a dagger and threw it, hitting the second owl squarely in the chest. It fluttered a moment, then fell heavily onto a nearby limb. It hung there for a second, then dropped to the ground. Breagle turned to scold Bili for what he'd done, but what he saw stopped him, open mouthed and gaping.

The owl changed form. The feathers disappeared and in their place lay a misshapen Sanguma priest, small but unmistakable.

Wulpai hurried over, and looked at the body for a moment. He made no comment, just stood over the priest. A burst of light took them by surprise as the lifeless body turned to ash, leaving Bili's dagger unchanged.

Breagle swore fluently, totally unnerved by what he'd seen. Bili, momentarily shocked, quickly reached down, taking his dagger. He hastily wiped it off on some nearby leaves.

"How did the Dark Lord manage that trick?" Breagle grated angrily. "I suppose the rest of those owls were spies as well?" He looked off into the darkness trying to see if the owls were still visible. He shook his meaty fist menacingly in their direction.

Bili followed his gaze, wondering the same thing. A deep chill struck his heart. Those owls probably were the Dark Lord's spies, he concluded. Nothing the group attempted went unseen. With a fearful heart Bili decided that the Dark Lord probably knew about their quest, and had plans to rob them of the stones when he could catch them off guard. That did not sit well with him. Fear gave way to feelings of panic.

Wulpai turned to them both and said, "Let's break camp. I don't think it's safe to spend the remainder of the night here. We're better off moving on. We should reach the Lake by noon, and can rest then. Tell the others."

Bili and Breagle left to spread the news. Everyone got up and as quickly as they could, packed their gear and met along the trail. Within minutes they were moving silently eastward. They traveled slowly because it was dark. Besides, the dwarves were scouting ahead to make sure there were no ambushes set for them. Hagred had healed up well enough to travel, and moved along steadily for one not completely whole. His companion Hergeth was still mending and needed help from time to time. Bili decided he would give him as much help as possible. It also gave him an excuse to be near Wesip. Yilmai dropped back from time to time to make sure they were successfully coping with the situation. He also teased Bili discreetly about ulterior motives whenever he got the chance.

Bili smiled at this welcome diversion, wishing there really could be something between himself and Wesip. Several girls had turned his heart in past months, but none fired his passions as this one. He watched her as she moved ahead of them along the trail. Even though it was dark, he could see her form silhouetted against the dark sky. The clouds had scudded toward the east, and now that the moon had gone down a few stars were visible. Bili's imagination wandered among meadows and streams, Wesip at his side. He pondered what it might be like to be married to someone such as her, a girl from the Western Lands. Bili had no idea what their culture might be like, nor what kind of houses they lived in. He'd never been outside his own area until he and Meri were forced from their homeland. Still his dreams plagued him as they traveled. But he didn't find these dreams particularly objectionable. He found comfort in them, for they promised life after tomorrow.

No ambushes lay in wait along the trail, so the night passed uneventfully. Toward morning, they stopped for a short time along the pass. The sun was about to poke its head over the horizon to shed light on the affairs of men.

Wulpai didn't want to miss the opportunity to see the colors and contrasts it threw on the mountains and cliffs below them. Bili was glad for the break. He was tired and ached from acting as a living crutch. He stretched, as one trying the pull the last stars from their lofty perch. With a soft groan, he sat down on a rock to await the dawn. Wesip saw him and came over to sit nearby.

"You must be tired, Bili. You've been awfully nice to Hergeth. I think we'd have had to make a stretcher to carry him if you hadn't volunteered to assist him."

"I didn't know I had so many bones and muscles in my body," jested Bili. "They're all protesting at once." He could see the outline of her face, but couldn't distinguish her features yet. "I'm glad that Hergeth is getting stronger. Soon he'll heal and be as strong as Hagred. That medicine my sister found in those caves is really something."

He was glad to have something useful to say. He felt awkward around Wesip, but wanted desperately to make a good impression on her. He knew Yilmai was right. He was deeply attracted to this Westerner in spite of their dangerous situation. He hoped this wouldn't endanger the others or keep him from his quest.

"Meri is close friends with the elven girl," Wesip whispered. "Did they just meet when you visited there?"

"Yes," replied Bili. "We stayed nearly a whole month, and she developed that friendship pretty quickly. I think they have a lot in common, so the bond came naturally. They're both deeply interested in natural medicines. Yilmai and I became friends when he saved our lives back at the goblin caves. We're pretty close too, as you've no doubt noticed."

She caught his smile in the growing light. "Uh, yes, I have noticed, she grinned. He also loves to tease you. He's discreet about it, but I'm not blind either."

Blushing furiously, Bili was glad that the low light hid the redness that came to his cheeks. He felt hot and embarrassed. He stood up and looked off to the east, glad that the sun, about to make its appearance, gave him an excuse to hide. Wesip quietly moved up beside him and looked over the mountains and valleys below them.

She was the first to break the silence. "I hope we get back home without more trouble. My father will be worried sick when he hears that our party was attacked."

"You'll get back safely if I have anything to say about it," Bili whispered protectively. "But you're right. I'm hoping against hope to get these stones safely in the right hands, and then get back to our home in the mountains. From what Wulpai says, the Dark Lord has great ambitions. If he's right, then this trouble we've experienced is only the beginning."

His voice trailed off as he watched the sun come up. He put his hand gently into Wesip's and squeezed slightly. She looked up at him and squeezed back, smiling knowingly. She laid her head against his arm and looked back at the rising sun. It felt comforting to have someone nearby she could trust. Her heart went out to Bili and his sister, for she understood the burden that had been placed upon them. She too wondered what the days ahead would bring. She savored this moment of tranquility and beauty.

As the day started, the sun exploded westward, lightening the sides of cliffs in a dramatic burst of yellow brilliance. There was a slight haze, but this only enhanced the color. Areas in shadow remained a dark blue, giving the valleys a sleepy appearance. Small pockets of fog covered the low ground near the river far below, and looked like a billowy blanket spread over a sleeping giant. Everyone stared at the scene, alone momentarily with his or her own thoughts.

Wulpai, moved deeply by the beauty of the scenery, said almost reverently, "This is worth all the days it takes to get here.

I've seen this twice before in my lifetime. I'm moved more each time I watch."

He stood there for a short time longer, then bent his knee in a gesture of worship or maybe recognition at the creator behind all this beauty. Then he stood, reached over and grabbed his gear, then moved a few steps down the trail. Suddenly he stopped, reluctant to leave such beauty. It was like a worshiper leaving the sanctuary of a cathedral after a moving service.

"Best to be on the trail again," Wulpai announced, clearing the catch from his throat. "With a bit of luck, we should arrive at the Lake around mid-day."

He then turned and walked down the path out of the pass. He worked his way down amid boulders strewn across the trail from the winter storms. The others, one by one, followed, casting longing glances at the scene around them.

Chapter 14

The Hermit of Lake Salduwe

The sun cast deepening shadows across the steep crags as the weary travelers crested the ridge overlooking the lake. It had taken longer than Wulpai had figured. Resting twice along the way enabled Hergeth to walk on his own for short periods. The others had welcomed the break as well. They had been walking a day and a half with little sleep the night before. The cool air at this altitude was refreshing, but made hiking more difficult. Bili set his pack down and stared. The lake was a deep blue, pure and clean. There was a small beach near the eastern end, kept free of brush by travelers who bathed there as they passed through. At the western end, the last rays of the sun highlighted a dark area beneath the water.

Bili continued staring, wondering if this lake held any grim secrets. There were fir trees and Ponderosa pines ringing the lake, with wildflowers of blue, white and yellow dotting the meadows above them. A few deer and elk grazed among them. These caught his eye. He nudged Yilmai, who was just setting down his own pack. "Hey, what do you think?

Yilmai turned, then looked in the direction Bili pointed. "Venison would make a nice meal. Wonder if they'll spook if we try to get near them?" he thought out loud.

"Looks like the others are wondering that too!" Bili replied. "We're downwind of them, so they can't smell us yet."

A small party of men quietly worked their way around the lake in hopes of bringing down meat for dinner. They moved slowly and carefully among the rocks and trees. Bili watched them from his vantage point near the crest. Meri, Wesip and Rimwai, the elven girl, joined them, seating themselves on a fallen log. The three girls took in the beauty of the lake and the surrounding hills. It looked so peaceful here, as though the area was a sanctuary. The ugliness of trolls, goblins and Sanguma priests seemed no more than a nightmare to be discarded in the morning light.

"I could stay in a place like this forever," Meri said wistfully. "All the ugly things that have happened to us along the way seem remote, you know, like they never really happened."

Bili looked back at Meri. "You can sense it too, then. This place feels different from any place we've been so far. The elven capital was similar, but this seems stronger somehow-like a sacred grove filled with powers of the priests, gathered to protect and help those who need it."

A shout startled them all! It echoed off the trees and rocks. The hunters leaped from their hiding places, taking wild aim at the bounding deer and elk. Their shafts fell short as the wild animals fled to the safety of the meadows and outlying forests. Some of the men shouted curses, frustrated at being interrupted in their hunt. Everyone looked around hoping to locate the source of the noise. The dying echoes were replaced by loud hearty laughter. Still they could find no one.

Puzzled by this strange laughter, Bili and Yilmai picked up their packs and started toward the lake. The girls trailed them at a distance. Yilmai noticed a small cabin up against an outcropping of stones at the upper end of the vale. "Bili, look over at the stone outcropping. A cabin is nestled against it." Yilmai said.

He pointed it out to Bili. They stared at it for a moment, then decided to walk that direction. They were almost half way there when someone appeared from behind the cabin. He started walking toward them. He was a grizzled old man, with a shock of unruly white hair. His britches were made of well-sewn buckskin, and he wore buckskin boots strapped halfway up his calves. A jacket of animal fur, possibly wolf-skin, covered his arms and chest. He carried a short staff in his left hand, while he pulled an unwilling goat with his right. He stopped for a moment, shook his head, muttered something inaudible to the goat, and then started again. The goat continued to twist, trying to break free. The old hermit paid no attention, but kept coming toward his visitors.

Walking within 100 feet of these outsiders, he stopped. He said nothing; just watched. Bili halted abruptly looking at Yilmai for support. The girls caught up and stood silently behind them. There was an awkward silence until the goat gave an angry bleat and butted the old hermit, knocking him off balance. He released the goat as he slipped backwards to the ground. The goat seized the opportunity to trot back to the cabin. With a sigh, the old man brushed himself off, muttering more epithets under his breath. Then he stared again at the young people. They were smiling to themselves.

"Well, well, what have we here? Visitors from the looks of you," he said, chuckling to himself at some private joke.

Meri broke the silence on their side. "Were you the one who startled us all with that great shout?" she asked. "We were hoping for some venison tonight, but that's no longer possible."

Again the old hermit began laughing. He seemed unable to control himself. He held his sides, and the tears began streaming down his face.

Bili, looking bewildered, then offended, asked, "What's so very funny?"

At that, the old hermit fell to his knees, then rolled over, helpless in gales of laughter. Meri seemed to find humor in the situation, and began laughing herself. Bili gave her a sharp look, but it made her laugh all the harder. Then Rimwai and Wesip started. Bili looked confused turning from one to the other, then began to smile as he looked at Yilmai. Finally, the old hermit got up and brushed himself off once again. Wiping the tears from his eyes, he looked at Meri and said,

"Not possible! Not possible, is it? Oh, It isn't often that I have the opportunity for a good laugh. It's like medicine in some ways; releases all the tension from living alone. It helps the body get back to normal."

He snorted into an old kerchief he pulled from his hip pocket. Wiping his eyes once again, he looked at the others, returning from the futile chase. Watching them as they approached, he singled out Wulpai.

"I've seen you several times in the past. What brings you to this part of the country after being so long away?"

Wulpai grinned, "Still protecting your animals are you? Hope you've got some meat curing up in that cabin of yours. We're out of meat and could use some. We've got a few more miles to travel before we reach the Western Lands."

"Something scaring the game east of here that you've come to the lake empty handed?" asked the old hermit, a wry grin splitting his face.

"Just some trolls, goblins and Sanguma," replied Wulpai. "Maybe us too with our noise at times."

"Yup!" Came the old man's terse reply. "I've sensed lately that somethin's amiss. I can feel it in my bones. No good will come of it all. Hawks and strange owls flying around at night, wild animals gettin' skittish and all. Makes a body uncomfortable being out here alone. Yet I'm not alone. Amethyst is a pretty good body guard."

"You still trust that mountain cat do you?" Wulpai smiled easily.

Bili's felt a shiver of fear run through him, and his eyes widened at the mention of the great cat. He'd seen a couple up in the mountains where he lived. After his close brush with death, he had a healthy respect for their powerful jaws and sharp claws. Yet here was a man who trusted the big cat like another man would a hunting dog.

"She's more reliable than many men I know. She keeps to herself most of the time, but keeps an eye on this place during the night. Not too many things approach the cabin when she's here. You're welcome to make camp and spend the night. Send a couple of your men and I'll fetch some meat for you. I don't like to see the wild game killed here in the meadows. It's been a traditional sanctuary for many years, and I'd like to keep it that way."

Breagle took off his hat and bowed low. "Many pardons old father. We had no idea this area was sacred. Accept my sincere apologies. We were but hungry men in search of sustenance."

The old hermit smiled. "No offense, friend dwarf. Just come with me and I'll give you what your stomach is grumbling for."

With that, he turned on his heels and walked in the direction of the cabin, chuckling quietly to himself again. "Not possible is it?"

Breagle suppressed a satisfied grin. Bili and Yilmai joined him and together they followed the old hermit. As they headed toward the cabin, the others turned and got to the business of making camp. Meri and Wesip gathered sticks for firewood, while Rimwai collected needles from the Ponderosa and Fir trees to make comfortable beds for the night.

The old hermit stepped around the cabin and went to the slab of rock behind. He touched a hidden latch, and a small door swung open on crude hinges. He walked into the darkness, took a torch from its holder, and used a small flint and tinderbox to light it. Then he led the way deeper into the cave. He brought them to a small room where several deer, covered in sheets curing, hung from ropes. He undid one of them and handed it to Breagle. Then he went to a shelf where he kept a store of dried jerky. He handed part of this to Yilmai and Bili.

"That should hold you for a while. Might even get you all the way to the Eastern Fortress if you're careful. I'd watch myself though, if I were you. Some mighty strange goin's on around these parts nowadays. A body can't be too careful you know."

They left the cave, thanking the old hermit once again, then went down to the camp to join the others. Soon the smell of roasting venison brightened the hearts of the whole party. Later, as they finished the last of their meal, the moon climbed over the tops of the trees casting its soft light onto the meadows. The lake remained a dark shadow at the heart of all this beauty.

Bili asked Wesip if she would go for a walk. She was delighted to join him. They wandered down toward the lake talking quietly. Bili looked at her from time to time, catching glimpses of the moon reflecting off her light hair. It was nice to take in the beauty here without having to think about what lay ahead. An owl flew off its perch ahead of them, swooping down to catch a field mouse that strayed too far from the sheltered meadow. It flew to another part of the lake to enjoy its feast. Bili wondered anxiously if this was another Sanguma priest keeping an eye on them. Feeling rather uneasy, he undid the strap holding his dagger in its sheath. *It's never foolish to be prepared for danger in situation such as these*, Bili thought to himself, glancing yet again toward the owl. *Otherwise I am betraying my training as a warrior.*

Sitting near the shoreline, Bili kept a wary eye on the owl, then turned his attention to Wesip who was watching a doe with its two fawns come from the meadows for a drink. The doe sniffed the air for a moment, then deciding it was safe, put her head down and drank. The little ones watched her, then wandered off a ways to lay in the soft grasses. Their mother grazed nearby. Wesip watched this in fascination.

"I've seen deer many times in the past, but I always enjoy watching the fawns and their complete trust in their mothers. They're quick to sense danger from her slightest move, but you'd never know they were nervous. They sure have quick reactions. We humans are so slow compared to them."

"I wish I had their kind of muscle and stamina," Bili mused. "They spring high over fallen trees and never seem to run out of energy when being chased. I could do with some of that about now."

Wesip turned to look at him smiling warmly. "If you were any friskier, you'd leave us all far behind on the trail! Just watching you and Yilmai wears me out. I don't know where you two get all your energy." She smiled at him then lay her head on his shoulder.

Bili's heart began to beat faster again. His animal passions were being aroused again. He wished this night would never end. The moon's reflection was cast back by the water in the lake, making the setting unbearably romantic. His mind wandered again over the past few days since he'd met Wesip. Since she had come into his life, it had changed completely. Things were now suddenly becoming more complicated-but delightfully so! Now he thought less of home, and more of these lands here. *I wonder if I'll ever have the chance to return to my childhood mountain country. It makes me feel like a traitor to all that I have grown to love and understand,* Bili thought sadly. *But here I stand here in this strange vale. Life for me is changing and now it seems there will be no going back.*

Something stirred behind them. Bili whirled around, dagger in hand. Two yellow eyes tracked him mere inches away.

"Easy Amethyst!" Cautioned the Old Hermit. "These are our friends. Bili, you can put the knife away. She's not going to harm you." Moving closer he continued, " I noticed a slight scar going down the side of your neck. Did that come from a mountain cat where you live?"

Bili was surprised how observant the old hermit was. Stammering he replied, "Well, ah, as a matter of fact, yes. I was learning to hunt on my own when I surprised one. I barely escaped with my life." He didn't go into more detail. *I wonder what else the old man has noticed?* he thought to himself.

"Wulpai tells me that you and your sister are on a quest to take the lost stones back to the Western Lands. I hope the Dark Lord isn't aware that you have both of them. From the legends that have been written, he's been looking for them now for a couple hundred years. He's anxious to get his hands on them."

Avoiding his question for the moment, Bili asked, "What do you know about the stones?" He was curious to know what the old hermit could tell him.

"May I see the stone around your neck?" the old hermit asked gesturing with an outstretched hand. "After I see the stone, I may be able to verify that what you posses is in fact what the Dark Lord scours the lands to obtain."

Bili untied the stone from his neck, then stood and handed it hesitantly to the old hermit. He felt strangely naked without it. *Have I come to depend on the stone this strongly in such a short time?* he asked himself in sudden fear. This unsettled him. He hadn't realized the stone held such power. Was he becoming addicted to the magic it held within? Sometimes, he had to admit, it was hard to let go. He felt more of a man with it around his neck.

The old hermit took the stone, held it up in the moonlight, looking at the several facets. Peering intently at the stone caused it to glow evenly. Bili could feel the power emanating from it. Small particles of glowing dust began dancing around the stone, spinning and whirling in circles. A strange music, wild and pure played on the wind for a moment. Then suddenly, it all disappeared, as though it had never been.

The old hermit gave the stone back to Bili. "Yes, this is one of the stones. Young man, you hold the future of this world in your hands. Guard it carefully! If the Dark Lord gains possession of this stone, there is no limit to the power he can wield."

Bili was at a loss for words. *Who is this old hermit? And how is he able to manipulate the talisman like he does*? He wondered? Bili felt quite unsettled, unsure of himself now. It had taken him quite a few days to attune himself to the stone. Yet, in just a few moments, this old man was making the stone do things he hadn't thought possible. Bili looked at the old hermit and suddenly felt constrained to blurt out a reply.

"Both my sister and I have had dreams about these stones. We were warned to get them to safe hands. Then shortly afterwards, evil men appeared in our forests, seeking information about a pouch that was lost. We knew they were looking for what the roc had dropped in the fight. They almost caught us at the caves of testing, and we were forced to go through them to get away. They provided our only means of escape. Those men weren't able to follow us, so we have eluded them for the moment."

The old hermit shook his head. "You people are going to need all the help you can get to arrive undetected in the Western Lands. Mark my words. The Dark Lord will catch up with you sooner or later," he warned kindly.

"C'mon Amethyst, time to be goin'." With that, he turned on his heels and walked back into the darkness heading for the camp.

The two figures blended into the dark landscape as they made their way toward the camp. Bili stood for a moment watching. Wesip looked up at Bili, but said nothing. Placing the stone in the small pouch this time, he placed it in a pocket.

Bili sighed. "Even though I'll miss this stone, it will be a relief to be shed of this burden. I feel as though it's trying to possess me. Not outwardly, but making me dependent on it. I'm becoming afraid of it."

Wesip nodded. "The sooner we get it to where it's supposed to go, the better it will be for all of us. I just hope we're able to take it to wherever…" Her voice trailed off into an uncertain silence. She stood and squeezed Bili's arm in an attempt to comfort him. Then, sensing the agitation and uncertainty building in his heart, she said quietly, "Let's get back to the camp. He's brought our short-lived dreams to an untimely end. He's such a jolly fellow don't you think?"

Bili turned and saw the beginnings of a smile betray itself on her lips. He grinned at her. "Jolly or not, at least his meat was tasty," He teased her back.

"He's sure quiet." She replied. "I didn't notice his presence until he purposely announced himself. He's really good!"

"We've managed well enough so far," asserted Bili. "I'm confident that we'll get through." Inwardly he knew this to be a lie, but he tried to sound confident for her sake.

With that Bili took Wesip's hand and together they too made their way back toward the camp. When they arrived, he noticed that the old hermit was talking with Meri. Bili wondered what he was telling her. He would check in the morning when he had opportunity. Bili realized that most of the fires had gone out, so he squeezed Wesip lightly and bid her goodnight. He found his way to Yilmai's spot, unrolled his blankets and curled up in them. He was soon fast asleep.

Chapter 15

Mountain Pathways

As light began to etch the eastern night sky, the aroma of nauka coffee filled the camp. Bili groaned, rolled over, then opened one eye. *Is it morning already?* He thought to himself? He struggled to sit it. His back was sore, even though he'd spent the night lying atop the bed of pine boughs. He stretched, attempting to get the kinks out. He finally threw the blankets off, sat up and began scratching his head. Yilmai had just gotten up, and was packing his bedroll. It was still dark, yet everyone was up. They had decided on an early start. The previous evening, they had all met after the evening meal, discussing at length the next leg of their journey. Everyone voiced feelings that the Dark Lord might send out a group of Sanguma priests and mercenaries big enough to capture them, so they planned an early morning start. They hoped to elude detection by hiding themselves in the vast mountain fastness that lay ahead. Once swallowed by this wilderness, it would be almost impossible to guess which of the many trailheads they were following.

Bili went down to the lake and plunged in. The water was cold, but it served to wake him up. He swam around a bit, then got out, shivering. Drying himself with a small towel, he caught a glimpse of deer again in the meadow. He was sorry to leave this haven, but knew his destiny lay elsewhere. He put his breeches back on and laced up his boots, then made his way back to camp. Breagle had a fire going, and venison steaks were cooking on a small griddle. The smell of cooking meat stirred Bili's brain. He could feel his stomach rumble in response. How could he be so hungry already after last night's feast? It seemed a sacrilege. Never mind, he thought, he could live with that. He poured himself a cup of hot nauka coffee before anyone could interrupt. He let the hot liquid slide down his throat, warming him. After a moment, he took another sip. It felt really good this morning in the nippy mountain air. His reverie was short lived.

"Bili, can I see you for a moment?" It was Wulpai. He came over and drew Bili aside.

"The old hermit says that Amethyst brought home the torn body of a goblin. He's gone out to see if there were others with him. He's worried that we're not going to make it through the mountains without being confronted by a group of armed men sent to capture us."

Bili winced. "Yes, I think that's what he was trying to tell me last night down by the lake. He's probably right about the Dark Lord, but I'm not too worried. After all, we've been able to handle all the trouble that's come upon us so far."

Wulpai smiled at Bili's self confidence, then said, "I know how you're feeling, Bili. I think we have been lucky so far. I believe that the Dark Lord is not yet sure you two possess the stones. Once he's convinced you each have one, he'll throw everything at us. Then the story will change fast. The old hermit knows a lot more than he's telling."

Wabran had been listening. He looked longingly at the crags, then shook his head. "I wish we were already over the tops of the mountains. I have a premonition that trouble is going to find us before long. Did the old hermit say when he would be back?"

"The big cat will smell out any companions pretty quickly," Wulpai answered. "If they're still in the area, it won't take long. He said it wasn't more than a mile or so from the end of the valley. Is everyone ready to move?"

"Almost," Wabran assured him. "We're packing the last of the dried meat, and have finished pouring water into the flasks. We should be ready before the old hermit arrives."

Bili turned to leave, but noticed a movement out of the corner of his left eye. Looking over he saw the old hermit working his way down the side of the mountain behind his cabin.

"I see the old hermit entering the valley now," Bili said. "Wonder what the news will be?" He wasn't sure he really wanted to know. *No news is usually good news- that's what the old shaman used to tell everyone.* Looking around, Bili noticed all activity had ceased. He could feel the tension rise as the others waited for the old man.

When he arrived, the cat wasn't with him. Yilmai and the girls joined them, anxious to find out what was going on. They didn't have to wait long.

The old hermit approached them, his face a mask of concentration. Bili looked at Yilmai, unspoken fear passing between them. Bili felt suddenly small and vulnerable. Events were taking a turn for the worse- he had no control over them. A sudden chill shot through his body, causing him to shiver convulsively.

"Well, it's as I figured," the old man began, clearing his throat. "The hillside back there is filled with boot tracks; small wide feet with several different designs. We found nary a soul, but those goblins have definitely been tracking someone. Looks like they headed off to the east after Amethyst got one of them. Since you're headed west, the trail should be clear. But I'd be moving pretty quickly if I were in your shoes. Never can tell what's up with those folk."

"Do you know any fast back trails that we might follow?" asked Bili. He looked at Wulpai, who just shrugged.

The old hermit replied, "There's only one. But you'd never find it. Better if I get my gear and show you the way. Amethyst can guard the valley, and find us if there's trouble."

Daniray, head of the dwarves seemed upset. "Old father, are you sure you're up to the journey? The way will be rough, and our pace must needs be quick. Wulpai is an Elf yet his is barely holding his own in these mountains. And besides, there will be no one to accompany you back to your valley once you've helped us."

The old hermit began to chuckle to himself. "Old and feeble they think me, eh?" imitating the mad hermits of the northland. "Well, there are more surprises ahead!" He gave no answer, but turned to get his gear from the cabin.

Daniray looked at Wulpai. "Did I say something wrong?" Wulpai just grinned.

Bili grinned at Daniray's discomfiture as well. Wulpai simply laid a hand on his shoulder. "I think you're going to be surprised at the stamina of this old hermit. He's lived up here for many years, and climbs the mountains all the time. He's pretty quick on his feet. I think some of the others may feel he'll be a liability, same as you. Just watch. I was with him once when he was in a hurry to get somewhere."

They waited for a few minutes for the old hermit to return. When he did, he outlined their trail in rough marks on the ground, then started off. He set a pace that even Daniray could not fault. He hurried to catch the Old Hermit. They went around the far side of the lake, cut through the meadows, making their way up through the gap at the eastern end of the sanctuary.

As they hiked steadily toward the crags, Bili dropped back to where Meri was walking with Rimwai and Wesip. He stepped in by Meri and asked, "Mind if I join you for a while?"

"Not at all, Bili. What's on your mind?" Meri asked, a trace of concern showing on her face. The two girls moved discreetly ahead to give them more privacy.

Bili struggled not knowing how to begin. "I suppose you've noticed there's something between Wesip and me." He blushed slightly as she smiled and nodded. "Well, last night I asked her to accompany me to the lake. While we were there watching the doe with her fawns, the old hermit surprised us with a visit. He asked me about the talisman stone I had in the pouch around my neck. He took it and did strange things with it. He has some sort of hidden power and the stone doesn't seem to affect him. I felt kind of naked and exposed without it. Much of what he told me we already know from what Wulpai has said.

"I'm just curious. I saw him talking with you when we got back to the camp last night. Did you learn anything new?"

Meri pulled off to the side for a moment to let the others behind her go on ahead. She looked at Bili then said,

"Well, actually, yes. After he looked at my stone, and made it do things I never thought possible, he handed it back to me too. Then he told me to guard it carefully. I guess just as he told you. He said you told him about the roc, the hawks and the men who came looking for the lost pouch. Then I asked him, 'How is it that the stones communicate with us? Do they have a life of their own or is someone behind their power?' The old hermit stood thoughtful for a moment, then leaned against a fir tree and started to explain it all to me. I didn't understand parts of it, but most of it made sense. He said,

'I think I'd better answer your second question first, then maybe we can talk sensibly about the first one. By now Wulpai has filled you in on the written records that his people have kept over the years. The stones once belonged in the realm of the Great One. They were stolen and brought here. He allowed it of course, to see what his rival could do with them. He had never explored their uses, and must have figured this would be a good opportunity to find out. Since he created them, they would naturally have his power in them. But I don't rightly know how they operate either. They just are, that's all. You have to attune yourself to them before you can do anything with them.

'As to your first question, these stones once belonged together, and weren't designed to be divided. They exist for one another, and are always seeking ways to be rejoined. I don't know how this will be accomplished, but I have a pretty good idea that the Dark Lord has most of that worked out. After all, he's had a few hundred years to do his figuring. They put a desire in the hearts of whoever holds them to find the other stones and rejoin them.' That's what he told me, Bili."

Bili looked at Meri for a moment, then up ahead at the old hermit. "What he's saying then is that the Dark Lord must already possess at least one of these stones, and the stone is now driving him to find these others."

"That's what I figured too," replied Meri. "Then He said, 'You're pretty perceptive there, young lady. I think you've got the gist of it. Like I said, just watch yourselves. Things are going to heat up a bit before this whole affair settles down again.'

"With that the old hermit turned away and went back to his cabin."

Bili was thoughtful. "That's why he's so insistent about accompanying us to the Western Lands. He knows that the Dark Lord is being driven and won't stop now until he possesses these stones. I didn't realize how much danger we're really in. He's right. When the Dark Lord is certain we have the stones, he'll kill us all to get them. So far he's just sent out his servants to pick up clues. If we can convince him we don't have them, we may have a chance of getting to the West. Let's stick pretty close together. Maybe the old hermit has something up his sleeve that will help us. Maybe he's the one that should have these stones."

Meri objected, "He would have asked for them if that were true, Bili. No, I have a feeling it's going to be up to us. The stones are probably harder on him than they are on us. I think he's afraid of their power, even though he knows how to use them. Power can be horribly addictive to those who crave it."

Finishing their conversation, they started striding out, soon catching the others. At a wide part of the trail, they regained their place in the group. Bili went up ahead to be with Yilmai again. Meri fell in line behind Wesip, who asked her what was going on. Meri explained the conversation she'd had with Bili. She also warned both girls to be ready for anything along the trail. The old hermit was expecting trouble.

The two elven scouts that had been sent ahead returned and reported that the way was clear. Everyone was relieved for the moment. They continued to climb in the fresh morning air of these glorious mountains.

Yilmai and Bili moved ahead as scouts, taking care to note the passage of any animals or unusual tracks. They moved steadily toward the crags. They were above the timberline now, so the path was filled mostly with dirt and small stones that had broken from the boulders above. They both felt exposed and hurried to reach the pass.

It was late afternoon when they finally did arrive at the top. Carefully, they looked for places that could conceal enemies. Finding none, they signaled back to the rest of their companions on the lower ridge. Soon everyone was enjoying the view. They felt as though they were on top of the world. Bili drank in the mid-afternoon sun, occasionally covered by cumulus clouds drifting toward the east. Wesip pointed out to Meri and Rimwai the direction of the eastern fortress. There were still too many mountains between them for it to be seen.

Wulpai suggested that everyone go down a ways on the other side, take a short rest and have something to eat. Their forms would be silhouetted to anyone for miles if they continued to stand atop the rocks here in the pass. Reluctantly everyone moved down to a less conspicuous rest area.

The old hermit stood, studying the terrain below. He squinted against the sun's brightness as he probed into every nook and cranny he knew could hold an enemy. Satisfied for the moment that there was no one, he sat down and began chewing on a piece of dried jerky. Yilmai and Bili discussed with Wabran who the next scouts would be. Wulpai joined them, helping them form a roster. The dwarves wanted to scout in the afternoon, so Wabran and Daniray would lead the party next. The elves would take the mornings, and Bili and Yilmai mid-day.

After resting long enough to feel ready, the party started along the switchbacks leading eastward. The scouts ranged well ahead, checking the trails and removing trash that the winter's harshness had strewn across them. The party moved quickly down the sides of the crags, entering the timberline area by dusk.

The old hermit consulted with the scouts, then moved on ahead, looking for one of the special trails. It took him the better part of an hour to locate it. Scrub brush and debris blocked the entrance. He carefully maneuvered around it, leaving no trace of his passage. All the others followed in single file. The elves were the last to follow. They thoroughly brushed out any tracks made by the others, then worked their way up the hidden pathway. They caught the others about a mile in. The old hermit had pitched camp underneath several overhanging rocks.

"I want a dry camp this high up. The rains and mist just appear suddenly at this altitude. You don't get any warning. No sense in making it any rougher than it has to be."

Following his lead, the others found shelter, then built a couple of small fires, cooking soup and the few plants the elves had collected once they reached the timberline area. No one spoke. Breagle, the best dwarf cook, put out the fires soon after everyone had eaten. With the exception of those on guard, everyone rolled up early in their blankets and tried to catch what sleep they could. Bili looked at the sky overhead through the trees. There were still a few stars shining, which had not been covered by clouds. The moon was not yet up. He lay with his sword and dagger handy. He rolled over and looked at the others, wondering if they were feeling as anxious as he. Outwardly he wanted to appear confident, to encourage the others. Inwardly, he was having misgivings, afraid of what might happen to himself or to his sister if they did end up in the hands of the Dark Lord. He lay awake for a long while, thinking of home and the meals he used to have with the family. Slowly, he drifted off into a dream filled sleep. Walking down a path, he was confronted with goblins, trolls, and Sanguma. He fought them off bravely, but they outnumbered him. They covered him with their sheer weight, pinning him to the ground, their ugly faces leering down at him, howling, laughing, and poking him with sticks. He struggled, trying to pull himself out of the nightmare.

He awoke with a start, grabbing for his dagger. Yilmai grabbed his arm. "Bili, it's only me, Yilmai. Calm down. It's our turn to go on watch."

Bili dropped back to the ground in relief, shaking violently. "I was sure you were one of the goblins in my dream. I was about to carve you up." He took several deep breaths to calm himself. Then he tossed off the blankets, rolled them up neatly, put them in his pack, and followed Yilmai to the edge of the camp. They stood guard as the half moon gave its light through the thickening clouds. They saw nothing, and felt relieved.

Dawn found the party back on the trail, moving at a steady pace along their new pathway. The old hermit led the way, taking various forks. Those in the rear kept busy brushing out tracks. Toward noon they came upon a small lake. Everyone felt the need to have a short swim. The girls went to one part, while the men went to another, bathing, splashing and enjoying the short break. Wulpai and the old hermit stood watch.

Three hawks came into view, rising on the thermals that the noon sun had created here in the mountains. They seemed innocuous enough, trailing each other in lazy patterns across the sky. They circled near the lake a few times, then moved off to the east, up toward the pass. Bili noticed them as he was drying off. He wondered how many of them lived up here in the mountains, a natural sanctuary for them. Few people if any lived in these parts. They were too far away from the towns of men, or elves and dwarves. It was too far to carry pelts or anything else to be traded.

After taking time to eat the cheeses and jerky they carried in their packs, the party moved on. They hiked across a couple of level hills, void of cover, then uphill into more trees. The Old Hermit knew this trail would end soon, and they would join the main path used by men traveling to the east. He hoped they would meet no one. It would be several hours again before they could gain access to another of his alternate trails.

The special trail ended abruptly, feeding into the common track. Bili felt uneasy out in the open, following a path like this. Walking here was risking discovery, but it couldn't be helped.

It was time for the dwarves to scout again, so Wabran and Daniray went ahead. Their path led downward through a narrow defile, bounded on both sides by limestone cliffs. They climbed the sides expecting trouble, but found no one hiding up above or in the few crevices along the path. Relieved, they signaled to the others to follow. Soon everyone joined the dwarves and passed warily through the narrows.

Chapter 16

Surprise Attack

The path continued downward through ever thickening cover. Fir and Ponderosa Pine stood as spires to all the small shrubs and saplings struggling to make a place for themselves in an already overcrowded environment. A few woodpeckers could be heard knocking, inviting unwary bugs and larvae to come outside and join them for dinner. Bili felt relieved that the path was winding through forest again. Yet the gnawing feeling that someone somewhere was monitoring their progress just wouldn't go away. He felt the stone around his neck. It remained cool in its cover. That at least gave him a measure of confidence. He felt there would be no surprises along this section.

The company traveled for another hour quietly wending their way through thickets, around rocky outcrops, and crossing swiftly running streams. The trail began to wind upward again into the face of the mountain. It narrowed here as the trail switched back several times. They crested the top, then started again down the other side. There was less cover on this side facing south, but still enough to hide them from anyone watching for them.

Up ahead lay another narrows through which they would have to pass. Wabran climbed to the top of one side, noting that the sun was beginning its final journey home for the day. He looked intently for intruders. Finding none, he gave the all-clear signal to those behind. Then he worked his way down the other side, giving them time to catch up. Daniray went on ahead looking for tracks made by anyone passing recently. He found only deer tracks and prints of smaller animals. Waiting for Wabran, he looked around. The trees were getting thick again, but that was good. It shouldn't be too long before they would leave the main trail once again to take another seldom-used route westward as suggested by the Old Hermit.

Wabran caught up and began following Daniray down the trail. A chilling snarl caught Wabran in mid-stride. He had time only to turn his head, as a poorly aimed sword bounced off his helm.

"Clang!" The sound echoed along the trail.

Wabran fell forward, pitching headlong down the trail, bowling Daniray over in the process. He lay there stunned for several seconds, helplessly rolling to one side. Daniray was up in a moment, drawing his battle-axe in one fluid motion. Side-stepping his fallen friend, he swung at the advancing goblin. The startled attacker drew back just in time, losing only his sword arm. Wabran, still dazed, staggered up, clumsily swinging his battle-axe, completing the job. The goblin, cut in half, was dead before he hit the ground.

The forest came alive with the sound of crashing feet all around them. Goblins seemed to materialize from nowhere, brandishing spears, their razor sharp edges broken by curled barbs, filled with oozing slime. Amidst a hail of thrown spears, Daniray yelled to Wabran,

"Retreat to the trees on the right. Maybe we can defend ourselves long enough for our friends to reach us."

Holding their round shields to cover their backs, they sprinted for safety, breathing heavily as they ran. Realizing they would be cut off from the main party just starting through the narrows, Daniray shouted again,

"Let's work our way back up the trail. It will give us more time. If we get surrounded, there will be little our friends can do for us."

Angry goblins poured in through the trees, trying by sheer numbers to capture the dwarves. Wabran's head had cleared now. He played a baiting game with them, all the while working his way back toward the narrows. The goblins misinterpreting his intentions as fear, thought only to pin the dwarves against the side of the cliff. Yelping encouragement to one another in their strange tongue, they drove headlong at Wabran. He shouted in the old tongue,

"Hani-pinak!"

With that, he launched himself at the goblins, swinging his mighty battle-axe as he moved. The loud crunch of the blade biting through flesh and bone could be heard above their frantic cries. Wabran was soon covered with gore as several leading goblins lay slain on the ground before him. Daniray had done the same, clearing a path around himself. The goblins yelped in surprise, stumbling over those rushing from behind them, trying to get away from the deadly blades. They fell in a heap.

Two trolls appeared, roughly shoving aside the goblins, clubs swinging as they charged. One crashed through the trees attempting to capture the dwarves. The other ran up toward the narrows, intent on taking the newly spied elves as prisoners.

Wabran swore loudly and took on the troll by himself. He lunged hard, feinting as he came. The troll swung down where Wabran had been, driving his club into the ground. Wabran braced himself, driving his battle-axe deep into the knee of the ugly thing. With an audible "Snap", the leg collapsed, bringing the troll down to the level of the dwarf. Wasting no time, Wabran beheaded him, dragging the grisly trophy behind him. Daniray screamed,

"Make for the narrows! The troll is almost upon the elves. If we don't help kill it, we'll be cut off from the others altogether."

With that, he leaped onto the trail again, slicing through the necks of two goblins hard on the heels of the advancing troll. The leading elves, seeing the fight break out as they came through the narrows, stopped, taking time to draw their bows. Quickly fitting arrows to their strings, they loosed them at the troll lumbering toward them. They stopped momentarily as they saw Daniray crash through the trees behind the troll. The advancing troll, now aware of the dwarf, had turned and began clubbing at Daniray, trying to pin him to one spot long enough to crush him. The four elves kept distracting him, hoping Daniray would be able to get away. They kept driving arrows into his massive neck and face, intent on hitting a vital spot. The troll just kept pulling the arrows out with one hand, while clubbing with the other, turning in frustrating circles Daniray was forcing him into.

"Thwack!" An arrow from above embedded itself into the troll's left eye. He bellowed, enraged at the pain. Plucking the arrow from his eye, he tried to look up, wondering where the arrow had come from. Blood began pouring from the eye, leaving him temporarily blind on that side. Yilmai fitted another arrow, trying to destroy the other eye.

Seeing that the troll would soon pin and kill Daniray, Wabran dropped the troll head, turning to help Daniray escape. Together they hewed the leg of the massive troll, in an attempt to bring him down too. The troll lunged clumsily, falling atop both dwarves, pinning them beneath his tremendous weight. He jabbed his club into them, trying to kill them. Bili, now able to see what was happening, leaped from the rocks above with a spear. Landing, he took aim at the mighty neck, and drove it with all his might into the carotid artery. Blood spurted everywhere. Grabbing the spear as though it were a small stick, the troll used it to flick Bili hard against the narrows wall, knocking him senseless. Ripping the spear clear of his throat, the troll stood up, eyeing his enemies one final time. Bellowing his rage, he stumbled forward. He didn't see the stone to his left, and stumbled over it. Wabran was up and on him again in an instant, hewing and hacking at his neck. With gore all over him, Wabran pulled this head away from the body as well. He knew that if the troll could find its head, it would heal onto itself and they would have to kill it all over again. Daniray had outguessed Wabran and ran back, dragging the head of the first troll into the narrows before the shocked goblins could take possession of it.

Moments later, the goblins and mercenaries had reformed to advance on the elves and two dwarves, keeping an eye on the single elf perched upon the rock. Two goblins sneaked out from the trees, trying to grab hold of the unconscious Bili's boot, but lost their hands in the process. Breagle had joined the fray and had seen them and hurried to stoutly defend the prone body of his friend.

Wulpai came through the narrows, taking in the scene at a glance. Jumping over the lifeless troll body, he helped Breagle

The Chronicles of Salduwe Book One

rescue Bili. Holding an arm each, they dragged him back into the safety of the cliffs, dodging arrows shot hastily at them. One caught Breagle in the leg. He winced in pain, pulling it out as quickly as he could, hoping there was no poison on the point to make the wound fester. Reaching the safety of the rocks, they pulled Bili to one side. Nothing seemed broken, but blood was oozing from his nose and a shallow cut behind his ear. Wulpai took some water and poured it in Bili's face. Spitting and struggling, Bili's eyes opened. Finding himself among friends, he relaxed and lay back, now aware of a thudding headache. Wulpai lifted Bili's head slightly and poured water down his throat.

Sputtering, Bili objected, "I'm all right! I'm all right! What are you trying to do? Drown Me?"

Yilmai looked down, concern changing to amusement. "Nothing's wrong with his mouth anyway," he shouted. Then he turned back to watching the trail ahead.

Goblins hurled spears that fell harmlessly into the mouth of the narrows. The Mercenaries, holding shields, decided to rush the pass and take anyone they could find. Fifteen of them yelled curses, and charged. The elves shot arrows at them, but these simply embedded themselves in the leather-covered shields held by the men. They kept coming, surrounded by swarms of goblins, yelping and yammering their excitement that battle was to be joined.

Wabran and Daniray, now flanked by the two younger dwarves, drew their battle axes and prepared to meet the mercenaries. The elves held their arrows and had drawn their short swords. Yilmai stayed perched above on the rock, bow in hand, watching for openings. Wulpai had drawn his sword, waiting for the clash. Bili, still unstable on his feet, was trying to uncross his eyes. The women were at the rear of the narrows, waiting to see what they should do. The old hermit left them and climbed the rocks, working his way toward Yilmai.

The dwarves took the offensive and charged the few feet down into the mercenary warriors. The loud crack of shields smashing together, and the ring of swords and battle-axes could be heard all over the canyon. Wabran shoved one of the mercenaries, then hewed his legs out from under him as he stepped back. The man screamed in surprise and pain. Another took his place and swung his sword down hard at Wabran's helm. Wabran's shield narrowly deflected the blow.

A sword jabbed at him from the left, driving into his mail shirt, shoved him back a step. Wabran pushed his shield in that direction, swinging his axe from the waist at the same time. He felt the axe cut through bone and knew that he had taken another mercenary out of action.

Beagle, fighting beside him, was hampered by the pain in his leg, but held his own. He traded blow for blow with a heavy mercenary, unusually quick for his size. Breagle was knocked off his feet by a blow from the right, and would have been killed had Wabran not seen the blow coming and deflected it on the handle of his axe. Dropping his shield, he reached for a dirk he had in his belt and drove this hard into the groin of the heavy man. The warrior grunted in surprise, then fell away in deep pain. Breagle gained his footing and was up swinging again.

The elves broke through the ranks of the dwarves from behind and began driving the mercenaries back under punishing blows, their short swords ringing off breastplates and helms. Yilmai found an exposed throat and shot cleanly through it. The man fell dead among his companions. The mercenaries gave way under the merciless blows rained down on them by the three elves, allowing the goblins to slip in around them.

As the mass of goblins attacked, trying to strike the legs from their taller opponents, the mercenaries quickly reformed and pushed in from the right side of the narrow pathway. The dwarves moved in to cut them off and the sound of steel on steel rang loudly along the trail.

The Old Hermit took in the situation at a glance and realized that more mercenaries had entered the enclosed area and were working their way toward the pass. It would be only a matter of time before they joined their companions in driving the dwarves and elves back up the hill. He began to laugh! He started low with deep powerful sounds as though an avalanche was beginning. He rose higher in pitch and continued laughing. Some of the stones nearby began to dislodge. Several fell onto the pathway crushing those pressed against the walls. There were yelps of dismay from the goblins who began to leap away from the falling stones. The Old hermit changed pitch and continued to laugh, this time louder and with more intensity. The ground began to pitch slightly and tremor, as though an earthquake had started. This caught the attention of everyone within sound of the Old Hermit's voice. One by one warriors stopped fighting, puzzled by the power of this laughter. Bili, still groggy from his contact with the rocks, began to smile. That familiar sound from up at the lake seemed to help clear his vision, enabling him to think clearly once again. Bili climbed to his feet, wondering what kind of healing could be embodied in laughter, although he had been taught that laughter was good for you, like medicine. His admiration for the old village shaman continued to grow. If he ever got out of this mess, he determined to sit down with the old man and listen to him. He held a lot of wisdom worth tapping into.

Bili looked around at those fighting. They were all looking up now, staring at where the sound was coming from. Bili turned and looked up as well, to see what he must be missing. When he did, he got the shock of his life.

Bili saw the Old Hermit, not as an old man, but transformed. He appeared as a fell warrior, filled with dreadful power. His image seemed to fill the afternoon sky, warping against the horizon as an image shimmering above the sands of a desert.

The goblins began yelping in dismay, holding their ears, trying to shut out the hurtful noise. The mercenaries, awed by this wondrous apparition, stood as if mesmerized. Two more trolls appeared along the pathway, then began rolling over and over with huge feet slapping the ground, hands to their ears.

Behind them, three Sanguma priests appeared, seemingly unaffected by the laughter. They stood on the trail for a moment looking up at the Old Hermit. They seemed to hesitate, then glanced at one another. They began conferring about something, then pulled small round silver objects from their pockets, chanting as they did so.

A loud humming started among the disks, like the sound of a thousand bees swarming about their nest. As the humming increased, the disks emitted three dull red lights. The sanguma moved these arcs of light until their ends meshed. The power of the light grew dramatically. In unison the Sanguma aimed the single beam at the Old Hermit. The buzzing changed to a pulsating high-pitched frequency, warping the air through which it moved. The Old Hermit staggered momentarily when the beam smashed into him. He put out his hand, pushing against the beam. He began to laugh harder. Everyone stood there watching the confrontation between the priests and the old man. No one dared move or interfere.

As the Old Hermit continued to push against the beam, it seemed to bend for a moment. Then with a loud crack, it turned around, hurling itself back to the senders. Bili saw the beam snap back and burst among the Sanguma priests, incinerating them in an instant. There was only time for a strangled scream before the sound of the explosion drowned everything else. The priests were vaporized, their charred bodies blown in all directions. The concussion knocked those closest to the Sanguma priests to the ground, senseless. Others standing further away, flattened themselves behind what protection they could find, fearing flying debris.

For a moment no one moved. The confrontation of such powerful beings had left everyone, dwarves, elves, humans, trolls, and goblins terrified. During that short interval of time the Old Hermit yelled with authority,

"Make for the old oak half a mile down the trail. Break through the ranks of our enemies before they can recover and try to stop us. Run! Now!"

With that, he leaped from the rocks, shoving down the trail past dazed trolls, goblins and mercenaries. They scrambled frantically to get out of his way.

Meri, Rimwai and Wesip ran after him, flanked by Wulmakai, Yilmai, Wulpai, Bili, Hergeth and Hagred. The remaining elves and dwarves followed closely behind, lashing out with axes or short swords at any foolish enough to get in their way.

Within minutes, they had all arrived at the rendezvous. The Old Hermit led them up into an overgrown area, where he began picking out another trail. The elves covered their tracks as best they could, and quickly caught up to the main party, perspiration dotting their clothing from the exertion. Bili noticed this, and wondered. He had seldom seen elves sweat, even after running for miles through their forests. Was it possible that they were far from their enchanted homeland, and the magic was wearing off? He looked at Wulmakai who was heavily winded from the long sprint. He too was covered in sweat and looking tired.

The Old Hermit left little time for idle speculation. His pace was necessarily hurried, and he urged his friends to all possible speed. They trotted silently, as though they were expecting another assault. Yilmai and Bili exchanged worried glances, nervous that the enemy was so close behind. The usually lighthearted Breagle's brow was furrowed in concentration as he followed closely behind Daniray. Wabran, as usual, was his taciturn self, carrying a scowl, as though inviting an enemy to start something with him. Yilmai was helping Wulmakai negotiate some rough parts of the trail, making sure he wouldn't fall. Some parts were narrow and sharp rocks bounded the pathway on either side. It would be easy to turn an ankle or break a leg on this treacherous pathway.

Wulpai was running right behind the Old Hermit, quietly exchanging ideas. At least that's what Bili surmised they must be doing. They were too far in front for him to hear.

After the group had slowed to a forced-hiked the better part of an hour, loud crashing started below them. Voices began calling to one another.

"I believe they have found our trail," called Daniray. "We're going to have to run for it." He ran on ahead to where Wulpai and the Old Hermit were waiting for him.

"Wulpai will lead you all to a flat topped dome called 'Fortress Rock'", instructed the Old Hermit. "You'll be safe there for a while. Try to sharpen stakes, collect rocks and brush as soon as you get there. We may have to make a stand before the night is through. Now go!"

Wulpai started off along the trail. Everyone followed, but the Old Hermit remained behind. No explanation- he just remained behind. Leading them to the left as they approached the first fork, Wulpai hurried on. There were a series of switchbacks as the trail began to lead upwards. Bili felt like a traitor, leaving the old man to the mercy of the angry, excited mob trying to close in on them. But he knew better than to question that decision. He had looked at the old man momentarily, unformed questions on his lips, then hurried down the trail after the others. The Old Hermit had just winked and patted him on the shoulder, then shoved him none too gently along.

Again the trail forked. Wulpai hesitated for a second, took the right path, this time leading down. Around a couple of curves, the trail began to climb. They made good time, and felt relieved hearing no more sounds of pursuit. An hour of hard hiking brought them to the flat domed bluff. The climb up the steep sides was slippery from scree scattered across the face of the slope, and it took some time to gain the heights. This trail obviously had not been disturbed for some time. It would be hard for anyone to climb the slope without being detected.

Collecting dead shrubs, rocks and anything else they could carry along the way, the small group worked its way toward the top. Wabran and the other dwarves had cut saplings along the way, and were busy sharpening both ends. As they worked their way up the slopes, they drove these stakes into the side of the hill, increasing the difficulty of any attacker trying to make a successful run to the top.

Arriving at the crest, Wulpai gave everyone a few moments to catch his breath then called them together.

"There isn't much daylight left. We're probably going to be attacked sometime during the night. The strength of the trolls and goblins is at it highest at dark.

"Wabran, Daniray, take charge of the northern slope. Build what barricades you can, rock traps, more stakes... anything you can to slow their advance. Bili, you and Yilmai go with them.

"I'll see to the eastern side along with the elves, Hagred and Hergeth. You three women collect as much brush into three piles as you can and bring it all to Breagle. He'll show you how to weave it all into torches. We're going to need firebrands for defense if we're overrun."

Everyone hurried, knowing they had little time to prepare the defense of their hilltop fortress. The dwarves were masters of defense, having lived in caves and mountains all their lives. They were experts with stone, knowing what it could do to others if properly placed in strategic positions. Both Bili and Yilmai had seen them set traps earlier in their travels against the trolls. They eagerly helped where they could, learning a great deal about rockslides.

Before sunset, the eastern side of the hill was bristling with sharpened stakes, and dotted with rockslide traps. Bili shuddered as he looked along the slope, almost feeling sorry for those below who would be hurt or crushed. Then he remembered what kind of beings they were: trolls, who lived on the flesh of others; goblins, whose only thought was cruelty; mercenaries, giving their allegiance to the only god they knew- gold and silver; Sanguma priests, the representatives of the Dark Lord, perpetrators of human sacrifices and other bestialities. *Maybe this is a proper end for those kinds of beings*, Bili thought grimly.

As the sun sank below the mountains, casting shadows of foreboding, the Old Hermit appeared. He looked rather haggard and short of breath. He climbed past the obstructions, eyeing all the preparations made in anticipation of an all out attack during the night. Reaching the top, he paused to catch his breath. Everyone stopped working and hurriedly crowded around him for news.

"I can't tell you a whole lot," the Old Hermit began. "I had to incinerate a couple more Sanguma priests, and sent the rest of the war party down the wrong trails. They'll discover their mistakes before too long and double back. It may have given us a few hours, but they'll eventually track us down.

"I also heard them talking about another group coming in from the West. Apparently they've made more raids on the outposts in that direction. So there's no point in running from here yet. We'd just face them with no particular advantages to help us out. I reckon by morning they'll have this place surrounded. It'll take a miracle for any of us to get out of here alive."

Bili looked at Yilmai. That certainly wasn't the kind of news they'd expected. Things were indeed going from bad to worse, as the old man had predicted. Yilmai shrugged, as if to say whatever happens, happens. In an almost automatic gesture, Bili put his hand to the little bag hung around his neck. Not for the first time he wondered why these gems had ended up in the possession of his sister and himself. *It will definitely be a relief to be shed of these burdens*, Bili muttered to himself. "And...it can't come any too soon!"

The Old Hermit continued, "You've all done a good job of getting ready. I couldn't have asked for better work. Now let's try to get some rest before they find us."

Wulpai set the watches, then with the help of the women, got some soup and meat boiling over a low fire. By the time the food was ready, darkness was upon them. Only Breagle and Hagred managed to sleep; the others were too apprehensive. Most of them spent their time either sharpening their weapons or talking quietly together in small groups. A spirit of dread seemed to hang over their hearts like fog above a river.

Wulpai's call for evening meal cheered the dwarves. Daniray had gone on watch, so Wabran woke Breagle and they brought some life back into the company. Breagle light heartedly told of the dream he had of climbing a tree to get its ripe fruit, only to have the fruit disappear and re-appear on the branch above. He continued to climb after the fruit until he realized that it suddenly was below him. He decided to trick the tree and let go, grabbing at the fruit on the way down before it could disappear. He caught the seat of his pants on a limb, which ripped out, causing him to drop the fruit. He landed at the base of the tree, and looked around for the fruit. It was nowhere to be found. He looked up in the tree again, and there was the fruit on the first branch. He was now too sore to climb again, so he picked up some stones near the tree and threw it at the fruit. The fruit got mad and spit juices at him. Then he got mad himself, found a long branch and tried to hit the fruit. It disappeared and re-appeared on the next branch above. Breagle was still shaking his fist at the tree when Wabran shook him awake. Breagle clipped Wabran's nose before he was awake enough to realize what he was doing.

Everyone laughed at the humor, then dished up soup and meat. Once all had been served, Breagle, as usual, took over and put the fires out. Darkness was to be their constant companion for the coming hours. Heads turned toward the east, eager to spy any signs of approaching enemies. Those near the edges kept a wary eye out for torches along the pathways leading to the rock. They were hoping to elude the hunters as long as possible. Clouds began gathering to the West of them, working their way slowly across the dark sky. A slight wind arose, bringing a chill to the camp.

Bili, worn out from all the excitement earlier, was beginning to tire. He moved over toward Yilmai and said,

"I'm feeling tired. I need to take a nap if I'm going to make it through tonight without falling asleep. What about you? How are you doing?"

Yilmai replied, "I'm not tired. Just worried. You sleep and if I see anything at all, or hear anything unusual, I'll wake you immediately."

"Thank you, my friend," Bili said, breaking out his bedroll. He pulled the blanket over himself and was soon fast asleep.

Yilmai smiled to himself, marveling at the quick emotional changes humans could make; one moment nervous, apprehensive, and the next, calm and peaceful to the point of being able to sleep. *Maybe it has something to do with the food they eat*, Yilmai chuckled to himself. *They usually do seem to be in better moods after they have eaten.* Yilmai knew he wouldn't be able to sleep until he knew the outcome of this battle. He spent his time waxing the string on his bow. He wanted to be **very** ready when the enemy decided to strike.

Chapter 17
The Passing of Two Great Warriors

An ominous silence seemed to settle on the darkened forest below the rock fortress. The night birds no longer warbled to one another in the trees. The crickets ceased to chirp. It was as though the very trees held their breath in apprehension. The wind had ceased again- nothing stirred. The silence was oppressive, and the darkness covered any movements that occurred below.

Yilmai felt a sense of dread enter his heart as he too succumbed to slept. In spite of his earlier promise to remain awake and alert, he found he suffered the effects of fighting and fleeing from those who sought their capture. Sharpening his knife for the fifth time didn't bring peace to his heart. He had thrown his knife into the ground in frustration, tired of the waiting game. Facing the unknown drained him of his vitality. Maybe Bili was right. Sleep might do him good. It was better than brooding over something he couldn't control, nor avoid.

Finally, making the decision and grabbing a blanket from his pack, he settled himself against a mound of dirt and stone, and moodily covered himself. He lay there thinking of home, wishing for a moment he could set foot in the sacred forests. How far away his homeland seemed to him now; how remote his family felt as well. All these were but pleasant memories in a world recently turned upside-down by conflict. Depression was beginning to gnaw away at his heart. He didn't like it.

In spite of those feelings, Yilmai found himself nodding off. Trying to stay awake once or twice, he realized the futility of fighting sleep; he might as well rest. Perhaps sleep would lift his black mood. Finally giving in to his body's needs, he fell into heavy slumber.

About the third watch, the guards began hearing noises in the forest below. Straining to hear, they moved forward among the stakes and rocks placed there earlier. They could hear muffled voices conversing. There was an occasional shout as others, moving into the area, identified one another.

The guards hurried back to the center of camp, where the Old Hermit sat resting. He looked up at them.

"So they've finally found us have they?" he said, resignation written on his tired face.

"It would seem so, sir," the anxious elf replied. "There is a lot of commotion going on down there. It sounds as though several groups have come together, possibly making plans to storm the hill in hopes of a quick capture. What do you suggest?"

The Old Hermit smiled. "You had better wake everyone, so we'll be prepared to meet our guests upon their arrival. Get the women to start at least one of the fires, so we'll have light up here. I don't want any more confusion than necessary if our defenses are breached."

One guard returned to his post, while his elven companion circled the camp waking the sleepers. Bedding was put away and everyone took the packs with what provisions were left, placing them towards the back of the bluff, away from the fighting. The Old Hermit looked towards the North, wondering whether there might be any route of escape if they were overrun. The bluff ended in sheer cliffs that towered 200 feet above the forests below. There was a narrow track to the west, but he had never taken time to see whether it led anywhere other than to a small cave.

Bili placed his pack with the others, then went over to check on the women. They were busy lighting the fire as instructed. Meri had set up her bow and arrows, so she could reach them at a moment's notice. She had waxed her bowstring, and had lined up the arrows in such a way she could get off three or four quick shots before an enemy could seize her. Wesip had her short sword strapped to her side, thrusting two knives behind her belt as well. She checked her boot knife just to make sure it was in place. Rimwai had set her bow on the opposite side of the fire to Meri, but her arrows were loosely placed in a quiver tied to the center of her back. Bili looked with satisfaction on their readiness. He turned to Wesip, taking a small animal horn off his shoulder.

"If anyone breaks through our defenses and gets to you, blow this horn. It will alert those of us up front that we need to break away and help you. Here tie it around your neck." He reached out to put the horn over Wesip's head. She took the occasion to embrace Bili.

"Be careful." she whispered. "I think these trolls and goblins want revenge, not prisoners. We've shamed them by evading their scouting parties."

She hugged him closely, desperately trying to calm her shaking hands. She was afraid, in spite of having been battle trained. She felt warmth and security in Bili's arms.

Bili was caught by surprise, but pleased. He dropped the horn over her neck, and hugged her in return. He knew that some of his friends would die here tonight, maybe himself included. He silently prayed they would somehow survive until morning light. Bili gave Wesip a tight squeeze, holding her close to him. Then he released her, looking into her eyes, emotions clouding his vision. A catch in his throat prevented him from speaking. He smiled reassuringly, then let her go.

Clearing his throat, he said to Meri, "Cover our backs. There are at least two trails up the face, and some of the goblins may get through. We'll do what we can to prevent them from getting to you."

Bili hugged Meri too, then turned and walked quickly to join Yilmai, who had talked in low tones to Rimwai, then headed to the edge of the cliff. Bili found him already looking down at the foe below them. In the dark it was hard to tell their number, but from the noise, Bili guessed there must be many.

"It sounds like several groups of goblins and trolls forming up down there." Bili said to break the silence.

Yilmai didn't answer. He just continued to stare. Bili glanced at him, then looked down again, wondering at the silence of his friend. Wulpai joined them, several arrows bunched in his left hand. Shaking his head he said quietly, "I can smell trolls. There must be a dozen of them down there. I hear some northern talk too, so there must also be a group of mercenaries. The groups that attacked the fort to the west must have joined those who are after us."

"Do you think they have any prisoners with them?" Bili asked nervously.

"If they haven't slain them all, I would guess they have a few." Wulpai replied.

"That's reassuring." Bili said sourly.

"Those groups are in a nasty mood right now," Wulpai reminded him. "They are on the hunt for the Dark Lord. They are free to do anything they like as long as they bring back useful prisoners to interrogate. They'll try to kill as many of us as possible in the beginning, then isolate and capture those of us who are still alive. If they break through our defenses, stick together. We'll have a better chance of survival."

On that note, Wulpai moved off toward the dwarves. Breagle turned as Wulpai approached, a grim smile creasing his dwarven features. Shaking his fist toward the cliffs, he grated softly,-

"If it's a fight they want, we're ready. I'm tired of running like a rabbit from a burrow. Let them have at us! They'll feel the bite of cold steel before this night's ended!"

Again he shook his fist towards the growing crowd below. Wabran stood impassively, looking down, then growled a remark.

"Just cover my back, cousin. I'll look after yours."

Wulpai clasped Breagle's left shoulder in a reassuring gesture, then moved off soundlessly into the night.

Bili watched them from the corner of his eye, remarking to Yilmai, "The dwarves really do become resolute when cornered. I think they would fight to the death rather than run, even if given the chance."

Yilmai finally looked over. "They have a highly developed sense of honor, you know. They'll give their lives protecting that honor, rather than suffer shame and go on living. They're a great foe in a conflict for that very reason. Retreating for them is hard. Wabran is one of the few that have overcome that dwarf weakness. That's why he's such a warrior of great renown."

"Among other things!" grinned Bili. "It helps to be as strong as a bull in his prime."

Bili's humor was catching, in spite of their circumstances.

"I hope he doesn't get wounded. I'd hate to be the one stuck with dragging him off to a healer. He must be 100 kilos. I swear he could lift a troll off the ground and throw him over a cliff if he got angry enough!"

"Heaven help the trolls tonight!" Bili replied lightly.

Hagred and Hergeth, who had joined them, smiled silently in reply.

The clashing of spears on shields interrupted Bili's answer. Great war cries echoed from below. The defenders on the top, startled, looked down into the darkness. Up the side of the fortress charged three great trolls, flanked by dozens of goblins. The side of the mountain seemed to be torn up by the savageness the trolls displayed in their charge. Rocks and dirt sprayed down on the goblins, as they tried to keep pace with their much larger companions.

Wabran watched impassively as they approached. At the last moment, he swung his battle-axe, severing the thick vine holding the logs to the first rockslide. With a deafening roar, logs, rocks and debris hurtled into the attackers. When the dust cleared, no goblins were to be seen, and only one troll remained. Angry yammering and yells filled the canyon as others rushed to take their place, careful to avoid getting crushed. The troll let out a loud bellow as he impaled a leg on one of the stakes. Angrily he pulled it out, then hurled it up at the defenders. It flew wide of the mark, but was met with a hail of arrows from the elves, trying the blind the ugly creature almost upon them now.

Wulpai, seeing that the troll would act as a distraction while others worked their way up the fortress, quickly wrapped an old rag around one of his arrows, and dipped it into a bit of pine pitch. Sticking it into the fire the women had started, the pitch ignited. Running to the edge of the bluff, he took careful aim and loosed the arrow. It embedded itself into the exposed neck.

The startled troll bellowed in amazement, losing his footing in an attempt to get away from the cursed fire. He fell heavily to one side, and rolled down the mountain beating at the flames. He took several unfortunate goblins with him.

Loud cheers went up from the dwarves and elves. Yilmai let out a wild shout of jubilation, then ran to get himself some pitch and a couple of lighted embers from the fire. Bili stood at the edge keeping watch while his friend brought back what he wanted.

"Now I know how to handle the rest of the trolls when they try to breach our defenses," Yilmai boasted. "I'm saving most of my arrows for them."

Bili smiled grimly, "I hope we can get arrows from the goblins we kill. From the sounds of things down there, we'll run short of arrows long before we run short of targets."

There was a second rush up the hill. This time there were no trolls, but several mercenaries had joined to drive the goblins before them. They were met again with a hail of arrows, many finding their mark. The goblins replied with arrows of their own, shot from the middle of their ranks. The dwarves hid behind their shields until most of them had gone by. The elves hid behind their leather shields, then spun around to loose a deadly volley of their own. The goblins kept coming. A group of closely clustered mercenaries pushed through the goblins and drove toward the dwarves. Wabran shouted a warning, then leaped over the stone filled barricade to engage them. Breagle swore, leaping over the defenses himself, nearly landing on the closest mercenary.

The fighting was fierce for several minutes. Wabran had killed the mercenary closest to him, and was busily engaged with the second, a great bull of a man. They were evenly matched. Breagle was fighting to his left, thrusting and parrying stroke for stroke with another. The two remaining dwarves worked their way to the right, getting behind their enemies, trying to encircle them. A stray arrow from one of the goblins took the lead dwarf, Beman, in the throat. Giving a gurgling cry, he fell from the mountain, where his body was chopped in pieces by the goblins. Daniray looked helplessly on as the wild yammering and yelping of conquest sounded from below.

From the corner of his eye, Wabran had watched his comrade Beman fall to his death. He heard the cries of the goblins below and knew what was going on. Greatly angered he drove viciously underneath the larger opponent, and drove the sharpened sides of his battle pike upward, ripping his belly wide. The startled mercenary gave an anguished scream, falling backward to his death. Wabran moved relentlessly on, ripping apart foe after foe to assuage the grief and anger he felt. Breagle fought and killed along side of him, understanding the anger that drove him.

The elves, seeing that the dwarves had over extended themselves, drew their short swords and leaped the barricades. Bili and Wulpai did the same, well to the left of them. They drove through the ranks of the goblins, slaying them on all sides as they went. The goblins yet alive hurriedly retreated behind the mercenaries, fearful of the powerful blades cutting great swaths in their ranks.

Wulpai was first to reach the dwarves, and helped dispatch three more mercenaries. Turning to Wabran, he said,

"Enough! We're well down the side of the cliff. If we go further, we're open targets for those below us. Return to the defenses and let them continue to come after us. It's our only chance."

Wabran, his eyes still battle glazed, didn't respond. He kept driving the remaining mercenaries down the mountain. Daniray rushed toward Wabran and grabbed him, and together with Brell, the other dwarf who had fought this far down the cliff, managed to restrain him. Realizing he was in no immediate danger and was once more among friends, Wabran came to his senses. He stopped struggling and turned to climb the hill.

Upon reaching the top, he shook his fist at those down below and roared, "I will be avenged on you for the death of Beman." Then he turned and made his way toward the fire, where Meri handed him a cup of coffee. He gulped it down in two or three mouthfuls, then returned to the edge to wait for the next assault. Breagle also made his way to the fire, tears still smudging his face. He accepted the coffee gratefully, his face an open book of sorrow. Meri attempted words of comfort, but was unable to speak. The Old Hermit put a hand on Breagle's arm and asked quietly, "Is this the first friend you've lost to fighting?"

Breagle mutely shook his head "yes" and turned quickly away, overcome by grief at what had taken place. He too went back to the edge after setting the emptied cup near the fire. Wesip looked helplessly at Rimwai, who nodded her resignation and turned to pour more coffee for the others who had arrived.

The Old Hermit looked up into the sky, which had begun to send down a fine mist. There was no moon visible at all, so he guessed the cloud cover must be heavy. Fearing it might rain heavily in the next few hours, he returned to the women with four long stakes. Cutting into the ground with his sword, he forced two stakes upright, then attached a wide bit of cloth he had gotten from his pack. He stretched this across the two uprights, then spread the other end out on the ground. He then tied the two loose ends to the remaining stakes, and pulled the whole thing upright, forcing the other two poles into the ground. This made an effective cover over the fire. Bili came by and saw what he had done, so he helped collect the brush from the other two piles and place it all under the hastily erected pavilion.

There had been no noise from the canyon area now for some time. This upset Wabran, who had been in many skirmishes during the past several years. He knew the enemy was up to something, but was unable to figure out just what it might be. Bili came along side him and stared into the darkness.

"Is there any way we can figure out what they're planning?" Bili asked, more to himself than to the dwarf. He knew his friend was still very angry about the death of his comrade.

Surprisingly, Wabran turned to Bili, a look of grim determination on his face.

"I plan to slip over the side of the lip into the darkness and see if I can spot anything. Would you and Yilmai cover my retreat? I may be spotted before I regain the heights."

"I'd rather go with you, than just hide and spot," Bili said, determination edging his voice.

"No, I'll go alone." Wabran replied gruffly. "One solitary figure is less likely to be spotted, and makes a smaller target in a forced retreat. But thanks for the support my young friend. I'll not forget."

Bili left him momentarily and pulled Yilmai from where he was hiding. Together they sought Wabran in the shadows off to the right. A narrow track led down into the darkness. Wabran, a black traveling cloak covering his features, was carefully working his way off the mountain. Soon he was lost to sight. Yilmai, whose sight was better in the dark than Bili's finally gave up and sat there immobile, waiting.

Off to the right, they heard a stone dislodged. Yilmai turned his head slowly, carefully. He could see nothing. Bili froze in position, his hand working its way slowly to his dagger. They both waited, scarcely daring to breathe. A twig snapped near the same place. Yilmai touched Bili lightly on the shoulder, and pulled him gently, signaling that they should work their way up the hill just a little, in the shelter of a large boulder. Bili followed Yilmai, careful not to dislodge anything or make noise, giving their position away.

"What do you think is going on over there?" Bili whispered hoarsely. "Is someone waiting for Wabran to return so he can ambush him?"

"We'll just have to wait and see," countered Yilmai. "I just hope I'm fast enough to get him before he has a chance to hurt Wabran."

Yammering and calling started down below, near the place where Wabran had hidden himself. Bili tensed, wondering whether Wabran had been spotted. He looked toward the right where some enemy was cleverly hidden. He had not shifted or made further noise. Yilmai picked up his bow, fitting an arrow to it, and stood facing the right. Bili, dagger now in hand, waited.

Suddenly, Wabran appeared below in the shadows, running hard, a group of goblins and mercenaries closing in on him. Yilmai decided to take a chance, and loosed an arrow toward the unseen foes. There was a sharp cry as his arrow found a mark. Bili jumped out, warning Wabran, "Keep running back to the fortress! They're right behind you!"

Startled by the outcry, the goblins and mercenaries paused, giving Yilmai time to catch two others in the throat. Those hiding in the shadows gave war cries, yammering and screaming their hatred. They called in the goblin tongue, but it was already too late. The trio had fled the trap and were almost to the barricades. The elves on watch covered their retreat, sending a volley of arrows in the direction of the noise.

Breagle, on watch above, realized what was going on, and timing their arrival as best he could in the darkness, cut loose another of the rockslides. Boulders, logs and dirt crashed down on the intruders, destroying any hope of launching a successful attack. But behind the slide appeared two trolls and a group of Sanguma priests. The trolls rolled boulders and broken bodies from their pathway, and lumbered on toward the barricades. Ten or more mercenaries, shields in place surrounded the priests, swords drawn.

Shouting to the others, Breagle grabbed his shield and ran to join his comrades down on the left. Wulpai and the Old Hermit rushed to join Brell and the four elves watching anxiously for any sign of movement in the dark shadows below them. Hergeth stayed to help stoke the fires and protect the women, but Hagred grabbed burning embers and chunks of burning pitch, rushing them to the barricades.

Yilmai was first to gain the heights. He grabbed two of the arrows he had prepared, and lit them in Hagred's burning pitch. Waiting his chance, he released the first arrow at the leading troll. It lodged in his neck, burning his beard, and causing panic. The troll staggered back, plucking out the arrow. He fell heavily, but only into the other troll. Neither fell from the narrow trail, and soon both were advancing on the defenders a second time, seemingly oblivious to the arrows that lodged in their unprotected legs and arms. Wulpai pulled the fletched feathers off on the flat side of both his pitched arrows before lighting them, hoping one would find its mark. Dipping them both into the embers until they were bubbling and spewing, he set them both to the bowstring. Taking aim at the second troll, he released smoothly, sending both arrows spinning. They spread apart several inches by the time they arrived at their target. The first troll, seeing them come, halted momentarily as he tried swatting them down. He missed. The troll following, was busy maneuvering around a block in the trail, and never saw them coming. They struck him squarely in the face as he looked up. One drove into his left eye socket, while the other tore through his cheek and into his throat. He bellowed in pain, grasping at both arrows. Brell leaped down from the barricade to hew away at the troll's right knee. Swinging his mighty battleaxe, he cut through tendon and bone to bring the great oaf down. As his head lolled within reach, two quick strokes severed it from his neck. Brell grabbed the head and raced back to the barricade amidst a shower of arrows from the group advancing from the shadows on the right. The clang of arrows bouncing off mail shirt and helm continued until he was pulled to safety. The headless body slowly arched off the trail, bouncing against the mountain in its heedless journey to the ravine below.

Bili cheered as the troll disappeared then prepared to meet the one now ripping at the barricade, trying to breach the wall of rubble. Goblins seeing their champion at the wall, rushed forward in swarms now, leaving the shadows in great boldness. Bili looked over at them, wondering what motivated them to take such chances, leaving the relative safety of the rocks?

Then the troll was upon them. Laying about with his huge club, he scattered everyone. Wabran ducked, dived, and rolled to one side, getting behind his foe. The troll took notice of him and turned to swing again and yet again at Wabran. As he spun chasing the wryly dwarf, Breagle and Brell chased around him trying to hew at his huge legs. Duranor, leader of the elves, hurried over with a spear, trying to jab past the armor plated joints into exposed flesh. Bili saw him and ran to help him bring down the troll, leaving the three younger elves to fend off the goblins storming the barricade.

Leaping upon a large boulder, Bili boldly launched himself onto the neck of the troll. Locking his legs around the thick neck, he drew his dagger and thrust it deeply into the right eye. The troll grabbed at the dagger, taking Bili's wrist with it. He yanked Bili off, but not before his other eye felt the second dagger push its way in. Dropping Bili, he reached for the second dagger, only to be brought down finally by the two dwarves. Sagging heavily, he collapsed by the boulder, nearly crushing Bili against it. As the troll attempted to roll onto his side, Wabran beheaded him. With a yell of triumph, he threw the head into the fire near the women. Bili and the two westerners rushed over shouting victory chants and began rolling the huge body toward the edge of the cliff.

"Eiyee," screamed Rimwai, as blood and hot ashes spattered her. She slapped at herself as the ashes burned through her clothing.

Disgust briefly marked her face as she wiped the remaining gore from her face and arms. She struggled to gain control of herself. Wesip grabbed a broken branch and shoved the head back into the center of the fire where the hot coals soon charred what remained.

"Rimwai!" Meri shouted. "Are you alright? I have some salve here to put on your burns. Quickly before you become infected. You don't want to contract "troll madness!" She grabbed Rimwai by her wrist and began dabbing the salve along both arms.

"Troll madness?" asked Wesip. "What is that?"

"It comes from the blood or saliva of trolls," called Meri. "Once it gets into your blood stream or you get it in your mouth and it burns the soft tissues there, it corrupts the blood in the body. It takes a few days, but eventually it lodges in the brain and makes you crazy. I've never seen it, but our shaman has stories about seeing several people during a war with trolls and goblins. One returned home but soon went crazy and leaped over a cliff in his madness."

"I hope we elves are not as easily affected as you humans, Meri. I must admit though, I'm really frightened about this," Rimwai managed to blurt out shakily.

Loud yells of dismay from the barricade interrupted them. The Old Hermit hurried to join the elves and Wulpai.

Emerging from the shadows was an evil creature of unknown origin. His red eyes bespoke cruelty, his slavering tongue, greediness for flesh of any kind. He carried no weapon, nor wore he any armor. He was a primeval creature, summoned from the depths. He lumbered toward them using heavy guttural sounds from an old forgotten language, and cursed the elves. They seemed to wilt under the barrage of curses. Fear could clearly be seen on their surprised faces.

Turning, then, toward the fire and seeing the Old Hermit, he bellowed a raspy challenge.

"So we meet again Old One!" he exclaimed. "You have had your way long enough," he spat. "The powers you fought to destroy have come back again to haunt you! We will be more than a match for you and your kind this time! You'll not get away again old man!"

The Old Hermit, looked at the creature, as though attempting to size him up. A look of bewilderment crossed his face momentarily. He moved closer for another look, then suddenly began laughing, sensing the great power beneath the huge ugly body.

His laugh enraged the beast-man that charged forward, eyes glowing, ignited by fury. Wulpai stood by the Old Hermit, drawn sword in hand. As the creature advanced, runes appeared on that sword, glowing brightly in the dark. The runes began dancing long the length of the blade, then onto Wulpai's arm. Wulpai blanched at the pain he felt, almost dropping his sword. Strange sensations began coursing through his body, making him giddy at first. He stumbled to keep his balance as it continued. He almost fell backwards, but a feeling of strength, filling him with courage, stabilized him. As the Old Hermit continued to laugh, Wulpai boldly stepped out from the barricade to meet the creature.

Giving a contemptuous laugh of glee the creature hissed,

"Yeesss, fool, come to me! I am hungry for bad fle-esh tonight. You shall make a fine dinner along with your bearded companion." The creature partially closed his eyes for an instant as though squinting in the sunlight. Suddenly they opened, hurling red hot bolts of power at Wulpai. The bolts bounced off the sword with a loud "Zap," shielding Wulpai as he attempted to work his way over the debris to engage the creature. "Zing! Zot! Zong!" Several more angry bolts hurled across the short space separating them, knocking Wulpai to his knees.

Bili and Yilmai watched in amazement as the creature continued to advance. Wulpai appeared to be overmatched! He staggered under yet a third blast of power. The creature roared his pleasure, knowing he would eat well tonight. He advanced again, hurling more power as Wulpai desperately thrust out at him trying to find a weakness. The sword cut through the thick hide of the creature and into its thigh, creating a blinding flash of light and thick acrid smoke.

The creature staggered back, swinging its huge ugly paw of a hand. Wulpai's sword was knocked from his hand, as he fell heavily to one side. The creature roared again, sending yet another burst of energy into Wulpai. He screamed in agony, Then lay still, unconscious on the trail.

Chapter 18

Wesip is Captured

A horn sounded in the background. Two, three blasts, one closely following another; then silence. Bili almost missed the sounds, so intent was he on helping Wulpai against the creature. The sound of the Old Hermit's powerful laughter nearly drowned the urgent calls of the horn as well.

Bili suddenly realized the women were in trouble. He broke off his attack, pounding furiously back toward the fire. Meri was releasing her last arrow as he arrived. Hagred lay on the ground, two arrows in one leg, a vicious cut on the other. Rimwai was holding a large firebrand that she had used to club a goblin into senselessness.

"Where's Wesip?" Bili yelled, panic welling up in his heart!

"Goblins have taken her," Rimwai screamed. "Over there by the path."

Bili, stopping only to pick up a fallen spear and thrust a fallen dagger into his belt, raced to the pathway, panic written all over his ashen face.

What if they killed her before I could reach them? Bili reasoned. What if I'm unable to find them and rescue Wesip? A thousand thoughts, each worse than the first, jammed their way into his mind, screaming to be heard!

Bili stopped, trying to get hold of himself. He knew he desperately needed to bring a measure of calm to his tattered nerves if he hoped to make any sensible decisions. He stopped momentarily to breathe deeply, centering on thoughts of peace, blotting out all intrusive thoughts, following the techniques he had been taught by his master back in the village. He dropped briefly to utter a prayer for help.

Instinctively he reached for the talisman. He slipped it from its pouch, and as he did, it glowed faintly. Concentrating his will toward it, and trying to attune himself again to the stone's frequency, his feelings of desperation began to fade. It's gentle pulsing seemed to reach out and fill him with peace. For a moment he felt as though he was standing beside himself watching someone else in his body. As the pulsing increased, the stone itself began to glow brightly, providing light. Aware once again of the urgency, Bili pulled himself from the sweet wash of the stone. It stopped immediately. The roaring in his ears ceased as he came to his senses.

Taking another deep breath, he leapt up starting down the pathway. Three or four turns later, he found himself facing the entrance to a cave. He entered without hesitation, anxious to find Wesip. Holding the stone above his head with one hand, and clutching the spear in the other, he looked for tracks. He had found fresh footprints of at least one goblin in the mud near the entrance. He hurried on, knowing the goblins would be rushing through the passages attempting escape. He settled into a jogging trot and ran as quietly as possible. Coming to a fork, he hesitated only a moment. The odor was strong in the left passage, so he hurried along its dark corridors; he was confident he had found their trail.

Rounding a section that had some fallen stones, he heard scuffling and sounds of cursing and swearing. Knowing someone was putting up a struggle, his hopes began to rise. Bili started running, intent on overtaking the goblins. He broke out into a wide cavern with multiple exits. He caught sight of someone disappearing through a passage on the right. He raced to that entrance, ready for a struggle. He had barely passed through when he ran into the rear guard, sword drawn, ready to stop him. Bili, noting blood oozing from a torn left shoulder, hesitated only a moment. Releasing the stone, he gripped the spear with both hands, parried the blow aimed at him and ran his opponent through. The goblin clutched the shaft as he crumbled to the floor. Bili pulled the spear free, retrieved the stone, then jumped over the prone body now covered with blood. He hurried on and as he did, he could hear Wesip attempting to slow her captors, hoping someone would catch up and rescue her.

A dull thud sounded in the passage. Suddenly the sounds of struggling ceased. Unable to discern its source, Bili lightened his footfalls as he continued his relentless pursuit. Holding the stone above his head again, he shortened the distance. Descending several carved stairs, he could see ahead as the passage veered to the left. He approached this with caution, expecting trouble. He found part of the floor fallen in, leaving a large chasm dropping off many feet into the darkness. Carefully, he sidestepped this, and plunged on. Coming to the end of this section, he caught sight of two goblins carrying the body of Wesip between them. They turned as they noticed the light. Dropping her, they drew their swords and prepared to fight.

Bili lowered the light, loosed his sword in its scabbard, and moved forward. He watched both goblins carefully, trying to decide which of the two to attack first. The goblins made the decision for him. They both rushed him, attempting to knock him from his feet. Bili moved to one side and lowered his spear, firmly placing the butt against a protruding rock. The leading goblin, seeing the point, feinted to the left, and avoided it. The second warrior tried to get past on the opposite side, but Bili swung it at the last second, impaling him. Bili instinctively dove to one side narrowly avoiding a sword that whistled past his ear. He was up in an instant, sword in hand, and turned, blocking the blows aimed at him by this remaining goblin.

Ugly snarls punctuated each thrust and stroke as the goblin sought to find a weakness. Bili maneuvered sideways, trying to keep the goblin from getting past him. He decided to protect Wesip at all costs. For all his size, the goblin fought well, and Bili was hard pressed to keep from being bested by his smaller opponent. Realizing he had thrust a dagger in his belt, he withdrew it with his left hand, and used this to parry the next blow while pushing the goblin back. The goblin stumbled for a moment against a large rock, then scrambled around it and thrust at Bili. Bili retreated from the sword point. The goblin stepped up on the rock and launched himself at Bili in a twisting motion, hoping to drive his point into a vulnerable spot as he dived past. Bili had seen this maneuver before. Dropping the dagger, he went to one knee with his sword held high in both hands. The goblin's sword thrust went high as Bili's blade found its mark in the goblin's swarthy neck. Gurgling in death throes, he hit the floor and rolled into the wall. He lay there bleeding profusely from a severed artery. He was soon dead.

Bili retrieved his dagger, got up and hurried to Wesip. She had a huge welt on her forehead. He picked her up gently, and started back along the passage. Looking back over his shoulder, he wondered how much time he had before other goblins found their way into these passages, or found these bodies and gave chase.

Bili chided himself for running off alone, like the hero he knew he wasn't. He had done it impulsively in order to save Wesip. He was proud he had managed to rescue her by himself, but now he felt exposed, vulnerable. She had not regained consciousness, and this worried him. If she was able to stumble along on her own with him, they had a better chance of regaining the bluff. Having to carry her the whole way would slow their escape. He would also have to lay her down to fight off the goblins if they caught him. There was no way out of this one, and he was keenly aware of his plight.

Turning a corner he remembered passing, he stepped over the fallen body of his first attacker. It was then that he noticed a slight trickle of water down the side of the wall. Setting Wesip's body against the cavern's rough side for a moment, he tore off a short piece of cloth from his shirt. Moistening it as best he could, he laid this against the lump on Wesip's forehead. He dabbed at it a couple of times, then put more water onto the cloth. He wiped her face with it, non-too gently, to see how deeply under she was. Wesip gave a low moan as he continued. Once more he placed the cloth under the water, then touched it to the lump. This time Wesip moaned, reaching up to push the cloth away. She opened her eyes tentatively, blinked a couple of times trying to focus. When she recognized Bili, she hugged him in relief.

Bili, anxious to be away, spoke in low tones.

"Do you think you can stand? The goblins will be after us again shortly, and we need to gain the bluff. We may be re-captured if we don't get some help."

Wesip nodded weakly, and with help was able to stand. She was dizzy for a moment, then stumbled forward, off-balance, holding on to Bili's shoulder. They worked their way upward, along the winding passages. Bili followed his own footprints through the intersections, careful not to make a wrong turn. Glancing back occasionally, he was relieved they had not yet been discovered.

His hopes were short lived. As they hurried along the tunnels, he began to hear yammering and shouting behind him. Wesip, in spite of a splitting headache, knew their only chance lay in speed. Being warrior trained, she immediately hardened her resolve against the pain. Stumbling from time to time, she trotted as quickly as she could. The goblins were gaining. She wasn't able to run fast enough. Nauseated, she stopped momentarily to retch. Precious moments were lost. She groaned, then stumbled on.

Hurrying through another junction, Bili yelled to Wesip. "This way. You're going down the wrong passage!"

Grabbing her hand, he yanked her none too gently after him, nearly causing her to fall again. Pointing her to the right one, he yelled, "Go ahead. I want to see how much of a lead we have on them. I'll join you when I'm done. Here, take my dagger."

Handing it to her, he ran back to the passage from which they had emerged, and waited. Looking around for some way to block the mouth of the passage, or at least constrict it, he found several large boulders. Leaning against one of them, he managed to move it only a couple of inches. Propping himself against another stone, he shoved harder. It began to roll. Bili kept shoving, trying to keep it moving, and rolled it into the entrance. The slight slope of the floor helped the boulder to gain momentum. It rolled down the passage occasionally bumping against the sides.

Bili didn't wait for the results. He ran after Wesip, hoping the boulder would crush some of the goblins that had just entered that passage. It took him a couple of minutes to catch up, and when he did he was winded. Wesip was moving steadily now, doing her best to reach the entrance. She halted so suddenly that Bili bumped into her.

"What's wrong?" Bili asked roughly, both surprised and irritated.

"Someone's coming up ahead," she replied. "It may be more goblins. No telling how many entrances this cave has."

Bili pulled her with him into a niche. They waited breathlessly as the intruder approached. Bili had his sword drawn and ready to use. Wesip held the dagger tightly, ready to defend herself.

A low burning ember shed some light down the tunnel as someone moved closer. Bili clutched his sword tightly, coiled like a spring, ready to pounce. A pair of buckskin trousers and shirt went past.

"Yilmai," Bili's hoarse whisper sounded loud in the passage.

Yilmai turned, startled. He knew his friend's voice. Holding the small torch above his head, he could see Bili, with Wesip hidden behind him.

"Phew! I'm relieved you two are all right." he breathed. "I saw you leave, but wasn't sure what was happening. I got away as quickly as I could. Meri and Hergeth told me what happened, so I followed. Your footprints weren't too hard to spot."

"I'll tell you everything when we get to the top. The goblins aren't far behind."

Yilmai led the way, with Wesip protected between them. They hurried to the entrance, only a couple of hundred yards ahead. Yilmai's ember was almost spent. Bili had put the stone back in its leather pouch. There was little light.

Coming out of the cave, they heard a lot of commotion ahead. Running to where Meri and Rimwai were piling all the brush on the fire, they stopped, their hearts filled with a dread chill. The Old Hermit was laughing, sword in hand, doing battle with some dark creature, this one mounted on a hideous bat-like flying bird. They were exchanging blows, all the while the bird thing attempted to claw the Hermit. Wulpai, conscious again, was fighting to work his way around the bird. He waited his chance to strike at a vulnerable spot. The elves and dwarves were doing their best to keep the goblins and Sanguma from over-running the barricades.

Realizing they would be set upon from both sides if they didn't do something quickly, Bili called to Yilmai

"We need to find enough rubbish and stone to block the pathway. If we don't, we'll be penned in soon."

Yilmai nodded, as they both rushed back toward the cave. Finding only small boulders, they began heaping these across the path. It wasn't much, but it would slow the goblins somewhat. Yilmai checked his quiver. He had only eight arrows left. That certainly wasn't enough to ward off a determined attack. He ran back to the fire to see if any more lay there. Rimwai gave him all but three of hers. Meri decided to join him near the path, arrows in hand. Rimwai stayed to tend the fire with Wesip.

It became apparent to Bili that they were going to lose this battle. It was only a matter of time. They were running out of arrows, and two of their company had been killed. Beman the dwarf had been taken by a goblin arrow.

Yilmai approached from the rear.

"Bili, I have some more bad news. While you were gone, Riyokai, the cousin-brother of Durathor was hit by Sanguma fire as he rushed to the barricade to engage the goblins."

"What?" exclaimed Bili in shock.

"That's not all!" Yilmai whispered fiercely. "Durathor took an arrow in the thigh trying to rescue his body, and Wulmakai was hit in the shoulder by a stray arrow as well. He's okay, but it was too close for comfort. We can't afford to lose him now!"

Bili offered no reply. He realized it wouldn't take long to overrun the fortress and overpower them by sheer numbers. At least that is the way things appeared.

Glancing up again longingly at the darkness overhead, Bili wondered how long it would be before first light. *Surely dawn can't be too far away*, he prayed desperately. *If only we can hold out until then, we may be able to figure a way out of this mess.*

The goblins interrupted his thoughts for they were soon upon them. They came out of the caves like angry bees buzzing from their jostled nest. Running toward the fortress, they came to the barricade. The two leading goblins hurriedly climbed the blockade, only to be met by Bili's sword. The two behind them fell from the path to their deaths, arrows protruding from their necks. Not expecting to be met with force, and realizing they had no cover and would soon be shot, the others hurriedly loosed their arrows and turned back for the shelter of the entrance. One of the stray arrows lodged in Yilmai's shoulder. He yelped in surprise. Bili, seeing what had happened, ran to and gently extracted it. There appeared to be no poison or barbed hooks on the head, so Yilmai let out an exclamation of relief. "Wow, I am truly lucky! Had I moved just slightly to the left, it might have entered my heart! I have a tear in my chain mail shirt from an early encounter this evening that I hadn't noticed! Thank the Great One for watching over me!"

The Goblins cheered that they had hit the elf, but refused to come closer. They remained near the cave entrance and from there they tried shooting the defenders. Few arrows managed to clear the barricade. Bili picked these up and ran them over to Yilmai and Meri who had moved closer to the fire.

As the Old Hermit continued fighting the creature of the darkness, Wulpai located the unprotected spot he had noticed earlier. Darting in quickly, he rammed the spear deep into the bird creature's side, slipping it past the armor plating. The bird gave a loud squawk, flapped its wings furiously, and then plunged to one side, mortally wounded. The creature nimbly leaped off the bird, turned to Wulpai and began thrusting at him with his sword. Wulpai dodged, drawing his own sword, and parried the blows. He backed up under the force of the creature's powerful swing, stumbling on a rock. Falling awkwardly, he rolled to one side to avoid being run through. The angered creature missed the blow, but recovered quickly and swung again, this time catching Wulpai a terrific blow across the head.

The Old Hermit got around the bird creature in time to block the final blow intended to kill Wulpai. The sword flew from the creature's hand. Hatred clouded his already hideous features. Drawing a dagger from his belt, he hurled it at the Old Hermit, catching him in the shoulder. The creature roared with triumph, moving in to finish the Hermit. Thinking him some minor warrior, the creature badly under-estimated the old man's strength. The

Old Hermit lunged as though nothing had happened, driving his sword deeply into the body of this nightmare. Black ichors burst from the wound, sizzling and burning as the dark sludge hit the rocky soil.

With an angry screech, the creature disintegrated before their eyes. Sanguma staggered under the death of the creature they had created, stumbling back helplessly down the trail. The champion of the goblins and trolls had been defeated. They too began to fall back. The elves, though wounded, and the stocky dwarves continued to push their advantage, killing those not fast enough to get clear of the trail. Then they rushed back to the barricades, trying to repair the breaches. Once the holes were filled with limbs, broken spears, shields and other debris, the dwarves and elves regrouped, hoping to stave off the next assault.

The Old Hermit pulled off Wulpai's helmet. It had saved his life, but he was unconscious for the second time that night. Lifting Wulpai over his shoulder, the Old Hermit walked unsteadily to the fire. Dropping Wulpai to the ground, he called to Meri.

"Wulpai's been hurt. Bring that stone of yours and the medicines. Hurry!"

Meri left Yilmai who she had been tending and ran to the Old Hermit. She looked down at Wulpai. He appeared dead. Looking in despair at the Old Hermit, she tried to voice her feelings. He forestalled her and muttered something of an assurance that Wulpai was too hard headed to be stopped that easily. Meri failed to see the humor in that statement.

Reaching into her pack, she brought out what medicines she had. She gave them to the old man. He in turn picked out a couple of leaves, and then borrowed the stone from Meri. He placed these on the bruise mark, crushing the leaves as he did so. Then he opened a flask and took a little water, pouring it on the leaves. A pleasant fragrance issued from the leaves, smelling lightly of jasmine. Laying the stone atop the leaves the Old Hermit quietly chanted words in an ancient tongue. Rubbing the stone over the bruise, he continued chanting, much like the shaman in the village where Meri grew up. To her relief, the welt began to shrink. The bluish mark slowly lightened, then disappeared altogether. It seemed that Wulpai was now only asleep, not badly wounded.

Taking the stone in both hands, the Old Hermit began to hum a tune. The stone began to glow. As it did so, he took it and placed it squarely on Wulpai's forehead. Feeling the stone on his forehead, Wulpai reacted, even in his unconscious state. His body began to convulse and tremble all over, trying to evade the power in the stone. There was a pulsing, buzzing sound. It sounded for only a moment, then the stone faded, losing its light.

Wulpai's eyes opened abruptly. Looking around, he saw his friends bending over him. He had a faraway look in his eyes. Sitting up slowly, he felt his head.

"I can feel that my head is attached to my body, to be sure," Wulpai mumbled fuzzily, "but somehow it doesn't seem like the same head. And it aches all over."

With a determined look in his eyes, the Old Hermit once again spoke words of power from some unknown language. As he did so, Wulpai lost that strange look, staring hard at the Old Hermit. He cocked his head to one side, as though trying to recall something he had heard long ago. When the Old Hermit had finished chanting, Wulpai mouthed words he couldn't recall ever speaking, in the same strange tongue the Hermit had used.

In dawning recognition, Wulpai stood, raised his hands high over his head, and gave a great shout, *"Girak epei kan kikak han kai. Girak epei kan kikak han kai. Girak kewato menmen yuwe nipa hi getenenim. Girak kewato menmen yuwe nipa hi getenenim."*

Everyone in the camp was startled. All eyes turned toward the fire and Wulpai. An awesome look of harnessed power passed across his eyes, a look that only Meri caught. It startled her and took her breath away. Her heart skipped a beat as she brought her hands to her mouth.

Who is this man? she wondered again. *Who is this man Wulpai? What are these secrets, these strange experiences happening to him?* He was fast becoming a growing enigma to her, yet she was strangely attracted to him. Her curiosity was peeked! *What does all of this mean?* She screamed deep down inside her heart More now than ever, she was determined to find out!

Chapter 19

Salvation from the Skies

With the first gray of dawn, and the encouragement of the Sanguma, the trolls and goblins regrouped, intending to capture or destroy the foul dwarves, elves and humans who had thus far thwarted their efforts to dislodge them. Fully aware the rockslides were empty, an elf and a dwarf lay dead, and a couple of them were wounded, the Sanguma decided to make a final push to win this battle.

Preferring stealth and trickery to accomplish what noise and bravado had not been able to achieve, they laid their plans. Under cover of darkness, and using hooks and ropes, they managed to secure lines off to the side, reaching to the top of the fortress. One by one, goblins worked their way into position. The mercenaries came next, followed by the Sanguma priests. The few trolls remaining decided to go ahead to make a direct frontal attack, diverting the attention of the defenders in this final attack.

By the time everyone was in place for the assault, the sky had turned red, great streaks pushing across the heavens. Bili sat near the dying fire utterly exhausted. He knew the enemy would try another assault before retreating for the day into the woods below.

It was only a matter of time, he felt, before they were either killed in battle or captured. There seemed no viable alternative. The battle had not gone as planned. That horrible creature riding the beast might come back, or possibly another like it. Bili knew they would be unable to withstand another attack of that nature.

Still lingering by the fire, he heard the bellows call again from far below. He knew only too well the meaning of those sounds. Grabbing a spear and loosening the tie holding his sword, he stumbled toward the barricades. His spirit indeed was willing, but his body was spent. It begged for rest. Moving up along side Yilmai, he watched the pre-dawn attack begin.

"The Great One only knows how we'll survive this attack!" Bili shuddered, dreading the coming battle. "Can you see anything yet?"

Yilmai looked at his friend, shaking his head sadly. "This is it, my friend. I'm guessing that all the trolls that haven't been killed will likely be in the front lines, trying to drive us back. If they gain the heights, we're finished. My shoulder is throbbing and it will spoil my aim. I'll be lucky to hit any of those pesky little goblins if I can't release immediately! Meri's salve has deadened the pain somewhat, but it will be a couple of days before it heals up again. We don't have the leisure of time. The Dark One's wrath will soon be upon us!"

Bili shivered, emotionally re-living the scenes of last night. The trolls, living on the flesh of others, would rend them apart, lapping up the blood as they devoured their bodies. How he longed to be far away, in the quiet of his own home woods, where he was comfortable and where he could rest, swim, or hunt in security. These past two days had drained him heavily, sapping his spirits.

His emotional strength had slowly ebbed from him, bringing him to the point of despair

Wesip, the only bright spot in his life now, was worn down as well, especially since her capture by the goblins. She seemed paralyzed with fear, knowing what lie ahead. How Meri and Rimwai kept to their feet he couldn't understand. They had tirelessly tended those among them with wounds. Some of them were partially healing, yet not fit to fight. Still, there was no other way out, if in fact, they would live long enough to get out.

Wabran, chewing on a tough piece of venison jerky, waited impassively. His presence lent strength to the others, as he anticipated yet another skirmish with those creatures he so strongly loathed. His resources seemed endless. He stood unmoved, and seemed to thrive on the tension and challenge. *"I wonder where he gets the strength to go on like that after all he's been through?* "He is unbelievable!"* thought Bili jealously.

Turning to Bili as though he could read his thoughts, Wabran put his huge paw on Bili's shoulder. "Perk up boy! There's still another chance to take down more of these evil creatures. Don't let it get the best of you. We're almost there!

Bili mumbled wearily, "You put courage into my heart again, Wabran. I don't how you do it! You seem to be a rock of strength. You go on against all odds! You are amazing!"

"It ain't me, boy!" Wabran retorted. "It's the whole dwarven nation! I'm fighting for my homeland, my family, and my future. If they get past me, everything and everyone I love will be destroyed. I'm just not about to let that happen. At least not while I can stand on my own two legs!"

Those words put some courage back into Bili's heart like a cool draft of water to a man stranded in the desert. Bili began to mull over what the old warrior was saying. Here on this lonely mountain, they really did have a chance to make a difference. Maybe that was why Bili was here. He determined to make a difference and stand with Wabran until he could stand no longer.

His mood began to lighten, even though he was scared. He knew he could live with the fear, but the depression and hopeless would kill him. He had to overcome that and overcome it now!

Wulpai came to the barricade, sword in hand, interrupting his thoughts. Bili glanced up at him. He hadn't had a chance to talk with Wulpai, but was keen to find out more about what had happened earlier. He had gotten snatches of it from the women, but knew little else. Wulpai had been knocked senseless when Bili had run off to rescue Wesip, and when he returned, there had been a new creature threatening them. Incredibly, Wulpai was fighting again as though nothing had happened. Then there were the questions about his healing and all that shouting in an ancient language. Bili wanted answers, and despite his weariness, decided to get them. Wanting to break the heavy silence, he ventured some questions.

"What happened when the Old Hermit laid the stone on you with all those leaves? Your body seemed to twitch and spasm for a few seconds, as though you were trying to get away from something."

Wulpai looked at Bili for a moment then spoke thoughtfully, slowly. "The Old Hermit called to me in the old language, the old language used long before men and elves dotted the landscape. I began to recall dreams of long ago, in another time, another realm. Pieces of memories began to invade my mind, things I thought were lost. There was an awakening in my heart and mind of days gone by, not years ago, but eons. At first my mind refused to accept these visions. 'That couldn't be me,'" I struggled. "I've never been there or done any such things. It was almost what people might feel in being re-incarnated. But I don't believe in that stuff!"

"Yet, I suddenly realized it was indeed me. I was capable of performing all that my mind saw. I am like the Old Hermit. We share a common heritage. He and I are both from another realm, another time. I don't even know if this is my original body! We've been sent here to protect these lands and those living in it from the Dark Lord."

Bili stood speechless. He was unable to process the words he was hearing. Wulpai, the man he rescued from the guardian; helpless, more dead than alive? Wulpai? Bili's mind recoiled, unable to believe it. Wulpai was thousands of years old? The Old Hermit too? How could this possibly be true? No, it was all nonsense. Too stunned for words, Bili just stared, his tired mind failing to take it all in.

"We'll talk about it later when your mind clears. Right now we have some unfinished fighting to attend to, Wulpai reminded him."

Bili turned to see several trolls loping up the side of the cliffs to form the shock troops of this displaced army. Wabran, just in front of him, was studying them carefully, making no move. The remaining elves and dwarves fidgeted, adjusting their bows, checking their arrows, or nervously fingering their battleaxes. The moment of truth would come shortly. Would they be able to withstand the first assault, or would the enemy gain the heights?

Bellowing loudly as they approached the barricades, the trolls grouped closely together, raising their huge clubs. Bringing them down together, they smashed at the barricades, hoping to open a larger entrance for their comrades who were to follow.

Wabran used this occasion to launch himself at the troll standing closest to him. Leaping up he drove his pike squarely into the right eye, gouging it out with a deft twist. He landed at the feet of his huge adversary, and ran past him.

Wulpai had followed a second later, driving his sword into the left eye of that same troll. Withdrawing it as he fell to the ground, he knew he had a few seconds before the troll could do anything. Taking this chance, he drove his sword deep into the groin, twisting hard as he went in. The troll buckled, and fell away, blinded and lame. His struggling body slipped from the path to fall far below and smashed against the stones of the valley floor.

The troll nearest Wulpai swung his heavy club, narrowly missing. Wabran chopped down hard and took that hand off at the wrist. Grabbing it, he hurled the hand down the mountain. The angered troll grabbed the club with the other hand and tried to pin the two warriors down.

Meanwhile, the remaining three trolls demolished the barricade. Several well-placed blows opened a passage. Bili, Yilmai, and Breagle worked as a team to distract the other trolls, enticing them to leave the barricade. Harassing their larger opponents with arrows, stones, and verbal abuse, they managed to slow down the barricade's final destruction.

At last, the Old Hermit, gaining a portion of his power again, moved to the front. He began to laugh, softly at first, then gaining in volume. His companions began to wonder why he was spending his energies now, instead of waiting when they were hard pressed. They had failed to see the goblins, mercenaries and Sanguma priests moving in from the right, still under cover of the early dawn skies.

Growing in volume, the Old Hermit's laugh began carrying across the fortress. The trolls stopped what they were doing and acting as though driven by some invisible force, rushed toward him, holding their ears and bellowing their war cries. The troll trying to kill Wulpai and Wabran dropped his club and held his remaining hand to his ear. Wabran promptly hamstrung him through a space in his leg armor. The troll fell sideways, unable to control his fall. As he did so, Wabran was waiting with a vicious blow to the neck that tore through a main artery. The troll gurgled as he rolled to one side, then joined his comrade on the valley floor.

Two groups of Sanguma clustered together, humming and chanting. They determined that the Old Hermit would not survive the battle. There was no sanctuary for him to run to- no one to ask to assist him. The Sanguma had him where they wanted him and planned to end his life. Honing their powers, they joined their small rays into one large pulsing force. The humming noise grew louder, the vibrations sending slight tremors across the bluff. The Old Hermit, looking tired, turned laughing to face them. Generating more energy than he looked capable of, he laughed louder. The trolls, almost upon him, suddenly fell to the ground, bellowing in agony. Wabran had to run to avoid being kicked or crushed by their violent thrashing. He turned his attention to the Sanguma. He knew they had power to kill him and all his friends, one by one. The Old Hermit had killed the ones before, but his battle with the ugly creature of the Dark Lord had sapped his strength.

Calling Breagle and Brell to him, he commanded, "We must work our way over to the Sanguma. We must destroy them, if we are to have a chance at surviving. They'll try to kill the Old Hermit.

We must get past their power beam and kill at least one, and then the others will scatter and the beam will be lost."

As one, the three of them waded into the ranks of the goblins with mercenaries surrounding their priests. They fought with great power, cutting a wide path through the goblins. Then they ran into the seasoned mercenaries. With shields up, they blocked further progress of the dwarves. A heavy pitched battle took place between them, as neither side was willing to give ground at all. Bili and Yilmai rushed to the aid of the dwarves, shooting and slicing as they went. Yilmai's arrows bounced harmlessly off the priests, who appeared to be shielded by some force thrown off by their light beam.

Wulpai suddenly jumped over a struggling troll. Leaving the others, he joined the Old Hermit. Laying a hand on the old man's shoulder, he spoke words of encouragement.

"I don't have a lot of power yet, but it is coming. I'm here to help deflect what they throw at you. I don't think they know about me yet. That may work in our favor."

The Old Hermit nodded his understanding. He knit his brows, putting up his shields to ward off the blows that would come any second. He felt his knees shaking unsteadily as he called on his reserves. He knew he would not be able to engage the Sanguma for long. If that failed, all that would be left for him would be the sword in its scabbard. Against the overwhelming odds, their chances were not good.

A change of frequency warned Wulpai that the beam was on its way. Grabbing the Old Hermit's left hand, he held it up at chest height. Then he raised his left hand and made a fist, as though drawing down power from the heavens. He was standing in this position when the beam struck them. Wulpai's head was engulfed in a deafening roar as the beam struck them both. He wanted to scream out in pain and anger, but held this in check as he worked to match the frequency of thought the Old Hermit was using. Finding it, their minds "locked in", and suddenly the loud roaring ceased, to be replaced by an unearthly silence. Wulpai mind cleared. He opened his eyes and saw that their upraised hands had absorbed the beam. It was doing them no harm. The Old Hermit began laughing again, loud, and louder still. Then he stretched forth his hand, pointing a finger at the priests and sent an energy bolt of his own. Bouncing off their shields, it tore fragments of rock from a nearby boulder.

Feeling secure in their shielded power, the Sanguma continued attacking. The beam pulsed with power again, spewing forth more raw energy. It burst over Wulpai and the Old Hermit. Wulpai seemed to gain strength from the beam, and this lent power to the Old Hermit. Several bursts of energy washed over them, seeming to have no effect.

Angered by their persistence, Wulpai released his grip on the Old Hermits' arm and drew his sword. He stepped over in time to catch the next surge full on his sword. It glowed brightly, looking as though it would melt. Then the surge ran up and down the length of the blade, raising runes heretofore unseen.

"Keriuwe gina ik hi are erekir yayiwe ke Mitik Kai Iuwe!" Shouted Wulpai in the old language. Filled with terrible rage and power, he leaped forward over the fighting men, swinging his sword as he came. He cut through the barrier protecting the Sanguma as easily as a man cuts the stem of a flower. The Sanguma staggered under the shock, losing concentration. The light that slammed into them from the Old Hermit held them momentarily. With a violent release of energy, they vaporized into ash.

The trolls had recovered, now that the Old Hermit was no longer laughing, and were beating the defenders back. Wulpai, his energies too now spent, staggered back, trying to gain enough strength to make a retreat. Goblins poured in where the Sanguma had been, and added their numbers to force the defenders away from the barricades. Clearly, they would be driven over the cliff to fall to their deaths below; that is, those who weren't killed first in the push to take the bluff.

Wabran continued his impassive, yet skilled defense against the trolls and mercenaries. But he was only one dwarf. Breagle called him,

"Wabran, fall back with the rest of us and form a group. Even though they surround us, we'll have more chance than if we get separated and fight only in pairs."

Reluctantly, Wabran seeing the wisdom of his plan, acknowledged his counsel, and began giving ground. The remaining warriors formed a circle to begin the retreat. The mercenaries now pushed past the trolls, who obediently held back. Using their shields to block the blows aimed at them, they closed in, forcing the defenders to give ground.

Bili and Yilmai helped guide the circle back to where the women were tending fires. They knew that fire was of no concern to the mercenaries, and the goblins were working themselves up into a yammering frenzy, awaiting the final kill.

Bili called out,

"Let's work ourselves back toward the caves. We'll have a better chance to escape or at least not be forced over the cliffs in that direction."

Steadily they retreated toward the hidden path, somehow dragging their wounded with them. It was a slow business. The goblins, thinking they were being pushed easily toward the cliffs, tried to force an opening. Several of them died in the attempt. They backed off as quickly as they could, not wanting to meet the deadly blades still being wielded by their determined attackers.

Wulpai, regaining his strength somewhat, joined in the defense of the perimeter. Yelling to the Old Hermit, he said,

"Unless something happens to get us out of this situation, we will shortly be scattered and hunted down one by one. Let the others get to the pathways into the caves first. We may be able to bluff that we have regained some power, and hold them off while the others reach the caves."

Nodding, the Old Hermit continued to parry blows aimed at his shoulder and sides. The mercenaries were pressing harder now, trying to make the victory complete. From the way they began to push, killing the Old Hermit and Wulpai seemed to be their first objective. Bili observed this and motioned to Yilmai to join him on the left side of Wulpai. Wabran was already on the right of the Old Hermit along with Breagle. This was where the fighting was hottest.

Suddenly, loud screeches rent the air! "Yareech!"

Looking up, Wesip saw giant rocs approaching from the west. Eight of them were majestically flapping their mighty wings, flying straight toward the bluff.

"Look," Wesip cried loudly. "Those are my father's soldiers! They have spotted us! They are coming to help!" A great shout went up from the defenders. They stopped giving ground, and began to fight, driving the enemy back a few yards.

The trolls came to the front again, pushing aside their puny companions. Looking skyward, they began to swing their clubs frantically, knowing they had but a short time before the great birds would be upon them. Some of the mercenaries, looking up, decided to retreat rather than be torn apart by those huge talons.

The rocs swooped in from two sides. The first rocs landed, dislodging the soldiers who ran to engage the fleeing mercenaries. The others swooped down on top of the goblins, scattering them in all directions. The soldiers leaped off, laying about them right and left, slaughtering many of the goblins and engaging the remaining mercenaries in severe hand-to-hand combat. The rocs leaped up, circled and swooped down, talons extended. Driving hard at the three remaining trolls, they tore their heads from them, carrying them high into the air. Tearing the eyes and brains from the heavy boned skulls, they feasted. Then returning, they tore into the mercenaries. Many, fearing the great birds, had decided to retreat, and had formed into groups of five or six. Frantically they drove through the ranks of the newly arrived warriors, rushing through the barricades and down into the cover of the adjoining forests. Others, unable to make the break or form into large enough fighting units, along with the goblins, were pushed back against the cliffs by the soldiers, and either killed outright or shoved to their deaths.

Once the battle was over, Wesip wearily hugged the leader of their rescuers, Captain Theo. She introduced him at once to the Old Hermit, Wulpai, Meri, Bili, and the others. Explaining as briefly as possible, she outlined the events of the past few days.

The captain, shaking his head looked at Wesip and said, "You're lucky to be alive! If our group hadn't happened along when we did, you'd either be dead or a very wretched prisoner of the Dark Lord."

Wesip looked shyly at Bili and replied, "Since they arrived I've been in good hands."

The captain glancing in Bili's direction smiled slightly then nodded. He continued with news of her father.

"Ever since the outpost was attacked and the defenders scattered, your father has been worried sick," he shared privately with her. "He's spent several sleepless nights, wondering whether he did the right thing allowing you to be part of the delegation to the Elves. He's sent patrols out daily scouring the forests for any sign of patrols from the north. He's regretted the decision to allow you to accompany them. Had he known the enemy was already moving about this far south, he wouldn't have allowed it."

Finishing the report, Captain Theo said, "Two days after you left, the outpost was overrun, and not three days later, our main fortress was attacked. The outpost was destroyed and several defenders there lost their lives. The main fortress is too strongly manned, so the attackers did little damage."

"Father's all right, then?" Wesip asked anxiously?

"Yes, he's well. Just worried for you and those who went with you, that's all. He hoped you'd already crossed the mountains by the time these patrols had entered. He wanted to send some rocs this far east, but today is the first day he's been able to get enough of us together to make it safe."

They were interrupted by the return of the rocs and riders sent off in pursuit of the remaining mercenaries and goblins, most of who had managed to escape. The sergeant, saluting smartly reported.

"Sir, we've chased the enemy as far as we could, but the forest cover grows thick not a half mile from here. The rocs were unable to penetrate the foliage because of the tangles and vegetation. I'm afraid they've pretty much eluded us for now."

"Very good, sergeant," the captain responded. "Now I think it's important that we get all these survivors to safer quarters. No telling what the Dark Lord may have in mind. Keep a sharp eye out for these flying beasts he sent. He may try yet again before we arrive at the fortress. Fly at tree top level until we have to cross the mountains."

Dismissing the sergeant, the captain divided the group into threes. Having lost four of his men in the fighting, he knew that by dumping some of the spare food, he had enough space to fit everyone on the rocs in one trip. There was no chance anyway to bury those who had been killed during the battle. The enemy had thrown them over the cliff as soon as they had killed them.

Shortly, everyone was mounted and held riding straps. The wounded were tied on as best they could be, and given leather strips to hold to steady them in flight.

Bili had never been on a roc before, but remembered vividly the fight that had taken place in his own forests. He shuddered at the memory, now aware how it had changed his life forever.

The captain took Wesip, the Old Hermit and Wulpai on his mount, while Bili rode with Meri and Rimwai on another. Yilmai rode with the remaining elves, while the dwarves sat astride another mottled roc. Hagred and Hargreth hugged their fellow soldiers and climbed behind them on two of the remaining birds. At a signal from the captain, the rocs rose as one, flapping their tremendous wings, and springing powerfully into the air. Wind from their wings scattered debris along the bluff, scarred with the battle that had recently taken place.

The flight was exhilarating. Bili could see for several miles in any direction. He leaned back, turning his neck toward Meri.

"I can't believe we're up in the air." He yelled over the sound of the wind. "This is like being on the tallest mountain top and seeing land in all directions!"

"It feels like a dream," Meri yelled back. "With these birds, we'll cover the miles in no time at all."

"Yes, it would really have shortened our trip to have one or two of these for transport," Bili called back.

He liked the feel of the wind in his face, but was a bit nervous and hung on tightly when the roc suddenly hit an air pocket and dropped 30 feet before stabilizing again. Rimwai let out of startled yelp, and hugged Meri in front of her, forgetting to hang on to the riding straps. Meri turned back, her eyes wide with fear, trying to find something helpful to say to her. She caught the flapping straps and handed them back to Rimwai.

The trip went quickly. By midday they had spotted the fortress in the distance. Wesip began pointing excitedly to the Old Hermit, yelling,

"That's my home ahead at the foot of the mountain!"

The Old Hermit followed her finger and shook his head, smiling at her excitement. Allowing the other rocs to catch up, the captain pointed down to their destination. All the others in the group were able to see clearly for themselves the heavy bulwarks, the jutting towers and the great gate, sealed up and heavily guarded.

A Short time later they landed in the courtyard. Wesip leaped from her position on the roc to embrace her father, Colonel Hargref, commander of the Eastern Fortress. He had come bounding down the stairs when he realized she was on the lead bird. He hugged her tightly; tears of relief managed to roll down his otherwise dignified face.

"Had I had any idea," he started out, brokenly as he cleared his throat, "that there were troops already about, I would have chanced sending a couple of rocs into the sky, rather than have you face the dangers of traveling through the forests!" The relief at having her back safely showed through his large frame. He shuddered slightly and just held her.

Wesip did not resist, but allowed her father to hold her, giving release to his pent-up feelings. She freely allowed tears of joy to flow down her cheeks. She was exhausted and wanted nothing more than to have a hot bath and sink into an uninterrupted sleep in a soft safe bed.

Captain Theo introduced the Old Hermit to commander Hargref, then he introduced Wulpai, Bili, and Meri. Wesip interrupted, explaining to her father the quest and the presence of the dwarves and elves, who were then introduced to the two men. Knowing the group was war weary, hungry and exhausted, he invited them in to the palace for food and drink. He also sent for a doctors to help clean and bandage the remainder of their still open wounds. Captain Theo went into the kitchen to alert the cooks to prepare something for their guests. The dwarves and elves kept together, although Rimwai and Yilmai moved about freely between everyone.

After allowing the doctors to tend the wounded and after providing an ample meal liberally accompanied with wine, the Colonel asked the group to explain in greater detail the quest.

"I have only heard short stories, and need to better understand what the quest will entail. Then I'll be in a better position to provide what assistance I may."

Bili and Meri started the story, and Wulpai added clarifications as needed. Then the Old Hermit capped off the story by giving a lot of background, and the purpose of the present conflict. He ended by stating for them all,

"That's why it's imperative we get these two young people to the Capital as soon as possible. If the Dark Lord knew how weak and vulnerable we are at this moment, he himself would come, take the stones and destroy us all."

Colonel Hargref sat listening intently, careful not to interrupt except for occasional clarifications,

Once the Old Hermit had completed his story, the Colonel replied, "The forces of the Dark Lord have overrun our outpost, and killed many of our people there. He probably has the information he seeks about our defenses, but he can't know as yet where you are. You should rest for a day or two before we fly you on to the capital."

Meri looked at the Old Hermit. Looking back at her, he saw the exhaustion in her eyes, and the unwritten pleas to be allowed to stay and look like a woman again. A brief smile touched his lips as he answered.

"I suppose we do look more dead than alive. Yes, it would do us all good to have a rest, mind you a short one. Then we need to hurry on."

With the decision made, Wesip took the two women with her to the bathing quarters. Meri, almost too tired to move, followed, looking forward to the tubs. She glanced back at Bili and Yilmai, who were trying to look brave and unconcerned. He glanced up at her as she left. She gave a small snicker, knowing that he was dying to have a hot bath himself, but must act the part of a brave soldier. She turned and left the hall.

Chapter 20

A Pleasant Relationship Develops

Dinner had been a rather somber affair. No one felt much like celebrating. It was true they had been rescued, but the dwarves and elves especially felt the bitter loss of two of their comrades. Those still recovering from their wounds were mute testimony to the recent hardships. Each one of them secretly knew this was just a respite, a brief interlude before the Dark Lord hounded them again.

It didn't help when Wesip's father made the announcements about the goblin patrol attack on the Puko outpost. Everyone in the hall felt the tension mount as Colonel Hargref described the violent clash, the merciless slaughter, the desecration of human values, and the appalling lose of life. Fear became a palpable demon, gripping the hearts of even the most courageous, squeezing confidence to nothing as someone crushing bread in his fist. Each person in the room, dwarf, elf, human, struggled with the growing apprehension. Inescapable war clouds were gathering in the north and that storm would soon spill over into their part of the land.

Wesip left the baths as quickly as she could. She gave her expected courtesies to those in positions of authority, and then left for the dining hall. She glanced over at Bili, then left. He was busily engaged in repeating the battle with the trolls and goblins to two interested young men. Looking up, he caught her staring at him. Bili blushed, but her attention pleased him. He watched as she left the noisy hall, noting that she was heading off toward the north battlements.

After a hasty conclusion to the battle, Bili yawned and excused himself. "I've had a very heavy day and would like to get some sleep before the conference in the morning. Hope you don't mind if I go now." With that, he too left the hall, but not in search of a warm bed.

Bili found Wesip waiting near the stairs. Approaching quietly, he wondered again what it was about this blond headed warrior that fired his blood so strongly. Wesip was different from the girls he had known. She had an air of confidence about her he liked, but seemed warm and friendly. Bili felt more of a man when he was around her. Wesip brought out things inside of him he didn't know were there. Just being around her sent tingling sensations coursing throughout his whole body.

"I'm glad you came," Wesip said excitedly. "I wanted to show you the rest of our fortress. And I, uh, never really got to thank you for what you did for me back there on the mountain.

"Come on, let me show you some of my favorite places."

Wesip took Bili's hand, guiding him over to a corner near the wall. A narrow set of stairs hugged the masonry, almost invisible in the subdued light. She went first, warning him of holes and ruts he needed to avoid as they climbed. Turning left along the wall Wesip stopped, pointing out the tall peak above Juniper

Point, Mt. Hodin. It still wore a mantle of white draped across its crest, tangible evidence of the hard winter snows. It was a majestic sight with the moon just beginning to illuminate it from the back. Shadows dotted the irregular surface, where boulders, strewn across its wide shoulders, jutted out their defiance to the harsh conditions. Its base was shrouded in fog, hiding the dense forests growing there as if seeking to protect its privacy.

"When we were younger," Wesip reminisced, "my father used to take us there before the spring thaw. He made narrow carriages with no wheels, and we would sit in these and slide down the hills across the snow. It was exciting to slide so fast toward the bottom. Sometimes we overturned and went sprawling in all directions. Then we would have snowball fights. When we were thoroughly wet, daddy would build a big bonfire and we would crowd around it, hanging our wet things up on lines.

Wesip went on, "One young boy had carved some planks and managed to stand on them and slide all the way down the hill without falling. For a while, we all copied the idea; that is, until my little brother rammed into a boulder and broke his leg. Father wasn't amused and put a stop to it."

"And just when you were learning how to have some real fun," mocked Bili teasingly. "It makes me cold just thinking about all that snow." Bili frowned in thought for a moment, remembering. "Up in the mountains, the snows come early, and we work hard to harvest our crops. If the growing season is too short, we aren't able to hold any festivals, and eventually fighting breaks out between the villages and clans. We pull sledges behind the horses and have contests to see who can knock the other young men from them first. The losers treat the one or two who are left standing at the end to a warm bath. But they usually half drown the winners, so I don't know whether it's an honor or not."

Wesip laughed at his comment and started walking toward the western wall. Bili decided he definitely liked the sound of that laugh. It sounded so clear and filled his mind with delightful thoughts. Her hair sparkled in the flickering torch lights, and was silhouetted against the rising moon. Never in all his days had Bili imagined such beauty. Girls from his nation were all dark haired. There was the occasional albino, but they avoided the light and hid indoors. No one thought them pretty!

Rounding the corner, Wesip pulled Bili to the edge of the wall again.

"Look down there. Isn't it beautiful!" Wesip looked down at the river as it emptied out of the gorge standing a mile above, spewing out water like an angry gargoyle guarding a palace entry. The river divided into two separate flows as it worked its way South. In the middle, a small island jutted like a proud peacock, covered with boulders and sparse trees.

"The island has a huge cave," Wesip said, pointing to a dark spot near the upper side. "It is said to have been inhabited by a dragon in years gone by. We used to swim over to the island and explore when we were younger. We found some beautiful stones inside and I collected a few. People say these are stones left behind by the dragon when he went north hundreds of years ago. I don't believe that myself, but it adds to the local color and mystery surrounding the cave.

"Daddy took some men once and followed the cave to its end. It comes out several miles away among the huge boulders at the base of a cliff. He mentioned another tunnel that they did not have time to explore, and has always meant to get back there to find out where it leads. "Sounds like it would be a perfect hideaway for people here if the war comes this far," Bili interrupted. "Do you go to the cave anymore?"

"I haven't had a chance to visit there for almost three years now," Wesip smiled. "But I would love to take you there if we get an opportunity tomorrow. I can't think of a person I'd rather be lost with," she teased.

Bili blushed furiously in spite of his futile attempts to remain poised. He couldn't help but be taken by her young innocent enthusiasm. It was obvious she was in love with life and all the adventures it held. She was so much more daring than girls he was used to being around. And she wasn't afraid to express herself. Life here in the Western Lands must be quite different. Girls had so much more freedom and were treated with greater respect.

How would she fit back home in his culture? Bili reflected. He knew Meri liked her very much. They had the potential of being close companions.

Wesip laughed at his discomfiture then began tugging at his hand, interrupting his thoughts. "Come on, the best is yet to come."

She led him down another flight of stairs, and they passed through several entrances, emerging at last into a beautiful garden off to one side of the main hall.

Here the tulips stood straight and tall, the promise of summer hiding in their new buds. Young dogwood trees had already flowered, spreading their fragrant scent into the peaceful night air. Wesip pulled Bili over to a bench set to one side of the pathway.

"Sit here with me," she asked, her eyes imploring him. "This spot is my favorite. All the smells seem to come together here when the flowers are blooming. I could spend days here taking in the peace and beauty."

Bili sat down beside her, looking over the garden in the darkness. The partial moon had not risen high enough to peep over the wall. He looked around, trying to see the garden through the eyes of someone who had grown up here. He turned to Wesip, captivated by the moment.

"I can see why you love it here. The garden is a very romantic place. Your father must be pretty clever to have designed a place such as this. There are so many plants and flowers. The grounds are so clean and well ordered. It's obvious that he cares for the garden as well, to have his staff spend this much time on it!"

Taking a deep breath, he turned away, letting himself enjoy the smells of the garden. Suddenly, he realized that all the fragrances in the garden weren't coming from the flowers. Wesip had on some lovely perfume. This only added to the fire that was already burning in his imagination. His heart began to beat so loudly, he thought Wesip would hear it!

Looking around again, he noted that along the far back wall there were what appeared to be statues and some kind of hangings with inscriptions on them. Maybe these were part of the famous religious art that he had heard so much of from his old friend back in the mountain village he called home.

He turned again to look at another part of the garden and found himself staring once again into Wesip's lovely face. He saw her gentle eyes looking deeply into his. Again, he began to blush. Hot flashes began to pour over him. He felt uncomfortable, like when his mother caught him doing things he knew he wasn't supposed to be doing. Yet this was different. He had done nothing wrong.

His breathing became shallow. He didn't realize he was staring at Wesip until she broke the silence.

"When you risked your life for me," she murmured, "That was one of the bravest things I've ever seen. I can never thank you enough."

Bili put his fingers on her mouth, stopping her.

"The fact you're still alive is thanks enough for me." he smiled shyly. Compliments made him embarrassed. "I've been warrior trained since I was small, and I really didn't stop to think about what I was doing. Besides," he stammered, "You're pretty special. I just saw that you were in danger. I got mad and I ran to help. Maybe I should be asking myself why I wasn't afraid. It was a bit daring and foolish to go off alone like that. The others have made that clear. But, now I'm so glad that I did it. I would never be able to forgive myself if I let you fall into the hands of the Dark Lord."

Bili looked down at his lap. Wesip smiled at his openness. She viewed this as an endearing trait. She knew she could love him very easily. Yet she held back. She was afraid of what the future held for them all. Could she afford to give her heart away if the object of her love were to be taken from her? She would be unable to bear the hurt. Yet her heart screamed at her to take the gamble.

"I'm so glad I met you, Bili. You've brought so much sparkle into my life in spite of these dangerous times. And your sister is such a dear. There's something special about her. I have a deep rooted feeling that she's important to the outcome of this war that's coming."

Bili looked up, troubled. "Let's not talk about the war. It's peaceful here with you and that's all I care to think about at the moment."

Absently, he felt the curls of her hair with the hand he had draped over the back of the bench. Her hair felt so smooth and silky to the touch. How different she looked from when he had first seen her on the trail. Her hair had been matted and she was dressed in warrior's garb, scratched and torn, covered with dust. Now she was in a dress and all woman. His heart began to race again as he looked at her.

"Besides," Bili continued, "your friendship and love are more than enough for anything I have done for you. I'm just glad I was able to help you get back safely to your father."

He gently took her hand in his, smiling as he did so. It was Wesip's turn to feel flushed. She blushed, which only added to the loveliness of her features. She looked into Bili's eyes and said,

"I know father is very grateful too. He was reluctant to let me go to the outpost in the first place, but I insisted. I also volunteered to answer the call of the elves when the summons arrived. We thought that by going on foot, we'd not draw attention to ourselves." It was her turn to look down at her lap, feeling ashamed.

Bili put his hand under her chin and lifted her face to his.

"If you hadn't, I'd never have met you. I'm so glad now that you did."

He stared at her a little longer. Wesip's heart skipped a beat. She could hardly draw a breath. Her lips parted slightly as she saw him lean toward her. He bent and kissed her lips tenderly. As he withdrew, her eyes sparkled brightly with desire. She stretched up again, and kissed, placing her arms around his neck. She kissed him long and hard, with all the newfound feelings welling up in that kiss. Bili responded passionately, embracing her strongly. Weeks of weariness and tension seemed to melt from him as he held her.

Wesip pulled gently away, afraid that she had gone too far this time. She tried to cover her embarrassment at being so forward. She need not have bothered. When she looked into his eyes again, she found only gentleness there, a look of unwritten 'thank you' showing on his face.

"Maybe that expresses a little of my feelings toward you, Bili. Oh, I wish this moment would never end!"

If this was what it felt like to be in love with a man, it was beyond words! It felt so deliciously right. She felt her heart melt within her. Her desire was to be with him forever.

Bili smiled and pulled her toward him. She moved, nestling into his arms, as he embraced her again. She pressed her head against his chest and felt the pounding of his heart, a strong heart. Bili tenderly caressed her hair again as he held her close. He too secretly wished this moment would never come to an end. He was miles from home and on a quest from which he might never return. What lay ahead of them along the trail? What would tomorrow hold? Would they reach their destination and complete their mission? Or would they have to fight for every inch to deliver the stones to those who knew how to use them properly? And... would he ever see this enchanting girl again? He didn't even want to think about it. He just wanted to live for the pleasure of this moment.

Sounds of voices began to drift to them from the other end of the garden. Bili looked across to see a couple of people moving their way. Wesip heard it too and looked up.

"Maybe we'll have some more time alone again before you have to leave here," Wesip said hopefully. "I'll miss you when you go." She felt a deep heaviness creeping into her heart.

"I'll miss you as well. I don't look forward to leaving here. This is the first rest we've had since we left home. It will feel strange to leave you and Hagred and Hargreth here. You've become so much a part of our group and my life especially. We'll all miss you."

"Strange how quickly you become attached, isn't it?" mused Wesip. "You, Meri, Yilmai, Rimwai, Wulpai, the Old Hermit. You've all stepped into my life. I'll never be the same."

"Speaking of Wulpai," Bili said softly, "He's a real enigma. He's been the real leader of our group, but there's something unusual about him. He's more than just a seasoned warrior. He never seems to need rest. He has more endurance than any person I've ever met. I wonder who he really is.

"He told me quite a story up there on the bluff; some crazy things about coming from another time and realm. It sounded like a lot of nonsense. Anyway, I'm anxious to complete our quest and see the wonders of the Western Lands. But, I wish you were coming along with us. That would be best of all."

He gave her a squeeze, then stood up. They broke apart and began moving toward the voices. Wesip puffed her hair lightly, knowing that it might betray what she had been doing there with Bili. He noticed what she was doing and smiled sheepishly.

"Sorry I messed your hair. Hope nobody takes too much notice of it in the darkness." He smiled at her reassuringly.

"Ah, there you are, intoned the colonel. "I thought you both had gone off to bed already." He smiled, knowing that this was Wesip's refuge. This had always been her favorite place since her mother had passed away.

"No, father," Wesip replied easily. "I was just showing Bili some of my favorite places. They hold so many pleasant memories. I'm sorry for leaving earlier than usual. It was getting so hot and stuffy;

I wanted a breath of fresh air. Bili was on his way to rest when we ran into one another, and I decided that I might not have another opportunity to show him the gardens if I didn't do it tonight."

"I understand," her father said gently. "Well, maybe the planning meetings won't take all day. That would give you young people time to visit the river or possibly explore the cave in the afternoon." He winked, knowing she had more on her mind than just exploring.

"Thank you, sir," Bili replied politely. "Knowing that we don't have to stay up all night, ready for an attack from goblins or trolls has already helped me to relax somewhat. I wish we had time to spend a week here. Unfortunately, I know that can't happen. Still, this is a lovely place."

With that, Bili took his leave. Wesip volunteered to show him to the men's quarters, which were located on the opposite side of the main hall. She guided him through the entrance her father had just used, then turned him right. There was still quite a bit of darkness. The moon, now risen, was completely hidden behind a bank of clouds making their way in from the North.

Standing outside of the men's quarters, Bili held Wesip's hands once more.

"Thank you for a very lovely evening. I appreciate you allowing me into your private life as you have. The gardens were beautiful, and if we are allowed, I would love to visit the river and see the famous island cave."

He reached down and kissed her again gently. Pulling away slightly, his eyes took in her face once more, trying to imprint in his mind the emotion and the beauty of the moment. He was all too aware that he might not see her ever again. Reluctantly releasing her hands, he gently whispered, "Good night, Wesip."

"Good night, Bili," She replied.

Stepping back, he turned and walked into the barracks, then veered left toward the room that had been given him earlier. He found Yilmai still up, waiting for him.

"Were you with Wesip?" he asked Bili rather boldly.

Bili couldn't hold back the smile that danced on his lips. He nodded in embarrassed silence.

"Well, don't be embarrassed about it! You act as though you've done something wrong! Actually, I'm glad for you my friend. I can think of no greater healing than to be alone with a woman who loves you."

"Who says she loves me?" Bili asked defensively, feeling threatened that his emotional involvement with Wesip was so obvious.

"Easy, Bili! We've all seen your relationship with her growing steadily. It's nothing to be ashamed of.

"Actually, I wish that I were in your place. We elves spend years cultivating relationships with one another and it's not very often that we get lucky and have one filled with deep passion. You are indeed fortunate, my friend."

Bili was mollified... and pleased. He knew he loved Wesip, but she was staying here. He had to move on. That bothered him. He had a quest to complete, and there was nothing for it but to go on and finish. Bili determined that if he survived the war, he would come back and ask for Wesip's hand in marriage. But what did he have to offer? Honestly, nothing! How could he ever hope to marry someone from the Western Lands? He was only an obscure person from an obscure place tucked high in some inaccessible mountains. Her father would never agree to such an arrangement. For that matter, Wesip might not be accepted in his culture either.

He hadn't thought of that. Maybe Wesip would not be happy to be in such a restrictive environment such as his, highly isolated and by all measures of what he had experienced, backwards.

Getting more and more depressed, Bili got his bed ready, then rolled up in it. He knew he couldn't share his feelings with Yilmai, who had already given up so much to come with him. Bili thought that maybe he could talk to Meri sometime tomorrow and share his feelings. Surely she would understand his plight. With that he turned his face into his blankets and found solace in as exhausted asleep.

Chapter 21

A Day Too Late

After a hearty breakfast, Colonel Hargref gathered his two top aids, along with several men of rank and ushered them into his private audience chambers. He then invited the delegation of dwarves, Elves and humans to join them.

"I've called you all here to discuss plans to get you safely to Witweis, the citadel, home of King Kelidor, ruler of the Western Lands."

Puffing nervously on a pipe filled with blended tobacco, he slowly surveyed the room, gauging the impact of his words on such a diverse group. "You are aware by now that the Dark Lord knows among your party there are at least two people who possess unusual powers. Sending one of his personal power lords is proof of that."

Continuing, he spoke briskly, "My responsibility is to plan the safest route to the capital. I suggest using the rocs, but flying low over the trees wherever possible to avoid detection. I am well aware that some of the Sanguma have the power to teleport and relay information to the Dark Lord. This presents one of the hazards traveling by this method. It is, however, an improvement over hiking the trails. It's faster, it's easier, and reliable."

He paused again, his eyes taking in the unity of purpose his words had created, as murmurs of agreement rippled through the room. Puffing again and exhaling slowly, he continued.

"It is rather late for you to start the perilous flight today. I suggest you rest just this one day, and be ready for flight at first light."

Clearing his throat softly, the Old Hermit made as if to speak. Glancing his way, the commander placed the pipe firmly between his teeth and nodded.

"It's not often that we have the privilege of being so kindly entertained. The night's rest has been good for us. I appreciate the need for caution. Our enemy is a wily one, and will be very difficult to outwit.' Looking down at the ground for a moment, like a man searching for the right words, the Old Hermit continued. "I am concerned, however, at our delay. By staying here another night, we place you and this entire fortress at risk. Possibly we might fly from here later in the day, and spend the night in some secluded area hard to reach by ground forces.

"By breaking our journey into segments, and flying in several directions, we may be able to throw our opponent off balance enough to actually reach the capital."

He looked around his companions for support. Bili looked at Yilmai and shrugged his shoulders. He for one would rather take the chance, and leave in the early dawn of a new day. He didn't relish the idea of leaving Wesip here in a place so unsafe and cut off from immediate help. He shifted nervously from one foot to the other, unwilling to join the decision making process.

Wulpai, seeming to read Bili's thoughts, smiled slightly at his young friend's predicament. Looking over at the commander, he suggested, "I believe that the Old Hermit has made his point well. I do wonder, though, if there are such places between here and the capital?"

One of the aides spoke up. "There are only two places of refuge that would suffice. One is four hour's flight from here bearing southwest, along a set of cliffs reaching up to three thousand meters. The other is equally far, but off course to the North. Both are difficult to find if the weather turns foul. You might find yourselves in a similar situation to the one two days ago if you were detected en route. I suggest, as the commander has already stated, you get an early start tomorrow. This will also give us time to prepare letters to the king, outlining our position and plans."

With a slight smile touching the corners of his mouth, the colonel turned toward the Old Hermit.

"Your point is well taken," the Old Hermit smiled knowingly. "I appreciate the situation. I have always been a man of action, often going on impulse. This has saved my hide more than once. I have one of those feelings now. Yet, I realize there is much to be finished here before even the rocs can be made ready."

Looking around at his companions he suggested, "Until tomorrow then?"

Hearing no objections, the colonel interjected, "Then it's settled. Tomorrow at first light, we'll have you on your way. May the Great One speed your journey."

"Now I would like to change the subject and hear in detail more of your travels through the Plains of Desolation and the trails you used between the lake and the bluff. We here at the fortress need to know what to expect in the days ahead and plan our strategy and defenses accordingly."

With that, they began a session that carried them right into the noon hour. They were heavily absorbed in planning when the bell chimed for mid-day meal. Reluctantly the commander broke up the meeting.

Leaving the chairs, Wesip took Rimwai and Meri's arms, directing them to Bili and Yilmai. With an innocent look on her face she said, "I made arrangements earlier this morning for an outing. We won't be joining the others at the dining hall. I have a surprise prepared."

Saying no more, she led them from the room and down the hall. Suppressing a satisfied grin, Bili threw a glance in Wesip's direction. She blatantly ignored him.

Arriving at the great door, she ushered them on through. Two great rocs were saddled, shifting from foot to foot, anxiously awaiting their passengers. Delighted, the two girls mounted the first behind Wesip, while the two young men mounted the second. In moments they were aloft, heading slightly North of West. Their flight took only a moment, with the rocs landing on the small island that Bili had spotted by moonlight the night before.

Disembarking, Wesip informed them, "This is one of my favorite places. I wanted to share it with you before you left for the capital in the morning. A lunch has been packed and we have the afternoon to explore, swim or whatever you might like to do."

The six guards accompanying them, took the baskets from the harnesses, and spread the lunch out before them. Meri gazed around her, taking in the beauty of trees, the huge boulders and the cave entrance not far away. She involuntarily shuddered, remembering the caves she had been forced to enter near her home.

Casting these thoughts aside, she turned back to the others intent on having a good time. She smiled as she seated herself, some unshared thought bringing brief pleasure to her heart.

As they ate the delicious fruits and nuts, sweet meats and savories, they talked excitedly about journey's end tomorrow. In spite of the excitement, Bili felt subdued, knowing that he would be leaving someone special. He wondered if there might not be some way he could convince the commander that she would be safer and of more use in the capital than here at the edge of the coming conflict. He nibbled at his food, deep in thought.

Wesip noticed, but it allowed it to pass unchallenged for the moment. She wondered if he was feeling the same as she. It would be very hard to say good-bye to these new friends. They were more than friends, now, she realized. She too would like to accompany them to the capital and see the wonders it held. She had only been there twice, both times when she was a young girl. The second occasion had been tarnished by the death of her mother. Her father had brought her and her mother to the capital to seek medical help, but the sickness was too far advanced for the physicians to do much more than ease her pain. A tear escaped her eyes at the memory of her mother.

Meri, sensing something amiss, looked at Wesip and inquired gently, "Is something the matter?"

Wesip, wiping the tear from her eye, looked up and replied, "I was just thinking of my mother who died a few years ago in the capital. I've missed her all these years, even with all the ladies here to care for me. Something died within me when I lost my mother. But let's not talk of that now. It's a time to enjoy ourselves."

With that she threw the core of her apple at Bili and jumped up running. He grabbed the core, and took up the chase. The others, laughing, jumped up and joined the fun.

Bili caught her at the river's edge. She had run him a merry chase. Grabbing her, he stumbled, and they both plunged into the cold water. Laughing and sputtering, they splashed each other noisily, as might younger school children. Then they climbed out of the water together, meeting the others who had come to join them. Yilmai pulled off his shirt, and made the plunge, feeling the cool water take away the heat of the day to refresh him. He surfaced, and splashed the two remaining girls, shouting at them to get wet. The girls backed away from the water, knowing his willing hands would gladly assist them in joining him.

Seeing they couldn't be persuaded to join him, Yilmai reluctantly climbed out and shook his long blonde hair vigorously. Satisfied with the squeals of surprise he got from the ladies, he grinned wickedly, knowing he had scored. Then using a small braided band, he tied his hair at the nape of his neck.

"Are you interested in seeing the caves?" asked Wesip, interrupting their fun. "There are some beautiful formations inside. The soldiers have two lanterns with them, and are quite willing to come with us."

Bili took her hand. "I'm willing to go wherever you lead." With that he nudged her, aimed a wink at the others, then took off at a trot for the caves, half dragging her there.

The caves were every bit as beautiful as Wesip had said. Meri and Rimwai were fascinated at the stalactites formed by hundreds of years of water dripping in the cave's interior. The lamps brought into bold relief the differences in color and composition of each one. There were groups of stalagmites that resembled small dwarves with long toadstool hats. Others were shaped like a long vacated throne room, with a king's chair and soldiers slumped at ease. In some places the ceiling narrowed and became plain with no decorations at all, connecting one room to another.

In the midst of their fun and exploration, one of the sentries outside the cave, came running in, working his way down the passages, finally locating and interrupting them.

"A roc has just been dispatched to us. Trolls and goblins have been sighted North of the battlements. You've been asked to return to the fortress immediately."

Without hesitation, the young people hurried to gain the entrance, feelings of misgivings showing on their worried faces. They well knew the menace that approached. They only hoped that they would be able to escape unseen back to the safety of the fortress walls. Rimwai touched Meri's arm as they hurried out into the sunlight, voicing what they were all afraid to ask.

"Do you think the Dark Lord knows we've found refuge here?" she asked tensely.

Meri stopped, and looked directly at her friend. "It may well be he's gotten word of our location. He has many spies throughout the lands. But if we gain the walls now," she continued, "He will have a very difficult time dislodging us. With the entire stockade to protect us, and the Old Hermit and Wulpai able to use equal force against those black beasts, he'll have to come in person to do so."

Wesip stopped suddenly. Turning she said to her friends, "I know this may sound silly, but I feel we should cross the river on foot and enter the fortress through the small secret door that we use to escape in times of great peril."

Beckoning to the soldiers she explained her plan. When they comprehended her idea fully, they hurried to the riverbank and crossed at the ford. The young people with their warrior escort were safely across and under cover of the trees leading to the entrance when the rocs rose majestically into the sky. Only the riders used to guide them were mounted.

As they watched apprehensively, the rocs gained the altitude necessary to glide over the walls and into the landing field adjacent to the stables. Wheeling for the final approach, they screeched their defiance as several war hawks materialized directly in their pathway. Both rocs and riders reacted immediately. The rocs cupped their great wings, reversing their bodies and extending their huge talons forward. The riders, reaching for sacks tied to the harness, loosed them in a shaking motion. Immediately the sky was filled with powder and dust as the bags flew open, their contents flung away by the wind. The hawks screeched in frustration, unable to fly through the blinding screen. Flying around it cost them precious moments. By the time they worked their way free of the dust, the rocs had landed safely, and men on the walls were scattering them, firing arrows high among them.

As the young people watched from their sanctuary, Bili sensing movement elsewhere caught Yilmai's arm. Pointing through a small clearing among the trees, they both watched a black flying beast circle slowly near the cave entrance, barely visible in the bright sunlight.

Hurrying their friends on, they arrived at the secret entrance. Taking a key she always carried while at the fortress, Wesip pushed it into the lock and turned the tumblers. With a rusty "Click", the lock released and the door swung open of it's own accord. Two soldiers went first, followed by the young people, and finally the rear guard, who helped Wesip close and bolt the door.

Once inside, they crossed to the landing field, where her father, his aides, Wulpai and the Old Hermit had gathered. He appeared relieved to see everyone back safely, but was astounded that Wesip had discerned that something was amiss. Explaining things to him she confessed,

"We have already had an encounter with his kind back there in the hills. Since we left the fortress I have felt someone watching us." Smiling in her endearing manner she said matter of factly, "I had a hunch that they had seen the rocs fly us to the island and would lay a trap that way if possible. So I decided to plan a trick of my own."

Smiling broadly at her bold admission, and proud of her resourcefulness, he hugged her closely. "You very well may have saved yourself and your friends today. I just hope we've made the right decision in convincing our friends to stay here the extra day," he finished lamely, looking apologetically at Wulpai and the Old Hermit.

Moving from the landing field, they went indoors. Bili pulled Wulpai and the Old Hermit aside for a moment, explaining what he and Yilmai had seen. When he finished, Wulpai hesitated for a moment, then smiled.

"Then he wasn't really sure we were here after all. This was just a scouting raid, unless of course, some of his minions spotted you on the rocs and then noticed you weren't on them when the hawk attack occurred. Even so, it's going to be hard to convince the Dark Lord you are in fact taking refuge in this fortress."

"Does that mean we can expect an attack tonight?" Bili frowned. "And if we join in on the defense, and are recognized by any of the Sanguma, won't the Dark Lord himself appear to deal with us?"

The Old Hermit spoke up. "No, Bili, he's not ready to show his hand yet, no matter how close he's getting to the stones. He has other plans he can't afford to upset by coming here himself." He paused a moment, then continued. "That won't stop him though from sending some of those dark beasts to capture anyone who can lead him to them."

Meri approached them, noticing that they had withdrawn for a moment to talk. "Is something wrong?"

"No more than we expected," the Old Hermit admitted ruefully. "We might have been better off taking our chances leaving today, but that is of no mind. We are here and we'll make the best of that decision."

Meri looked from one to the other. "Then we've been found out? Is that what you're trying to tell me?"

"That's only one possibility of several," Bili said quietly. "Yilmai and I didn't say anything to the Commander, but we saw one of those black beasts fly into the cave entrance as we were waiting for Wesip to open the secret door. I think they have a pretty good idea we're in this area, and will be watching all movements closely for the next few days."

"All the more important to make a quiet departure in the morning," added Wulpai. "Let's just hope there's a lot of ground fog or mist to cover our departure."

Hurrying down the hall, they caught up with the others. They decided to gather in one of the Commander's private rooms to plan their trip to the capital. They laid out all the facts, then tried to come up with good plans for deception and evasive action should their party be set upon in the air.

After the meeting, the young people gathered together again with Wesip. She took them to the supply building, allowing them to pick whatever they needed to restock their empty food sacks. While the others were deciding on what few things they could take with them, Bili pulled Wesip aside.

"What a way to spend our last night together, eh?" he said rather grumpily. "I had hoped we might have some time together alone."

Wesip smiled warmly, asking, "Just what did you have in mind for this evening, may I ask?" Her dimples were showing, betraying her teasing.

Bili caught the look, and smiled grudgingly. "I just wanted to be alone with you for a while. Wesip, I just don't like you being here in this fortress when so much is about to happen. Who knows whether your father and his soldiers will be able to hold this place, especially with the power the enemy has. You saw what they can do! Without special help, those beasts could easily overrun your defenses and you would be in the hands of the Dark Lord as hostages to do with whatever he pleased. I just don't like" ...his voice trailed off to a whisper.

He was interrupted as the others joined them again. They had made their choices and packed them into their travel packs. Yilmai brought over a couple of well-balanced daggers that were sitting among the food stores. "Are these for the taking as well?" He asked.

"Anything you want you may take," Wesip responded. "Just remember to travel light. The capital is only a day's flight away."

Bili looked at the daggers, then looked over to see if more lay about. He walked over and picked up one as well as a small throwing knife. He tucked the dagger into his belt, and hooked the smaller knife into a sheath over his shoulders to lie between his shoulder blades. Wesip watched as he adjusted it, and tried pulling it from its sheath. Noticing that he was having trouble getting it free, she moved behind him, tightening the strap so that it sat just a little higher. He gave her a satisfied nod as it slid easily from its place.

They left the room then, the girls going back to the women's quarters, and the two young men out into the courtyard. The sun was getting low in the sky, and a chill came up as clouds began moving in from the mountains bringing a veil of darkness to the hills.

"It looks to be a dark night," Yilmai observed. "Just the kind of night those uglies out there like," he commented sourly. "It won't surprise me if they ruin our sleep with their bellowing and curses."

"They're more likely to attack us, either to harass us, or test the defenses," Bili snapped back. "I'm going to get a bit of sleep before evening meal, so if we have to fight, at least I'll be able to stay awake for the ride to the capital."

Turning back indoors, Bili went to his bed, pulled a blanket over himself and was soon asleep. Yilmai smiled, not unkindly, then went over to the library room to look through the selections placed on the shelves.

During the meal, everyone was subdued, awaiting the dreaded call from the walls that would signal the beginnings of a night filled with the noise of fighting. Colonel Hargref had talked with the Old Hermit and been briefed on the situation. He had stationed extra men along the parapets and tower windows, keeping a sharp lookout for any movement in the adjacent forests.

Everyone drank sparingly, especially of the wine. This was no time to be drunk. Only the dwarves seemed unaffected by the threat of war. Wabran, Breagle and Beman all packed away enough food to last for a week... including the wine. They seemed impervious to its effects. The elves, for their part, were judiciously picking at their food, their keen hearing alert for any sounds which might indicate intruders. The young people sat together talking quietly, trying in vain to make light conversation, knowing tomorrow would come all too soon.

Colonel Hargref got up to make a short speech. Motioning for quiet in the hall, he began,

"As you are all aware, we will soon be embroiled in heavy fighting. The war clouds have been slowly gathering these past months in the North. Our friends have already run into trouble east of here. The news is grim. It appears that the Dark Lord, so long a character of myth, is again preparing to stalk the land. We must do all we can to fortify our position and hold out until reinforcements arrive from the West. No sacrifice..."

"Ba-room!" The loud blare of the horns interrupted the colonel, drowning out his final words. Everyone arose, hands to sword hilts, rushing to the windows. Nothing, of course, could be seen because it had become dark. Yet, it gave the warriors something to do. Tension ran high and this was the moment to break the tedious monotony of waiting.

Colonel Hargref raised his sword, and yelled above the din, "Men, to your battle posts! Keep a sharp watch overhead. We may have flying visitors. Be ready!"

With no further comment, he turned to his guests. "I don't know whether to tell you to stay indoors or join us outside."

Wulpai gestured, saying, "We will keep watch for any activity overhead. Otherwise, we will save our strength for the long flight in the morning. The walls are stout enough to help you cope with the trolls and goblins. If any other evil pranks are planned, we stand ready to aid you at a moments notice."

Taking his leave, Colonel Hargref left the hall, hurrying to marshal his forces.

Chapter 22

Night Attack

Goblins with ladders and grappling hooks came against the walls, intent on storming the heights and gaining entry. Trolls, bellowing their anger and hatred, brought heavy logs crashing against the fortified gates. The complete darkness had worked to their advantage. They arrived at the walls uncontested, and with no loss of life..

Above them, soldiers shouted angrily, shooting arrows and hurling spears, attempting to keep their foes from gathering in force to storm the fortress. Torches were hurriedly set in holders, throwing bursts of light in the growing wind, but not nearly enough. Smoke blinded the defenders as the wind suddenly picked up, a storm roiling over the crags.

"Get those torches back off the walls," Shouted Colonel Hargref, fighting to breathe in the dense fumes. "The wind is gutting the torches. We can't see anything below. The smoke is choking everyone on the walls. It's impossible to fight."

Captain Theo rushed back to direct the defense on the northern wall, while Colonel Hargref took control of the eastern wall. The trolls had determined that the eastern gate was the weaker, and began busily pounding it. Loud thudding broke out as eight huge trolls rammed a thick log against the cross braces.

Looking down at the hot grease and sludge that had been brought from the kitchens, Captain Theo considered. They were set to dump on the trolls, who had leather hauberks covering their tough hides. This would certainly spoil their sport, he thought. And it might even slow them down for a spell. Making his decision, he yelled out, "At my signal lift those vats and spray the contents down on those trolls," Barked the captain. Several soldiers rushed to obey this orders. They lifted the vats, emptying their contents down on the unsuspecting trolls. The hot grease hit them as they charged against the gate. Dropping the log, they furiously ripped at their hauberks, now trapping the hot grease that had soaked smoothly through their clothing and holes in their armor. Pots of hot oil were set on small catapults and released into the goblins milling near the wall, waiting to mount the ladders. Surprised and dismayed, their howling and shrieking filled the night. The grease spattered them well. Arrows from the night clattered against the walls, some finding their mark among those defending the wall. Several bodies sagged against the wall, or slipped over and fell to the ground outside the fortress, where they were hacked to pieces by the angry attackers.

On the North wall, the goblins made a concerted effort to breach the defenses. Drawing their bows they launched scores of arrows at the defenders. Then hurriedly throwing their hooks, they scaled the walls. Others, with ladders, set them against the battlements, scurrying toward the top. The defenders fell back momentarily, recognizing the plan of attack. They let them come to the top, ready with pikes and spears.

As the first goblins gained the heights, Captain Theo blew his horn. His men advanced to the edge, driving the ladders back, and hacking at the ropes holding the goblins. Cries of fear and anger rent the night air as goblins fell to be impaled on the stakes driven into the ground at the base of the wall. Others, including hired mercenaries managed to hang on and gain the parapets, fighting hand to hand with those around them. The many defenders bunched together in the fort soon overpowered them. Those that surrendered were taken and bound in chains. Others, not willing to be taken captive fought and died. Their bodies were thrown back over the wall, the disgust of the defenders obvious, as they smelled the stench of the filthy, unwashed bodies.

Colonel Hargref soon deduced orders were being issued by hidden commanders who were stationed in the woods not far off. Whether they were Sanguma or mercenaries was impossible to guess. He watched as the enemy kept coming despite appalling loses against the walls. The trolls, meanwhile, though burnt and angry, worked their way back to the walls, their tough hides healing rapidly from the burning grease. They again attacked the posts and straps with a vengeance.

Commander Hargref knew it was but a matter of time before the trolls destroyed his gate. Though they would have to destroy two more gates to gain entry, the colonel felt they would do so before the night was through. Attempting another distraction, he called for a detachment of soldiers, seasoned in fighting trolls in the northlands. They slipped over the walls on the Southern side, which as yet had not come under attack. Its naturally steep sides made it impossible to find footing to plant ladders. These soldiers carried special pikes with which to pierce the leg armor of the trolls. Their intent was to hamstring them, then behead them. It was a dangerous mission, but the only recourse the Commander felt would work against such powerful enemies.

Waiting until the goblins attempted to scale the walls a second time, and were repelled, the unit charged. They easily broke through the back of the scattered goblin ranks, rushing determindly at the unsuspecting trolls. Several pikes found their marks, toppling the trolls to the rear. In a roar, they fell, to be beheaded from behind. The trolls to the front, now alerted at the danger behind them, picked up discarded spears, rushing their attackers. The soldiers gave way before them, drawing the rush off to the left. The soldiers holding the heads of the beheaded trolls rushed to the walls, lifting the grisly trophies on their pikes to be taken by those from above. Turning, they rushed back to try to help their comrades.

"Stop them! Stop them!" yammered the goblins, rushing to block the commandos from engaging the trolls again. Their sheer numbers momentarily stopped the warriors from joining their comrades. Spears from the walls flew among them, impaling many, but still they blocked the soldiers. The trolls, using what they could, drove the soldiers toward the forests, away from help.

The lieutenant, seeing their plight, shouted, "Men, fight your way down the side on the right. Maybe we can regroup there and make a stand!" The soldiers rushed to make a break, attempting to out-maneuver their more clumsy opponents.

Out of the forests rushed mercenaries, who fell upon these men, separating them from each other. One by one the soldiers who hadn't seen the mercenaries coming and broken off the attack were killed either in hand-to-hand fighting or torn apart by trolls who managed to reach them. The Commander, standing on a knoll, watched them being driven between this pincer movement yelled,

"Men! Regroup and retreat to safety!" Those near the wall helped the others fight their way safely back. They reluctantly left the few who had no chance, fighting their way back to the South wall, where others had come out to aid them. The goblins, now fired with frenzy at the taste of blood, tried driving them down away from the wall. A great hail of arrows and spears rained down stopping them. Using the momentary lull, the soldiers rushed ahead, reaching the safety of the walls once more. The remaining trolls left the gate, temporarily, to feast on the blood of those whom they had killed. Angry shouts rose from the walls as their comrades shouted defiance. The trolls, looking up from their bloody feast, grinned, then turned to crunch more bones and tear more flesh.

Bili and Yilmai stood in the shelter of the main castle, looking out upon the battle. Both knew what was going on, and were sick at heart. "We should be out there fighting along side these men," groaned Bili, near tears. They've rescued us and shown us great kindness. Here we stand unable to aid them." Anger and frustration laced his voice as it trailed into silence.

The Old Hermit, sensing their feelings, spoke quietly but firmly to them both. "Better a few die at the walls of this fortress, than you fall into the hands of the Dark Lord. If that happens, thousands will die the way these soldiers are dying tonight. Be prepared for the trip tomorrow, and set your sights on getting to the capital so carnage such as this can be stopped."

Bili looked over, sorrow etching his features. Yilmai put a hand on his friend's shoulder.

"He's right you know. There is nothing to be gained by our risking our lives there tonight. Our battle lies elsewhere."

Bili nodded. "Thank you for your encouragement. It just doesn't seem right to let someone else fight our battles. I feel unworthy of their allegiance. They are dying in my place." Tears welled up in his eyes, rolling down his cheeks.

"We are all in this together," Wulpai added quietly. "We all know you would give your life in place of theirs. You have been given a different charge. Don't allow them to have died in vain; you've had your share in this battle along the trail. Rest while you may and be grateful."

Bili nodded mute assent at the encouragement, then moved off to weep quietly by himself. The others left him alone, allowing him time to come to grips with his feelings.

Meri, standing a ways off with Wesip and Rimwai commented,

"This is one of the rare times I've seen my brother shed tears. He's always tried to hide his emotions, and bury them deeply from the sight of others. He has been deeply moved by what he's seen here tonight."

Wesip, having grown up among men, understood. She too remained where she was, feeling a deeper love for this young man. Waiting until she felt the moment appropriate, she approached Bili. He turned at the sound of her coming, and embraced her. He held her for a long time, then looked into her eyes.

"I love you very much. I don't want to leave you."

She looked into his eyes, deep feeling welling up into her heart. She tried to speak, but her throat was thick with emotion. She choked back a sob and replied,

"I love you too, Bili. I'm just sorry we're caught up in this maelstrom of greed and hatred." Wesip was silent then for a few moments, feeling his strength as she pressed her head into his shoulder.

Suddenly she tensed, and looked up.

"Bili, I forgot. Last night I had a dream that upset me. I fear that my father is in great danger. I don't know from what or whom, but I'm afraid for him."

"Have you spoken to him about it?" Bili asked her.

"No, but even if I did, he would just laugh and tell me not to worry. But I am worried. I have one of those feelings!"

Bili chuckled quietly in spite of her fears.

"I guess I shouldn't laugh because the same things happen to my sister. She's usually right."

"Then what do you find so humorous, Bili?" She pressed.

"I guess it's that you women are so alike. Maybe predictable is a better word. You tend to rely on feelings much more quickly than we men do. Maybe I should take a lesson from the Old Hermit in that area."

"Well, he's shown himself to be correct several times along the way," Wesip said reproachfully. "Except, he's different. It's as though he has a sixth sense about things, and has some inner voice helping him. Oh, I don't know, but I feel safe around him."

Wulpai came over as they continued talking and interrupted them.

"I think we should all get some sleep if possible. Tomorrow is going to be a long day, and who knows what it will bring. The servants have set up beds below, near the dining hall. They feel we'll be safer if we all sleep near one another. They say this is by far the biggest attack they've had. The gates may not last."

"Is there nothing you can do?" Wesip asked Wulpai. "I'm so afraid for my father."

"The Old Hermit and I will remain awake," promised Wulpai. "If it looks safe, we will use some of our power and assist your father so that the gates are not broken nor the wall breached. Trust him into our hands. You try to get some rest with the others."

Smiling, she briefly hugged him, then turned to follow the others. Meri lingered behind, waiting for the others to go. Then she moved closer to Wulpai.

"It's pretty bad isn't it?" She said, more statement than question.

"Yes, something's going on out there. I have a feeling that we're going to have a rough time getting to the capital. Something's definitely wrong. I don't like it. But I don't think these attackers are the main concern. I feel the presence of some evil not far away, biding its time, out there waiting."

Looking out into the darkness, Meri shivered in the cool night air. Goose flesh covered her skin. She felt naked, exposed to whatever or whoever was lurking beyond her senses. Noticing that Meri seemed cold, Wulpai pulled off the cloak he had been given by the Commander earlier that day, and wrapped it securely around Meri's shoulders.

"Oh, thank you," she responded, embarrassed. "I didn't realize how cold I'd gotten standing here."

Wulpai let it pass, knowing that she was trying to hide her true feelings. He knew trying to appear brave even at the best of times was hard. She was a brave woman, of that he had no doubt. He was becoming more and more aware of the strength of her character. Reaching out gently, he put his arm around her shoulder.

"I'm sorry. I didn't mean to scare you unnecessarily," he said gently. "I have become aware of new sensations ever since the Old Hermit awakened something in me that has been asleep for a long time. It's almost as though I can feel that which can't be seen, and when it moves, I sense it."

Meri, relieved that he knew her feelings, moved closer to him, feeling the security of his presence. "Thank you, Wulpai. I don't mean to be afraid, but I'll be so glad when this awful nightmare is over. I just wish I were back home again in the quiet and beauty of our own forests."

Wulpai felt his own heart stir within him. He knew he was more than he looked, and no doubt had some important role to play in the coming conflict. At the same time, though, we was becoming more and more aware of his manhood, especially with someone like Meri around. He knew he had to harness those emotions if they were to survive the coming days.

Noise from the walls interrupted their thoughts. Wulpai pulled away and joined the Old Hermit who had climbed up the edge of the palace wall for a better look.

"I think the Trolls will soon have the gates torn asunder unless we do something to confuse them," he Old Hermit gestured. "We need to get down there, but disguise ourselves, lest any among those attackers be warriors we've run into before."

Silently they both hurried down the stairs and out into the courtyard. Making their way to the gates on the East, they stood wrapped in gray cloaks, their heads wrapped against the wind. Concentrating, they began to weave a web of confusion in the minds of the trolls. As they worked to smash through the final pins holding the front gate, one troll slipped sideways, pulling the other off course. They stopped, while he regained his footing and had another go at it. This time the lead troll pulled the log off to one side, hitting the mortar, giving his fellow trolls a solid shock. They began to bicker and bellow angrily, in frustration at first.

After a couple more attempts that miscarried, they became angry at one another and started grumbling. One of the lead trolls drew back and threw a slap that would have beheaded a horse. The troll he hit went down in a heap, but jumped up a moment later, ready to fight. The log ram was forgotten as the trolls vented their fury on one another. The mercenaries and goblins backed away as the huge brutes battered one another.

Having fought until they rid themselves of their rage, they sat for a while, getting their breath back. Then they picked up the log and tried again.

This break had given the defenders time to go down to the gate and place some heavy timbers against the inside. They also threw up as much debris as they could find to make it harder to open.

It was well after midnight now, and the fighting had slowed somewhat. The trolls had given up trying to destroy the gate. Every time they attempted it, something would go wrong. The Commander had wondered at first what was happening, then he spotted two unknown figures nearby. Walking toward them, he realized it was the Old Hermit and Wulpai. He muttered under his breath as he passed by,

"My thanks to you both! But for you two, those trolls would have broken through both gates by now." He continued toward the eastern wall and his men.

Fighting continued sporadically through the night. The goblins and mercenaries, sensing the truth, understood the fact that the trolls were unable to destroy the gates. They had been told this would be an easy victory, but had been deeply disappointed. Not willing to risk further spears and shafts from ever-vigilant bowmen, they began to retreat into the edges of the forests. By dawn, the enemy host had withdrawn completely, melting into the surrounding terrain.

Chapter 23

Broken Paths

Slowly, majestically, the rocs rose in the early dawn, their wings roiling the cold moist air, blowing the caps from attendants running for safety. Gathering speed, they lifted over the sanctuary of the walls, flying just above the trees lining the riverbed. All the rocs had been put to flight in this desperate attempt to help the group reach the capital. Captain Theo led one squadron, while Colonel Hargref led the other.

It was a last minute decision to leave the fortress in the hands of his two capable lieutenants. Feeling there might well be a spy among their ranks, the Commander kept his plans to himself and his closest officers.

In the early dawn hours, when he was sure the attack was over, Colonel Hargref issued orders for the rocs to be saddled; then he sent orderlies to awaken their guests. He also took steps to transport several prisoners for questioning in the capital city, including two Sanguma priests who had been dressed in battle armor, trying to scale the walls. They had been tied securely, blind folded and gagged. They were to be questioned by the Seer, a trusted aide of the king. The Seer had a noted reputation for his ability to probe into the minds of those who were in the service of the Dark Lord. It was rumored that some screamed in unendurable agony at his touch, while others died immediately as their befouled minds came in contact with the searing power of his probe. Colonel Hargref knew that if anyone could draw out the secrets of the Dark Lord, the Seer would.

They flew in two close formations, one behind the other, 17 huge birds flying in rank. The lead roc acted as airfoil for the others behind him, flying much as geese did during their winter migrations toward warmer climates. The Commander had Wesip, Rimwai and Meri behind him, along with two shield bearing soldiers. Captain Theo had the Old Hermit, Wabran and Yilmai on his roc. Wulpai, Bili and Breagle rode behind on the next roc, suited and bearing shields as well. The remaining dwarves and elves were positioned behind on following birds.

The chill morning air was laden and damp creating the fog that still clung to the ground. It was an ideal time to leave, hidden by the mists that were getting thicker along the riverbanks. No one spoke as they flew along the rugged gorge, which wound itself through the mountains to open up later toward the southwest. Here the river disgorged its frigid waters into the plains of Leserel, the series of valleys that divided the Western Elven nation from the Nomads of the Southron Plains. Jagged rocks stuck out in the narrows, reaching out their twisted hands as if to pluck the great birds from the sky.

Within the hour, the fugitives were safely through the gap, hugging close to the northern side of the mountain, bearing westward. There was little cover here, but the enormous cliffs that barred the way of all but the hardiest of travelers dwarfed even these great rocs. They all knew there was little fear of detection.

At last the air began to warm as they left the mountains. Bili, feeling the warmth touch his neck and hands, stretched, then looked off to the South, wondering what kind of people the Western Elves would prove to be. He knew they would have to return here to bring the messages they carried from the East, but right now their destination lay firmly in the West.

Bili enjoyed the power of flight that the rocs gave to him. He could feel those great strong wings pumping in continuous rhythm as the scouped the invisible air and forced it behind them. Often as a young man, Bili had watched their smaller cousins, the Rock Eagle, as they caught the air currents and circled high above the forests, never dreaming he would someday be flying above them himself.

As the valleys became wider, the two formations broke into three, flying five to a group, much like ducks on migratory flight. The two extra rocs, with the Commander in charge, flew directly behind the lead roc, which broke the wind ahead and eased their flight. If they needed to make a run for safety along the way, they would be fresh. When one lead roc tired, its rider would allow it to drop below the rest, and the one of the left would assume its place. The one below would then catch up and fly near to the rear.

It wasn't long before the rocs began flying over grassland. It was sparse at first near the base of the cliffs, but as they continued west, the jagged peaks receded and the grass became lush. With heat from the rising sun, the morning winds warmed, stirring the grasses to move gracefully in undulating motions, moving this way and that like a giant carpet being shaken by a cleaner woman.

Bili could see rolling hills in the distance, giving way to dark brooding mountains behind them. Bili wondered bleakly what dark secrets they might hold, especially if the Dark Lord had any minions in those areas. Turning away to look elsewhere, Bili attempted to shed his mind of these depressing prospects.

The wind whistling in his ears had a numbing effect, and Bili began to feel drowsy, at peace with his surroundings. He tightened the cinch around himself, and adjusted the riding straps. Then he allowed himself to doze.

What awakened him, he wasn't sure! He sat bold upright, as if someone had slapped him hard across the face. He gave a strangled yell as he realized he was still flying. Now the scenery had changed. They were almost through the rolling hills and gaining altitude. Looking around rather embarrassed, he caught the eye of Wulpai, who gave a short laugh at his discomfort. Yelling above the wind he commented,

"Who haunted your dreams? I hope she was pretty." Bili flushed, feeling hot, knowing he was blushing furiously, but unable to stop it. He smiled, and shook his head. This elicited another hearty laugh from his friend, who reached out and clasped his shoulder.

"We need all the joy we can find for what lies ahead, my young friend."

Bili nodded his agreement, then looked on ahead as they approached the gap that led into the mountains. Broken clouds partly hid their way, but he could see again the jagged peaks, their spires standing as mute sentinels over the forests below.

The rocs moved again into two formations as the airways narrowed ahead of them. Eyes turned to both sides as they flew into the defile, high above a roaring river which ran out of its bed, falling several hundred feet below in a spectacular splash into a large pool formed over hundreds of years.

Flying on, they continued to follow the natural channel formed by the river, keeping as low as they dared. Going up river, they passed a narrow gorge, the flume spraying strongly as the waters were forced from the wider bed upriver. The whitewater here was rough, partly from the narrows, but more so from the water rushing down from the heights above. Bili watched with fascination. He had never seen such a large body of water. Wondering if it could be navigated, he noticed large boulders just below the surface, and concluded that no one would survive such a trip.

At the base of a cliff, the river divided. The confluence of two rivers made this mighty waterfall down-river. The rocs turned right, following the larger river. Not long after, they reached another gap. The rocs left the river, flew south through the gap, and turned west. Here there was nothing but forest, set upon rolling hills and jagged outcroppings. Calling back over his shoulder, the rider yelled,

"It's about an hour's ride yet to the capital. With any luck we should be there by lunch time."

Bili nodded, acknowledging that he had heard. He looked at the Old Hermit, who was scanning the skies. Glancing over at Wulpai he noticed he was doing the same. Looking up himself he saw nothing but a few clouds drifting in from the West. Wondering what they were looking for he started to speak, but was cut off before the words came out. The sky tore open suddenly right in front of them! The pressure of that tear nearly unseated the lead riders, pushing the great roc backwards.

Dozens of screeching war hawks suddenly materialized ahead of them, flapping their wings, diving to intercept the rocs and their riders! The commander's formation peeled off to the left, narrowly avoiding the raking claws and poisoned metal spikes. The formation behind had more warning, so with drawn swords and fixed shields, they peeled off to the right, slashing and thumping the hawks with their shields. The din and noise of battle was deafening.

Sickening thuds could be heard as the hawks slammed into the shields, almost unseating the soldiers and knocking them senseless with the speed of the impact. The "Clang" of the swords as they bit into the mail plating of the hawks echoed off the hills below.

Suddenly in front of the rocs, large pterodactyl like birds appeared, armor plating on their necks and sides. Riding astride each of these were Sanguma priests, holding long lances held tightly in stirrups strapped to the great birds. Aiming these lances, a red power bolt sizzled forth, narrowly missing one of the rocs. It reacted in fear, nearly dislodging its riders.

The Old Hermit yelled to the rider ahead,

"Move directly toward those Sanguma, quickly, before they have a chance to intercept the other rocs."

The rider pulled the leather thongs hooked above the eagle's beak. He changed course instantly. The Old Hermit began laughing, building up the force hidden within. As they drew near, a Sanguma aimed his lance at them. The Old Hermit lifted partially from his seat, to draw attention to himself. The Sanguma aimed for him and released the bolt. It seared from the tip, hurtling at the Old Hermit. Reaching out his hand, he deflected the bolt, and sent flaming blue light into the priest. Surprised, the Sanguma caught the bolt squarely in the chest, and was instantly incinerated. The pterodactyl, caught in the power wave, was rolled over and went spinning helplessly toward the rugged terrain below.

Seeing the fate of one of their number, the other priests broke formation, attempting to distance themselves from the Old Hermit. Chasing after other rocs, they hurled power bolts among them, causing panic and confusion. The hawks closed in, trying to rake rocs and riders alike. The first formation circled back, bristling with swords, bows, and spears, attempting to help their comrades. Several hawks managed to drive their talons into riders' unprotected areas, injecting poison into their systems. They soon slumped unconscious in their riding straps.

Hawks were circling and attempting to find places to strike the great rocs, thick with feathers, and tough hided legs. The riders took their toll of the hawks, slashing or shooting those that flew too closely. The Sanguma, were hunted down by Wulpai and the Old Hermit, one by one. As they tried to close with a solitary roc, they had to dodge arrows fired at them and the power bolts of the two strange men riding two of the leading rocs.

Wulpai, closing his eyes in concentration, released a power bolt, striking a pterodactyl squarely in the chest. The whole armor glowed brightly for a moment, then exploded, rending the bird. It fell lifeless from the sky as the Sanguma priest disappeared. Screeching their fear and anger above the din of the aerial battle, the pterodactyl re-grouped, and flew in formation toward the Commander and his rocs. Red power bolts issued from the lances once again, striking violently on the shield of the Commander and his riders. Several were torn from their seats, falling to their deaths in the forests below.

After making their pass, the Sanguma banked away to the left, avoiding a direct confrontation with the Old Hermit and Wulpai. This gave the two formations a chance to fly near one another. The Commander yelled out,

"Let the delegation group together and fly toward the capital. Captain Theo will fight these priests and hawks. Let us escape while we can."

With those words, he headed his roc westward, the great wings flapping strongly, out-distancing the hawks and the leather winged birds of the Sanguma. Feeling they might have a chance apart from such a heavy escort, the Old Hermit consented to breaking away. Soon six rocs stroked for the West while the others continued to circle and fight. The hawks, no match for the speed of the great rocs, were soon left behind. They would have to be teleported by someone again if they were to be effective.

Gaining distance and altitude, the Commander was confident they would reach the capital. He gave the thumbs up sign to the rest of the riders and motioned them on.

Suddenly the sky above filled with darkness. Three black beasts appeared, enveloped in magical armor. Apparently this separation was what they had been awaiting. They swooped down on the rocs, their ugly beasts screeching out an unearthly croaking sound.

Colonel Hargref barely had time to look above him and pull the reins to one side before the beast struck the roc. The thud of impact was sickening. The great roc was thrown sideways, just managing to keep its balance and fly. It wheeled in mid-air, it's sharp beak tearing at the armor of the beast. The beast clawed out at the roc, catching it a blow across the head just above the eye. The roc in turn fastened its claws on the beast, ripping great chunks of armor and flesh from its back. The beast pulled away to make another pass.

The next beast landed squarely on one of the rocs bearing soldiers. They fought the beast, but couldn't penetrate its armor. The dark power being riding above sent a power bolt amongst them, hitting the roc squarely. It screeched as the bolt seared its back, turning upside down with its claws raking the beast. The soldiers were torn from their straps, plunging helplessly into a stand of trees near a knoll. They disappeared into the forest canopy. The beast croaked angrily, dark blood pouring from the soft underbelly opened by the roc's powerful talons. The straps holding the magical armor were torn to bits, and flapped uselessly in the wind. Using his powers, the dark power being brought the straps together again, and partially closed the wound of the great beast. He then turned his attention elsewhere. The rider still clung to the roc, fighting to bring it under control. Then he flew down to see if any of his companions had survived the fall.

Wulpai and the Old Hermit sensed their presence just before the beasts materialized and attacked. They had turned their attention and powers upward. As one of the beasts plunged towards them, the Old Hermit and Wulpai both sent searing blue power into the beast, hitting it in the neck, where no armor covered it. The beast croaked in pain, and began falling uncontrollably. The dark rider put his power into the beast enabling it to right itself again, but the roc by then had put quite a distance between itself and the beast. It attempted to pursue them again.

Above them, one of the Sanguma riding a pterodactyl clone materialized and plunged into the roc before any power bolts could be used. There was a tangle of feathers, claws and people. The Sanguma, sensing the time was right, fired energy from the point of his short lance. Wulpai deflected it while the Old Hermit, sword now drawn, drove the point into the unwary priest. He screamed in pain as the blade drove deeply into his chest, then slumped in his harness as the big bird fought to disengage itself from the eagle. The Old Hermit was just barely able to free his sword before the roc pulled away under the direction of its rider, flapping its wings strongly once again.

Commander Hargref didn't fare as well. The third beast, losing the advantage of surprise moved over from one side and croaking its hate, drove its claws into the eagle, attempting to drag it to earth. The soldier at the rear, shot at the power being, trying to distract him. The evil lord, looking at the soldier in disdain, pointed his lance at him, sending a bolt of power pulsing into his body. He was killed and his straps were burned away. His charred body fell away. Colonel Hargref, sensing what was happening, made a daring move. Giving the reins to his daughter, and drawing his dagger, he leaped onto the head of the beast, driving the dagger through the eye of the beast, before the power lord could act. Croaking now in maddened pain, the beast began plummeting, dragging the roc with it. The power being, certain that this would end in their deaths, teleported elsewhere, leaving them to their fate.

Wulpai, taking in the battle below, shouted to the Old Hermit, drawing his attention to their desperate plight.

"Use what strength you have left to help me slow the fall of that roc. Otherwise the Commander and those with him will be killed."

The Old Hermit looked down and back, and stretched out his hands. A blue aura reached down and enveloped them, slowing their descent. This gave the roc time to thrust powerfully with its legs, disengaging from the dying beast. Wesip began pulling on the left rein in an attempt to get the roc's attention, a scream of fear escaping her lips as they continued to fall. She regained control not far above tree level and the roc began flapping, desperately trying to stop its fall.

Colonel Hargref was not so lucky. Unable to make the leap back to the roc, he clung fiercely to the beast as the roc thrust it away. They fell together toward a thick stand of Poplars on the side of a hill.

Wulpai seeing that the Commander would be killed, attempted to slow his descent as well. At the same time, the Commander, knowing he would be crushed by the weight of the falling beast, jumped clear to fall freely. Just before he disappeared into the trees, the blue energy beam held him momentarily. Then he was gone. The beast fell heavily, snapping large limbs from the trees where it fell.

Seeing her father fall, Wesip's first instinct was to turn the roc around and go after him. After all, Wulpai and the Old Hermit seemed to be coping with the power beings. Turning to Meri she said,

"I'm going down to check after father. He may still be alive and will be pretty badly hurt if he is. I can't leave him lying there."

Meri started to reply when a bolt of red power pulsed with a loud buzz, narrowly missing them, but striking the soldier who was seated behind them. He was charred and he tumbled off the back of the roc, spiraling slowly to earth. Looking up they saw three more Sanguma trying to close in on them. Wesip, instantly changing her mind, urged the angry roc back into full flight. In a moment they pushed ahead of the Sanguma. Wesip yelled to Wesip and Rimwai, We can outdistance the enemy if we can just keep the bolts from striking the roc." The great bird was bristling with anger, and wanted to claw and tear at those who pursued. It was all Wesip could do to keep control and force him to fly forward.

Hurriedly Meri and Rimwai released the metal shields that were tied to the straps, looping them through their arms. Then half-turning toward the Sanguma, they raised them, attempting to deflect the bolts fired at them. Three times the Sanguma pointed their short lances and sent energy bolts hurtling towards them. Twice the bolts narrowly missed the roc's head. The third bolt, aimed at its body was caught full force on Meri's shield. She was knocked back in her seat, the shield flung from her arm. The bolt was deflected, but Meri's left arm now hung limply from her shoulder. Grimly she hung on with her good arm as they pulled away from the Sanguma.

Crossing a narrow range of peaks, the women saw the capital before them. Wesip, looking back again, saw that the Sanguma had given up the chase and had simply disappeared.

And just in time too, she decided. Flying towards them was a formation of rocs, soldiers from the city mounted astride their backs. As the women drew nearer the city, the soldiers encircled them giving them escort, recognizing the emblem on the Roc as that of Commander Hargref. Wesip began to cry in relief as she realized they had made sanctuary.

There had been no time to turn back and look for her father. Wesip felt badly about this, and through her tears hoped against hope that Bili or Wulpai might locate him and give what aid he could. She knew their only chance had been in flight. She felt she had done what her father would have wanted of her. That didn't lessen the pain she felt stabbing deep in her heart. Tears fell down her cheeks only to be blown away by the wind.

Minutes later, the rocs landed in the field adjacent to the palace, the heart of the citadel. Dismounting, the soldiers hurried to help the women. They were greatly surprised to note that one was an elf maiden.

The other, a dark haired girl from the mountains, was obviously hurt. Hurrying to unbuckle the harnesses, they raced for the palace where they were met by the old Seer. He ushered them all into the safety of the building.

End of Volume 1 Salduwe